FOREBODING

FOREBODING

ISBN 978-184426-400-1

First Published 2006 by
UPFRONT PUBLISHING LTD
Peterborough, England.

Printed by Lightning Source

FOREBODING

JILL PAINTER

With Best Wishes

Jill Painter

Chapter One

Foreboding. That was the word drumming in Jilly Kenworth's head. Loud and persistent it dragged her from sleep careless of the fact that she was still tired. The time was a little after seven on that particular July morning. With her pansy-blue eyes flickering and unsure, she focused on the ceiling seeing the watermark left by the winter's storm that had ripped the tiles from the roof. Although they had been replaced the stain remained. It reminded her of a sad-faced moon that stared at her with incomprehension. It also reflected her feeling of disquiet. Why this feeling of foreboding? Had she been dreaming again? Was it a dream or imagination which, when in a half-waking state, appeared as life? Either way it was disturbing and recurring.

Dreaming of Richard was both sweet and sad. Their happiness had been shared. Their marriage fulfilled when their daughter Becca was born. Now sadness was the state Jilly bore alone. Death was so final. Unexpected, death, incomprehensible. The constant question was – why? She knew how. A hit-and-run driver. Never traced. Did he know his actions had shattered a happy family? Did he care? She thought not. The facts were the basis of her dreams. But they were not orderly as they had been in life. They were confused. Sometimes Richard died before the car hit him. At other times he was driving it. The worst scenario was when he wasn't there at all but he was still dead. Nothing made sense. And so the dream became a nightmare, if it was a dream. She was never quite sure.

The sun lanced its way between the yellow curtains, its beam creating a raked stage on which dust motes danced. Jilly lowered her eyes and watched them. Gradually her feeling of foreboding retreated into the back of her mind. There it would remain only to re-emerge later. And that, she knew, was inevitable.

The cottage was quiet except for the friendly creaking of ancient timbers. The low beams spanning the ceilings were gouged and scarred by life as it was a hundred years ago. Then it had been a fisherman's cottage. Festooned with nets and lobster pots it had belonged to a bygone age. History said it had also been a smuggler's hideout, a cache in which to secrete kegs of rum and Oriental silks. Then it could have been cold, dark and mysterious. Now it was bright, comfortable and safe.

Outside, a wild flower garden bloomed. Its flagged path led to a wooden gate that opened into a rutted lane. Beyond that stood a low stone wall. Beyond that again lay an expanse of dark, springy turf enhanced by clumps of wild, Cornish flowers. They embroidered and partly framed the cove with its small beach. Edged by the sea where that morning it gently lapped, it was the stuff of which picture postcards were made. Without the backing of a south westerly the tidal ferocity was non-existent. There were no storm clouds on the horizon, but that was soon to change. For the moment a light southerly breeze danced through fluffy clouds creating thermals on which the gulls soared, while other birds plunged to snatch hapless fish from the sea.

All was tranquil. The sky and the sea, both azure, merging at the horizon made a vast canvas. Smudged vapour trails criss-crossed as aircraft flew to countries where Jilly and Richard had taken exotic holidays – and their honeymoon, but those days were over.

Now the smell of cooking bacon drifted through Jilly's half-open window. It came from the holiday let along the lane. The Armstrong's had occupied it for over a week. They were an odd couple and somehow seemed out of place in their City clothes. He generally wore a suit though not always with a shirt and tie. Sometimes he aimed for casual, wearing round-necked sweaters boasting designer logos. For him they didn't seem to work. Slightly portly with thinning dark hair brushed forward it framed unexpectedly sharp features and darting eyes. The left one had a slightly demonic upturn caused by a scar running from the outer corner. She was younger. Much younger, but of the same ilk. Frilly blouses, short skirts and heels too high to cope with the local terrain, she tottered unsteadily about. Attractive in a coarse way her raven-black hair, short and spiky, framed a face that could have been beautiful. But whenever Jilly had seen her, her face was always over-laden with make-up and mask-like, only her grey eyes were animated.

As visitors to the area they didn't seem to do much other than limited shopping in the village and visiting The Mariner's Head, the popular pub at Welda Point. The local pub was not on their itinerary. Jilly wondered why. It had a lot to offer. Perhaps they had friends at Welda Point. Not that Jilly cared. It was just a passing thought. She'd never had a long conversation with them, only polite uttering about the weather and the merits of the local ice-cream. Nine-year-old Becca was the mine of information. She loved talking to new and different people. To her it was exciting and it didn't take her long to make their acquaintance.

"Mom, they are nice," she told Jilly at tea that particular afternoon. "The man has been poorly but he's better now. And Mrs. Armstrong has long, pearly fingernails. She said she needed more varnish, but our chemist didn't sell the colour she wanted. I told her about the chemist in Penzance and how to get there the quick way."

"Becca! You must not intrude," Jilly told her patiently. "I'm sure they appreciated your help, but if Mr. Armstrong has been ill, he may need to rest."

Becca bit into cake and said, "He seemed to be all right, Mom! And he was interested in finding a short cut to Penzance. He said the main road was a pain! And it is, isn't it? It's OK in the winter but when all the Emmets arrive in the summer – well!"

Jilly laughed and reminded her that at one time they had been Emmets.

"Had we not been down here on our summer holidays, we would not have found this cottage. Had we not found it we would not be living here; you would not know our neighbours and that includes Davy and Alex, and we would not be having this conversation!"

Becca looked bemused and with the cake mid-way between plate and mouth, asked, "Mom, how do you do that?"

"Do what, Becca?"

"Sort of undo everything. Go backwards, then talk forwards?"

"I guess it's a trick," Jilly laughed. "Now will you promise not to pester people? Offer to help, but don't be pushy."

"OK!" Becca agreed and, cramming the remains of her cake into her mouth, she reached for another slice.

Jilly looked at her daughter with a slight frown. Sometimes her overt friendliness was a worry. The world could be a dangerous place even in this quiet corner. Not that anything untoward had ever happened, but that did not mean to say it never would.

Becca understood and heeded warnings most of the time, but sometimes she forgot them. If she was out with her dog, Benji, Jilly felt she was safe. That was why daily walks to the village were allowed. It was familiar territory.

Now, after several months, the little girl with the red-gold curls and her brown and white dog were well known. Dick Rogers, the butcher, who could be crusty tempered, sometimes produced a meaty marrowbone wrapped in a plastic bag. Handing it to Becca he would warn: "If Benji doesn't keep his teeth clean they'll drop out! So you give 'im this bone, my bird!"

Becca was never quite sure whether to believe him or not. In due course Benji would get the bone only to hide it. Jilly had a sneaking feeling that the land between the lane and the sea was a secret burial ground for Benji's crunchy treasures.

Becca was in her room. With its brightly painted furniture and walls covered with pictures of pop stars and dogs, she lay wide awake on the top sheet of her bed. Her duvet was a crumpled mass on the floor. In the corner, curled up in his basket, Benji slept, his nose buried in his blanket and his paws twitching. He knew his place. This was his bed. That was Becca's. Sharing was not allowed.

With the back of her left hand across her mouth and her right hand twiddling a curl on the top of her head Becca was in thinking mode. Today she wanted to think about – today. When she had thought about it she would talk it over with Mom. Their morning discussions during school holidays were the norm. Becca treasured them. They made her feel grown – up. Sometimes she thought she was the grown – up. That was when Mom was sad, though sad days were not around as much as they used to be. Sometimes Mom would talk about Daddy remembering only the fun they shared. At other times her eyes would shine with unshed tears. Those moments worried Becca. She did not know how to handle them.

Now a smiling Mom, holding a towel, peeped round the door.

"Morning, Becca! What are you going to do today?" As she spoke, and after kissing Becca, she sat on the end of the bed curling up her lightly tanned, slender legs.

Becca sat upright and crossed hers then, dropping her chin into her hand, she summarised thoughtfully, "First I'll walk Benji to the village. Then I'll ask if Davy wants to go to the cove. If he does we might swim out to the raft." She paused, looked at the ceiling and added, "Or we might paddle to the next bay. Or we could explore the cave for the millionth time." This was said with a huge sigh of boredom.

Jilly frowned. She didn't like the children going into the cave and said so.

Becca sighed again. "Mom, I keep telling you it's safe."

"I know! But I don't want you trapped by the tide."

"We won't be! Even at full tide we won't even get wet. Mr. Rogers said so. He should know. He was born in the village."

"All right, darling, just be careful." Standing up she draped the towel over her shoulder saying, "I'm going to have a shower, OK?"

"OK, Mom."

Benji whined and, scrambling from his basket, scuttled through the door before Jilly closed it. Unworried by the house being open she watched him race down the stairs and head for the kitchen door. Once in the garden he wouldn't go far beyond it. He might hop over the wall to do a bone inspection, but that was all.

Still sitting on her bed, Becca uncurled her legs and thought about Davy. He lived next door and was home from boarding school for the holidays. Tow-haired and stocky, he was two years older than Becca and challenged her in many ways. Who could skim stones the furthest; climb cliffs the highest; and swim under water the longest? Their mutual competitive spirit was part of their understanding of each other. The age difference and gender didn't seem to matter. They liked each other. They shared worries and sometimes secrets. Perhaps they were close because each lacked a parent and they empathised. Not that they talked of their situation. It was enough to know it existed.

Alex Hunter, Davy's father, having moved into his cottage just before Christmas was still considered by the locals to be a foreigner. Jilly had spoken to him several times and found him pleasant if slightly reserved. On the other hand Davy and Becca became friends immediately. Yet their burgeoning one-ness was not enough to persuade Alex to accept a glass of Christmas wine from Jilly. His refusal was charming but disappointing. After that Jilly did not venture again. He obviously guarded his privacy and she could respect that.

Not so Becca. She wanted everyone to be friends with everyone. Mom liked Alex and, according to Davy, Alex liked Mom. So why didn't they meet and talk to each other? Becca didn't know and couldn't guess, and so she made up her mind to change the situation.

With the arrival of Spring and the garden fence remaining a barrier over which Jilly and Alex exchanged vague pleasantries, Becca decided enough was enough. It was half-term. Davy was home. He was her friend. Mom should have a friend. Telling no one of her intention she took it upon herself to invite Alex and Davy for coffee. Now that Davy was around and they had so much fun together, it was only fair that Mom and Alex should have fun, too. She and Davy did children's things, so why couldn't Mom and Alex do grown-up things? There was no reason at all! So she would make them be friends. That was her plan and she saw nothing wrong with it.

Standing at the Hunter's closed kitchen door, her red-gold hair tousled by the breeze, she rattled the brass knocker and waited.

Alex appeared and smiled at her.

"Hello, Becca! Everything all right?" He asked only because, as a rule, Becca did not come to the door. She usually yelled for Davy over the fence.

"Yes, thank you, Mr. Hunter. Mom says she would like you to come to our house for coffee – now!"

"Now – coffee?" he repeated, his face blank. Caught unawares he stumbled and tripped over his words. "Er – why – er – yes. Thank you. That would be very nice. Davy?"

Davy, hovering in the background, eyed Becca suspiciously. He knew she was being crafty but he didn't know why. Looking at her he said to his father, "You go, Dad. I'll stay here."

"Oh, no!" Becca said quickly. "You have to come too, Davy. It's not just for grown – ups. Mom wants us all to get to know each other. Be sort of neighbourly. Then afterwards we can go down to the cove. Just you and me, Davy." Adding as an unconvincing afterthought, "You can come, too, Mr. Hunter."

Alex raised an eyebrow, winked at Davy and politely refused.

Davy grinned.

Becca was relieved. Alex joining them on the beach was not what she wanted. She wanted him to stay with Mom.

The invitation was almost a disaster, for when Becca ushered Alex and Davy into the kitchen, Jilly was on her hands and knees cleaning the oven.

Alex said, "Oh, dear! Are we too early? Sorry!"

Scrambling to her feet, looking confused and embarrassed, wondering what they could be too early for, she said, "I guess oven cleaning takes longer than I thought!"

Knowing she looked grubby and unkempt her personal pride wilted in the heat of her embarrassment. Yet Alex didn't seem to mind her appearance or even be aware of it. For that she was grateful.

When, a moment later Becca, walking round the scrubbed kitchen table, asked if she should make the coffee, for Jilly everything fell into place. Coffee! That explained the situation. Becca had not paused to think. She had issued the invitation expecting it was all right to do so. Normally it would have been. This time it wasn't. Now Jilly felt at a disadvantage. Still flustered she gave an apologetic smile and suggested Becca should take Alex and Davy through to the sitting room.

Alex said, "We'll be quite happy in the kitchen. Or shall we go away and come back another day?" He spoke with a warm smile and by the look in his eyes he had grasped the situation.

Relieved, Jilly laughed and pushed a strand of fair hair from her face

"Are you a kitchen guy?" she asked.

"I'm an anything guy! Easy to please, domesticated in a ham – fisted way, and totally ignorant about cleaning of ovens!"

"Keep it that way!" Jilly advised him, her eyes sparkling. "It's a lousy job!"

As far as conversations went it wasn't the most scintillating opener. But it was an ice-breaker. It was also safe. It revealed nothing and begged no questions.

When, after an hour of friendly, light-hearted banter, Alex made his excuses and left, Jilly sparkled. Becca was well pleased. Mom hadn't sparkled since Daddy died.

With her mission accomplished she, Davy and Benji went down to the beach. Because it was little more than a patch of sand mostly hidden by overhanging cliffs, it was usually deserted. The locals preferred the next bay where the water was deeper and they could dive from rocks. Becca and Davy were content with the cove. It was a place of safety that had parental approval and few visitors.

Over the following weeks Jilly's relationship with Alex became more friendly and, just occasionally, they would share a bottle of wine while sitting in the early evening sunshine.

Conversation was always casual. Neither spoke of the past, yet there developed between them a kind of understanding that the time was not yet right to talk of things that mattered.

Becca was delighted by the situation. Even Davy grudgingly admitted his Dad seemed happier.

All these thoughts trickled through Becca's head as she lay on her bed twiddling her hair. Mom had said something about her being a match-maker. She wasn't sure what that was, but it sounded nice. Suddenly hearing the click of the bathroom door she remembered it was her turn to make the coffee. Sliding from her bed she scuttled down to the kitchen, made coffee and scuttled back forgetting to call Jilly.

Jilly returned to her room and opening the curtains flooded it with sunlight. It was going to be another nice day. With Becca and Davy pursuing their own activities, Jilly felt free. A day without grazed knees or bumped heads would be bliss. Optimistically she held up crossed fingers, and waited for Becca to call her. It didn't happen.

* * *

Delza Pascoe clumped along Jilly's garden path in her black lace-up shoes. The garden gate, having been slammed too hard, had bounced out of the latch and was now swinging open. Grunting, Delza returned to the gate and kicked it shut. Pulling her dark-green anorak hood over her sparse hair, she wiped her nose on her sleeve and clumped back along the path to the front door. Once there she kicked off her shoes to leave them sole upper-most on the doormat. Mrs. Kenworth said she must not wear her shoes in the house. Slippers were all right, but not shoes. Mrs. Kenworth had bought her some slippers. They had flowers on them. Behind Delza's broad, flat face her brain struggled to get to grips with the problem of shoes and slippers. Sometimes she went into the garden in her slippers, and then when she returned to the house she would take them off and patter about in bare feet. Mrs. Kenworth didn't like that. She would make Delza wipe the soles of her slippers and put them back on. This puzzled Delza, making her stubborn and difficult to handle. The fact that this procedure happened only when the garden was muddy she did not understand and so she thought Jilly Kenworth stupid.

At fifteen years of age Delza, christened Demelza, had the mental age of a seven-year-old. Unemployable, in a commercial sense, lacking any kind of skills she helped Jilly around the house. If shown how to perform a task she would do it to the best of her ability – albeit painfully slowly, but it would be done with a willingness to please. In her own way she was a mimic. Verbal instructions were lost on her, but she could copy. Because of this she secretly learned from Becca. She watched her through half-open doors, from behind curtains, or from a distance. She didn't always understand why Becca did certain things but Delza would become a mirror image of her. The one thing Becca did that Delza could not do was – talk to Benji. Delza was afraid of dogs. Even so she still tried very hard to talk to him. But Delza could not talk to anyone. Delza was dumb.

Until the age of five she was, within her own mental capacity, able to make herself understood with monosyllabic sentences. Then something happened to her. Exactly what only the family knew. Whatever it was it took away her ability to speak leaving her even more incapacitated and vulnerable than she already was. Yet despite this, for the most part, in her own way, she was happy. The bouts of temper she had were usually short-lived and, Jilly suspected, they were brought about by frustration rather than anger.

Tom Pascoe, Delza's grandfather, also worked for Jilly. A grizzled, taciturn man he tended the garden and dealt with never-ending odd jobs. Many irritating household problems were solved by his gnarled hands. Originally he had been a fisherman out of Newlyn. He'd also played a part at Dunkirk. He was only a boy at the time. He'd sneaked aboard 'The Merry Sue' looking for adventure. The slaughter he witnessed affected him deeply. He rarely spoke of it and when he did it was only to say he was there.

His daughter Audra was Delza's mother. She had never married or, outside the family and close friends, named Delza's father. Rumour said it was Hal Polglise, a layabout from the area. Rumour also said that Delza was one of several off-spring. That came as no surprise. But wherever else he philandered it was known he loitered near the Pascoe's cottage. It was just after Delza became dumb that Audra died of a heart attack. Polglise being the rogue he was left the scene. And so Tom raised Delza, stubbornly fighting off the authorities that wanted to put her in a home.

Now he trailed after Delza swearing quietly as he secured the gate. She'd broken it again! Another job to do! Following the path he passed the front door, then turning right he skirted the side door. Ahead stood a wooden shed into which he disappeared. Cluttered with garden tools and bicycles he gazed at Becca's rear tyre. It was flat and down to the canvas. It was no longer roadworthy. It needed replacing. But Mrs. Kenworth said to leave it. Becca didn't ride it all that often. Her own bike was used now and again when visiting friends. Taking the car along the narrow lanes, meeting tractors and having to reverse, was not Jilly's strong point.

Now Tom toed Becca's worn tyre. It was too dangerous to be ridden. He'd have to disable the bike. There was no point in dismantling the back wheel. Given time Davy could put it back. He would have to think of something else. After several minutes of pondering he decided to remove the saddle. That he could easily hide!

Minutes later, satisfied he had done his best, he then took down a long-necked oilcan from the shelf and proceeded to grease a pair of garden shears.

* * *

Jilly, having showered and dressed, appreciated the freshly-made pot of coffee left by Becca and managed to drink half a cupful before Delza arrived. Giving her the task of cleaning the two brass frogs, which squatted either side of the sitting room fireplace, she returned to the kitchen and topped up her cup of coffee. She then heard someone at the front door. Glancing at the clock she saw it was just a little after eight. It was early for visitors unless it was Davy. When he and Becca were off on an adventure they often had an early start. Had Becca forgotten to mention it? But it wasn't Davy. It was Mrs. Armstrong. Heavily made-up, wearing a short, black skirt and a custard-yellow blouse she apologised for the intrusion.

"I'm sorry to bother you," she smiled. "I'm Marilyn. Next door?" It was said as a reminder rather than an introduction. "Could you lend me an egg, please?"

"Yes, of course," Jilly smiled back. An egg was a new departure from the time-honoured cup of sugar. And why was she not surprised to learn the woman's name was Marilyn? It suited her.

Widening the door, Jilly invited her in, saying, "I'll get the egg from the fridge. Is one enough?"

"Plenty! I don't eat brekky – well – maybe a bit of toast, but that's all." She patted her slim hips and laughed, "Storage space if I'm not careful. Arthur's the one for full English. You name it – it's on his plate! I've just dropped his egg on the floor. You might know it was the last one!"

Jilly flipped open an empty carton and put in two eggs. "Just in case!" she smiled again.

"That's very kind of you! Thank you. I'll return them this afternoon."

"No hurry," Jilly told her.

Marilyn scanned the room and appeared to be taking in every detail.

"You've got this really nice," she complimented. "It's a lot better than our place. And the rent's a rip-off." She scanned again and sighed, "Still, there you go! You don't always get what you pay for, do you?"

"'Fraid not," Jilly had to agree.

It was some minutes later, after Marilyn had tottered away on her high heels, that Jilly wondered what had happened to the cooking bacon she had smelled earlier. Perhaps Marilyn was not domesticated, or perhaps she had just got her timing wrong. Or at some time had Becca said something about the cottage, that made Marilyn curious to see inside?

She had certainly made a point of looking at everything. Her eyes had lingered here and there, particularly on the equipment. Was she one of those women who hankered? If Mrs. Jones had it, then she must have it, too? Not in a holiday cottage, surely!

Gazing round the empty kitchen her thoughts were sliced by the sharp ringing of the 'phone. Her heart lurched. She knew what was about to happen. She would pick up the 'phone and the line would go dead. Steeling herself she felt compelled to go through the motions. To go through them time after time to hear only silence.

Trembling she reached and then listened.

Nothing.

She hung up and chillingly the familiar sense of foreboding returned.

Someone was playing some kind of game. A child? A prankster?

Whoever it was knew how to play, but was it a dangerous game?

Chapter Two

Benji butted through the open back door, nosed his empty water bowl and gave Jilly a pathetic look. At the same moment Becca came down from her bedroom and, without being prompted, filled the bowl and set it down. Wiping her damp fingers down her grubby T-shirt, she then hitched up her shorts, and stroked Benji's back.

Jilly looked at her, and did a double-take. "Becca!" she cried, "That T-shirt looks disgusting!"

"It's OK for the beach, isn't it?" she asked, fingering an ice-cream stain.

"I suppose so," Jilly sighed. "Is that where you've decided to go? Have you spoken to Davy?"

Pouring cereal into a dish, Becca said, "I talked to him from my bedroom window. He says going to the beach is OK with him, so that's what we're going to do. Who came to the door just now?"

"Mrs. Armstrong. She borrowed a couple of eggs."

Becca spooned cereal into her mouth, crunched it and said slightly guiltily, "I forgot to tell you I'd made the coffee, didn't I? Shall I leave the beach early and ask for the eggs back as a sort of 'Sorry'?"

Jilly smiled, "There's no need. We're not desperate. Just put your brain into gear and hurry up. Otherwise Davy will go without you."

In the blink of an eye the dish was empty and both Becca and Benji disappeared.

Delza lumbered into the kitchen holding a screwed-up duster and a tin of Brasso in her blackened hands.

Jilly sighed. She had forgotten to tell her to put on rubber gloves. It was no good scolding her. If Delza wasn't told Delza didn't do. Patiently Jilly helped her to wash. That involved playing 'Round and Round the Garden,' on her soapy palms. Delza gurgled making Jilly wonder, not for the first time, why she could make sounds but could not speak.

Patting her hands dry, Jilly said, "Delza will you make Becca's bed, please, and put Pogo on Becca's pillow?"

Delza beamed. She loved Pogo almost as much as Becca did. Given to Becca by her father a few days before he was killed, Pogo was a small toy in the shape of a white, fluffy bear. Loved and treasured he lived only on Becca's bed. At night she held him until she fell asleep. In the morning she picked him from the floor, kissed him and sat him on her stool. It was a ritual. Delza knew nothing of rituals. She wouldn't remember them anyway. All she knew was that Pogo felt soft against her face. She liked that. Although once, when she saw his stuffing poking from his back, she was afraid. But she showed Mrs. Kenworth and she made him better by pushing cotton wool into the hole and sewing him up with a big needle. He didn't cry. He was very brave. Now she would go upstairs and make Becca's bed and, for a moment, hold Pogo against her face so that he tickled her cheek. That would be heaven to Delza.

* * *

As Marilyn Preston put the egg carton on the kitchen table, Arthur Armstrong didn't look up from the notebook in which he was writing. The pages were dog-eared after weeks of scribbling. Not that he'd written anything of importance. He hadn't, but even the smallest detail could be valuable. Every scrap of information had been meticulously recorded even down to the times of sunrise and sunset. One never knew.

Now he looked up. "Anything? Did you see anything relevant?" he asked.

"Not really," she shrugged. "I borrowed a couple of eggs."

He looked at her and said sharply, "You were supposed to ask the times of the buses. That was what we agreed."

"I know! I know! But bus time queries would not have got me into the house. Borrowing an egg did".

"You said eggs!"

"Oh, for goodness sake! Don't be so pedantic! She offered two. I accepted."

"She's very generous!" he said without sarcasm. "So what else?" he then asked.

"Nothing. The layout of her place is more or less the same as this one. There's nothing special about it. One or two bits of pretty pottery hanging from the rafters."

"That figures. Her folks were into pottery. They had a ceramic business that they sold and then retired. They are now what is described in financial terms as 'comfortable'."

"How do you know?" she asked, her head to one side.

"Read it in the paper. It was a headline thing. Something like 'Business closes after a hundred years of family trading'. Not that it matters. What about the Kenworth cottage?"

"There's no sign of wealth – at least not in the kitchen. The equipment is top quality…"

"Ah!" Arthur cut in, smirking.

"…and well-used."

"Oh," he said, sounding disappointed.

"So, everything on view was just ordinary. No extravagance. No crystal. No silver! Incidentally I've promised to return the eggs later today."

"Very thoughtful," he told her absently.

"It's more to do with forward-thinking," she told him. "Although I found the woman very nice we don't want her knocking on the door getting friendly, do we?"

"Not really," he said, hunching his shoulders.

"Which is why I want to take the eggs back!"

"Good idea! D'you think you could get another look inside the house?" he asked hopefully.

"Maybe," Marilyn said, but her voice was edged with doubt.

Unwilling to press her, Arthur changed tack.

"By the way, I've just spoken to your better half. Whenever you ring him, for the rest of the day, you're like a dipso in a spa! So I rang him. He's bored, unhappy and missing you, but he wants us to stay on track."

"So, what's new?" Marilyn sighed. "No one seems to care about my feelings!" which she knew to be untrue. Jack cared. And he hated their separation as much as she did. She knew he would never give way any more than Arthur would. For a moment she wallowed in self-pity. It was an indulgence but it was comforting. She then said in a low voice, "I want to go home! I hate this situation! I know we have a purpose, and if we're lucky we'll win, meanwhile, what?"

"Meanwhile – nothing. Eventually some kind of recompense."

"What good's that?" she demanded angrily.

Arthur didn't answer.

Picking up the empty frying pan Marilyn stared at it and accused, "You've scoffed all the bacon! You greedy guts! What now?"

"Another couple of rashers and two eggs," he suggested, patting his stomach. "It must be the Cornish air whetting my appetite."

"Cornish air? More like gluttony!" She stared at him for several seconds and then asked wearily, "How much longer must we wait, Pop?"

Angrily he hit the table with his palm." Don't call me Pop," he yelled. "Down here you are Mrs. Armstrong, my wife."

"I don't think Mum would like the idea," she said, stony-faced.

"She had her chance. She blew it. She's not around. Who cares?"

"I do!" she told him, her eyes bright with anger. "Are you completely heartless?"

Ignoring her he turned back to his notebook and continued writing.

Knowing he would not be drawn into any further discussion, she moved towards him and put her hand on his shoulder. Lightening her tone of voice she asked what he was plotting.

He closed the book and said, "Nothing. I just need to keep notes on how things are going."

"To me they aren't going at all. They are static. Stuck. Immovable!" She crossed to the fridge and yanked open the door.

"Did you say two rashers?"

He frowned and ignored her.

Spreading pink, lean back across the pan, she switched on the hot-plate. With food to comfort him he'd soon be smiling again.

* * *

On the beach Becca, shading her squinting eyes from the glare of the sun, stared out to sea.

"There's a man on the raft, Davy!" She was surprised. At that hour everywhere was usually deserted.

The raft, an amenity provided by the Council, gently bobbed some fifty metres off shore. Anchored by a thick chain to a massive block of concrete it was rarely used by the locals, but visitors appreciated it.

Skimming a flat pebble across the water Davy said, "I wonder who it is?" He purposefully sounded disinterested.

Becca was always talking to strangers. He wished she wouldn't.

"It'll be a visitor," Becca told him, her eyes still on the raft. "Shall we swim out and talk to him?"

"Boring! Boring! Boring!" he said, adding, "We can't swim. We haven't put on our cossies!"

"I can swim in my shorts," she told him. "And my shirt's dirty, so Mom won't mind."

Davy shrugged, "You go. Dad's not keen on new gear being dunked." He flicked sand from his crisp, navy shorts and smiled. "You go," he repeated. "I'll stay with Benji. You know how he hates being left behind and dogs aren't allowed on the raft."

Needing no further encouragement she ran down to the water's edge. The moment she plunged into the sea, Benji tried to follow.

Davy grabbed his collar.

Benji reared, pawed the air and made odd noises in his throat.

Becca's head bobbed away.

Benji fussed, straining for freedom.

Davy's grip tightened, but he stroked him and spoke quietly telling him Becca would be back in no time.

Benji licked Davy's chin and again pawed the air.

Becca clambered on to the bobbing raft and wiped her wet face on the crook of her arm.

The man, lying on his back with his head cradled in his clasped hands, opened his eyes and smiled.

Becca saw he had brown teeth and wondered if she should tell him about the new toothpaste on the market. Perhaps not. She smiled back and then crossed to the far corner, sat down and leaned against the upright post. Would the man notice her grubby T-shirt? She glanced down. Now that it was wet it looked all right. Folding her legs and with her elbows on her knees she asked him if he was a visitor.

"Just for a few days, are you?" He spoke easily, his eyes friendly.

"No, I live here."

"Lucky you!" he said, lifting himself on to his elbow and looking towards the shore.

"Is that your brother with the dog?"

"No. He's my friend but the dog is mine. His name is Benji and he doesn't bark."

"Why not? Has he got a sore throat?" he asked with a smile.

Becca looked at him with disdain. Sometimes grown-ups were so ignorant.

"No, he hasn't got a sore throat!" she told him, trying not to sound cross. "He's a Basenji hunting dog and Basenji hunting dogs can't bark!"

"Is that a fact?" the man said, his head to one side. "How very interesting." He then went on, "Although I suppose as a guard dog he's not much use."

Becca did not reply. Benji had his own way of dealing with situations.

"He's a very good friend," she said, side-stepping the suggestion. "And this raft is the only place I go without him. NO DOGS," she said in a deep voice while pulling the stern face of authority. "Although he goes to lots of places without me."

"I'm sure he does," the man laughed. Again looking towards the shore he admired the prettiness of the cove and the cottages on the skyline.

"It's a bit like a picture postcard. I'll bet those little houses would tell wonderful tales if they could speak."

As an opening for further conversation Becca saw it as an opportunity not to be missed. Within seconds she was not only recounting the history of the cottages, but also of the whole village. Flattered by her attentive and almost silent audience, her flow broken only by his occasional and appropriate comments, she chattered on.

Finally the man said, "Everyone sounds so friendly, I think I'd like to live here! Maybe when I retire I will. We might even become neighbours! Would you mind having a policeman as a neighbour?"

"Is that what you are?" She looked at him thoughtfully and went on to ask, "Who do you work for?"

"The Queen."

Becca's jaw dropped in awe.

"At the Palace?"

He gave a short laugh. "No! I'm teasing. I am a policeman, and sometimes I work near the Palace but not in it. I'm not posh enough for that."

She giggled at him. She enjoyed having her leg pulled. Later, using the same ploy, she would tease Davy. Yet in a way the man did work for the Queen so that made it only a little leg-pull.

A moment later he looked at his watch and said, "Heck! Is that the time. I must be getting back. My wife will start to worry."

With that he stood up, and crossed the raft making it rock. Standing with his toes curled over the edge he said, "It's been nice talking to you, Becca. See you again."

"Are you staying in the village?"

"No, at The Mariner's Head."

She was about to ask him if he knew Mr. Armstrong and then she decided not to. Mom said she was not to be pushy.

At that point he dived into the water and, using a slow crawl, swam towards the next bay.

By the time Becca returned to the beach Benji was in a frenzy. Becca hugged him whilst saying to Davy, "The man on the raft is a policeman. He has brown teeth and wears a fab watch, but he's very nice."

Davy was not particularly interested, saying he was hot and hungry and they should be getting back for lunch.

Becca looked at him in surprise. She had no idea she had been away for so long. Benji, satisfied that all was well, wandered off. Nosing between the rocks and marking his territory he disappeared, only to return minutes later with sand on his muzzle.

Becca brushed him down and then, with all three chasing each other, they made their way home.

Jilly had made a huge Spanish omelette, a mixed salad and laid the big kitchen table for four.

Alex casually leaning against the cupboard door said, "I don't know how many lunches I owe you, Jilly. It's good of you to bother."

"You supplied the eggs," she reminded him. "The rest came from the garden – courtesy of Tom."

"And where did the thoughtfulness come from?" he asked. "You are such a generous soul!" he added.

Jilly shook her head, saying, "Not really. It just seems silly not to share. In any case you took us all out last week."

"A Pizza Parlour! Oh, big deal!" he said, belittling the gesture scornfully. "What I'd really like to do is take YOU out somewhere special. Not exactly black tie, just something a little classy. There's a new place near Land's End. I've heard it's superb – equal to a five star rating. How does that grab you? It could make a very pleasant evening out."

"Dream on," she laughed. "There are two children to be considered."

"Couldn't we get sitters? Or, how about one sitter and both kids sleeping under one roof?"

"You're serious, aren't you?" Jilly said, feeling mildly fazed at the thought of dressing up and dining out. And with the children organised, why not? Thoughtfully she went on, "If you like I can ask Mrs. Atkins to sit for us. And as there is a bed already made up in the little back room, I'm sure she wouldn't mind listening for both children. I've used her before. She's very reliable, but ..." she paused, "One of us would have to run her home. It's too far for her to walk alone and in the dark."

"No problem!" Alex told her. "We can have a taxi both ways and, after our return, Mrs. Atkins can be driven home in style. What do you think?"

"Wonderful!"

Jilly felt a sudden inner glow. It was almost like returning to her old way of life where wining and dining were the norm. Sophisticated was the only appropriate word to describe that, which used to be. High living. First-night tickets. Red-ringed calendar dates. The whirl of life. The hustle. The bustle. The excitement. All ended when Richard was killed.

Her body stiffened with the memory.

"What is it?" Alex asked, his face creased with concern. "What's wrong?"

"Nothing," she said, as her eyes searched the middle distance. And then she blinked and went on brightly, "When are we to embark upon this fabulous outing?" She spoke lightly conveying she was not expecting more than was being offered.

"If it can be arranged at such short notice, how about Saturday?"

"I'll ring Mrs. Atkins and see what she can manage."

At that point the children and Benji arrived. Tramping sand into the house they complained, loud and long, about the heat.

Benji slurped water thirstily.

Becca said, "It's absolutely boiling on the beach, Mom. I swam in my shorts and top, and they're already dry. That proves how hot it is!"

"Talking of which," Jilly said to Becca, "can you have a word with Delza? She's put on her anorak and I can't persuade her to take it off. She's so hot she's crying. She must be absolutely sweltering and extremely uncomfortable."

"OK, Mom! Is lunch ready? I'm starving!" With that she disappeared to return moments later with Delza's anorak draped round her shoulders.

"How did you manage that?" Jilly asked with amazement.

"I told her I was cold," Becca grinned.

Jilly and Alex exchanged amused glances. Sometimes answers were so simple.

During lunch Becca spoke of the man on the raft.

"How do you know he's a policeman?"

"He said so," Becca replied, scrunching celery. "He's staying at The Mariner's Head with his wife. And when he retires he wants to live here." She then added brightly, "You can sell him this cottage. I told him all about it. You know, the pirates and stuff. He said it sounds great, so I expect he'd like to buy it."

"And where would we live?" Jilly asked, amused by Becca's chain of thoughts..

"I could bunk in with Davy, and you and Alex…"

Cutting in quickly Jilly said, "I get the picture. Now, please eat your lunch and don't speak with your mouth full."

From the corner of her eye Jilly saw Alex's shoulders moving in silent mirth. She had a strong urge to join him.

"Dad," Davy said frowning, "what happens to a watch if you wear it when you're swimming?"

"Nothing if it's waterproof. Otherwise it ceases to work. Why? Don't tell me you've ruined yours already."

"Course not!" Davy scoffed. "I don't wear mine when I swim, but the man on the raft does, doesn't he, Becca?"

"It was super," she said. "It had lots of dials, and a really posh strap."

"I know the kind you mean," Alex said. "They provide all sorts of information at the press of a button. Very useful, particularly, for police work and such like."

"Perhaps he isn't a policeman," Becca said in her flight of fancy voice. "Perhaps he's James Bond!"

"And perhaps you've got too much imagination," Jilly laughed, "and please don't talk with your mouth full!"

"Sorry, Mom!"

After lunch Alex excused himself saying he needed to catch up with correspondence. "I'm not the world's best communicator, and I tend to let things slide. However," he sighed, "my bank manager is not the most patient man in the world."

"Bank managers! Huh! Are they ever!" Jilly grimaced.

The children and Benji went back to the beach leaving Jilly to idle away the time. The garden beckoned. Scent-filled but somehow airless it sweltered under a brassy sun. Pulling a striped lounger into part shade Jilly sank on to it and closed her eyes. From within the house came the sound of Delza crashing dishes and rattling cutlery. At least she was no longer crying – thanks to Becca. It was odd how Becca instinctively knew how to handle Delza. They seemed to have some kind of affinity, or was it to do with being young? Looking back Jilly knew that, in her own way, Delza was protective of Becca. Jilly recalled the time Becca had a wasp in her hair. Delza hit it with her fist knocking Becca to the ground. Becca, to break her fall, put out her hand, wrenched her wrist and burst into tears. Delza did not connect her action with Becca crying, but she was immensely pleased at having killed the wasp.

Poor Delza! It was possible she would always need a Becca in her life.

Jilly's thoughts switched to the man on the raft to wonder how much Becca had told him about the house. Its history was interesting and, when described by Becca, slightly over-stated and colourful. The date, carved on the granite chimney breast, was 1792. The time of George the Third. Becca was not into history as it really was, only how she imagined it to be. Jilly just hoped the family history had remained private. There was nothing to hide, but that which existed was painful to remember. Becca both knew and understood that Jilly did not encourage her to speak of it to strangers. It was for her own protection. Becca could not deal with sympathy, and once her tears started to flow they were difficult to stop.

Jilly had never spoken to Alex about Richard, and Alex had never discussed his marital status. The only inkling she had came from Becca via Davy who, just occasionally, would mention his mother in relation to school holidays. Jilly never questioned, believing that in so doing she forfeited the right to remain silent about her own life.

Although lost in thought she became aware of no longer being alone. Opening her eyes she saw Delza, silhouetted against the sky, holding a glass of lemon balm tea. It was ice-cold and looked like crème de menthe. It would seem she had been a mite heavy with the food colouring.

Sitting up, Jilly took the tumbler with both hands, and thanked her. She then suggested Delza should take a glass to the shed for her grandfather.

Delza looked blank.

Jilly sighed. She'd confused Delza again! Delza did not understand 'grandfather' In her world grandfather was 'Papa'.

Jilly smiled and said, "Take a drink to Papa?"

Delza shook her head, grunted, pointed to the shed and laid her cheek on her closed hands.

"He's sleeping?" Jilly said. "I expect he's hot and tired. Take it to him presently."

Delza shook her head and pointed towards the village. She wanted to go home, which she was allowed to do, and she also wanted her anorak.

"It's in the hall, Delza," Jilly told her.

Grunting happily Delza pattered away on bare feet.

Jilly sighed. Would she ever solve the problem of shoes versus slippers? Never in a million years!

Delza wandered back wearing her anorak with the hood strings crossed under her nose and held in place by her pouting lips. She looked like a Chinese Mandarin. It was a trick Becca had taught her and, when they did it together, it always made Jilly laugh. The challenge was for the girls not to laugh just to see who could hold the strings the longest. Becca always won, but having a generous heart she often conceded to Delza. At that Delza would smile for the rest of the day.

Now Jilly laughed and told Delza she was very clever. Delza grunted and, holding the strings in place with her lips, returned to the house.

Jilly saw she was still barefooted and called out, "Delza! Put on your shoes."

A few minutes later she heard her clump along the front path obviously well shod.

It was then that Jilly went into the house to telephone Mrs. Atkins about sitting with the children on Saturday. The arrangement was made and an assurance was given that caring for two children was just as easy as caring for one! Although Alex had not suggested a time, Jilly settled for seven-thirty. If Alex was unable to make a reservation, they would still have time to look elsewhere to eat. But that would not be necessary. For a few minutes later as Jilly returned to the garden Alex called over the fence, "If we've got a sitter, it's all set for Saturday, Jilly! Get out your tiara!"

"I'll wear mine, if you'll wear yours!"

"Does that mean the children are organised?"

"Seven-thirty on the dot!"

"You are an amazing woman!" He waved cheerfully and disappeared into his house whistling.

Suddenly Jilly had a mild panic. What on earth was she going to wear? What did she own that was neither too dressy nor too casual? Not much. Perhaps she could cannibalise and come up with something suitable. She hoped so.

The 'phone rang. Her heart twisted. She hesitated then hurried indoors. She knew what would happen next. It was like watching the trailer of an old movie. She picked up the 'phone. The line went dead. There was no message. There never was. Un-nerved she trembled, rubbed her damp palms together, then squared her shoulders. She would not give way.

Pushing the incident aside she returned to the garden, settled into the lounger and mulled over the contents of her wardrobe. There was sure to be something appropriate, therefore there was no problem. The only cloud in the sky briefly blotted out the sun relieving her skin of its daggered heat. Unexpectedly she shivered. The ringing 'phone, the silence, they had frightened her. Glancing about she now had the feeling she was not alone. Was she allowing her imagination to take over? Or was there a hidden threat in the air?

Forcing herself to relax she settled back into the lounger. She must not give way.

* * *

Arthur Armstrong held the feathery branch of tamarisk away from his face. While shielding him from sight it also gave him a good view of the Kenworth garden. The children couldn't be seen or heard. The old man wasn't in view, the girl had gone and, Mrs. Kenworth was settled and relaxed. The only thing about which he was unsure was the dog. If he sniffed him out, and exposed him, then everything would be jeopardised. Having found this secret spy-hole he wanted to hang on to it. Marilyn had been some help, but not enough. He needed to know more about everyone's movements. He needed to get into the house. Now was not the right time. He would have to wait. Silently he let the branch fall back into place, and then just as silently he slipped away.

Chapter Three

The heat on Friday was almost unbearable. The children squabbled endlessly. The whole day was filled with discontent. Alex was away and Davy was in Jilly's care. Where Alex had gone she was unsure, and if Davy knew he wasn't saying.

Alex returned home at teatime. He seemed remote as if he had a lot on his mind. Jilly, feeling it was not her place to ask, spoke only of the day's happenings, which amounted to little worth talking about.

Just after seven Alex and Davy returned to their own cottage to leave Becca in a peevish mood. With so much daylight left in which to play she felt cheated. Finally, and far earlier than usual, she went up to her room taking Benji with her.

Jilly, relieved to find herself alone, offered up a silent prayer of thanks, poured herself a glass of chilled Chablis and browsed through a glossy magazine. It was still daylight when she finally went to bed.

That night she didn't sleep well. She roused several times thinking she heard unaccountable noises. Twice she peered out of her open window to see the landscape, bathed in moonlight, as still and silent as a painting. Even the sea could not be heard. That was disturbingly unreal.

A tired household greeted the dawn and a snoring Benji was reluctant to move from his basket. Eventually, Becca yawned her way to the kitchen, made coffee and took a cup to Jilly.

By the time they were both up, showered and dressed the sun was beating down from the buttermilk sky. There was the smell of melting tar as roads shimmered and smudged the horizon with heat-haze. Aiming to keep cool, Jilly wore shorts and a loose top. Becca settled for her bikini. Looking for shade, Benji finally dug a hole under the escallonia and curled into it.

When Delza arrived crying because she was hot, no amount of coaxing could persuade her to take off her anorak. Despite Jilly opening all the doors and windows the house remained airless. Undeterred Delza still tackled her chores while weeping with discomfort.

In the garden Tom, his leathery and wrinkled face scowling, grumbled at having to water the plants.

"Fat lot o' good it does!" he mumbled. "No sooner do it hit the soil when it 'vaporates. Slugs is 'appy, though." He jetted water on to a half-eaten lettuce and snarled, "Little blighters!"

Just after ten Davy called for Becca and taking Benji with them they went down to the beach. Unexpectedly Delza unzipped her anorak and although he face was flushed she had stopped crying and seemed happy. Jilly was just beginning to think everyone was settling down when Tom banged on the door and told Jilly he would have to buy two new hinges to mend the gate.

"Our Delza broke it, Missus," he said, "so you take the money out of her wages. 'Taint fair that you should be forever forking out. 'er knows 'tis wrong to kick things."

"Don't worry about it, Tom," Jilly told him. "Just fix it."

"That's all very well, Missus," he said, sounding injured, "but it don't teach our Delza no lessons. At 'ome she do kick the sideboard. Ruined it, she 'as. It were a nice bit o' furniture 'til she got 'er size nines on it!"

Jilly laughed.

"Tom! You know full well that Delza takes a size five!"

He gave her a sheepish grin and said, "It's a good thing, too. With nines she'd have kicked the 'ouse to bits, never mind the sideboard!"

With that he wandered off, shaking his head.

Later Jilly gave Delza the feather-duster and showed her how to use it on the ornaments. This was something new for Delza. Usually she was not allowed to touch the china figurines. Now she was and that pleased her. Jilly's motive was purely to help her to cool down. Doing something which took little effort seemed to be the answer. The figures standing on the broad sills were pretty but of little value, a breakage would not matter, as long as Delza remembered not to touch anything else. Having settled her, Jilly went up to her room to find something to wear for that evening.

For some reason she had kept what Richard called her 'posh frocks'. They were extremely glamorous and totally unsuitable. She was beginning to despair of finding anything even remotely wearable when, inside a cardboard box wrapped in tissue, she uncovered a cream, silk blouse. Unable to remember when it was last worn it held no memories. It was beautifully cut. Worn with her black, velvet skirt perhaps, as an understatement, it would show good taste. A pair of pearl-trimmed black shoes and a matching bag completed the ensemble. She decided against jewellery. She wasn't out to impress. Keeping things simple sent out the right message. Alex was a good friend and that was all.

Suddenly she experienced a surge of pleasure, and the feeling of foreboding that had haunted her for so long disappeared. She felt a lightness to her heart. Temporary it might be, but she was glad of it.

Sitting at her dressing-table she peered into the mirror and scrutinised her face. Faint lines round her eyes appeared when she smiled, otherwise her skin was smooth, even if it did lack the bloom of youth. She wondered if Alex liked blondes. Being blonde himself he might prefer contrast. Yet there was contrast. Jilly was slight and slender against Alex's chunkiness. Davy was the same. Tow-headed, sturdy of body. Side by side he and Becca could be miniatures of Alex and herself – apart from Becca's red-gold hair. That came from Richard's side of the family. And what of Davy's mother? Was she blonde, too? As if it mattered! Jilly didn't know and she didn't want to know!

Opening a drawer she took out a black velvet box containing a bottle of Chanel No. 5. Rarely used, the bottle was almost full. Wistfully she wondered if there would ever be other occasions to warrant its use. She smiled at herself and said aloud, "You dismal Dolly! Get on with it!" And with that she felt the evening was going to be very pleasant.

Almost at the same moment came the sound of shattering china. Jilly's heart plummeted. What had Delza broken? And where had she broken it? Running downstairs she found Delza sitting on the floor, rocking and whimpering, the broken china scattered over the granite hearth. To Jilly's relief she recognised the bits as those of a vase. One of her mother's hand-made rejects. Something Delza should not have touched, but something that didn't matter.

Crouching, Jilly comforted her. "It's all right, Delza. It was an accident." She put her arm round her shoulders only to be shaken off. It was a warning sign. Delza was frightened. The noise, the disobedience and being discovered had made her retreat to somewhere within herself. For the rest of the day she would be completely intractable. Not wanting to cope with her difficult mood, using the heat as an excuse, she eventually spoke to Tom about sending her home. Minutes later, after being bribed with the promise of sweets at bedtime, Delza scuffed away slamming the gate behind her.

* * *

On the beach the children made plans for their evening together. They decided on a midnight feast in the garden, unaware that Mrs. Atkins was going to sit with them.

That news was given by Alex when they were at lunch in Jilly's kitchen.

Davy protested loudly, "Aw, come on, Dad! Why do we need a sitter?"

"Because it's against the law to leave you on your own," Alex explained patiently.

"Who's to know?"

Alex's jaw tightened.

"We are! And if you're going to make a fuss, Davy, the whole evening can be cancelled. It's up to you."

Becca nudged Davy, her expression conveying, "Big mouth!" She then went on, "Mrs. Atkins is OK, Davy. She isn't bossy. She just sits and watches the telly. We can still go to the beach, can't we, Mom?"

Jilly looked at Alex, "What do you think? It's what they would normally do."

After a moment Alex agreed, adding, "But home by half past eight and not a second longer, understand?"

"Thanks, Dad," Davy said, grinning. "Shall I wear my watch when I swim?"

Alex grinned back, drew his index finger across his throat and said, "If you do…!"

Becca joined in the laughter. They might not be able to have a midnight feast but the beach was a bonus.

Alex wondered if it would be a good idea to have the taxi pick up Mrs. Atkins before collecting himself and Jilly.

"What do you think?" he asked.

"It sorts out the timing," Jilly said. "And Mrs. A will be delighted. I doubt if taxis feature in her life all that often."

"Will you arrange it with her, Jilly? Coming from you it might sound better than coming from me."

"Will do," she happily agreed, appreciating his thoughtfulness.

With lunch over the children made for the beach and were surprised to see Delza on the clifftop. Mom said she had gone home. Although some distance away, they could see she was on her hands and knees with her face hidden by the tall grass.

Intrigued they paused and watched her.

"What's she doing?" Becca asked, frowning.

"Looking for her anorak?"

"Stupid! She's wearing it. Maybe she's lost something."

"Her head?"

"Idiot!" she cried, pushing him.

He pushed her in return and, Delza forgotten, they shouldered each other all the way down to the beach

By mid-afternoon they returned home saying the sand was too hot to walk on, and the raft had been taken over by a group of rough, noisy lads.

Retreating to the garden Becca was restless. She wanted to do something. A bike ride would be nice.

Jilly refused permission.

"Your bike is not roadworthy, Becca. It isn't safe."

"I can ride yours," she argued.

"No! It's too big. When you're on the saddle you can't reach the pedals."

"I can so," she replied sulkily.

"Becca, no!" Jilly said with finality.

Davy, sensing the friction, suggested playing a board game. Becca refused. She wanted a bike ride. Davy argued it was too hot, and again suggested a board game.

"How about Ludo? You always win at Ludo!"

Jilly secretly smiled. Davy was becoming quite a tactician.

Reluctantly Becca agreed, but it was not what she wanted to do.

The game lasted less than half an hour. Disinterested Becca threw down her counter and said, "Why don't we go and find out what Delza was doing on the cliff top."

"What for?" he asked, folding the board.

Becca shrugged, "It's something different to do."

Taking the game from him she went into the house.

Jilly was not in sight.

Benji trotted in, his nose covered with a mixture of sand and black soil. Making straight for his water bowl he lapped thirstily then crawled under the table and went to sleep.

Pushing the Ludo box into the cupboard Becca shouted, "Mom! We're going down to the beach."

"Why did you say that?" Davy asked, as they headed from the garden towards the cliff top.

"I couldn't tell her I thought Delza was eating grass, could I?"

Davy gave her a quizzical glance. Sometimes she had a really wild imagination. Just because Delza was on her hands and knees!

Pinpointing the place where they had last seen her was not difficult. The flattened and broken grass evident. The intriguing part was the bare patch between the rocks. Smudged hand prints on the sandy soil were clearly visible. Filled with curiosity Davy knelt, placed his hands, leaned forward and peered into a narrow fissure.

"Hey! Becca!" he said excitedly. "I can see into the cave."

Pushing him aside she knelt, peered, then sat back on to her heels grumbling, "There's nothing to see except rocks."

"Did you know you could look into the cave from here?"

"No!"

"So, what was Delza doing?"

"Looking into the cave?"

"Why?"

"I don't know," she said crossly. "Oh, come on, Davy. I'm thirsty. Let's go home."

Jilly was alarmed when Becca recounted the incident and decided Tom should be told.

"Tom, is it safe for Delza to be wandering about? I thought she always went straight home."

Tom, on his knees thinning radishes, got to his feet. After wiping his face on his shirt sleeve he asked if Jilly had scolded Delza.

"Has 'er done something wrong?"

"Absolutely not! There was an accident with a small vase. I told her breaking it didn't matter and although I was not cross with her, she was still upset."

"Ah!" Tom said knowingly. "That was why 'er was on the cliff top!"

"Doing what?" Jilly asked.

Tom's expression became guarded as if he had already said too much.

"Just wandering about," he shrugged dismissively. "Now I'd best get on." And without further explanation he abruptly turned away.

Mystified by his attitude Jilly hovered. It was unlike Tom to be disrespectful. She then decided that Delza's safety was more of a worry to her than to Tom. If she was allowed to roam, then it was no concern of hers. Even so, there was something odd about the whole incident.

To Jilly's relief the rest of the day was uneventful. After tea Davy arrived with a small overnight bag containing toiletries that he put in the bathroom. Becca bossily told him although he was welcome to sleep in the spare bed he was not to touch anything of hers that was kept in the room. Davy took her orders in his stride. He was used to her ways. Remaining cheerful he then followed her into the garden.

Jilly was just touching her wrists with perfume when Mrs. Atkins arrived. Wearing a white hat and a floral dress, she stepped out of the taxi looking pleased. She was always happy to sit for Mrs. Kenworth, and it was a comfortable way to add to her income.

Mindful of her duties she asked what time the children had supper and how late they should go to bed. Having listened to Jilly's instructions, she then told her how nice she looked and wished her a happy evening. After that she sat down and switched on the television. There was a good film on. A love story. Mrs. Atkins liked a bit of romance.

When Alex collected Jilly he was unprepared for how she looked. He had expected her to turn heads, but to look so absolutely stunning amazed him. She was truly beautiful and he told her so.

The warmth of a blush touched her skin as she stuttered her thanks. Compliments were so rare she had almost forgotten how to accept them gracefully. Delighted that the evening had started on such a high note, she wondered what other good things were in store.

⋆ ⋆ ⋆

The restaurant was elegant. The service efficient and unobtrusive. With the meal ordered they then sat in comfort overlooking the sea, and drinking chilled wine.

Alex, at ease with the world, looked at their surroundings and asked Jilly if she was impressed.

"Very," she admitted. "It's really beautiful and on décor alone well worth top rating."

"Is that the voice of appreciation, and experience talking?"

"Very much so," she smiled.

He looked at her for a long moment, and then said thoughtfully, "It's odd how, although we know each other quite well, we know very little. We've never discussed the past."

Inside herself Jilly shrank.

"It's irrelevant! There's no need, is there?" she asked in a tight voice.

"I'm not sure," he said, again thoughtfully. "If I owned a thoroughbred horse I'd want to know its pedigree so that I would treat it properly. Isn't it the same with people? The more you know the better you understand them?"

She looked at him over the rim of her glass. Sipping the wine it suddenly tasted sour. He was asking her to talk about her past with Richard and she didn't want to. She could not share her memories with a stranger. Was Alex a stranger? Almost, yet at the same time she felt she knew him. How could that be? Emotionally she felt tangled and dreaded the idea of the evening slipping into a black hole.

Her fears were wiped away by Alex's generous and warm smile.

There was an ease about him which embraced her as he said, "Let me start the ball rolling, Jilly. Let me tell you about yesterday."

"Alex, you don't have to!"

"No, I know! But I want to. I don't want to build barriers. I would much rather tear them down. So … yesterday I went to Bristol to see my ex-wife."

She looked away from him. Did she really want to know about his domestic upheavals? Did she care? Did it matter? Oddly it did.

Alex went on, "Every now and again there is a crisis. Usually to do with money, which I have to sort out."

Against her will, Jilly asked, "Aren't you divorced?"

"Yes, but I still feel responsible for her although it won't be for much longer," he added, sounding relieved. "She is about to remarry and this latest debt is for her wedding outfit!"

"You're joking!" Jilly uttered, struggling not to laugh at the absurdity.

"I wish," came his rueful reply. "Designer clothes do not come cheap!"

"They most certainly do not!" Jilly exclaimed. Remembering her own once extensive wardrobe she asked if his wife had been accustomed to labels.

"And still is! Originally it was a way of life for her. I had my own furniture-making business, doing all the designing." He held out his scarred left hand, "I also learned the practical side, as you can see." Withdrawing his hand he went on, "Life was pretty good – or so I thought – then everything went wrong. After my marriage folded I sold the business and got out. I still do freelance designing, but nothing practical."

With her curiosity aroused she wanted to ask why the marriage failed. Alex gave the answer in a distant voice. "It was another man – though not the one she is about to marry." He gave a wry smile. "This chap is one of many. The latest. The poor fish is rich and he's in her net."

"Were you rich when you married her?"

"Funnily enough, no!" He then gave a broad, if slightly bitter, grin and added, "I expect she saw my potential! But enough about me, what about you? What line of business was Richard in?"

Now that the subject was broached she shrank from it. It was so hard, so difficult to speak of Richard. It brought him to life. He was dead, and nothing could change that. It was deeply painful to even voice his name, but could she avoid doing so forever? Now she must test herself.

Taking a deep breath, and without looking at Alex, she told him Richard was an agent – a courier.

"Do you mean a representative type of thing?" he asked, totally misunderstanding. His error seemed to ease Jilly's noticeably strained expression.

"No," she said, with a faint smile that held forgiveness. "He was self-employed, undertaking to collect and deliver articles which might not have been safe if transported through normal channels."

"What sort of articles?" he asked, his brows drawn together.

"Anything. Papers to do with business or even at times to do with Government. Valuable artefacts. Paintings. Jewels. As long as they were legal he would accept the commissions."

"Couldn't they be dangerous?"

"At times," she nodded. "It was always risky. That was part of the challenge. He loved the idea of danger. Not that he met it very often. It was just a chance which added spice to his life."

"And did he take one chance too many! Was that how he was killed – because of his work?"

Dumbly Jilly shook her head wondering if she could continue. It was a long time since she had spoken of Richard's actual death.

Perceptively Alex said gently, "Look, Jilly, if you'd rather talk of something else..."

"No. I'm all right." She took a sip of wine and went on," Richard's death was nothing to do with his work. He was the victim of a hit-and-run driver. It happened in Finchley."

"It that where he worked?"

"No. His office is in Soho." Having used the present tense she gave a quick smile. "The lease still has a year to run, and I can't bear to give it up. Silly, isn't it?"

He shook his head and asked where Finchley fitted into the picture.

"I don't know," she admitted. "I've never known. I can only guess it might have been a pick-up point for a commission."

"Aren't you curious?"

"I was. Very. But there were no answers. The accident was investigated. The other man involved survived and, as far as I know, is fit and well. The driver was never traced."

"The other man? Was he a friend of Richard's?"

"No. Just a passer-by in the wrong place at the wrong time." At that she looked away. "Let's change the subject," she said, her voice brittle her face stone-like. Her memories were now crowding in to suffocate her.

Alex looked at her sharply. Something was hurting her.

"Jilly, what is it?"

She lowered her head to avoid his searching gaze and said, "I'm not sure."

"Tell me."

She bit her lip. She had not intended to let things go so far. It was getting too personal and too painful. She remained silent.

He reached for her hand and gently pressed it.

"Jilly, please. Whatever it is you can tell me."

Aware of his touch, glad of its comfort, she said with a calmness she did not feel, "The day before Richard was killed he left the house extremely early and came home late. He gave no reason. That was most unusual. He also seemed pre-occupied. Again that was unusual. Richard never brought business home. It was almost as if he lived two unrelated lives."

"Did you ask him if anything was wrong?"

Jilly nodded. "He assured me it was nothing serious. He'd had a celebratory lunch with a friend and had too much champagne. I didn't believe him. It wasn't the kind of thing he did. I wondered if there was a woman involved." She avoided Alex's steady gaze, feeling traitorous to Richard's memory.

"And was there?"

"I don't know. I ran away from the situation. I didn't want the inevitable heart-break which might have followed."

"That's understandable."

"Now," she said, "I have untarnished memories of picnics, trips to the zoo and all the little things that made us happy. Family celebrations were always wonderful. My parents' wedding anniversaries were the annual highlight. Richard used to joke, saying our marriage would never last as long as theirs. How right he was," she added bitterly.

Alex covered her hand with his own to ask, "And the other woman?"

"Non-existent! That's what I tell myself. The following day he was the Richard I knew." She pulled her hand away. "In fact he was at his very best!"

"You remember?"

"I remember every moment of that day

"Richard had an early 'phone call from his secretary. There was an unexpected offer of a commission. Some sort of papers had to be collected from somewhere in the late evening, but he didn't say to where they had to be delivered. Although it put Richard's schedule out he thought it worthwhile. He then cancelled his morning flight to Paris and booked on to one leaving at midnight. That in turn meant he would be at home for longer than usual. Becca was delighted. She loved having Richard to herself. Because I had a hair appointment I'd arranged with Mrs. Garland, our cleaner, to remain in the house until Becca was collected by friends for a trip to the zoo. Even though Richard was at home, Mrs. Garland was happy to stay on as arranged. The morning was slightly hectic and it did throw me out of gear, but it was a fun time, with lots of laughter."

Her voice suddenly tailed away and she looked into the distance as if fearing to lose sight of the memory. She then shook her head and went on, "The last time I saw Richard he was on the 'phone. He mouthed he would be leaving at noon. When I returned home, having lunched with a girl friend, the house was empty. Becca arrived about seven and had a few tears after I was cross with her for playing with my manicure scissors. Scissors were a big no-no. As it turned out I was wrong. Mrs. Garland said that just after Becca left, Richard had gone into his study and asked not to be disturbed. Later he asked to borrow the kitchen scissors and then refused them as being too big. He must have used the manicure scissors though why in Becca's room and for what purpose I have no idea."

Alex didn't even try to guess, but he did store the information in the back of his mind.

With a sudden look of embarrassment she said, "Alex, I'm so sorry. I'm rattling on, spoiling the evening, what must you think of me?"

"I think you're gorgeous!" he said.

"I think you're drunk!" she countered, with laughter.

"I'm happy!" he told her.

She believed him.

The waiter arrived and led them to their table. At the same time there came a violent clap of thunder and a storm broke with incredible fury. Momentarily the lights dimmed, flickered, and then glowed steadily.

Jilly and Alex smiled at each other. Let it rain! They were comfortable and dry. Their meal held promise and the champagne could not be wasted.

They were halfway through their dessert when Alex's mobile rang.

"Damn!" he said, "I meant to switch it off. Sorry, Jilly."

A moment later, having taken the call and put his 'phone away he said, keeping his voice level, "That was Mrs. Atkins. It would seem Benji has gone missing."

"Oh, no!" Jilly exclaimed. "Missing? He can't be. He never wanders off. Is Becca all right?" she asked, knowing she wouldn't be. If anything had happened to the dog she would be inconsolable.

Alex, having been told that Becca was distraught, tempered his reply by saying she was tearful.

Jilly knew that to be an understatement.

Rising from her chair she said, "Alex, I'm sorry, but you'll have to take me home."

Calmly he replied, "Of course. Finish your wine first."

She refused. "I can't. You don't understand. I must get home."

"Jilly," he said firmly, "listen to me. Everything is in hand. Mrs. Atkins had the foresight to arrange for a taxi to collect us as soon as possible. We can do nothing without transport; just try not to worry."

Jilly hardly heard him. She knew Becca would be in turmoil. She adored Benji. He was a gift from her father which made him extra special to her. She firmly believed that if she were ever really naughty then Benji would die. Jilly, dreading this was part of the problem, explained it to Alex. That left, both wondering what Becca might have done to cause so much upset.

The taxi arrived within fifteen minutes. The storm had heightened and the rain was a wall of grey water. St. Michael's Mount, lit by fork lightning, appeared to swirl in distortion as white horses pranced at its rocky base.

Pale-faced, Jilly hunched forward willing the rain to stop as flood water slowed their progress. It wasn't until they started to climb the slight rise to the village that Jilly's leaden heart lightened.

They found the cottage ablaze with light. At the front door Mrs. Atkins hovered anxiously. Careless that her hair and flowered dress were sodden, she retreated into the hall, saying, "We've all been out looking for Benji but we couldn't see much. Not in this rain." She dabbed her streaming face with a crumpled handkerchief. "I've never seen nothing like it!"

Becca flung herself into Jilly's arms, her face pale, her eyes red and shining with tears.

Davy, too, was white-faced, his wet shirt clinging to his body.

Alex gripped his shoulder to ask if he was all right. Davy nodded.

Alex held up his hand spreading his fingers. "I'll be five minutes," he said. "Can you hold the fort?"

"We'll be fine, Dad!"

Alex, bundling Mrs. Atkins into the waiting taxi, climbed in beside her. She protested. There was no need for him to ride with her. She was all right. She was wet but that was nothing a dry towel couldn't take care of. He patted her hand and said there was no way he would allow her to return home alone. At that she settled back into the seat. Perhaps the evening had not been of the best, but at that moment she felt cherished.

Becca clung to Jilly and sobbed out her fears.

"Mumma, what if Benji's fallen down a hole, or into the sea? What if he's trapped? What if…?" The possibilities tumbled from her mouth in a stream of fear.

Softly Jilly suggested, whilst gently rocking her, that it was likely he was just digging up his bones. How she remained so calm she did not know, for deep down she knew Becca was truly frightened. Calling her Mumma was something she did only when she was deeply troubled.

Suddenly huge, uncontrolled sobs burst from her, and unstoppable tears flooded her face.

She was sorry! When she took the stopper from the bottle she had meant only to smell it. Now it was all spilt. It had marked the dressing box Daddy had bought, and the bottle was empty.

For a moment Jilly did not understand, and then she realised that Becca smelled of Chanel No. 5. She had dropped the bottle and damaged the box! So that was the crux! Becca thought her naughtiness was why Benji was missing! Swiftly Jilly reassured her that was not so. A reprimand she would deliver later. Davy was standing quietly at her side looking lost and forlorn. Holding out her free hand she drew him to her. Willingly he sat next to her showing no embarrassment at having her arm around his shoulders.

Gradually Becca's tears gave way to small sniffs while Davy tried to account for Benji's disappearance. There was nothing mysterious or dramatic about it. He just hadn't followed them home from the beach.

"We'd been playing 'Piggy in the Middle' with him," Davy said, "and we came home at half past eight."

"That was when I spilt your perfume," Becca confessed, her eyes welling with fresh tears.

Davy cut in swiftly, "We thought Benji had followed us, but we didn't really miss him until it started to rain."

Becca lifted her head from Jilly's shoulder and added, "We spent ages looking for him. Davy even went down to the beach, I went along the lane and Mrs. Atkins searched the garden. We called and called, but he didn't come home."

Tears spilled and she buried her face in Jilly's neck.

That was when practicalities took over. Damp clothes had to be discarded, and warm drinks provided after hot showers. By the time Alex returned, both children were clad in nightwear and ready for bed. They were much happier having been convinced by Jilly that come the morning – if not before – Benji would be home leaving muddy paw marks on the kitchen floor.

There was no suggestion that Davy should return to his own bed. Jilly insisted the original arrangement should stand. There had been enough disruption for one night.

Later Alex asked, not without embarrassment, if Jilly would object to him also staying the night.

"I'll doss down on the couch or the armchair – whatever. I need to be nearby for Davy. On the face of it he's settled, but he's not quite at ease. I'm pretty sure he feels responsible for the situation."

"Poor Davy!" Jilly said sympathetically, "The blame lies entirely with Benji! Davy must not feel guilty! You should be proud of his sensitivity."

"I am!"

Jilly went upstairs to retrieve bedding from the airing cupboard aware that the landing held the faint smell of Chanel No. 5. Poor Becca. Jilly could imagine her fright. When she returned to the sitting room Alex was pouring red wine into china mugs.

Jilly laughed, "I do own appropriate glassware! Where did you get the wine?"

"From home. After I'd delivered Mrs. Atkins, I nipped indoors and grabbed the first bottle I saw. The only reason we are drinking from mugs is because I knew where to find them!" He then added, "They are not quite as delicate as flutes, or as exciting as champagne, but do you mind?"

"Not at all," she told him, piling the bedding on to a chair. "I'm just sorry for spoiling the evening, Alex. It was going so well. Everything was turning out right, and when it all went wrong I couldn't cope."

She took the wine he offered and they sat side by side on the settee.

"Tonight is in the past, Jilly. We can always have another evening out!"

"I really am sorry," she said through a sigh of regret. "All this fuss over a missing dog! And spilled perfume!"

"Ah, yes! That didn't help, did it? And I'm assuming Benji doesn't go walk-about very often."

"Never!" she told him frowning, "But there's a first time for everything, isn't there? If Benji has found himself a ladyfriend…" She smiled, "Becca's into birds and bees so she'll understand."

In her own mind Jilly decided that was the answer. It was acceptable and normal.

Alex was talking about Mrs. Atkins not being able to throw any light on the subject. She was slightly put out about getting so wet. It seemed her dress was of the dry-clean-only variety, and she thought it would now be unwearable. That being so she would have to put it in the church jumble sale. Jilly made a mental note to tactfully offer a replacement.

The conversation drifted back to Benji. If he hadn't found a lady friend, could he be shut in somewhere? Most of the cottages in the vicinity had out-houses of one kind and another, but if he was trapped then his inability to bark did not help matters.

Outside the storm continued to rage. Although the thunder grew fainter, and the lightning less frequent the oppressive heat remained.

After a while Jilly checked on the children. Davy's breathing was regular, his bed smooth and unrumpled. Becca was softly whimpering, the duvet on the floor, her pillow serving no purpose. Jilly left her undisturbed. The night was so hot she was unlikely to feel chilled.

* * *

Arthur Armstrong tossed the empty cigarette packet into the dead hearth. The ashtray, full to overflowing, had already spilled its contents on to the small side table. He wiped the grey ash away with the heel of his hand to leave a tell-tale smear on the ring-marked surface. Closing his eyes he leaned back into the winged chair, steepled his nicotine stained fingers and wished the storm would pass. Storms gave him headaches. It was something to do with air pressure – or so he had been told. Not that he found all explanations of life's mysteries acceptable – he had his own theories. Which was why he found himself where he was; tucked away at the back of nowhere looking for answers to questions that might prove to be hypothetical.

He knew for certainty that Richard Kenworth had been murdered by accident – if that wasn't a contradiction in terms. In his own mind Arthur thought the 'accident' was meant only to scare instead of which it killed. Either way it was likely threats would have been made. If so, what lay behind them and who made them?

With deliberation, and not for the first time, he mentally went back to the morning of the day Richard died. Despite the passage of time, and a great deal of reasoning, he could not convince himself everything was normal. It wasn't. He couldn't say why. Richard was short-tempered. That was not unusual. It came hand-in-hand with his responsibilities. Arthur had become accustomed to crisply delivered orders. And after four years they were both expected and accepted.

And so the fateful day began.

Safety was paramount, and so a set procedure was always followed. Richard would ring Arthur at home. Time round about 10.00 a.m. Conversation would be mundane. Fifteen minutes later Arthur, using a public telephone, would ring Richard on his mobile.

Arthur would be given instructions for his pending duties. Sometimes they involved travelling abroad, at others it was local work. That particular day it was local but, because of circumstances, Arthur had to break with procedure.

After he dialled Richard he heard him say in his precise way," We'll leave from the office and go to Victoria. The time has yet to be arranged but I'll let you know by noon. You won't need your passport this time round, OK?"

"Guv, I'm sorry," Arthur said.,"I can't do it. I'm down with a stomach bug. Can things be delayed until I'm back on my feet?"

He heard Richard swear before replying, "No can do. This is urgent and important. I've already had one set-back."

He didn't explain further. Arthur knew he wouldn't – even if he asked. He did, however, suggest Richard use Escort 2, "if he's available."

"He isn't!" Richard replied, his voice tight.

Arthur felt a shaft of annoyance. Why the hell did Richard have to keep everything and everyone in separate compartments? There was no teamwork! He employed three staff. Two Security Escorts and a secretary. None of them had ever met. His wife, Jilly, was an unknown quantity. Arthur had no idea why, any more than he knew why Escort 2 was unavailable. Risking Richard's anger he made a suggestion.

"Guv, as it's a local job and you need an escort, how about using Jack Preston my son – in – law?"

"For God's sake, Arthur!" Richard exploded

"Hang about!" Arthur said calmly. "He's a one-hundred percent good guy. He's on leave from the army, and he knows how to take care of himself – and anyone else for that matter. He doesn't need to know anything. All he has to do is keep his eyes peeled. Right?"

There was a long silence before Richard replied doubtfully, "Using someone untried and untested? I'm not sure. I'll be taking one helluva risk."

"Not as far as the lad's concerned, you won't," Arthur told him stoutly. "But it's up to you, Guv. All I can say is he's tough and trustworthy."

"Thanks," Richard said. "I'll think about it and get back to you."

With that he rang off.

Just before noon he rang back. The usual precautions were not observed, and the conversation was brief.

"Ask Jack to wear his uniform, as means of identification, and to be outside Bartlet Wine Bar just off Finchley Road at nine-thirty p.m."

Arthur, seeing no problem with the arrangement, agreed.

Now, looking back, he again wondered why the change of venue. It was not unusual, but why Finchley? Cancellations were one of the hazards calling for fast re-organisation.

A hoax was rare and potentially dangerous, but it was always checked out. Had this assignment slipped through the net? Had Richard been sucked in? If so by whom, and why? They were the imponderables. There were no clues. No leads. The only certainty was that as Richard lay dead in the gutter someone searched his body. That brought Arthur back to the imponderables. Who and why?

Jack witnessed the search. After being hit by the same car, and despite having a broken leg and severe bruising, he clearly saw and remembered what happened. The car was a black Ford. It hit Richard full on and then swerved and hit Jack. A white man came from nowhere and searched Richard's body. Finding nothing, he then kicked him and ran off. The next thing Jack knew was being stretchered into the ambulance. Pain set in, and everything became hazy. When he came round and was questioned by the police, instinct told him not to mention the man and the body search. He knew nothing. As far as the police were concerned he was merely crossing the road and couldn't recall much at all.

After proving his identity and being kept in hospital over-night he was allowed to go home. He heard nothing more about the incident. If it was reported in the local paper he didn't see it.

The fact that his injury had ruined his career was something he was learning to live with. The Army didn't do limping soldiers. That did not stop him from wanting to even the score. Arthur had always spoken very highly of Richard, and Jack felt it was his duty to take some kind of revenge. As far as Richard's wife went, she was an unknown quantity. Did nice guys marry bad girls? It happened.

Now Arthur shifted in his chair, his thoughts sour. What use was the information he had? He needed evidence that, he felt sure, could be found in the cottage next door. It was a case of waiting for the opportunity to search it and find ... what? He didn't know but something would turn up. Inwardly he cursed Richard's mania for secrecy. If Escort 2, the nameless, faceless counterpart to Arthur, was also trying to solve the mystery, their working together could bring about a swift conclusion. There was no chance of that happening. Searching for Escort 2 would be a waste of time. Arthur had no starting point. The man's profile was a complete blank except to Richard. Another enigma was the secretary 'Miss Smith'. Arthur had never seen her. The files in the office contained only data of dates and destinations. Arthur knew that only because he recognised some of the information relating to assignments in which he had been involved. About the remainder he knew nothing. And the computer? He didn't want to know it. He preferred to use his brains.

Wearily he glanced at his watch. Earlier there had been a lot of noise. What with the thunder and yelling and shouting from the kids next door, it was pandemonium. Now everything seemed to have quietened. So it should. It was gone midnight and time for bed. Would he sleep? He didn't think so.

* * *

Jilly, sipping the last of her wine, was comfortable and drowsy. Her disquiet about Benji had subsided although she was still worried about Becca. While the situation no longer appeared out of hand, life had not yet returned to normal despite Alex's calming influence. He was not easily ruffled. In that respect he was like Richard. He too was always calm in a crisis. Quickly she pushed Richard from her thoughts. She didn't want to go down that road tonight. It was late and she needed to sleep undisturbed by recurring dreams.

Yawning, and after bidding Alex goodnight, she was in the hall on her way to her room when the telephone rang. Someone had found Benji! Expectantly snatching up the 'phone she breathed, "Hello?"

"Mrs. Kenworth?"

"Yes!"

"Remember Pontivy?"

Before she could reply the line went dead.

Expectantly Alex moved to her side. She stared at him in bewilderment.

"What is it?" he asked urgently.

"I don't know," she faltered. "It was something to do with Pontivy."

"Pontivy?"

Haltingly she explained it was a small town in Brittany where she and Becca stayed with her friend Mitzi." It was just after Richard's funeral. The man on the 'phone said to remember Pontivy."

"Why, what happened there?"

Her mind was blank.

"Were you and Becca in a hotel?" he asked, looking for a starting point

"No, we were staying with my friend Mitzi who was converting a barn," she told him. "We had gone to Pontivy to buy floor tiles."

"And?"

"Nothing. We shopped, had lunch and then went back to Mitzi's."

"And that's all?"

"Yes. Becca, because she didn't speak French, had a fit of the giggles but other than that…" she shrugged, and spread her hands helplessly. Yet, as she did so she felt a shaft of unease. She couldn't pinpoint it, but it was there. Realising she was too tired to pursue the matter she gave a wan smile and said, "I'd rather not talk about it tonight, Alex. Perhaps tomorrow?"

"Whenever," he replied, easily.

With a look of gratitude she lightly touched his arm and said, "I did so enjoy our time together, Alex. Thank you."

Smiling he saluted.

Reaching Becca's door she decided to check on her and found her sleeping quietly. The earlier whimpering had stopped and she appeared settled. As Jilly tip-toed towards the door her eyes fell on Becca's cluttered dressing table and the tiny toy telephone. Doll-size, Becca had seen it in a shop window and bought it in … Pontivy!

Jilly's heart lurched.

Now she remembered.

Becca had gone missing for several minutes.

Mitzi found her clutching the unwrapped telephone.

Jilly, relieved to find her safe, pushed the incident aside. There was no reprimand. The incident was over and unimportant.

Now she asked herself, was it? Did Becca really wander away, or was she lured by someone English-speaking?

Jilly's heart lurched again.

The voice on the 'phone – a man – he was English-speaking! Was he in Pontivy on the day in question?

If so, who was he and what did he want?

Chapter Four

At dawn, tearfully, Becca crawled into Jilly's bed and curled into her arms. Jilly, heavy-eyed after a restless night held her tightly and lulled her to sleep. Her thoughts crowded in. She had to dismiss Benji. If only she could dismiss the anonymous caller's reference to Pontivy. Could it be to do with Becca's disappearance? Becca could know the answer, but now was not the time to ask her. She would be thinking only of Benji. Beyond that she would not go. She had her father's single-mindedness and it was not easy to deal with. For now, all Jilly could do was offer comfort and hope Benji would soon be found.

Despite the early hour Alex had already left. A note on the kitchen table told Jilly he was going to scour the cliff tops towards Penzance, and would be back to search further afield if need be. He said nothing about his feeling of unease. The reference to Pontivy could be a veiled warning – even a threat – against Becca. He needed to be on his guard.

Before leaving, he roused Davy from sleep and, without offering either an explanation or reason, he asked him to watch over Becca.

"Don't let her do anything silly."

"Like what?" Davy asked, knuckling his eyes and yawning.

"Oh, you know! Girls can be so nutty when they want to be. Who knows what mountains she will climb, or holes she will burrow into to look for Benji."

"He hasn't come home?"

Alex shook his head.

"OK, Dad. I'll do my best, but you know what she's like."

Alex ruffled Davy's hair, and said, "Thanks, son. I'll try not to be out for too long."

Once away from the cottage Alex quickened his pace. Time was of the essence. He didn't want to be away from Jilly longer than need be. The 'phone call had really disturbed her, and her reluctance to discuss it in depth worried him. He half hoped the caller could be an admirer – even an ex-lover. He instantly dismissed the idea as being frivolous. The timescale alone made that possibility unlikely. No, the situation was such that it could be serious. And it had to be talked about.

Ahead lay towering cliffs and at their base a dangerous and rocky shoreline. If Benji were down there he would stand no chance at all.

Davy was still in bed when he heard Tom and Delza arrive. Crawling out he quickly pulled on his shorts. He wanted to tell them about Benji. Creeping out of the cottage he made his way to the garden shed.

Explaining the situation to Tom was easy, but Tom explaining to an open-mouthed Delza was a different matter. She appeared to be listening but gave no indication that she understood. She just kept zipping and un-zipping her anorak.

Finally Tom said, "Now you listen to Papa, Delza. By-and-by, you go down to the village and look for Benji. If you see him you come back and tell me. All right?"

Delza grunted and stretched her face into a smile.

"How will she be able to tell you?" Davy asked intrigued. His boyish mind thinking in terms of secret signs.

"Her'll manage," Tom said abruptly, and with that Davy had to be content.

Jilly arrived with a mug of tea for Tom and orange juice for Delza. She then told Davy to help himself to cereal in the kitchen, and if he wanted toast Becca would make it for him. "Only if you ask nicely!" she added, her eyes twinkling.

Davy grinned.

As Davy left, Tom said between sips of tea, "Sorry about the dog, Missus. In a minute Delza's off to the village to look for him – if that's all right with you. Not that 'er'll touch him if she do find 'im, but 'er'll tell me in 'er own way."

Jilly recalled from past experience that Delza passing on information could be a lengthy and puzzling business and so a sudden idea offered a short cut

"Tom, what if I gave Delza a scarf? If she wears it we will know she hasn't seen Benji, and if she takes it off and waves it, we'll know she has. Would that work, d'you think?"

Tom emptied his mug, wiped his mouth on the back of his hand and told her he thought that was something with which Delza could cope.

Jilly hurried into the house and returned with an emerald-green, silk scarf which she tied loosely round Delza's neck.

That pleased Delza. She liked the bright colour, and the softness against her skin was a delight.

Tom looked and flattered her." You'm 'andsome, my bird! Now you hear me. If you see Benji then you come back to me and give me the scarf."

Delza scowled.

Reading her mind he went on, "I'll give the scarf back to you, then you show Missus where you've seen Benji. All right?"

Delza grunted and hid her chin in the silk.

Jilly looked at Tom with doubt.

He gave her a rare smile and said, "'er'll be fine, Missus. Don't you worry. 'ers a good girl when 'er gets a little reward – like wearing your scarf. And 'er can be sharp-eyed when 'er wants to be."

Not entirely convinced, Jilly hovered uncertainly then, deciding Tom knew best, she returned to the kitchen.

Becca had cheered up. Although her eyes were still dull her face didn't look quite so pinched. She and Davy were munching toast and marmalade while having a mild argument about where to look for Benji. Before they could agree Alex returned.

Hot and mud-spattered, he pushed his fingers through his damp hair.

"No sign," he said drawing a glass of water. "I asked several people if they'd seen him. No one had."

Becca's face puckered.

Jilly said, with forced cheerfulness, "He'll be around somewhere! We'll just have to keep looking."

She then suggested that asking neighbours to check their out-houses, garages and sheds would be a good idea.

"Delza has gone to look round the village, so that area's covered."

"Delza?" Alex repeated with surprise.

Jilly smiled, "Yes, it's all been taken care of."

Becca said she wanted to look on the beach and in the cave.

Alex gave Davy a quick glance.

Davy responded by agreeing with Becca. He then boosted her ego by saying he thought it a really good idea. He then went on to remind her that, as the previous week it was she who found the iron ring in the wall of the cave, it was more than likely she would find Benji.

"Not trapped!" she half shrieked in horror.

"Course not. Silly!" Davy laughed.

Jilly cut in, "With all points of the compass covered, one of us is bound to find him."

Becca's clouded eyes cleared and she beamed. If Mom said so, then it would happen.

Jilly went in search of Tom and told him of their intentions. She was more than grateful when he offered to man the 'phone.

"I'm a bit slow on my legs to go wandering about, but I can deal with callers and messages. If Benji do come back on his own, then he'll be safe with me."

Uneasily she wondered about the silent calls. Then dismissed them, saying, "It might be a good idea if you were indoors, Tom. Out in the garden you might not hear the 'phone."

"That's fine by me, Missus. You put me a chair in the hall, and I'll be as right as nine pence." He then added, "I wouldn't say no to a glance of the 'paper."

"I'll leave it on the hall table, and if you want more tea – just help yourself."

* * *

The children set off for the beach but didn't actually go there. Instead they sat hidden by the cliff overhang and had a fierce argument. Becca was determined to have her own way, and Davy was just as determined she wouldn't.

"You're not to go!" he told her angrily. "Your bike isn't safe and your Mom's is too big for you to ride"

"I don't care!" Becca shouted back, furious at his opposition to her plan. "I'm only going through the lanes to The Mariner's Head."

"It doesn't matter where you're going! Your Mom said you were not to ride either bike!"

"That was before Benji went missing," she cried rebelliously.

"It doesn't matter when she said it," Davy yelled. "She meant it!"

"I don't care!" she repeated hotly. "The man on the raft is a policeman. He'll know how to find Benji."

"Don't be so stupid! He's not going to spend his holiday looking for a lost dog!"

Becca's eyes filled with tears.

Davy looked away disconcerted. All he was trying to do was his father's bidding. He knew it would be difficult but he had not allowed for Becca's tears. They always undermined his resolve. He had to give way. If he didn't Becca would go it alone, and that would make the situation even worse.

Scrambling to his feet he said, gruffly. "Oh, come on, then! Let's check the beach first."

"First?" Becca queried, blinking away her tears, "Then what?"

"We'll look for your policeman," he told her, disgruntled at having no alternative. Becca immediately brightened.

"And you won't tell Mom about the bike?"

Davy shook his head and crossed his fingers behind his back. No, he wouldn't tell. Not unless he had to.

Seeing the policeman on the beach was totally unexpected.

Wearing cream Chinos and a blue, open-necked shirt Becca recognised him instantly.

Almost incoherent with excitement and urgency it was several minutes before she made herself understood. He then listened gravely, offering both sympathy and advice.

"Dogs are a bit like people," he comforted. "They have routines which they like to follow. Know what I mean?"

Becca nodded.

"So," the man went on. "If you know his routine then check it out. If that doesn't work then look for him in his favourite haunts. If he has doggy pals, talk to their owners."

He glanced at his watch and said regretfully, "I'd like to help, but I've promised to take my wife to Land's End. Sorry."

"That's all right," Becca said hiding her disappointment. "I expect someone will find him. Lots of people are looking for him. My Mom, Davy's Dad. Even Delza and although she can't talk she can still look."

"The more eyes, the better!" he told her. "I'll be on the beach in the morning and if he's still missing, come and talk to me and I'll see what I can do." Again he glanced at his watch. "Try not to worry. I'm sure he'll turn up." At that he patted the top of her head and strode off following the edge of the tide to the far bay.

Davy had kept his distance but hovered within earshot. Becca often embroidered repeated conversations. It wasn't fibbing it was just her way. But under these circumstances, truth was essential.

After watching the man disappear Becca turned to Davy and beamed. "See! I knew he would help if he could."

"He didn't tell us anything we didn't already know, Becca," he pointed out. "We've followed Benji's routine. We've checked where he snuffles for bones. And the place under the hedge where he sleeps when he's hot was empty. We've looked everywhere, so what now?"

Becca shrugged and said, "At least we're doing everything properly, aren't we?"

"I suppose," Davy admitted.

Now that the need for the bicycle ride had been removed, he felt more at ease. To keep her mood sweet he suggested they paddle to the next bay.

To his surprise she agreed. Her reason being that although it wasn't one of Benji's haunts it didn't mean he never went there. And so with a sudden exuberance they kick-splashed each other while following the route the policeman had taken.

The bay was empty. Of Benji there was no sign.

* * *

Jilly and Alex had walked round the wide sprawl of cottages, tapping on doors and asking for information. People were concerned and obliging. They knew Benji by sight and would keep an eye open for him. As they neared the neighbouring holiday-let, conversation revolved round the telephone call of the previous night. To rationalise it was impossible, but answers had to be found. Quietly Alex wondered if the toy telephone was somehow part of the mystery.

"I'd completely forgotten about it," Jilly admitted. "In fact, looking back the whole holiday is little more than a blur."

"Why did you decide to go to France?" he asked.

"We were invited. It was another chance to get away. After the funeral we stayed with my parents in Derbyshire. We then had three weeks in Scotland after which we returned home and left, almost immediately, for France. After returning to the UK I found living in the house without Richard unbearable and so we then went to the States for three months. I really was running away, wasn't I?" She gave a sad smile, shrugged and went on, "Within weeks of coming back I sold the house and moved here. The constant upheaval had a bad effect on Becca, she was tearful and clingy. So I thought the best thing to do was to settle and start again."

Alex listened closely and then asked if, since being on her own, anything untoward had happened.

"Like what?" she asked, puckering her brow.

"I don't know," he said, hunching his shoulders. He had plenty of ideas but kept silent. There was no point in suggesting possibilities that could make her feel even more uneasy.

"Do you mean something like thieves getting into our previous home?" she asked, as if reading his thoughts. "No chance!" she told him firmly. "We had an alarm system which was connected to the police station, and electronically controlled gates. Richard was extremely safety-conscious – because of his work – and we were well protected."

"And was it all in full working order when you were away?"

"Absolutely! And had there been a problem the police would have dealt with it, and kept me informed."

She then paused in her stride and toed the damp ground saying slowly, "Now I come to think of it there was an incident, although it was nothing to do with me. Just after we went to Brittany my parents' house was broken into. Nothing much was taken, and the police put it down to children."

"How did they get in?"

"Through the downstairs toilet window – which now has a metal grille," she told him with a wry smile.

"It does sound like kids, doesn't it? Good for a laugh! Was there anything else? Such as strangers hanging about, odd 'phone calls?"

"My parents have never said. "

"And at the time of the break – in, did they know where you were?"

"Oh, yes," she smiled. "I'd told them we were to stay with Mitzi; and in case they forgot Becca bought a picture postcard of the ferry, wrote out our timetable and posted it in Plymouth before we sailed." She tilted her head and looked at him through narrowed and questioning eyes.

Shrugging he said, "I'm trying to find a beginning to the mystery of the 'phone call. There has to be one, and there has to be a reason for it."

He didn't add that he thought it sinister, nor did he add his disturbing thoughts on Richard's death. Was he really a victim of hit-and-run? Not knowing the answers filled him with frustration. He needed to question Jilly. Was it possible, that without realising it, she knew of something important? He hesitated to ask her. He was too afraid of opening old wounds that might force her into silence. Pain did that to some people.

He would wait. For now he would make finding Benji the priority.

The curtains of the holiday-let were closed. Was the hour too early for visitors to be up and about? Jilly wondered if they should return later. Before she could voice her thoughts the downstairs curtains were pulled aside. Screened by yellowing nets Jilly could not see beyond them, but guessed they had been opened by Marilyn.

Because the basic layout of all the cottages in the area was the same, Jilly was surprised at the length of time it took Marilyn to answer her knock. Wearing a blue satin wrap, and a towel round her head she half opened the door looking embarrassed.

"Sorry," she said. "I didn't hear you. I was washing my hair."

Her eyes fluttered and she looked away. Her words, hollow and unconvincing, hung in the air.

Jilly wondered why she had lied. There was nothing sinful about keeping callers waiting. Smiling and apologetic Jilly explained their reason for such an early call.

Remembering the noise of the previous night Marilyn feigned surprise. Frowning, she shook her head and said with apparent concern, "Oh, dear! What a worry. I haven't seen Benji, but you are welcome to look round the garden and in the shed. Mind how you go, though. The shed's dangling with cobwebs! It's so bad I haven't even thought about using the deckchairs. Tatty old things! Makes me wonder what we're paying for!"

She then invited them in and led them through to the kitchen. Turning to Alex she suggested he made a search and then returned for coffee.

Jilly was so surprised she was on the point of refusing when Alex said, "That would be most welcome. We seem to have been traipsing about for hours." He then held out his hand and introduced himself, "I'm Jilly's neighbour."

Marilyn accepted his warm clasp, although her attitude was distant. She said, almost automatically, that coffee would be ready when he was, and then added brightly, "Which, if you're thorough, will give us ladies time for girlie talk!"

"Meanwhile I'll try not to make any noise." he said.

Marilyn looked at him blankly.

Alex pointed to the ceiling.

"Just in case your husband's still sleeping."

Marilyn's expression was momentarily one of confusion. She then stuttered,"D-don't w-worry about him. He'll sleep through anything except the sound of a pint being pulled!"

"A man after my own heart!" Alex laughed. "On that score we could be blood-brothers!" With that he saluted her and, leaving by the side door, went into the garden. Side doors were things he had yet to get used to. It seemed all the local cottages had them as opposed to back doors. Legend said they made escape easier for felons when the Law came calling. Quite how, Alex could not fathom but to argue the point with a Cornishman was something he would rather not do. They had a queer kind of logic that seemed to work and impress the uninitiated.

The garden path, soggy after the storm, showed a set of footprints leading to the shed. Where they went after that Alex was unsure as the path came to an abrupt end. To the side a cinder path looped back to the cottage door, but from where he stood the way forward was across grass. It couldn't be described as lawn. It was too sparse and patchy with daisies and dandelions. Beyond was a wooden gate which led on to swaying marram grass growing in tall tufts in the sandy soil. A vague track skirted the boundary of the cottage and then led back into the lane. Alex studied it for several moments. It looked trampled. Was the man of the house really in bed? If so, who had walked up the muddy path to the shed? Marilyn? Not unless she wore enormous shoes! The shed *was* hung with cobwebs and it smelled musty. Yet someone had been in there recently. There was a smudged patch where something, maybe a sleeve, had rubbed against the surface of a shelf. That was the only evidence of a disturbance. As for paw marks there were none – not on the path nor in the shed. Leaning against the timber wall were two grubby deckchairs. Marilyn could be forgiven for not using them, they were awful.

In the kitchen Jilly was trying to be friendly without revealing too much about herself.

The girlie talk had progressed from films and fashion to more personal aspects and Jilly was wary of the questions. Her answers though truthful were slightly evasive. Marilyn talked openly about her own life and indicated that her marriage to Arthur was happy if dull. She sounded quite genuine, making Jilly feel guilty at her own attitude.

It was only when Marilyn started to ask about Richard that Jilly felt a real need to be devious. Telling Marilyn that Richard was an accountant who had died of a heart attack was delivered in a level voice with an unwavering stare. Had she travelled abroad, she was asked? The exotic every time, she replied. Europe? Of little interest. The lies fell from Jilly's lips in a smooth flow. Did Marilyn recognise them as such? If so she gave no indication. It seemed to Jilly that within the last few minutes circumstances had forced her into giving herself a completely new past life.

Why? Instinct? Yes!

Alex came in from the garden saying there was no sign of Benji, "With everywhere being so muddy had he been around it wouldn't have been difficult to follow him."

"One dog's tracks are pretty much the same as another's to me," Marilyn said.

At that Jilly explained how Benji had a missing claw.

"He lost it as a puppy and it never grew back."

"A sort of doggy ID," Marilyn commented chirpily. With that she took the coffee pot from the stove, filled a mug for Alex and offered cream and sugar.

Helping himself to both he asked how long they would be staying in the area.

He was told just a few more days. Arthur had been unwell, but now that he was on the mend they would be returning home.

"And where's that?" Alex asked casually.

"Leeds."

"Really!" he said in a voice which held both charm and interest." I was once taken to Leeds when I was small. I seem to remember spending the day at – would it be – Kirkford Abbey?"

She nodded vigorously.

"Oh yes! I've been to Kirkford loads of times." Her intonation suggested it was the place where people went as a matter of course.

Alex wanted to pursue the subject but before he could do so Marilyn stood up, crossed to the fridge and took out two eggs.

"While I remember," she smiled at Jilly

"There's no need," she told her.

"I'd rather," she replied. "And now if you'll excuse me I'd best see to Arthur's brekky. I'll keep my eyes open for

Benji and if he turns up I'll check his paws to make sure he isn't an impostor."

And on that light-hearted note she ushered them into the hall, and then out of the front door.

Once in the lane Jilly, holding the eggs in her cupped hands said, "What did you make of her, Alex? I thought she was quite lively but I was wary of her."

"With good reason! She's something of a tall-story teller!"

"What do you mean?"

"She no more lives in Leeds than I do. The Abbey there is Kirkstall not Kirkford."

"Could she have mis-heard?"

"Only to repeat the mistake? I don't think so."

Jilly thought for several moments and then sighed, "Things do not ring entirely true, do they? If Arthur was still in bed, who opened the downstairs curtains? Marilyn? But she said she was washing her hair. Could someone else be staying with them?"

"Possible, but unlikely. The whole business could be some kind of charade."

"And the purpose?"

"I have absolutely no idea!" he confessed.

Jilly fell silent then after a moment told Alex she hadn't been truthful with Marilyn.

Pausing in his stride he asked her why not.

Shrugging Jilly said, slightly perplexed, "I think it was a sort of native caution. Her questions were too probing and so I fibbed in reply."

"As long as you remember what you fibbed about you shouldn't have a problem."

Her troubled expression caused him to smile sympathetically and say cheerfully, "All good liars have phenomenal memories."

"Be serious!" she chided.

"I'm trying, but I really do not see you as some kind of female Pinocchio, you look far too honest. No, serious lying is not in your make-up."

She didn't argue because she didn't know. She had never been tested. All the same she would have to remember her conversation with Marilyn just in case they met again. Not that it was likely. They had no reason, and nothing in common.

Alex had wandered across the lane and was leaning against the stone wall looking out to sea. Everything was so calm and peaceful it seemed unfair that it should be spoilt by vague tremors of disquiet. If that was how best to describe the happenings. Deep down he knew it wasn't. There was more to the situation than vague tremors of disquiet. There was a brooding darkness that held threats.

Straightening up and squaring his shoulders he said he thought it time to return home adding, as he walked back to Jilly, "Because today is going to be a good day. The children will be wearing halos and Benji will be in his basket chewing a bone."

"I wish," Jilly sighed, looking troubled. "I truly wish."

Strolling back to the cottage there was a silence between them that was heavy with anxiety. Each concerned for the other, but as neither was willing to speak it held them apart. It was the accidental brushing of shoulders that took away tension and made them smile.

"It'll be all right, Jilly. You'll see," Alex told her. His conviction was such that she almost believed him.

On reaching the house and walking into the hall Jilly's breath rasped and the eggs fell from her nerveless fingers. Tom's prone body was on the floor, an empty mug beyond his reach, his breathing barely audible.

Frozen by shock, Jilly stared.

Alex knelt and felt for a pulse.

Wide-eyed, Jilly shivered and suppressed a cry of fear as her feeling of foreboding returned.

***

Earlier, using stealth acquired through years of practice, Arthur moved towards Jilly's cottage. From the yelling of the previous night he knew the dog was missing, and the house would be empty. His understanding of human nature told him everyone would be out searching – except the old man. He would be in his shed. That made everything easier – and safer. A quick sift through belongings by an expert often found more than prolonged delving by an amateur.

Arthur was an expert.

To almost fall over Tom's sprawled body was a shock.

What the hell had happened?

***

Arthur hesitated. He wanted to help, but there was no time. He had to get out. His plan to search the cottage had to be abandoned. He knew Jilly Kenworth was not the assailant. He'd seen Tom looking out of the side door after Kenworth left. If only he'd watched him, he might have seen the intruder. Now he cursed his bad luck. He'd missed what could have been of vital importance. The chance of finding the cottage again empty *and* unlocked was nil, making it impossible to probe the place in safety. It was not his day! There had to be another way, and he had to find it. Guiltily he stared at Tom. He didn't like leaving him, but he had no choice. Arthur knew that unless he left at once he could be caught. Jilly Kenworth may already be making her way home.

He moved swiftly away. Panting, he neared his own cottage following the path where he had earlier trampled the marram grass. He kept low, ready to throw himself full length if he had to. He didn't want to be seen by anyone.

He'd dodged the callers helped by Marilyn's delaying tactics, and now the faint smell of frying bacon told him they had left.

His sigh of relief was audible.

Still panting he stumbled into the kitchen and slumped into a chair. "Well, what did the Kenworth woman want? Did you find out anything?" He held his chest, afraid it was about to burst.

Marilyn, busy with the frying pan, didn't look up. Flicking the bacon over she said, "She told me her husband was an accountant and that he died of a heart attack."

"Did he now?" Arthur gasped, "And what other fairy tales did she tell you?"

"None!" She picked up a plate and hooked the bacon on to it. "I still think you're on the wrong track. If you could have seen her look of distress when she spoke of her husband you would know she couldn't have hurt him."

Arthur tossed her a cynical smile.

She replied with a frown, saying defensively, "All right so she lied probably with good reason, but that doesn't make her a criminal!"

Arthur said nothing.

Marilyn's frown deepened. What was wrong with him? He wasn't arguing and he was still panting. Why?

Still searching for breath he said, "Someone attacked the old man! He was in Kenworth's hall out cold on the floor!"

"Dead?" she mouthed, the plate wobbling.

He shrugged.

White-faced. she cried "Bloody 'ell. We didn't bargain on this! It's time we pulled out.

We're on dangerous ground, Pop!"

"I know," he told her grimly, then tightening his face he said, "And don't call me Pop!"

The unexpected anger in his voice left her dumbfounded.

* * *

Delza was crying. She was hot, tired and her legs were muddied from sprawling on the ground. She had been trying to find Benji in the cave. Dogs went into caves. Squinting through the crack she had peered into the gloom below. It terrified her. She could hear snarling and growling but could see nothing. It was always the same. The noises. The smells. They frightened her. Delza was not brave. Many things disturbed her. Earlier she had seen the big man talking to Becca. They were on the beach. She'd also seen the man from next door. He wasn't on the beach. He was…? She didn't remember, but she had hidden from both. She didn't like men. They all scared her. Except Papa.

Minutes later, going to the village and then to the harbour, being among people she knew, calmed her. They gave her sweets and biscuits. And, sometimes, small toys unwanted by more fortunate children. Despite her years, Delza remained a child. Today she scrunched barley sugar. Mrs. Atkins at the bakery had given it to her. She had also given her a bun which was in the pocket of her anorak with the sweetie papers. Papa made her save sweetie papers to put in the dustbin. The bun was hard but it didn't matter. When she got home Papa would pour milk on it and let her eat it with the red-handled spoon.

Delza would be in heaven.

The harbour was already busy. Trips round the bay were on offer and would-be sailors queued patiently under the clear sky. At the helm of 'Blue Gull' stood Dick Rogers. Hal Polglise had failed to turn up again and so Dick had stepped into his place. Leaving young Bernard to cope with the shop wasn't a worry. Hot weather and fresh meat were not ideal partners, and so Dick had done his preparation. People were more likely to want ham on the bone and spit-roasted chicken rather than steaks and chops. All Bernard had to do was wrap the food and take the money. Sunday opening, in the holiday season, while inconvenient, was lucrative and therefore a nice little earner. Bernard was a good lad and reliable. The only problem was Hal. A black-hearted scrounger with no sense of responsibility, he thought only of himself. Dick knew, without being told, Hal would have had a better offer for the day's work. For all Hal cared 'Blue Gull' could sink without trace. Dick wagged his head. How could a bloke be so irresponsible? At that moment he saw Delza ambling along the cobbled quayside. Again he wagged his head. She was another responsibility Hal Polglise had thrown off. He wanted horsewhipping.

Delza kept her eyes on Mr. Rogers, but when he waved to her she looked away to meet the curious stares of strangers. Those who didn't know her nudged each other and whispered. Delza smiled, her lips juicy with barley sugar. Contentedly she weaved through the busy streets and eventually into the lane known as 'The Narrows'. With darting eyes she looked for Benji. Although afraid of him she wanted to catch him. That would please Papa. Taking off the scarf she trailed it then dropped it as she saw the tall pink spikes of valerian growing in the hedgerow. How pretty. She would take them home for Papa. After a moment they too were dropped. She didn't like the smell of them. Grimacing, she wiped hands down the front of her anorak. It was time to go back to Papa.

Un-noticed, a light breeze wafted the scarf into the air, carried it over the hedge and across the field where it finally became entangled in a hawthorn bush. Delza was unaware.

* * *

Tom, sprawled in Jilly's hallway, was grey-faced and had a cut above his left eyebrow.

At Jilly's cry of alarm his eyes swam into focus. Momentarily confused he lay there. Helped by Alex he then struggled to his feet and stumbled to the chair while insisting he was all right.

Jilly, ignoring the spread of spilt tea and broken eggs, gathered together plasters, cotton wool and a bowl of warm water. Gently bathing the wound she was relieved to see it was neither wide nor deep although the inevitable bruise promised to be colourful. Meanwhile Alex produced sweet tea and insisted Tom should drink it.

"It's good for shock, Tom."

"That's as maybe! But what's good for clumsy?" he grumbled fingering the newly applied plaster. "I fell over me feet, didn't I? Silly old fool that I am. I'd just made a cuppa when I thought I heard a noise."

"What sort of noise?" asked Alex

"Dunno! Just a noise. I thought it might be Benji. I started to move but you know what my legs are! I tell them to go left – they go right." He took a sip of tea and added, "I think that's when I must have tripped, and I must have banged by head on the table. 'Course I dropped me tea, too." Glancing at the carpet, seeing yellow yolk and broken shell, he gasped, "I never touched no eggs, Missus! Honest!"

Quickly Jilly reassured him that the mishap was down to her.

"Don't worry about the mess, Tom. You take care of yourself. I think it would be wise if you went along to the Cottage Hospital and had your wound properly treated."

"Don't hold with namby-pamby," he said as a flat refusal. "Give me a minute and I'll be fine." With that he leaned against the high back of the chair, winced and groaned.

"What's wrong?" Alex asked.

"Blowed if I know," Tom said, fingering his left shoulder. "I feel sort of numb and I've a bloomin' great swellin'! How'd I get that?"

Jilly and Alex exchanged surreptitious glances. Alex wondered about some kind of karate chop. Jilly's mind was blank, but she knew there was room for speculation. Not that she could have dealt with it at that moment. She needed time to get over the shock of finding Tom hurt. Although he wasn't seriously harmed the picture of him lying there was still sharp in her mind. So much so that it would make a constructive input difficult and floundering would be of no help.

After a while, and wearing a plaster, Tom insisted on returning to his shed. He had things to do and he needed to get on. Alex, recognising that Jilly also needed time to herself, made an excuse to leave by saying he wanted to change out of his muddy trousers.

In the hall, Jilly cleaned up the mess of spilled tea and broken eggs; after which, in the bathroom, she splashed her face with cold water and, returning to the kitchen, focused on preparing lunch. She had to do something normal. She also had to be in control of herself. Inwardly she was shaking. Too much was happening too quickly. If she wasn't careful her wild thoughts would spill over and revealing them could be frightening.

Channelling her mind, making herself think in terms of practicalities, she glanced at the clock. The children would be home soon and, with or without Benji, they would be hungry.

Unexpectedly Tom knocked on the kitchen door and said apologetically, "Missus, I'm real sorry! It's only just come to mind. I expect it was the bump on my head that made me forget!"

"Forget what?" she asked kindly.

"The 'phone call. Someone wanted to speak to you. I said you was out looking for Benji and he said he would call later about the key."

"What key, Tom?" she asked perplexed. "Did he mean he would ring again or come to the door?"

"I don't know, Missus! And before I could ask he rang off."

Thinking it odd Jilly probed: Did Tom recognise the caller's voice? He didn't.

"What time did he call?"

Tom thought for a moment then said with certainty," It was before I banged my head! And it was likely to have been just after eight I remember hearing the church clock strike the hour!" He looked at her, his rheumy eyes uncertain. "I've not done nothin' wrong, have I, Missus?"

"Not at all, Tom," she assured. "And thank you for telling me."

She watched him as he plodded away, his shoulders hunched, his hands clasped behind him. Turning into the kitchen she leaned against the table as her mind raced back to earlier that morning.

When they arrived at the holiday cottage it was to be told that Arthur Armstrong was still in bed. Was he?

Or had he made the 'phone call or, worse, had he attacked Tom hoping to find a key?

To what? It was anyone's guess.

A key? Pontivy? Were they connected? If so, how?

Chapter Five

Tom was painfully aware of his throbbing head. Sitting in his shed he tried to collect his thoughts. They were like the rolling tide; one minute they were there the next they were gone. Opposite, perching on a wooden box, her eyes vacant sat Delza. Twice she had tried to touch Tom's plaster and twice he had pushed her gently away. Although he knew she would not understand the situation he had to explain it. And so, being pre-occupied, Tom did not miss the scarf and it was forgotten by Delza. As she made to touch his head for the third time he held her back by her wrist. She trembled. He knew she was afraid, not of him but of her own incomprehension.

"'Tis nothing, my bird," he repeated for the third time. "I was clobbered. Not that you'll understand. No one's to know. Just you, me and Missus, d'you hear? You're not to get upset. Takes more than a clout on the head to hurt Papa!" With that he started to pull faces making her laugh. If only it was a laughing matter. But it wasn't. Someone had it in for him. Hal Polglise? More than likely.

Delza pulled the bun from her pocket and gave it to Tom. He dropped it into his haversack promising she could have it later.

Delza smiled and again tried to touch Tom's plaster.

"No!" He then smiled.

The bun told him she'd been to the harbour taking her usual route. After that she would have turned into The Narrows, picked a few flowers and thrown them away, leaving streaks of pollen down the front of her anorak. He didn't mind about the messy anorak, but he didn't like her wandering the lanes on her own. They were too quiet and lonely. He always worried about her when she was not in sight. It was only then that he saw she was not wearing the green scarf.

Anger hit his already thumping head as he touched her bare neck where the scarf should have been.

"What you done with it, girl?" he barked. "You silly turnip! You been and gone and lost it."

Delza's eyes immediately swam with tears. Papa was cross. What had she lost?

Whimpering she zipped and un-zipped her anorak.

***

Outside the shed Becca and Davy were eaves-dropping. Having returned from their search for Benji, intrigued by Tom's words they had listened with round-eyed amazement.

Tom had been clobbered? Now they were open-mouthed. Tom had been attacked! Who by, and why? And what had Delza lost?

Their intention to tell him Benji was still missing was forgotten. Both frightened and excited they slipped silently away to take refuge at the far end of the garden. There, hidden by a bramble patch and the hedge, they sat on the grass and stared at each other. Who had hit Tom? And why? Should they ask, or would they be fobbed off with parental mumblings? They had heard Tom say no one was to know, but that did not diminish their curiosity, so how could they find out what had happened?

After several minutes of silence Davy came up with what he thought was the only explanation.

"I think someone tried to break into the house and Tom tried to stop them. He told Delza only because she can't tell anyone else!"

Becca nodded, sighed and reflected forlornly, "It wouldn't have happened if Benji had been home." She paused to chew on her thumb and then said, "I wonder if Mom knows what really happened."

"Dad might."

Becca shrugged, "If they do I bet they won't tell us."

"We'll make them! Let's take them by surprise and just ask. It's what Dad calls shock tactics."

"Does it work?"

"Let's find out!"

Scrambling to their feet they headed for the kitchen.

Jilly was prepared for their anticipated verbal attack. She and Alex had already agreed that if questions were asked, they should not be answered with the full story. Without looking up from the magazine she was reading she casually explained that Tom had tripped and bumped his head. It was nothing to worry about.

Becca was about to argue when Davy nudged her into silence. Clamping her lips she stared at the floor. Mom had fibbed!

Dismissing the subject of Tom, Jilly talked about Benji feeling sure he was around somewhere. "He'll be out having an adventure. Finding bones – or maybe burying them." She spoke absently, as if life was smooth and trouble-free.

Becca's heart sank. Mom was pretending about Benji and Tom. She was pretending about something else, too. If only she knew what.

During lunch Becca was silent. Words were tied up in her tangled thoughts. Everything seemed wrong. Someone had hurt Tom. Would they hurt Mom, too?

The possibility terrified her. In rising panic the only person she could think of to turn to for help was the policeman. He would know better than anyone what to do.

Later when Becca and Davy were again at the bottom of the garden and out of earshot Becca said fiercely, "You've got to come with me, Davy! I need to find him. We'll use

Mom's bike. You can stand on the pedals and I can sit on the saddle."

"No, Becca! It's dangerous!" He was appalled by the suggestion.

"No it isn't! And even if it is we've got to do it. Walking to The Mariner's Head will take too long."

"There are short cuts we can make."

"No, we can't! There aren't any! And if you won't come with me I'll go alone on my own bike."

"It's got a flat tyre." he reminded her.

"Don't care!" she stormed.

Angrily they stared at each other. Finally Davy looked away. Knowing she had won the battle of wills Becca scrambled to her feet and in so doing stumbled backwards into the overgrown bramble bush. Yelping with pain she blinked back tears. Pulling her free Davy carefully picked thorns from her scratched and bleeding arms. Perhaps the incident would make her change her mind! If anything it made her more determined. Knuckling her tears she marched towards the shed.

Reluctantly Davy followed.

Of Tom and Delza there was no sign. Perhaps they had gone home.

Becca's bicycle, propped against the wall, was minus its saddle, but Jilly's was alongside and usable.

Becca grabbed it.

Davy's heart sank. He was not happy or confident about that which he had promised to do. He knew it was dangerous AND against the law. Becca was so headstrong! She never stopped to think! Neither did Dad. Asking Davy to take care of Becca was like asking him to wash quicksilver.

Minutes later, furtively and precariously, they moved off.

Becca's plan was simple. If the policeman had not returned from Lands End she would leave a message asking him to call at the cottage. Mom wouldn't mind. She needed help and what better person to give it than a policeman?

After wobbling through the lanes and meeting a herd of cows they finally arrived at the hotel, red-faced and breathless.

The Mariner's Head was bordered by a small beer garden, a play area, and a car park which held four cars. One housed a barking dog. Becca's eyes filled with tears. Was Benji locked inside a car?

Leaving Davy at the roadside with the bicycle, Becca mounted the four wide steps. The heavy door, when opened, led straight into the bar from behind which the barman said she should not be there – she was under-age! Undeterred she stood her ground and asked to speak to… It was only then she realised she did not know the policeman's name. Determined not to be beaten by lack of information she gave the barman a lengthy and accurate description only to be told he was not a guest nor had he been. It was a family hotel and so far only families were in residence.

Bewildered Becca returned to Davy. Near to tears she tried to understand the disquieting situation. She wanted to rush home and tell Jilly. Davy didn't think it a good idea.

"She's already worried about Benji and Tom. If you tell her we've been riding her bike and trying to find someone we don't really know she'll be very cross!"

"I don't have to tell her everything!" Becca argued.

"Oh, come on, Becca! She's sure to find out sooner or later!"

"I know! I know!" she shouted, frustrated by his argument.

"Well, then! How about telling Dad?"

"He'll be cross, too," she said sulkily.

"Not if I can get him on his own," he coaxed. "If I explain what's happened he'll know what to do, Your Mom might not."

"Are you saying my Mom's stupid?" she asked, flaring with indignation.

"'Course not, silly. Oh, come on, Becca. It's no good getting angry with me. I'm trying to help."

Knowing he was right she gave a half smile, grabbed a handlebar and, walking either side of the bicycle, they eventually turned into The Narrows and headed for home.

* * *

Sitting in the garden Jilly and Alex were trying to find innocent reasons to explain the incidents of the last few hours.

"So much has happened that coincidence has to be ruled out," Jilly said, reluctantly relinquishing the hold she had on that idea. "Somehow it's all linked. The attack on Tom can't be explained. Benji missing? He could be chasing the girls, though I doubt it. The 'phone calls? They can't all be wrong numbers."

"Particularly as Pontivy is now in the equation," Alex cut in. "And that's where we should begin," he said decisively. "Ring your friend," he urged. "She might remember the incident with the toy telephone. Then ask Becca for her version. It doesn't have to be interrogative, does it?"

"No," Jilly said thoughtfully, "A teasing, jokey approach would be better."

Alex patted her hand.

"Go and ring your friend. She might come up with something new."

She didn't.

After an affectionate greeting and the usual questions about life in general, Jilly broached the subject of Becca's telephone.

"Do you remember the incident, Mitzi?"

"I remember your panic," she laughed over the crackling line.

"Can you remember who bought the 'phone for Becca?" she pressed.

"Vaguely, but why? What's so important?"

"I can't explain," Jilly told her, her voice rising," But I need to know! Please. Mitzi! Think!"

The line went quiet, then Mitzi said, sounding unsure, "I seem to remember a middle-aged woman with … maybe blonde hair … or maybe high-lights, I can't be absolutely certain. It's too long ago. But she looked English and she spoke English. Middle class. Not too posh."

"Are you sure?"

"Absolutely! I remember the voice but not the face. Any help?"

"Could be. Thanks, Mitzi. I'll be in touch." And before Mitzi could question further Jilly hung up.

Alex, waiting restlessly, was disappointed by the lack of information.

"I don't know what I was hoping to hear – a full description and a blow-by-blow account, I suppose. But at least we know that the woman could be a middle-aged blonde."

Sinking back down on to the grass, Jilly said ruefully, "She will be easy to find! There can't be more than half-a-dozen middle-aged blondes in the whole world!"

Again patting her hand Alex chuckled, "At least we can ignore brunettes and redheads!"

At that Jilly, too, chuckled. Alex was good at positive thinking.

After a while he said, "Jilly, I don't want to open old wounds or pry into your past, but could all these happenings be somehow connected to Richard?"

He heard her faint intake of breath. Was he treading on dangerous ground? Her unexpected reply told him he wasn't.

"I've been thinking along those lines too," she admitted. "Richard's work was high-risk. He handled valuable commodities for all sorts of people."

"All sorts?" he queried

"All sorts of honest people," she told him firmly. "Richard was no fool."

"Do you have a list of his contacts?"

She shook her head.

"Richard never disclosed anything about his business. He didn't discuss or confide."

"Didn't you resent being shut out?"

"I did at first. Then later, when I understood his reasons, the isolation was acceptable. Particularly after Becca was born. All Richard ever wanted was our safety and happiness. He gave us both."

"Until now."

Although she made no reply she looked wounded.

For a time the silence between them was heavy: Jilly, looking back at her life as it had been, wondered if Alex was casting his doubts upon it. If he was, should he do so? Should she do so?

Within that same heavy silence Alex's thoughts raced. Was it possible Richard was mixed up in something unsavoury? Had he been forced into a dangerous situation by circumstances? That could be the answer! Anyone could fall into the trap of getting in over one's head. Misjudgement happened to the wisest of men. Had that happened to Richard? Alex believed Jilly's claim that she was in total ignorance about Richard's business. And because of the risks involved he could understand her exclusion. What he did not understand was how a group of people could work for the same man and never meet. That was taking security too far. How were gaps bridged? What happened if someone was ill, or there was some kind of family crisis? When asked Jilly merely shrugged and said because Richard didn't work to a strict schedule, he coped.

"He juggled time," Jilly told Alex.

"How do you know? You were never involved!"

"Wives develop a sixth sense," she told him with a faint smile.

Alex knew that to be true. Within his own marriage the demands for jewels or designer clothes or, on one particular occasion, a huge Chinese carpet, always coincided with an upsurge in his business. Yes! He knew about the female sixth sense!

Looking at her he asked tentatively," How would you feel about my going to Richard's office?"

Startled by the suggestion she asked for what purpose.

"Just to look round. I might find something which could be a pointer."

"There's nothing there! Apart from a couple of chairs, a desk and an empty filing cabinet."

"What about his secretary? Did she have her own office?"

"No. She worked flexible hours, and used Richard's office when he wasn't there. When he was she just took notes."

"About the business? Writing to clients and that sort of thing?"

Jilly gave a really deep frown and said, "I honestly don't know, and what I do know is only what I gleaned from Richard's 'phone calls."

Alex sighed, "And I suppose his secretary's name is 'Smith'?"

"I don't know that, either," Jilly told him with a feeling of inadequacy.

"So," he continued, "assuming there is nothing to be found in his office, where else can we look for some kind of lead?"

"Nowhere," Jilly told him. "There are a couple of boxes in the loft which hold some of his things."

"What sort of things?"

"Sporting trophies. Books. University stuff. Bits and bobs. Just things he treasured. They don't amount to much, but I've kept them for Becca. She has a right to family history – such as it is. It's not much of a heritage, is it?"

Alex didn't reply.

* * *

The children were halfway along The Narrows walking in gloomy silence. Becca was angry at having been conned by a policeman. She didn't understand why. All she had asked him about was Benji. She did not ask him for his help – he offered. He volunteered guidelines and a follow up if they led to nothing. To discover he was not, nor had been, a guest at The Mariner's Head, compounded her anger.

"I hate him," she stormed at Davy. "He's a horrible man!"

Davy remained silent wondering why the man had behaved as he did.

Suddenly Becca said, pointing over the low hedge and into the field, "What's that, Davy?"

"What, where?" he asked, eyes in darting search.

"Over there! On that bush! Something green!"

"Leaves?" he teased

Becca scowled. She was in no mood for his silly jokes. Leaving him to hold the bike she ran along the lane until she found a gap in the hedge. The Public Footpath sign had been torn up and tossed aside, but it didn't prevent Becca from mounting the over-grown stile. Kicking aside brambles and nettles she dropped down into the field and made towards the bush. Davy, discarding the bike, followed. He had no option. He had to keep Becca in sight. He had promised his Dad. Unexpectedly Becca yelled, "It's Mom's scarf!"

"How d'you know?" he yelled back, running towards her.

"I bought it for her in Pontivy."

"Where's that?"

She told him. He was impressed.

As she spoke she reached up trying to tug the scarf free from the fiercely thorned bush.

Being almost beyond her reach the more she pulled the tighter it became. Davy tried to free it and failed. Finally, putting his hands on his knees, he offered his back as a platform.

Becca refused. "Stand on your back? You'll let me fall," she wailed.

"No, I won't," he told her firmly, adding the taunt, "But if you're too scared…!"

Glowering ferociously, unable to ignore his challenge she clambered on to his back and within moments the scarf was freed. Triumphantly waving it, she jumped to the ground to ask Davy what he thought the scarf was doing in a bush.

Davy didn't reply. In bending over a damp patch of soil, he'd seen something he recognised. He blinked and looked more closely. It was Benji's paw print! It was smudged but unmistakable. One claw was missing. Should he tell Becca? No. She would race around in a panic. If Benji was dead and she found him she would be hysterical. Then what would happen? How would he cope with her? He glanced after her. She had draped the scarf round her neck and was now walking back to the stile. Quickly Davy looked again at the damp patch of soil. He had to be sure his eyes were not tricking him. No, they were not! Benji had been in the field at some time, but where was he now? Knowing he couldn't handle the problem alone he thought it wise to share it with his Dad. Telling anyone else might raise false hopes.

* * *

When Tom told Jilly that Delza had lost the scarf it came as no surprise. His offer to buy a replacement did. She refused. She had plenty of scarves, but that one was a gift from Becca and irreplaceable. When Becca arrived home saying she had found the scarf in a bush – which was why it was torn – Jilly was relieved. Explaining why Delza was wearing it and how she might have lost it, was easy. Not so the disappearance of the man on the beach. Becca had believed in him so implicitly, it was sad to see her trust betrayed.

Now wrapped in Jilly's arms as they both nestled in the comfort of the settee, Becca was pale-faced and tearful.

Jilly, hiding her own increasing alarm, tried to comfort her.

"Sometimes, Becca, grown-ups tease. I expect he was having a joke with you. Once he realises what he's done he'll feel really guilty. And if his wife finds out I expect she'll give him a good telling off!"

"Serve him right!" Becca sniffed, secretly hoping he was having an awful holiday.

Fingering the scarf she asked if Delza was going to wear it again.

"Not if you don't want her to," Jilly said.

Becca thought for a moment, then said in a small voice, "Perhaps she should. It might help her to find Benji." She then added in an even smaller voice, "Mumma, you don't think he's dead, do you?"

Jilly could hardly reply for the lump in her throat.

* * *

Alex and Davy had returned to their own cottage and were sitting in the kitchen. Because it had been closed up for some time the whole place was airless and didn't feel like home. Neither of them had appreciated the feminine touch until now. Jilly's kitchen was always bright and welcoming. Their own was stark and soulless. For now it didn't matter. It was a refuge. Here they could talk in private.

Alex looked across the table and asked Davy if he was sure the paw mark was Benji's.

"It had to be, Dad. Because of his missing claw Becca and me have tracked him thousands of times. It's a game we play."

"Except that it isn't a game any more," Alex told him seriously. He then fell silent. He needed to say more but hesitated. Davy was sensible but he was still only young. There was no way Alex wanted him entangled in what could be a dangerous net. Over a lost dog? Was it that simple? He thought not. And what about the man on the beach? What the hell was he playing at? Becca was a trusting child. He had no right to hurt her. Keeping these thoughts to himself he said, "You did the right thing in not telling Becca about Benji's paw marks. In fact I think we should keep the information to ourselves – just for the time being. That way we don't raise anyone's false hopes."

"OK, Dad," he agreed, relieved that the decision was made for him. He then went on to ask if anything could be done about the man on the beach?

"I don't see how. If he walked in now, what could we do that would serve a purpose?"

Davy shrugged, "Nothing I suppose. What if he's a policeman on some kind of mission? He could be, couldn't he?"

"It's possible," Alex said with a conviction he did not feel. If that theory was believable to Davy, then let him take comfort from it. For himself he had strong doubts. Dismissing him, Alex realised that ideally he would have liked to go to The Narrows just to check Davy's discovery. He knew he would not have been mistaken but maybe there were other clues that Davy had missed. He glanced out of the window. Daylight was fading fast. The Narrows would soon be shrouded in darkness. He would have to wait until tomorrow.

Just before they returned to Jilly's, Davy said, "Dad?"

"Yes, son?"

"Me and Becca know what happened to Tom. Someone hit him, didn't they?"

"I'm afraid so, Davy. But don't make too much of it, will you? We don't want Becca having nightmares."

"Jilly told us he'd fallen."

"I know. It was the best we could do on the spur of the moment. Someone stumbling is less frightening than someone being attacked."

Davy looked at Alex with pride. It wasn't easy being a Dad.

At Jilly's request Alex agreed that he and Davy would again be happy to stay overnight. To make things more comfortable Becca was to move in with Jilly, Davy was to have Becca's bed, and Alex was to occupy the small back bedroom, "Which," Jilly promised, "has a very comfortable divan."

"It's got to be better than your couch," Alex quipped, laughing.

"Anything's better than that!" Jilly laughed in return.

It was after the children were in bed that Alex suggested it might be a good idea to look through the boxes in the loft.

"In search of what?" Jilly asked.

"Anything that might lead to Pontivy."

"Alex! Those boxes came here after we'd been to Pontivy," she reminded him

"Yes, I remember you saying, but I still think it will do no harm to look. By the way, did you ask Becca about her toy telephone?"

"Yes, I did, and it's a bit of an odd story." She paused then went on, "Before I tell it I think a glass of wine would be a good idea, don't you?"

It was a wise and comforting suggestion that took away tension.

Holding the stem of her glass she gently swirled the dark-red wine and said, "We'd bought the floor tiles and been to the jeweller to collect Mitzi's ring that had been cleaned. While she was paying the bill she asked me to show the assistant a pair of diamond earrings that were in the window. Mitzi's into diamonds! She liked them and bought them. After that we just wandered about window-shopping. That must have been when Becca saw the telephone. Although she didn't speak French, unseen by both Mitzi and myself Becca went into the shop to ask the price. She couldn't make the assistant understand, so she took her outside and pointed to it."

"Where were you when this was happening?"

"I think both Mitzi and I had drifted on, each thinking the other had Becca's hand. When we realised that was not so, Mitzi dashed off in search, whilst I waited. I was unwilling to move just in case..."

"Becca said that when she went back into the shop with the assistant, an English lady admired her hair. Telling her that she looked so much like her granddaughter she would like to buy Becca the telephone. As it cost very little, Becca was not to worry about the price. The woman then put the money on the counter, the assistant took the telephone from the window and, unwrapped, gave it to Becca. The woman spoke to the assistant in French, spoke to Becca in English and left. That was the bit Mitzi overheard."

Alex had listened carefully. On the surface it all seemed innocuous and what Becca had said tied up with Mitz's version, but he was still uncertain on how to interpret the event.

"If we choose the very worst scenario, what do you think the anonymous 'phone message could mean?" he asked.

Jilly put down her glass and shook her head. She couldn't even guess. Her straying thoughts led her to ask if Alex thought Benji's disappearance had anything to do with what was happening.

"The idea had crossed my mind," he reluctantly admitted. His voice was low, and almost lazy.

Matching his pace Jilly replied, "So much appears to fit the picture, doesn't it? When the order of events is analysed everything seems planned to have a disturbing effect."

Although he agreed he remained silent. Trying to decide whether or not to tell Jilly about the paw prints had pushed him into a corner. If Benji was part of the mystery and she was kept in ignorance, could she unwittingly become involved? Could she be put in danger? Was she already in danger? Without knowing the answers he had to make a decision about the next move. He and Davy needed time and opportunity to check what Davy thought to be Benji's tracks. And that had to be done in secrecy. If they were his paw marks then Jilly would be told. But how did one practise subterfuge? Jilly was sharp and not easily fooled. How could he get her and Becca out of the area? He was at a total loss when an idea hit him. What better than a day out? A day in Truro? Shopping? That could be the keyword to unlock enthusiasm!

He made the suggestion casually whilst topping up Jilly's wine.

"How about a day out? Go shopping. Spoil yourself! Go tomorrow – on the bus. Becca will love that."

"Why the bus?" Jilly cut in

With split-second thinking he reminded her of parking problems. It was a valid argument. For his own part if they went by bus he would know where they were for at least two hours. He would also know they would be safe. Maybe he was being over cautious, but better that than careless.

She looked at him, her expression unsure. What about Benji? If he wasn't found, shouldn't she be looking for him? Going on a shopping spree might suggest she didn't care about him.

"Looking for Benji can be left to me, Davy and half the village! Many people are so willing to help that no-one will begrudge you a couple of hours away. Go. Jilly," he urged. "Forget everything. Buy something pretty for Becca and half a dozen chews for Benji." He squeezed her hand. "How's that for optimism?" Smiling, he added, "Go! It'll do you good."

She still hesitated. Truro would be busy. Would they be safe in the crowds? Would she and Becca become separated? Not if hands were firmly held at all times! Alex was right! They needed to get away. She needed to escape from the cocoon of worry in which she was wrapped. With that thought in mind she finally agreed that a day out was an excellent idea.

With the decision made, she leaned back and closed her eyes. Time spent exclusively with Becca was such a rare happening it would be fun. Her spirits lightened and then fell into darkness as again the feeling of foreboding returned. It hovered like an enormous full stop. Forbidding any movement, forcing her into gloom. With her hand touching her throat she said she couldn't go. She'd been warned. Becca was vulnerable. And she dare not expose her.

"I'm a prisoner! We both are. What can I do, Alex?"

He pulled her hand down, his fingers strong and compelling.

"Listen to me. If there is a watcher then he must see the usual pictures. He must not know he's suspect. Nothing must change. You and Becca together. Davy and Becca playing, going to the beach, doing the things they like to do."

"No," she protested, wrenching her hand away. "That's impossible. I can't let Becca run free – not now."

"You must, Jilly! It will be wrong to change the pattern," he told her urgently. "You could have found a starting point. You mustn't lose it. Let the kids play. When they are together Davy will take care of her."

"He's only a boy," she protested. "Becca is wilful and hot-headed. He cannot be held responsible for her! What if, at some dangerous point, she decides to go her own way?"

"Davy will stop her! He knows something's amiss. He doesn't know what but he is aware. He'll be careful, and he'll try to anticipate events." He gave a gentle smile and added, "He also knows how your wayward daughter's mind works!"

"You're very reassuring," she told him through trembling lips.

"I do my best," he told her, adding, "and you really do need to take time out."

She still hesitated and then doggedly told herself the unknown must not imprison her. She had a life to live and she would live it as she chose. Smiling at Alex, hiding her misgivings, she bade him goodnight, and went upstairs.

Her room felt cold. Her bed colder. The night air held a chill that drifted through her open window to settle like a cloud above her head. Staring into the black sky she shivered. Would tomorrow, spent away from the whirlpool of worry, carry her and Becca into an oasis of calm and safety? Or would she feel they were walking on a treacherous path of quicksand?

Chapter Six

As the 8.42 bus to Truro pulled away from the kerb Becca, kneeling on the back seat, waved to Alex and showed the tip of her tongue. He laughed and waved back. They were due to return at 4.20 when he had promised to collect them in the car. For Davy and himself that meant their plans to track Benji would be free from interruption. They had already agreed to walk to The Narrows. Taking the car would be a problem. In any case the distance was not all that far. Alex still wondered if their secrecy was necessary. He could have told Jilly about Davy's find, but not without raising her hopes. If Benji was lost, or worse – dead, what then? False hopes led only to pain. Silence hurt no one.

After returning to Jilly's, Alex was concerned about leaving the cottage empty. He thought Tom might be unwilling to be left in charge again.

Tom was unperturbed by the request.

"Lightning don't strike twice," he said gruffly. "And if it do, I'm ready for 'un!"

With that he pulled from his pocket a stubby, hickory cudgel that he caressed with gnarled fingers before pushing it back into his corduroys. "You go on," he said. "Me and Delza will mind each other."

The thought of Delza minding anything did not fill Alex with confidence. Then after looking doubtfully at Tom and seeing his face lined with grim determination Alex felt reassured.

Minutes later he and Davy were crossing the harbour. The shopkeepers were busy but not too busy to ask about

Benji. Dick Rogers called from his door to say he'd saved a marrowbone. "It'll keep in the fridge," he said, adding, "I don't go much on little dogs, but Benji's all right. I hope he soon turns up. Meanwhile I'll keep my eye about. You never know. I might spot him."

Mrs. Atkins, at the bakery, showed concern. Standing in the doorway she asked. "Where've you looked? Have you been up the cliff path?"

Alex admitted they hadn't but that they were about to do so.

Davy looked surprised. He didn't know that was part of the plan.

Alex went on, "I've been told there's a little lady Pekinese living in the house at the top."

Mrs. Atkins laughed and said, "Oh, you mean Mimosa! She's Mrs. Lang's dog. Benji won't stand much chance there. The poor little thing is never allowed out alone. Still, you never know," she added, her eyes twinkling. "Anyhow, it doesn't hurt to look, does it?" Ruffling Davy's hair she said, "Call into the shop on your way back and I'll find you something nice for your tea."

Davy's mouth watered at the thought.

Returning along the cliff path, as they came to a stile Davy clambered over and paused before jumping down on to the other side.

"Dad," he said, looking serious." Are you very worried?"

Alex, his face level with Davy's, creased into a frown.

"Yes, I am, son. I'm worried about things I can't talk about."

"Why not?"

"In the first place the problems are Jilly's and therefore confidential. Secondly the less you know the safer."

At that he silently swore. He had meant to say 'better' not 'safer'. But it was too late, Davy had already picked up on the word.

"Safer!" he repeated his voice rising. "What do you mean, 'safer'?"

Alex stared at the horizon and said distantly, "Let it go, Davy! Just let it go."

Davy hesitated, clamped his lips together holding back an argument, and gave his father a hard stare before jumping from the stile. Branching to the left he said, over his shoulder, "We can get to the field this way."

Wordlessly, but still silently cursing, Alex followed.

Turning into The Narrows, with its high hedges of valerian and cow-parsley, the trapped heat was overpowering. Underfoot the melting tarmac was uncomfortably sticky to walk on. Ahead the road shimmered. Above, black against the blue sky, a buzzard silently menaced a screaming crow as they hurtled to earth. Alex watched pitying the terrified victim and its inevitable end.

Davy lost no time in locating the field. The signpost lay where he had last seen it. Nettles and brambles still entwined the stile. Climbing it, Davy's heart sank when, on the other side, he saw a mixture of footprints of varying sizes and patterns following the rough path. Had they obliterated Benji's paw marks? In the distance, the single blackthorn beckoned. Davy ran towards it. Crouching clear of its thorned branches he stared at the naked earth. Trampled and churned there was nothing to show that Benji had been there.

Alex gazed at the top of Davy's head saying regretfully, "It was too much to hope for, Davy. After all this is a public footpath that crosses private land."

"I know," he replied, his voice trembling with disappointment. Standing up he pushed his hands into his pockets and said, "But just because the marks have gone, that doesn't mean he wasn't here, does it? We can still look for him, can't we?" he pleaded.

"Why not!" Alex replied. "We've nothing to lose!" Although sounding optimistic, it was not how he felt. Privately he thought the dog was out of the area if not out of the county. Benji was no run-of-the-mill canine and someone could have found him interesting. He pushed the idea away. That was defeatism!

The field, lumpy with hillocks, sloped gently down to a copse while the narrow, beaten path meandered away at right angles. Alex suggested Davy should follow the path.

"It'll be easier to track, and you are more familiar with Benji's paws than I am. I'll take the wooded area. It looks pretty hopeless and dense so don't try to follow me. Just give a shout when you've had enough."

Davy set off, his step firm, his shoulders square.

Alex watched him. He was a gutsy kid! No matter what he met, he'd cope! Davy would never give in until he knew Benji's fate.

The copse was fenced off with ancient wooden posts and barbed wire. Dangling with rabbit fur it spanned a fox run of rutted earth and twigs where the scent of animals could have lured Benji under the fence. Ducking between the wires Alex felt his shirt snag and rip. He swore, then thought: better the fabric than the flesh!

Scanning the area he saw several vague paths leading in various directions. None looked promising, and so he just plunged ahead and hoped for some kind of result. Dodging low-hanging, lichen-covered branches, he skirted bushes and boughs that criss-crossed his self-made path. Pushing himself deeper and deeper into the undergrowth, he shouldered his way through, careless of his scratched flesh. It seemed everything was challenging him. He knew Benji would never have ventured into such deep undergrowth but Alex felt compelled to go on. There was no point in trying to track, everywhere was too densely overgrown and treacherously laid with hidden roots. He would be lucky if he got away with something as simple as a sprained ankle.

To suddenly find himself looking on to a clearing came as a surprise. To see a parked, dark-green camper van was even more of a surprise. How did that get there? There must be a farm gate beyond the trees. Partly hidden by foliage, he was able to take in his surroundings and study the middle-aged woman sitting on the top step. The door was open and she was reading a newspaper. She looked unkempt, poorly dressed and wore a dark triangular scarf tied round her dark hair. As he took a pace forward a twig snapped beneath his weight and, startled, she looked up.

Boldly stepping into the sunlight, he approached and apologising for the intrusion he explained he was looking for a lost dog.

"What sort?" she asked shielding her eyes.

"Small. Brown and white," he told her. Describing the colour was easier than describing the breed.

She shook her head.

"Haven't seen it. How long's it been missing?"

"A couple of days."

"Poor thing," she said, without feeling. She then pushed the paper under her arm, stood up and went into the van slamming the door.

Momentarily surprised he stared after her then shrugging off her disinterest he turned and re-entered the wood.

Finding himself back in thick undergrowth and surrounded by ferns he knew covering the ground would not be easy. It was too dense. Pushing aside branches, tripping over dead wood and fighting brambles he lost his way. This was not the terrain he had travelled earlier. Underfoot was no longer crisp with last years autumns leaves, but boggy.

Suddenly there was gunfire.

One shot.

Crows flapped and called raucously.

Un-nerved he paused.

Davy?

He listened.

Silence.

Grimly he shouldered his way through thorn bushes shielding his face with his bloodied arm.

Urgently he pushed on.

Finally, he broke cover to find himself barred by the wire fence. Damn!

Silence deepened, and then faintly in the distance Davy's voice, high-pitched and urgent, called him.

Careless of safety, Alex vaulted the fence. Racing across the uneven field, yelling Davy's name, his eyes swept the area. Where was he?

Was he hurt?

Trapped?

Fear kicked in as he thought about the gunfire. He powered on. He blanked his mind. He needed a clear head.

Suddenly, in the distance, Davy appeared. Standing in a hollow he was only part visible. Waving his arms, his words faintly carried by the breeze.

"Dad! I've found him. I've found him!"

Alex raced on. Davy, thank God, was safe!

He found his son sitting on his heels his blood-covered hands gently stroking Benji's head as it rested in his lap. Alex could see the dog was alive but only just. Eyes glazed, tongue lolling, his back leg tightly held by barbed wire attached to a fallen wooden post, the dog couldn't move.

It took time and care to free him. Alex wondered if he would survive. He was weak. Lack of food didn't matter. Thirst did. Davy found a puddle, soaked his handkerchief and dribbled water into Benji's mouth. His licking was feeble. The dog needed swift attention. If only they had brought the car! Now the best thing he could do was carry Benji and send Davy ahead to contact the vet.

He arrived within minutes of Alex laying Benji on Jilly's blanket-covered table. The vet's prognosis was optimistic. Apart from dehydration, superficial cuts, a lacerated back leg which he stitched, Benji should be fine within a day or two.

"Keep him quiet and don't let him drink too much water. It'll make him vomit. I've given him a shot to keep any bugs at bay, and I'll see him in a week unless you have a problem. You never know with rusty barbed wire. It's an absolute menace."

Patting Benji's head and playfully knuckling Davy's chin, he said, "Well, done, young man," and left.

Davy flung himself into a chair and sighed with relief.

Alex knew exactly how he felt. Benji's return held significance. There was no mystery attached to his disappearance. Evidence said, having become trapped, he was unable to free himself. Why he'd wandered so far from home would remain a canine mystery. Now asleep in his basket, his paws gently twitching, it was good to have him home.

Davy said, "Just wait until Becca sees him. She'll go absolutely scatty!" He then said, "Ooops! We didn't call into the bakery, did we? Mrs. Atkins promised us a treat. Shall I go for it now, and tell her we've found Benji?"

"Good idea! Pick up a couple of pastys for lunch, will you? And tell Mr. Rogers the news, too."

Whistling cheerfully, buoyed by the possibility of cream cakes for tea, Davy left for the village.

Tom's head appeared round the door. He'd seen the vet arrive and depart, now he wanted to know about the dog. When Alex told him about the barbed wire, Tom scowled.

"Typical!" he said.

"Who owns the land, Tom. D'you know?"

"The Polglise lot. Most of 'em live at Treveden." He spoke with disrespect making it clear that he had no time for the family.

Alex went on, "I had to fight my way through an overgrown copse..."

"Ah, that'd be Hanging Wood," Tom said.

"... and I came across a parked camper van in a clearing."

"Always the same this time of year," Tom told him. "The proper campsites fill up quick. Letting out that bit o' ground gives the Polglise lot a backhander the tax man don't get to know about."

"But there didn't appear to be any amenities. No water. No electricity."

Tom touched the side of his nose. "Don't be fooled. Hal will have tapped into someone's supply to get a freebee."

"That's theft!"

"Which don't matter to some folk!"

Delza wandered in, bare-footed, gave Benji a nervous glance and grunted. When he was asleep in his basket she was unafraid. If he moved she would cower. As he slept on so she inched closer. Peering at him she saw the blood on his fur. Fearfully she backed and grabbed Tom's hand, her grunting loud, her face distressed.

"'Tis all right, my bird," Tom comforted. "Dog'll not move. He's poorly."

Delza backed further away.

Tom shook his head and holding Delza's hand said, "I best take 'er outside. 'er's not 'appy. Glad the dog's back, though. Missus'll be pleased, and the little 'un. Go on, Delza, my bird. Let's find your shoes, shall us?"

Delza grunted and smiled. Papa knew where to find them. Delza didn't.

When Davy returned from the village he was smiling broadly, carrying two freshly-baked pastys and a cake box.

"Look, Dad," he said, flipping open the lid. "Mrs. Atkins said it was to celebrate finding Benji. The pastys we owe for. I forgot to take the money."

Sliding the pastys on to plates Alex then looked into the box and there sat a cake thick with rich, yellow cream. Across the top, sprinkled in hundreds and thousands, a smudged message read 'Welcome Home Dog'.

"Mrs. Atkins couldn't spell Benji," Davy giggled, "But 'Dog's' all right, isn't it?" He touched the cream with his finger, licked it and said, "We're having a really good day, aren't we, Dad?"

Alex had to agree. Finding Benji was one worry out of the way, and something of which Davy could be proud. Now, having achieved far more than expected, they put the cake into the fridge, ate lunch and lazed until it was time to meet the bus. Although Alex had intended to look at the boxes in the loft, he decided against it. Tomorrow would do. Jilly was sure they contained nothing of interest or value – except to her. Richard's possessions were treasured even if they had remained untouched since his death. The idea of searching through his things was merely a shot in the dark. They might reveal a clue, they might not.

Davy, sprawled on the lawn, was absorbed by a nest of scurrying ants. He suddenly asked when Becca was to be told about Benji.

Alex thought for a moment. Davy had already said she would go scatty once she knew. An overwrought child bouncing about in the car was not an ideal passenger. Because Benji was hurt it might be wise to wait until they were home before she was told or – better still – let Jilly explain the situation.

"Can I tell her when she gets off the bus?" Davy asked, expecting to be there to meet her.

"Sorry, Davy," Alex said regretfully, "But someone will have to stay with Benji whilst I collect the girls."

"Da-ad! That's not fair!" Davy protested. "Can't Tom do it?"

"No!" Alex said firmly. "Tom can't."

Davy scowled and pouted.

Alex sighed wondering if he would be in a bad mood for the remainder of the day. It wasn't often Davy sulked, but when he did there could be no mistake about how he felt.

Alex, being in no mood to deal with sullenness, was about to say so when Davy asked if he could go to the beach. The request solved the problem. It was still sunny with only small clouds drifting across the sky, and the sea looked calm. After being reminded to be back in time for Alex to leave, Davy padded away, a towel slung over his shoulder.

Alex wandered off to find Tom. He was transplanting lettuce. Delza, happily wearing her shoes, had gone home. To Alex there was a feeling of emptiness about the place due, he thought, to Jilly's absence. He had become so used to her being around, now that she wasn't, there was a void. He wondered if she felt the same about him. He doubted it. Richard occupied her thoughts for most of her time. Thinking of Richard reminded him of the past few days and the mysteries they held. Was it only a few days? Was Richard the catalyst, and what about the key? Pontivy couldn't be dismissed. Having been deliberately referred to on the 'phone, then it was relevant. Whoever was involved had proved how easy it was to separate a child from its mother. His thoughts jerked to a standstill. Had sending the girls to Truro given the stranger another opportunity to repeat the performance?

He suddenly felt uneasy. Although he had been watching Tom spraying the transplanted lettuce he hadn't actually seen him.

Lack of concentration!

His mind was now crammed with unappealing thoughts. Returning to the house he knew he had been stupid in suggesting Jilly should take Becca shopping. Truro would be crowded. Fine weather did not keep everyone on the beaches. Jostling crowds would be a good cover in which to commit a crime or to cause fear. Now Alex felt an urgency to talk to Jilly. To warn her without frightening her. Had she taken her mobile?

He was unsure.

Where should he look?

Downstairs yielded nothing.

Her bedroom?

He found the 'phone next to her dressing box. Fingering it he swore under his breath.

Damn! She was out of contact.

Checking his watch he saw there was still an hour to go before they boarded the bus for home.

Could he drive to Truro in time to collect them?

He could, but where was the point? If anything was going to happen it would already have taken place. Time would have been of the essence and acted upon accordingly.

Alex was chilled by a cold sweat.

There was nothing he could do except meet the bus and pray the girls were on it.

Restlessly pacing he waited for Davy to return from the beach.

Benji was still sleeping and snuffling. The vet's knock-out drops had done a good job. And Alex had no worries on that score.

Eventually Davy came back with sand on his shoulders and his hair sticky with salt.

"I'm going to have a shower, Dad."

"Fine! I think I'll make a move," Alex said, looking at a spot above the boy's head.

"Won't you be too early?" Davy frowned.

"Better than late!" he said. "You'll be all right won't you? Benji's asleep, and Tom's in the garden."

"Dad!" Davy said his voice holding a note of protest. "Stop trying to make me into a Mummy's boy!"

Alex blinked. Was that was he was doing?

"Sorry!" he said and left.

* * *

Tom had been forced to send Delza home. With Missus gone for the day and the dog asleep in the kitchen Delza wouldn't go into the house alone and get on with her chores. Sending her home was all he could do. She'd be all right. She'd find the bun and the red spoon on the drainer, she knew where the milk was and she'd be quite happy looking at her picture books.

Now, having fiddled about with young lettuce, he was sitting in his shed unravelling a bundle of twine. He wished Benji had not come to grief on Polglise land. It worried him. Hal Polglise was into dogs. Any size, any breed as long as they were different. They attracted him. He could always see a money-making scam with unusual dogs. Labradors? Retrievers? Ten a penny. Benji? A pretty good price. If Hal got his hands on him, then Tom didn't fancy his chances. Mulling over the possibility he took comfort in the fact that few people knew Benji's breed and even less about his peculiarity.

With the twine unravelled and wound into a tight ball, Tom dropped it into an empty coffee jar. A job neatly done! If only life was that easy! But it wasn't. There was always something or someone causing tangles.

Earlier, Dick Rogers had told him how Hal had failed to take out 'Blue Gull' on the morning tide. It wasn't the first time he'd missed a sailing over the last few weeks. A law unto himself, he didn't give a damn about anyone else. As long as he could legally, or otherwise, line his pockets he'd go his own way.

Tom, fingering the plaster on his head, would not have been surprised to learn it was Hal who had hit him. He wouldn't need a reason, or payment, to use violence. Such was the enmity between the families.

Tom sighed. All this feuding was nothing to do with Benji. It was likely he just wandered off in search of a lady friend. His being trapped on Polglise land was sheer bad luck.

Although Alex had started out with time to spare, heavy traffic used up the minutes. Driving slowly made him impatient and edgy.

The roads were crowded. Sunburnt people dawdled as they made their way home after spending time on the beach. Jilly and Becca should have done the same. That would have been safer and wiser. But life's mysterious plan had deemed otherwise. That was the dark side. But Benji had been found and saved from what could have been a slow and agonising death. That thought lifted his spirits and, if the Gods were willing, dog and child would soon be re-united. And if the Gods were even more willing the day would end happily for everyone.

* * *

For Jilly the trip to Truro was not as therapeutic as she hoped. She was plagued by thoughts of the mysterious man and his demands for the key. What key? And why was he now silent? Had he attacked Tom thinking the cottage was unoccupied? He could have done. Half the village was out looking for Benji. Why not the family? Had he hoped to search and find the key? What stopped him? These thoughts dogged her all day. At the same time she kept reminding herself this outing was Becca's treat. It should be fun-filled and happy, but could it hold danger? She tried to dismiss the thought without success.

For the first hour Becca was bright and chatty. In and out of shops she wanted everything she saw. Knowing that was not possible did not spoil her game.

Suddenly the game stopped.

Jilly, preoccupied with her own thoughts, did not immediately notice Becca's silence. Her clinginess Jilly put down to the density of the crowds and so put her arm about her. Becca nestled and clutched the back of Jilly's blouse.

They lunched at a pavement café. Becca toyed with her meal and refused ice-cream. She looked pale.

Jilly wondered if she was unwell.

Becca said she was fine.

In vain Jilly tried to jolly her along but Becca either couldn't or wouldn't respond

The day seemed doomed.

It was only when on their return journey that Becca became bright and chatty again. And then, as they left the bus, her mood changed.

Now worried that the child was not at all well Jilly, anxiously searching for Alex, was dismayed when he was not in sight.

Becca looked hot, her hands were cold, and she was again clingy.

Agitated, Jilly suggested buying a giant puzzle book. If Becca was really unwell, she would not be comforted. But she brightened. Clutching Jilly's hand Becca led the way to the shop across the road. Then without warning she held back on stiff legs.

Oncoming traffic neared.

Angered by the silly behaviour Jilly cried, "For goodness sake!" and dragging Becca towards the shop, she pushed her through the doorway.

Alex arrived to an empty bus. He scanned the crowd, his heart thumping.

Minutes later he saw them weaving through gridlocked traffic and then they were scrambling into the car.

His relief was enormous. Now he could almost laugh at his uncharacteristic paranoia – if that's what it was. He silently admitted to being afraid for them. He did not like the strange happenings that surrounded them. All he could do was try to shield them from possible danger.

Now they were together, his heart slowly returned to its natural rhythm. For the moment they were both safe.

It wasn't until they were clear of traffic that he asked if they'd had a happy day. Somehow he didn't think so. Twice he'd looked at Becca in the rear mirror to be met with scowls.

Jilly was quieter than usual. Should he mention Benji, just to cheer everyone up? Explaining injuries and all that went with them? Not a good idea. He would wait.

Jilly suddenly started to talk about their trip.

"Truro was very busy, wasn't it, Becca?" she said brightly. "We shopped, had lunch and shopped again!" Jilly went on even more brightly. "Becca has two new sun tops, we bought Davy a pair of trendy shorts. I treated myself to perfume and for you Becca bought a book on wood carving."

The brightness seemed so forced that when Jilly fell silent there was a wake of trailing darkness.

Again he glanced at Becca in the mirror and again he was met with a scowl. Cheerfully he thanked her for the book." I'll look forward to reading it."

She didn't respond.

Switching on the radio he felt, rather than saw, Jilly's surprised reaction as raucous music blared out. Not to his taste, but to Becca's. She leaned back in the seat, closed her eyes and banged the rhythm on the arm rest.

Under cover of the noise he drew Jilly's attention and in semi-profile mouthed, "We've found Benji. Injured but alive."

Immediately relief flooded Jilly's face. Furtively and constantly glancing into the mirror Alex outlined the situation.

"If you explain to Becca that the vet his given him a shot, and he has to be kept quiet! She'll understand, won't she?"

"Leave it to me, Alex," she said, gratefully. "And thank you. A happy ending to a not-very-happy day."

"It isn't over yet," he told her smiling.

Within moments of arriving home and being given the news of Benji, Becca's excited squeals shattered the peace of the garden. Squirming she tried to escape from Jilly's firm hold.

Davy raced from the cottage leaping and whooping. Arms outstretched they fell into a group hug while Alex watched as they eventually bustled indoors. He was content to remain in the garden knowing he would not be missed. Davy would describe Benji's rescue with high drama. Becca would listen with wide-eyed amazement, and their friendship would be cemented even more firmly. That thought, while pleasing him, made him reflect on his own relationship with Jilly. He knew they were good friends and would always remain so, but he wanted more than that. If only Richard didn't keep getting in the way.

Jilly emerged from the cottage smiling.

"Oh, Alex! Thank you so much," she said, "What an ordeal for you both! But thanks to you and Davy I now have a very happy daughter."

Taking his hand she led him to the bottom of the garden. Sitting on the grass they faced each other. Jilly plucked a daisy and twirling the stem between her fingers said, her eyes clouded, "We did not have a very good day in

Truro. Becca was in such an awful mood. Your rescue of Benji could not have come at a better time."

"I thought she looked grumpy," Alex said. "In fact, I almost told her about Benji just to make her smile."

"I'm glad you didn't," said Jilly. "You saw her reaction! Almost out of control! She is so besotted with him. Maybe worrying spoiled the day. She was so mercurial! And for some of the time, I was going to describe her as..." Jilly paused to search for the right word, "I was going to say – 'sulky'. But it was something else."

"Like what?"

"Don't ask me," she laughed. "I've had only nine years experience of such moods! And as I don't understand them now, what will I do when she's in her teens?"

Alex, too, laughed. He could foresee the same problem with Davy. "Except," he added, "now and again Davy and I have a sort of role reversal. I become the child. He becomes the master. Using jargon learned at school – all to do with computers – he blinds me with science. It's a weird feeling being unable to understand what he's talking about, but it works. Kids have fresh ideas that hold new slants on life and I'm not too proud to learn from him."

Jilly gazed at him in silence then said, "Alex Hunter you are a wonderful man!" Getting to her feet she held out her hand and said, "Come on! I believe there's a cream cake waiting to be eaten."

Looking at each other, and hand-in-hand they went into the kitchen.

* * *

Becca, kneeling at Benji's side, could not be lured away, not even by a slice of cake. All she wanted to do was sit by his basket. Twice he roused and lapped water from the dish she held, other than that he slept.

Davy, delighted with his new shorts had taken them, and his cake, home. Trying shorts on in Jilly's house was risky. He didn't want to be caught in his underpants. Later he bounced in and gave Jilly his thanks and a hug.

"They're great, Jilly! Where's Becca?"

"In my room with Benji."

"Is it OK to go and talk to her? I thought we might play cards. She cheats like mad, but it makes us laugh."

"Don't be too long," Alex said. "You both need a good night's sleep, so, bed earlyish!"

"Can I read?"

"Lights out at ten!"

Davy grinned, gave a thumbs up sign and quietly closed the door.

Left alone Jilly and Alex listened to music. Soft and soothing it was Jilly's choice and it suited her mood but only to a certain degree. To become perfectly at ease she needed to know why Becca had been so unhappy in Truro. It might have been caused by worrying about Benji, but Jilly didn't think so. It was something deeper and heavier than that and Becca was too young to carry a weighty problem.

Outside, twilight brought out the bats. Swooping soundlessly they feasted on unsuspecting insects whilst skimming through the air. Jilly's attention was drawn as they darted across the garden silhouetted against the moon.

A sudden ringing of the door bell startled her.

Alex half rose.

She held him back.

"I'll go," she said, wondering who would call so late in the evening.

It was Marilyn asking about Benji.

When told he was safe she looked pleased and pushed a paper bag into Jilly's hands.

"Sweets for Becca," she explained. "A sort of cheer-up. They're gobstoppers. Kid's love 'em, don't they?"

"That IS kind of you," Jilly exclaimed with delight. "Would you like to give them to her?" she invited.

"Better not! Pop … er … Arthur will be wanting his supper. He suffers from E.O.D."

"E.O.D.?" Jilly repeated blankly.

"Ever Open Door! Always hungry!" she complained sliding her eyes upwards." Love to Becca! G'night!" And she was gone.

Smiling, and returning to Alex's side, her smile faded when he asked if he had heard correctly.

"Did I hear her refer to Arthur as 'Pop'?"

"Yes, she did!" Jilly told him, creasing her brow. "Maybe it was just a teasy thing. She's a lot younger than he is."

"Or maybe it was a slip of the tongue," he said objectively. "Oh, I know she made a quick correction… but…" He frowned then looked at her saying, "I'm becoming more and more intrigued and curious about those two. The galling thing is having no foreseeable way of satisfying my curiosity."

"Our curiosity," she corrected. "Whatever it is we are in this together. I know it's my battle, but I can't fight it alone, Alex." Resting her head on his shoulder, she asked, "Where would I be without you?"

Before he could reply the telephone rang.

Jilly took the call in the hall returning moments later, her face devoid of colour.

Taking an urgent stride to her side, Alex asked, "What is it?"

For a moment she could not speak. Trembling, the pulse in her throat wildly beating, she looked at him with fear-flecked eyes.

In a low voice she said, "It was a man asking if we'd had a nice day in Truro.

And did I want Becca or the key? I couldn't have both!"

Her eyes were suddenly empty as she said, "Alex, I don't have a key I can't account for."

He shook her gently. She looked so lost and vulnerable he held her close. He had to protect her. Take away her worries.

She drew away from him and brushed her hand across her eyes.

What was she thinking about! Why was she worrying about a key, when Becca was at risk? The watcher had been in Truro. He'd seen them. He knew how to track them!

Alex's mind was also racing.

Who knew the girls would be away for the day? Only Tom and Davy.

Someone was definitely watching the cottage!

The holiday couple?

Their cottage was a vantage point.

Was Marilyn's visit an excuse to make some kind of check on the household?

Such as what? And sweets for Becca didn't fit the equation.

Someone heartless was making threats, and the heartless did not buy gobstoppers for intended victims!

The 'phone rang again.

Jilly blanched.

"I'll take it," Alex said, his face set as he went into the hall.

A moment later he looked round the door and smiled, "It's your Mum! And I get the feeling she thinks we are up to no good!"

Jilly half smiled. Her mother could think what she liked – she'd be wrong!

Late calls from her parents were not unusual. They led a busy social life and ringing Jilly was a question of fitting in. The arrangement suited everyone. Tonight's call was to say there was a parcel in the post.

"Daddy had a little win on the Lottery, so we went shopping," her mother told her excitedly. "Nothing much. Just sharing our good luck with you. Now don't ask me what we've bought. You'll spoil the surprise."

They chattered on exchanging news and views, except that Jilly said nothing of her own worries. There was no point. Her parents were too old and too far away to be of practical help.

Suddenly her mother said, "We thought we might do a tour of France. You know how Daddy loves driving. Would you let us take Becca?"

For a moment Jilly panicked. France? No! Yet a refusal would lead to questioning.

"When are you going?" she asked as a delaying tactic.

"When we can get a ferry booking. We thought to use the one you sailed on. You spoke very highly of it, but we can't remember the name. Was it the White Swan?"

"White Eagle!" she corrected. "You have a picture of it which Becca sent to you," she hastily reminded.

"We used to have a picture!" her mother said crossly. "Remember when those naughty children broke into the house? Well along with one or two ornaments they took the picture from the mantelpiece. I suppose, being boys, they liked the ship. Any way, darling, it's gone. What did you say the name was?"

"White Eagle," Jilly said, trying to keep her voice steady.

"And what about taking Becca?" her mother asked.

"Another time," Jilly quickly suggested. "She has so many invites and things to do before school starts."

The excuse sounded lame, but it was the best Jilly could do. There was no way she would let Becca go to France! As things stood she wouldn't let her go anywhere.

"That's all right," her mother said, easily. "Another time. Perhaps next year we can all go together? Now don't forget about the parcel. And by the way, your young man sounds charming! Goodnight, darling! Hugs to Becca." And the line went dead.

Moving to the open doorway of the sitting room, Jilly, looking stunned, said in a disbelieving voice, "Alex, Pontivy. I'm sure it was a set-up! I'm sure we were tracked!"

"What! How?"

Churning with apprehension she told him about the stolen postcard. How it held all the details. Mitzi's address, when Jilly and Becca planned to return to the UK and heaven only knew what else Becca might have written.

"That was why the postcard was stolen!" she said. "It couldn't have been children who broke into the house. It was someone with an ulterior motive."

Quietly, angrily Alex swore. It all made sense, it all added up, but what was the answer?

They talked in hushed tones as if hiding a secret plan. They had no plan. All Jilly had was her feeling of foreboding.

Hours later, tense and sleepless, she had to accept that someone was monitoring their every move. The thought was frightening. Had they been watched ever since Richard died?

Recently Alex had hinted that Richard's death may not have been what it seemed. The idea was preposterous. Who would want to harm Richard? The question churned in her mind. Earlier Alex was convinced that if they were to get anywhere at all then the missing postcard could point them in a new direction.

A direction to what?

Murder?

Chapter Seven

When Jilly opened her bedroom curtains she was met with heavy rain and a sea fret thicker than a blanket. She welcomed both. They solved problems. Becca, disliking rain, would walk Benji no further than the bottom of the garden. After that her puzzle book would keep her occupied. Alex, eager to search the loft, would think it a good way to dodge the weather and Davy would be keen to help him. It was unlikely that Tom and Delza would show. Jilly discouraged Delza during wet weather. She created problems with her shoes – or the lack of them – depending upon her mood. As things were at that moment everyone within the house was content except Jilly. Contrarily she was feeling rebellious.

She would not allow circumstances to make her a prisoner in her own home! Providing she could leave Becca in the care of an adult, then life, as Alex had suggested, must follow the normal pattern. Therefore she would go to the village as usual. She might window-shop, she might not. Sometimes she did, sometimes she didn't. She would thank Mrs. Atkins for the cake and pay for the pastys Davy had collected. She would be an ordinary Mum doing ordinary things. If her heart should flutter with apprehension that was her problem and it wouldn't be shared.

Walking in damp misty weather did not worry her. She was happy in any element except a Force 12. That was something to be reckoned with. Today was uncannily still. Sounds were muffled and no birds flew. The harbour was bereft of visitors. One or two fishermen were mending nets, their boats bobbing gently on a half tide. Out of the corner of her eye she saw and recognised Hal Polglise. He was someone she instinctively disliked.

Lazily leaning against a bollard he watched her with a mocking stare, saluted her then ran his eyes over her body, a carnal sneer twisting his features. Repulsed, her head held high, she walked on, her pace unfaltering. He whistled tunelessly matching her rhythm. She did not move out of sync. There was no way she would give him the satisfaction of knowing she was aware.

By the time she reached the bakery her heart was racing and her breathing was hurried. Relieved to find the shop empty, Jilly fumbled in her purse paid for the pastys, and thanked Mrs. Atkins for the cake. This simple action gave her time to regain her composure.

Taking the money, Mrs. Atkins beamed. "The cake was my pleasure and I'm pleased to know the little dog is safe. Mind you, anything that gets trapped on Polglise land comes as no surprise to me. Careless lot! Don't deserve to own land. As far as they are concerned what falls down, stays down. You should see their outside lav'! It's a disgrace. Still Benji'll know not to go courting that way again, won't he?"

She stacked a pile of warm scones under a glass dome and went on, "And don't you worry your head about my frock getting wet. My niece put it right for me. Works in a dry cleaners. Did a proper job, too!"

"Then you must let me pay for it," Jilly insisted.

"Don't see why. Got it done free!" As she spoke her eyes moved beyond Jilly and her expression hardened.

"Yes, Hal?" she snapped.

Jilly's skin crawled as she felt him standing behind her almost touching but not quite. "I'll have a pasty," he said adding spitefully, "Today's. None of yesterday's left-over rubbish."

Wordless, Mrs. Atkins reached into the warmer, chose a pasty, wrapped it, took his money then put the parcel on the counter.

"Ta!" he said. Removing the food from its paper bag he screwed it into a ball and threw it on to the floor. He then crammed his mouth and left.

Jilly retrieved the bag and dropped it into the litter bin.

Mrs. Atkins, her face flushed with anger, said, "That Hal's a real nasty piece of work. Don't you never have nothing to do with him. In fact don't have nothing to do with any of that family. And," she went on becoming more and more heated, "If he has a go at you about Benji being on his land, you tell Dick Rogers. He'll soon sort him out." And so Mrs. Atkins went on spilling out words of anger about the Polglise clan, but mainly about Hal.

What she had to say about him came as no surprise to Jilly, it merely confirmed that he was not a man to become involved with at any level.

Some minutes later, when she left the bakery, Hal was leaning against the shop wall his mouth bulging and flaked with pastry crumbs. Aware of his insolent stare she looked through him.

His face darkened. He didn't like being ignored.

Walking home under the lifting clouds Jilly recalled Mrs. Atkins' words. If what she said about Hal was true, then he could be dangerous. All his life he had been a layabout and a womaniser. Involved in a bitter feud with Tom Pascoe, about which Mrs. Atkins refused to talk, Hal did all he could to make Tom's life uncomfortable. He was also involved in some kind of illegal sport that, again, Mrs. Atkins refused to discuss. All she would say was that money-wise he knew how to play the game to his own advantage.

"But," Mrs. Atkins finally said, "Dick'll get him in the end. You mark my word."

Jilly believed her, convinced by the firm ring to her voice.

Dismissing all thoughts of Hal Polglise she hurried on. The day was dreary enough without having him in the background.

* * *

Much earlier Alex had been roused from a troubled sleep by Jilly's laughter and the chatter of the children in the kitchen. Needing time to pull his thoughts to order he sat on the edge of the bed and stared into space. Somehow he had to think up a plan of action. He felt responsible for everyone's safety and he needed to be on his guard. If only he knew against what.

The smell of coffee finally lured him to the kitchen where Becca and Davy, sitting at the table, were again playing cards while Benji, almost fully recovered, slept in his basket. Jilly smiled a greeting and, as she was about to leave the house, reminded Alex that if he intended going into the loft it lacked lighting.

A few minutes later, knowing it warranted the effort, he rigged up a cable and lamp-holder which he could run off the power point in the hall. Becca wanted to know why he was going into the loft. He told her Jilly had asked him to find a photograph album. At that Davy looked at him sharply. It was not what he had been told! Wisely he said nothing.

At the thought of photographs Alex remembered the stolen picture postcard written by Becca to her grandparents. It had contained a lot of information; Mitzi's address, the date when Jilly and Becca were due to return home, and promised shopping sprees. Postal deliveries being what they were from abroad might have given the girls two or three days grace. After that the information about them could have fallen into the wrong hands making tracking them through France a simple exercise. But why the time lapse between then and now? Had they been under surveillance all that while? If so then the time involved must have been costly. In turn that suggested the anticipated reward would be enormous. That, surely, was the motivation! There was also the mysterious demands for a key. What type? Door, suitcase, cash box? No. Any of those could have been forced. What about a safe? A possibility! Except that with the right expertise any safe could be opened. But – if it was a safe – where was it? Not in Richard's office, Jilly would have known. Not in the house. So where? And what about Richard's staff? Did they know if it existed? Why had they disappeared? Were they at the funeral? Jilly didn't know. Most of the people who attended the service were strangers and only friends spoke to her, which was all she could remember about the day. After that her parents took over.

Alex felt he was floundering in a quagmire that was determined to suck him down. It offered no foothold. Grimly he knew if he was to make any kind of progress then he would have to find his own footings.

Switching his mind back to getting into the loft he was faced with the first problem. The hatch hinges had seized up through lack of use and neglect and it was only by using force that he gained access. The hinges snapped. Alex swore. Davy offered to go to the village for replacements. Alex refused. Where Davy went Becca went. And the children roaming about would be against Jilly's wishes. Alex told Davy he had spare hinges at home. Davy gave him an odd look. For Dad to have a spare anything was a miracle. Spare hinges? No way!

The loft was boarded over and a number of boxes and packing cases were stored at one end. Holding up the light Alex could see several containers. This surprised him. Jilly had led him to believe there were only three or four.

Perhaps she had simply forgotten. Hitching the lamp cable over the crossbeam, he began to search. Seven boxes held nothing but crumpled paper and cardboard. The three remaining boxes contained a mixture of brassware, plus a pair of miniature copper kettles with the likeness of Queen Victoria stamped upon the lids. Would the contents of the remaining two boxes prove to be of more interest? He thought so. They would be the cartons of which Jilly had already spoken. Those holding personal belongings.

Swiftly he opened the first two to find they held books, boyhood annuals, one or two comics, books containing handwritten work, and text books relating to them. There were boxes within boxes that held faded personal letters, some greeting cards and photographs. Two silver cups, for sporting achievements – running – carefully wrapped in wadding and that was all. He had felt so sure he would find the missing key among the contents that when he didn't he was acutely disappointed.

There remained one more box. And if the key existed at all was this where he would find it? His curiosity was put on hold when Jilly, having returned from the village, called out that coffee was ready. Reluctantly, and followed by Davy, he clambered down the ladder and went into the kitchen.

Jilly, her hair sparkling with droplets of water, having suffered the affront from Hal Polglise, angrily recounted the incident.

"He's an absolute moron, Alex," she said, her hand shaking as she poured the coffee. "And Mrs. Atkins warned me, in no uncertain terms, to avoid him. She also said if there's trouble about Benji being found on his land then to tell Dick Rogers!"

Alex listened in silence and appreciated he could have an ally in Dick. He might be glad of him one day.

Putting down the coffee pot Jilly said, "Having got that off my chest, tell me what you found in the loft."

When he reminded her of the number of boxes stored there her look of dismay made him laugh.

"Oh, no!" she exclaimed. "I had truly forgotten! Richard had a huge collection of brass and copper. Most of it was sold, but one or two choice bits were kept for Becca."

Becca, sitting next to Benji's basket, clapped her hands and scrambled to her feet asking if she could see them.

Alex asked Jilly if later would do. "Everything is strewn about and with one more box still to open."

"Yes, of course, Alex."

"Mom!" Becca wailed.

"Later, Becca." Jilly promised.

Lowering his voice Alex told her he hoped the missing key might be found in the final box.

"In a way I hope it isn't," Jilly told him unexpectedly. "Finding it could cause even more trouble. It could lead us into a situation that might be difficult to get out of."

Alex made no comment. She had a point, but he wasn't sure it was a good one.

Finishing his coffee he returned to the loft and, after much pleading from Becca, he lowered the boxed brass down to Davy. It was immediately pounced upon and excitedly dragged away. Davy made his escape by scrambling back into the loft.

The remaining box was much sturdier than the others and had reinforced metal corners. There was no trademark on it and it looked unused, even custom-made.

Davy fingered it and said tentatively, "Dad, I know something's going on – something's wrong." With his head on one side he asked, "Are you in some kind of trouble?"

Taken aback by his directness Alex pulled on his bottom lip. The question could not be side-stepped, but how much should Davy be told? He was bright. He would see through lies. Would half-truths suffice? Or should he stick to his original comments? He decided on the latter.

"Davy! As I've already told you, the problem is Jilly's. It's nothing too serious, it just has to be handled with care and discretion."

"Is it to do with Benji?"

"Benji!" Alex exclaimed in surprise. "What gave you that idea?"

Davy shrugged and didn't answer. If it wasn't to do with Benji, then what?

Life was suddenly very complicated.

To avoid discussing the matter further Alex busied himself with the remaining box. Crouching, he tore off the gummed strip holding down the divided lid, pulled it open, and exposed the contents. Neatly packed and level with the top was a sealed, unmarked manila envelope. Below that lay a number of flimsy cardboard files containing papers. Carefully handling them he passed them to Davy asking him to stack them in order, explaining it might be important to Jilly that he should do so. There was nothing to indicate the subject matter held within the files yet, at some time, they must have been important. They were too precisely stored to be otherwise.

Davy placed the last file on top of the unsteady pile and held it safe with his hand.

"There are twenty, Dad, plus the brown envelope. Does that sound about right?"

"I've no idea, Davy," Alex told him absently. Frowning, he looked at the files, then getting to his feet and standing with his hands on his hips he peered into the empty box.

"Something's not quite right," he said with slow deliberation. "When I opened the box the contents were level with the top. Now with contents and box side by side there's a discrepancy of at least a couple of inches."

"Dad! We're metric!"

"Who cares?" Alex said, crouching and reaching into the box." Well, now!" he said after prodding at the base. "I thought it was empty, but it appears to have a false bottom. Holding...?"

"More files?" Davy chipped in, sounding bored.

"Who knows?" Alex replied. Files were a possibility, but would there be a key? To find anything at all the box had to be virtually torn apart, but only after Jilly had climbed into the loft to identify it.

She stared at it. It was vaguely familiar, or was it? One cardboard box was pretty much like another. This particular one? She was unsure.

"I'll have to hack it open," Alex warned.

She shrugged. What did it matter? If the contents were merely mementos they could be stored in another container.

Given the go-ahead, Alex set to work but even with pliers and a knife it took him several minutes to prise the box apart and remove the false bottom. Only then, when the bits were scattered, did he see, packed in a thin layer of plastic foam, a laptop.

Open-mouthed, Jilly wondered why Richard had hidden it and the contents from her. She looked at Alex with questioning eyes.

"You didn't know, did you?" he said.

She shook her head, "No, I didn't. I knew about his office computer, but that was sold."

"Who bought it?"

Again she shook her head saying, "I haven't a clue. The solicitors handled everything to do with Richard's estate. Why do you want to know?"

"Because it could hold information which might be useful to us, Jilly." He paused for a moment then searched her face. "Are you sure you haven't seen this laptop before?"

"Absolutely! If Richard kept it in his study I wouldn't have known. Not that the room was out of bounds, but I rarely went in there. I had no reason. The cleaning lady did what was needed about once a month – usually when Richard was away. He left everything neat and tidy, so if I'd had the inclination to poke about I doubt if I would have found anything I wasn't meant to find. The box, as far as I remember, was already packed before we moved house."

"Didn't that strike you as odd? Weren't you intrigued by a heavy, sealed carton?"

"Not really. I guessed it was something to do with his work. Had I opened it, I wouldn't have known if the contents were important or not. The laptop?" She shrugged. "It means nothing to me, and to be quite honest I really don't remember that particular box."

"Are you sure?"

"Of course I'm sure!" she told him edgily. Her eyes flickered as she asked in a taut voice, and with a defensive attitude, what was he really asking?

He told her he was merely trying to learn and store facts that he could call upon later.

He looked at her and added calmly, "If I'm prying, I'm sorry, Jilly. I didn't mean to."

She turned away from him and said in a voice that remained slightly unforgiving, "I must think about lunch." And with that she disappeared down the ladder.

Davy looked at his father, his eyes questioning.

"Don't ask me," Alex said shrugging. "I don't always understand women!"

"I don't think I do, either," Davy told him.

Alex ruffled his hair, picked up the laptop and said, "But you do understand these, don't you?"

"We've got them at school – well – we've got big computers. Laptops might be a bit different to use but I expect I can work it out. D'you want me to have a go at it?"

"Not unless Jilly agrees. If she does, you're not likely to damage it, are you?"

"I'll be very careful" Davy told him in a voice that said he wasn't an idiot.

Alex grinned.

Gathering together the files and the laptop, they went down to lunch.

The atmosphere was strained. Only Becca was unaffected. Delighted by her box of treasures she described each one in detail. After that she talked about Benji, vowing never to let him out of her sight again.

Jilly smiled. Becca had unwittingly eased the tension with her extravagant promise. That trait she had inherited from her father, although his promises were never seriously made – not in that context. Becca could also be secretive. Another inherited gene? That possibility prompted Jilly's thoughts to return to Truro. What had caused Becca to be so moody? Had it been a cry for help? She needed to know. And what about her own flaring anger with Alex? He wasn't the real target, Richard was. The sudden contact with his belongings opened the wound made by his death. The hurt she felt was overwhelming. She hid it with rage. How unfair! Alex was a good friend who wanted to help her. Now she looked at him as he listened to Becca's ceaseless chatter. His face calm and strong, his attention focused. If only he could read Becca's mind. Whatever secret it held she knew Alex would be able to deal with it. Except it wasn't down to Alex. Becca was her responsibility. If Becca lacked the confidence to talk about whatever was worrying her, then it was up to Jilly to find a way round the problem. There was no point in guesswork, she had to ask. And given the right moment she would.

It came a little later when Becca asked if she could wear one of the new sun tops bought on the previous day.

"Now that it's stopped raining, it's lovely and sunny, Mom. I can take Benji into the garden and read to him. Or we could play ball. I know he's got a poorly leg but I'll be very careful. Promise."

"Play ball in a new sun top!" Jilly teased. "Benji will be flattered! By the way," she went on, "can you remember the name of the shop where we bought them? I thought we might go there again next week."

Becca's face closed. She'd shut out a memory, a mental picture, or was it something she heard? Jilly didn't ask. Instead she suggested they go upstairs and choose which sun top she wanted to wear. At that Becca's face cleared, and she raced ahead leaping the stairs two at a time. Minutes later, with the top chosen and donned, Jilly sat on the bed and opened her arms.

"A hug?" she suggested. "A sort of thank you for yesterday?"

Again Becca's face closed and she looked at Jilly with troubled eyes. She then sat beside her and rested her head on Jilly's shoulder.

"Mumma," she began.

Jilly's nerves tingled. So something was wrong! It was Mumma instead of Mom!

Becca went on in a small voice, "Yesterday I was frightened."

Jilly's heart lurched.

"Frightened, of what, Becca?" She spoke softly, treading lightly, knowing Becca could easily clam up if her voice held anything but sympathy.

"I was frightened of the man."

Again Jilly's heart lurched.

"What man, darling?"

"He followed us all day," Becca whispered. "When we went into the shops he waited outside, and when we had lunch he watched us."

Holding her close, her own thoughts verging on turmoil, Jilly asked if she knew who the man was.

"It was the policeman, Mumma." There was a long pause. "Mumma," Becca went on asking in a tiny, frightened voice, "Have you done something wrong?"

The question cut into Jilly's heart. What agony had Becca been through! No wonder she had been moody. She must have been so frightened. Jilly's mind darted about. The man on the 'phone! He asked about Truro. But he already knew about them. And Becca knew about him. Becca had been scared for most of the day! She had been afraid. Not for herself, but for Jilly. Filled with dread Jilly looked for a simple explanation, but couldn't find one. How could she assure Becca her world was safe? At that moment because her own mind was so cold with fear, she had no answer.

Becca provided her own solution.

"I think…" she said, slipping away from Jilly and standing to face her with hands on her hips. "I think, because he's a horrid man his wife has left him and, because you are pretty, he wants to marry you." She didn't actually say "so there!" but Jilly heard it in her voice.

The seriousness of the situation did not take away the humour of Becca's whimsical idea. And if the idea removed Becca's fears then Jilly would not undermine it. For Jilly the situation remained serious. Was he really a policeman? If so, why had he followed them and would he continue to do so?

Becca, having unloaded her fears on to Jilly, skipped away eager to show off her new sun top and take Benji into the garden. Jilly hoped Davy would join them. She needed to talk to Alex alone. She needed to see his reaction to her discovery, and she needed reassurance.

His gaze was direct. His surprised whistle low.

"No wonder she was moody," he said of Becca. "I can't imagine what thoughts were running through her mind.

She must have been really scared. The next thing is how do we find out what the guy was up to?"

"Where do we begin?" Jilly asked at a loss. "There are so many loose ends, all disconnected yet somehow tied in."

She fell silent as thoughts scurried through her mind. Alex had spoken of murder. Richard's murder. It was a road she had no desire to go down and she shuddered at the idea. And what about the missing key? Alex had hoped to find it in one of the boxes but hadn't done so. Her mind switched to the policeman. Did he know Becca had seen and recognised him? If so, was she now in real danger? Were they all in danger? For herself she didn't care, but she was afraid for Becca. Perhaps she should have let Becca go to France with her parents. After all the enemy would be unlikely to keep her in sight if she was abroad. The key they wanted was here in the UK and this was where the action would take place. With a sudden resolve Jilly made up her mind. Becca must go away. She would ring her parents now and make arrangements. She would find a convincing excuse for her change of heart, and so Becca would be safe.

Tom knocked on the side door and handed Jilly a package.

"I was at the gate when it arrived, so I signed for it. All right, Missus?"

"Thank you Tom. Is Delza with you today?"

"I left 'er at 'ome. She be in one of 'er moods. You know what 'er's like!"

"Indeed I do, Tom," Jilly laughed.

Shaking his head and smiling Tom ambled away.

The package was from Jilly's parents.

Inside she found a pair of exquisite opal earrings for herself, and a gold chain bracelet for Becca. Such extravagance and such generosity! As Jilly rang to thank them Becca danced with delight pausing only when she heard Jilly say, "I know I refused your offer earlier, but having thought about it I'm sure missing a few parties won't worry Becca and she'd love to go with you."

"Go where, Mom?" Becca cried, tugging her arm.

"We've decided not to go," Jilly's mother said faintly.

"You've changed your mind?" she asked masking fear with disappointment.

"Not at all! We've decided on a cruise. Round the Med. The Cudesa no less! Stateroom with balcony. Sailing from Plymouth the day after tomorrow!"

"How wonderful!"

"So, can we still take Becca? It can be arranged. In fact we have already tentatively sorted it out."

Jilly's spirits soared. A cruise! What could be better? What could be safer? Within hours it was all settled. When Alex offered to drive them to Plymouth everything fell into place. Even Benji, Becca's biggest worry, was catered for. Knowing it would be unkind for the dog to journey so far in one day, Mrs. Atkins was approached and promptly volunteered to care for him. She asked no questions, and Jilly gave no reasons, yet between them there was a mutual understanding that the less said the better. For the remainder of Becca's absence Davy promised to guard Benji with his life. Everything that needed to be investigated was put on hold. Jilly's main concern was getting Becca to safety. The key, the laptop, the mysterious man became of secondary importance.

For the next few hours the house throbbed with excitement and activity, and even a dawn start on the day of departure was looked upon as an adventure with spirits remaining high. If their leaving in Alex's car was observed, Jilly didn't care. Becca was being whisked to safety.

The journey to Plymouth was uneventful, marred only by a few tears when Becca realised she had forgotten to pack Pogo. Then the moment she saw the ship, gleaming white in dark water, Pogo was forgotten. After waving goodbye from the quayside Jilly felt as if an enormous weight had been lifted from her shoulders. Becca would be safe for two weeks.

"She'll have an amazing time," Jilly said on the drive home. "She'll be utterly spoilt and completely out of hand when she returns. And," she went on, lowering her voice, "if the situation is not resolved by the time she's due home, she can stay with my parents until it is."

In the back seat Davy, listening with strained ears, picked up the thread of the conversation. Becca had been sent away on purpose? Was it all to do with the policeman? Becca had told him what she saw in Truro, now he wished his father would tell him what was really wrong. Perhaps with Becca out of the way he would.

Conscious of Davy's presence, Jilly closed the conversation realising that whatever she and Alex discussed would still have to be guarded.

After arriving home, Davy was despatched to collect Benji, Alex checked the cottage to see if anything had been disturbed, and Jilly made sandwiches.

"Everything seems to be in place," Alex told her as he returned to the kitchen. "And," he went on, "I think we have to tell Davy about the situation. He's growing more and more suspicious. At first he thought I was in trouble. I got out of that by saying you had a small problem."

She gave a faint, rueful smile, at the understatement then looked at him anxiously. "I don't know what to say, Alex. He's still only a boy."

"The truth is kinder than leaving him with guess work, Jilly. And he knows when to keep his mouth shut. Think about it! When we found Benji he could not have behaved more sensibly. He was so eager to tell Becca the second she arrived home, but he didn't. At the moment he's trying to figure things out for himself. He's worried. I've tried to reassure him but…" he shrugged, "he's a bright boy."

Jilly halved the sandwiches, set them on a plate and switched on the kettle.

"You're right," she agreed soberly. "He is bright. He is also discreet. Unlike Becca who is the original loudmouth!"

At that she burst into tears.

Instantly Alex held her.

"Darling, Jilly," he said gently. "It's OK. She's safe. Cared for. Out of harm's way."

"I miss her," Jilly said her voice muffled against his shirt.

"We all miss her, but you have done the right thing."

She felt him kiss the top of her head and, and suddenly he was kissing her lips. Time was soundless and still. She was in a strange and new world. Locked in a loving embrace where nothing intruded, she savoured the moment. Drawing apart they looked at each other to smile and kiss again. Alex said with great tenderness, "It had to happen."

"I'm glad it has," Jilly told him, as a single tear sparkled on her lashes.

He brushed it away with his thumb and said, "We'll take it slowly, Jilly. Yes?"

She nodded, afraid words would break the circle of magic in which she was held. Her next thought was for Richard. Was she being disloyal to the memories she cherished? Sharply her emotions fragmented leaving a void that rapidly filled with guilt. Her body stiffened and she withdrew from Alex's embrace.

He understood and let her go.

"We'll take it slowly," he repeated, his eyes searching hers. "I promise."

She gave him an uncertain smile, turned from him and asked, "Is instant coffee all right?"

"Absolutely!"

★ ★ ★

Davy arrived with Benji who, glad to be home, scurried about, slurped water then went in search of Becca. Unable to find her, he hopped into his basket on three legs, then curled down and went to sleep.

Davy asked if the dog could sleep in his room that night. "Otherwise he might keep everyone awake by looking for Becca."

Alex raised a questioning eyebrow in Jilly's direction. Did she want them to sleep over again?

"Would you, please?" she asked. "Davy does have a point. Benji might well become restless during the night."

"Fair enough," Alex said, not averse to the idea of everyone being under the same roof.

"Right, Davy! It's dog duty for you from now on."

Davy grinned. Dog duty suited him just fine.

* * *

Sometime after lunch, when Arthur was standing at his front door gazing out to sea, he saw Alex, having driven from Plymouth, draw up at Jilly's garden gate. Intrigued, Arthur watched as they all piled out of the car. He was then left wondering where Becca and the dog were. He'd seen them all leave just after dawn, so what now? Almost at once he saw Davy disappear down the lane only to return with Benji on a lead. That was really odd. He thought the dog and Becca were inseparable.

Now indoors he looked into his mug of tea, swirled it absently and said, "It's a rum do, isn't it? I wonder where they've taken Becca? They left early enough to take her to the moon!"

"Maybe she's gone to stay with a schoolfriend," Marilyn suggested. "It's what kids do."

"Yes, I know!" he said testily. "But where's the dog been all day or, more to the point, why didn't it go with them?" He sighed and went on," If everything is open and above board, why didn't the mother mention the kid was going away when you took round the sweets?"

"Why should she? If the house was to be empty all day, why advertise the fact?"

"I wish I'd known!" he said regretfully. "I could have had a good scout round."

"To find what?" Marilyn asked in exasperation.

"Anything!" he retorted. "We are trying to solve what could be a murder. And don't you forget that, thanks to Richard, you now have a crippled husband."

"Don't talk such rot!" she flared. "Richard was not to blame. He, too, was a victim. The difference being that while Jack is lame at least he's alive."

For a moment Arthur looked crushed as he said heavily, "I'm sorry, love. I'm not blaming Richard. In fact if I go back to the very beginning I'm the one to blame. If only I had been fit. If only I hadn't picked up that bug."

"Stop it!" Marilyn cried, her voice shrill. "Saying 'if only' doesn't work!"

"Yes, it does!" Arthur argued. "It makes you rationalise things. If only Richard hadn't been so damned secretive! Let me ask you this: is there another man in the world, running a high-risk business where none of the staff know each other? I don't think so."

"It prevented collusion."

"Granted, but look at the problems it's caused!"

Grudgingly Marilyn agreed. It was a bizarre set-up but it worked – well – it almost worked. But the system held a rotten apple. At first Arthur thought it was Jilly Kenworth, now he was fairly sure it wasn't. That was the only hurdle he had managed to clear. Marilyn sighed. Living the charade was not easy. Pretending to be her father's wife was not the happiest role she had played in her acting career. At first she had refused to do it. She didn't see the point.

"It's simple," Arthur patiently explained. "I need someone with me. If we live as father and daughter it could lead to questions like – where's your mother? Do you have a mother? That sort of thing. If we pretend to be husband and wife, because of the obvious age gap, people will speculate. It'll be nudge nudge, wink wink, but they won't actually ask questions about us."

After giving it some thought she had to agree he was probably right.

The garb she wore embarrassed the few people they did encounter. She too was embarrassed. She hated the black, spiky wig. The too-short skirts took away her dignity, and the thick make-up brought her out in spots. But Marilyn was created for a purpose, and she had to be believable. She was. She was avoided, and ignored. Mentally she gave herself an Oscar for her convincing performance. But there were days when she rebelled. It was only the thought of Jack that strengthened her will. Her Jack who loved the Army life that was no longer his. Remembering him, and desperately wanting to find payback time, she gritted her teeth. Pushing Sarah Mason, Jack's loving wife, to one side she took on the role of Marilyn. RADA trained she knew what to do. But to play the part on stage was one thing. Playing it to nice people with problems was another. She liked Jilly Kenworth but Jilly had lied to her saying Richard had died of a heart attack. That was not true as Marilyn knew to her cost. And so, suspiciously and warily, the charade continued with determination.

Now Arthur was worrying about Becca. Marilyn didn't know why. She wasn't connected to her father's death, so why was Arthur so concerned about her? Perhaps one day he would explain. Having been highly critical of Richard's penchant for secrecy, Arthur was not exactly Mr. Open and Friendly

Sighing she looked out of the window. She would have loved to go to the cove and swim, but while the Sarahs of the world would have done so, the Marilyns wouldn't. Resigned to yet another boring day, she picked up an out-of-date magazine and, slumping into a lumpy chair, she listlessly turned the pages.

Arthur stared at her from beneath his eyebrows. She looked like a 'Marilyn'. Not the Munroe kind. The tarty kind who aspired to glamour and missed it by a mile. She was a convincing and dedicated actress and he was proud of her. As a human being she didn't measure up quite so well. She didn't understand why he needed to bring Richard's murderer to justice. Thirty-five years ago he had failed to find his brother's killer. Jim, as a twenty-three year old copper, was gunned down outside a jeweller's. He got in the way and was brutally disposed of. Arthur was still unable to accept his death. He could not see it as part of the past. To him it was as real now as it had been then, and within himself he still mourned. To catch Richard's killer might bring him the peace he sought. To achieve that he was prepared to watch and wait for as long as it would take. So far he had discovered very little, but he was convinced he was now looking in the right place. Somewhere, at some time, something would confirm his belief. If only Sarah understood how he felt. Maybe she did for to mention Jack put a glint of steel into her eyes. That was something which heartened Arthur. Like Jim, she'd inherited the family gene. They all had that kind of strength.

* * *

By early evening all those in Jilly's cottage were tired. It had been a long day. For the most part Jilly had sat at the kitchen table going through the files. She had learned nothing. With few exceptions everything was in code. Some of the files were ten years old. The most recent of them seem to hold a great deal of information that was totally indecipherable. It was all a jumble of letters and numbers that didn't appear to follow any particular pattern.

Alex had spent time trying to break down the numbers. Following the trail of a particular digit led nowhere. Everything seemed to be random, but logic told him that was not so. There had to be a common denominator, the problem lay in finding it.

Davy was itching to get into the laptop, and while Alex would have given him the go-ahead, Jilly hung back.

"As I see it," she said, resting her chin in her hand, "The whole business will become impossible if we weigh ourselves down with even more mysteries."

"Who's to say there will be more mysteries?" Alex reasoned. "The laptop could hold answers."

"I don't see why! Why should there be simple language on a machine, but coding on paper? No, everything will be unreadable. Richard was always consistent." She furrowed her brow and added, "Even predictable."

Alex wondered if that was what led him to his death. Had someone anticipated his moves and acted accordingly? It could be a valuable slant, but what was the motive? Revenge? Maybe. Theft? More than possible.

Davy was looking pale and heavy-eyed. Alex suggested it was time for bed.

"What about the laptop, Dad?" he protested.

"Tomorrow, Davy," Jilly cut in. "Tomorrow we'll all be feeling fresher and more able to cope."

Davy shrugged. He wasn't the least bit tired, but if Dad said it was bedtime then to bed he must go.

When, a few minutes later, Alex looked in on him he was sleeping soundly.

By the time he returned to the front room Jilly had opened a bottle of wine and put on a Streisand CD. The curtains remained open and a huge moon shone from an indigo sky dotted with twinkling stars. The atmosphere was without tension and for the first time that day Alex felt at ease. Had it not been for Jilly's pale face bearing blue shadows of fatigue he would have thought he was far removed from the events of the last few days. Sensing her worry he turned his mind to practicalities.

"Davy's out cold. I doubt a bomb would waken him." Taking the offered glass he smiled at her over the rim.

"He's had a long day. You too must be tired." She patted the cushion at her side and, as he sank beside her, she went on, "What with all the hours of driving and then trying to solve endless problems, which," she said with a grateful smile, "are not even yours, how do I thank you? Particularly for Becca's safety. The rest of the world is a problem with which I can cope." She smiled at him and said softly, "At least I think I can."

"I'm here for you," he told her just as softly, "and between us we are indomitable. We are strong and determined! What more can I say? What more do we need?"

"I wish I had your faith," she sighed wearily. "I also wish I knew what was happening to my world. I truly believed that the tranquillity I had found here was for always, but it's been shattered. I don't know why, or by whom."

Alex saw her knuckles whiten as she squeezed the stem of her glass. Taking it from her he set it on the low table.

"It's time you hit the hay," he told her lightly. "I'll give Benji a quick trot round the garden, lock up, and see you in the morning."

The sudden squaring of her shoulders told him she was about to protest.

He laid a finger across her lips saying, "Tomorrow. We'll talk tomorrow. Go on," he insisted firmly. "I'll make everything safe."

Moving to the door he paused, turned and said, "Goodnight, Jilly. Sleep well," and left.

* * *

She looked at the closed door with a sense of disappointment.

In her room, sitting on the end of her bed, she gazed out of the open window. The night was quiet except for the gentle hiss of the rolling tide. Such outer peace belied her inner turmoil. How was it all going to end? Why had it started in the first place? If Richard had known his work would cause her so much fear and endanger Becca, would he have changed direction? She didn't think so. He would still have followed his own path, but he would not have left her and Becca so vulnerable. He would have protected them. Therefore was she right in assuming that Richard's death WAS a tragic accident? It was what she wanted to believe, but deep down her doubts grew stronger with each passing day. Looking back she now wondered how she could have been such an innocent. She had never questioned the circumstance of his death. Not even when the police repeatedly questioned her about their lives, and Richard's business. She never asked them to explain. If they had their suspicions, she was never told.

Now her mind would not go beyond that point. She was too tired, too depressed to think about the past. Tomorrow it would be clearer, wouldn't it?

She shivered. She did not know.

Slipping between the cool sheets she turned away from the window. The moon's brightness would not encourage the sleep she needed, but blotting out the light did not help. She was too edgy. Her mind was filled with disturbing thoughts that bordered on nightmares. Her feeling of foreboding returned to smother what little optimism she clung to. Fear of the unknown presented itself as a kaleidoscope of grotesque shapes which writhed and threatened her. They loomed. They hovered. They swooped. Unable to deal with the turmoil, she leapt from her bed, dragged on her wrap and ran on bare feet downstairs. Nothing was familiar. Nothing was real. The silence hurt. The cold froze her skin. Unable to breathe she swayed.

Alex caught her as she crumpled.

Bewildered, unable to focus, it was some minutes before she was able to drink the offered brandy.

Sitting close to her, his strong body protective, he held her.

Encouraging her to drain her glass, he told her with a humour he did not feel, "I'm not sure brandy is the best thing to be drinking at three o'clock in the morning."

"Three!" she echoed with incredulity. "I've been to sleep?" she asked with disbelief.

"It's possible you've slept," he told her. "You went to bed about five hours ago. So I suspect your dreams turned into nightmares."

She gave a slight shudder as she vaguely remembered.

Guiltily she said, "I disturbed you. I'm sorry!"

"I was awake," he assured her, "So no harm done." He scrutinised her face and pushed a lock of hair from her eyes. "Do you feel better?"

She nodded.

He smiled and said, "Good. Go back to bed." He gave her a hard stare, "And stop worrying!"

"I'll try," she told him shakily. Putting down her empty glass she said, "I'm sorry I made such a fuss What's a nightmare, eh? Absolutely nothing! See you in the morning."

"Sleep well," he said for the second time that night.

Back in her own room Jilly could not believe she had slept for several hours. To then find herself downstairs with Alex was incredible. He must think of her as the complete idiot – if he thought of her at all!

Crossing to the window she looked out into the night. It would soon be dawn. The sun would replace the moon and, with daylight, she would see things more clearly.

Turning away from the window she swiftly turned back. What was that?

Below in the garden a shadowy figure was silently easing through the garden gate.

Holding her breath, narrowing her eyes, Jilly watched

A lone cloud fleetingly hid the moon.

When its light flooded back the figure had gone.

Jilly stared into the night, her heart beating heavily.

The shadowy figure, darkly clad and, wrapped in silence, she felt sure was that of Hal Polglise.

Was it?

Chapter Eight

The morning sky was washed with a rosy glow while, on the horizon, a grey mist swirled above a calm sea. In the distance the sound of church bells, one slightly cracked, swelled and faded on the light breeze as wedding hats bobbed along the hedge tops.

Someone was about to have a happy day.

Alex, already showered and dressed, sat at the breakfast table and filled the coffee cups for the second time.

"Jilly, are you sure it was Polglise you saw?" he asked.

She shrugged uncertainly, "As sure as I can be under the circumstances. Although the moon was bright, he was wearing dark clothing and he was also half-hidden by the shrubs. But – there was something about him. I can't really explain what – but, yes, I'd say it was him."

Alex toyed with the spoon in the sugar basin.

"You could be right," he said, without looking at her. "Someone has tried to force the dining room window."

"When? Last night?" she asked fearfully.

"I'm not sure, Jilly."

"Was the window actually open?"

"No. That's not possible. The sash cord is broken and someone's wedged the frame."

"That'll be Tom," Jilly said, suddenly remembering. "The cord broke ages ago. I thought he'd repaired it."

"It's just as well he didn't! He's accidentally made the window burglar-proof!"

"Who did?" Davy asked, appearing at the door. Tousle-haired, yawning, he was still in his pyjamas.

"Morning, son," Alex said dodging a reply.

"Toast?" Jilly asked.

"Um – please. Dad, are we going to have a go at the laptop today?" he asked, having forgotten the subject of burglars.

Alex raised an eyebrow. The laptop? Jilly would have to decide about that. Having glanced through files and found them useless, the laptop might be the same. How would they know without exploration? They wouldn't. Pushing thoughts of Polglise to one side he looked at Jilly and waited.

She gazed at him with uncertainty. He understood her reluctance to take the next step. Entering into the unknown may still reveal nothing. That was the risk. It still had to be taken. If it was the wrong path then they would have to find a new one.

Fingering the laptop she said, "It's no good ignoring it, is it?" She half smiled. "What we are searching for may well be here. So, yes please, Davy. It's all yours – within reason!"

"Brilliant!" Davy enthused.

The toaster pinged.

Alex said, "Breakfast first, shower then dress, OK? After that we'll get down to playing detective."

Davy, grinning, howled like a bloodhound.

Setting up the laptop took only minutes after which, and at Davy's request, they left him sitting at the kitchen table fingering the keys. He needed to familiarise himself before accepting responsibility. Not wanting to commit anything to memory, he found pen and paper and helped himself to a glass of orange squash. A deserved reward.

Jilly then went upstairs. Alex disappeared into the garden to inspect all the window-frames more closely. Finding one had been tampered with left him feeling uneasy. He'd made the discovery only that morning, just before Jilly told him about the dark figure in the garden. Now, running expert fingers over the frames, he found them rotting and in need of paint. The salty air and the wind-blown, abrasive sand had laid bare the wood. The damage he'd found earlier although slight was newly made. The gouge, having had no time to weather, looked pale against the remaining green paint. It was the sort of evidence that gave credence to what Jilly saw. Not that he doubted her. Despite the earlier nightmare, by the time she returned to her room she was in control.

If it was Polglise in the garden, then something would have to be done about him. Would Dick Rogers offer guidelines? It was a possibility. Had the problem affected only Alex then he might have gone in with fists flying. As it was he couldn't. Jilly's safety had to be considered. Polglise was a thug and needed cautious handling.

Jilly was still in her room when the 'phone rang. Her heart jolted. Was it the man making demands she was unable to meet? If so she would listen and say nothing. With her hand trembling she lifted the receiver.

She almost wept with relief when she heard Becca's voice.

A ship-to-shore call! How wonderful! Becca, so excited, could hardly speak and what she did say made no sense. Finally Jilly's mother took over. All was well. They were having a magical time and Becca had already become a favourite with several passengers.

"The only thing she seems to be worried about is a policeman. Have you seen him? If you have do you know the answer?"

"Yes, I do," Jilly lied. "Tell Becca it was all a misunderstanding, he is very sorry, and now he's gone home with his wife."

"It all sounds very mysterious! Is everything all right, Jilly?"

"It couldn't be better, Mummy," Jilly told her brightly. "And tell Becca that Benji is fine and that he keeps looking for her."

They chatted on for a few moments then Jilly's mother, having been assured that all was well, rang off.

Jilly's palms were sweaty. She hated lying. But she had no option. Becca had to be reassured that the policeman had gone away – forever.

Jilly hoped she had been convincing.

Leaving the house she searched out Alex to find him standing by the front gate contemplating the veronica bush. There was nothing to suggest anyone, shadowy or otherwise, had been near it. Alex toed the ground and pondered the situation. If it was Polglise and he'd been trying to get into the cottage, what was his purpose? Theft? Pay-back time for Tom? Or did he have a thing about Jilly? Did he want to own something which belonged to her? Something personal? A fetish? He found the idea distasteful and hoped he was wrong.

Jilly touched his shoulder to jolt him from his thoughts.

"You were miles away," she said. Then she went on to tell him about Becca. "She's having an absolute ball! Although I think she was worried in case I married the policeman!"

"I think I'd be worried, too," Alex told her through laughter.

Jilly blushed and then said in a low voice, "We still don't know who he is, or his motive."

"It's worrying, isn't it? Is he friend or foe? Who knows? But we will find out – eventually."

Benji limped into the garden followed by a despondent Davy.

"What's wrong, son?" Alex asked.

"I can't open the laptop. All it tells me is 'Access denied.'"

"What does that mean?" Jilly asked.

"That some of the information it holds is protected by a code or password. Without it we can't read what's written." He hung his head and went on, "All I've found are some thumbnail pictures of you and Becca when she was little, and other photographs that could be family." Shame-faced, he confessed he had found them only by accident. "Sorry, I'm not as clever as I thought I was. I'm not even sure I know how to work the laptop properly," he added forlornly

"You're doing your best, I'm sure," Alex told him.

"And I'm grateful," Jilly added.

Although disappointed by the outcome Jilly asked to see the photographs, wondering if Becca looked any different now to how she looked at least a year ago.

Davy grinned at her. Yes she did! She had fat legs with dimples! Laughing, they went indoors.

There were ten pictures. Small, coloured and in a block.

"Like you said, Davy," Jilly told him squinting at the screen. "They are thumbnail size."

Peering at them intently, Becca was recognisable only by the colour of her hair and dimpled legs. Jilly recalled her own dress, long discarded, and thought she looked plumper. The remaining pictures were of strangers. One woman and seven men.

"Do you recognise any of them?" Alex asked.

"Not really," she told him shaking her head. "They're too small to see details."

Davy immediately enlarged the picture of Becca.

Seeing the scatter of freckles across the bridge of her nose, Jilly said, "Gracious! Becca will be furious if she ever sees this. She hates her freckles! But doesn't she look cute!" she added with maternal pride. "That snap was taken in my parents' garden when she was about four."

Davy clicked the mouse and Jilly's image filled the screen.

"Taken on the same day! I wonder why Richard chose these particular snaps? There are far better one's in the album."

"Could the garden have meant something to him?" Alex asked.

"I doubt it. Richard was not a man of the soil. Daddy grows roses but only to please Mummy."

Davy asked if he should enlarge the remaining pictures.

"Yes, please, Davy. I'm quite intrigued by them."

One by one the strangers stared at her from the screen. No face was familiar. Jilly thought they could be pictures of clients, then concluded they were more likely to be photographs of staff. Character references could be held under code. It was the kind of safety measure Richard would use.

Alex wondered if Richard had devised a code. If so could it be based on a family connection?

"Common sense says it had to be something which could be easily remembered by him, while remaining obscure to strangers. Think birthdays, anniversaries, even car number plates. Any one could be converted into a code."

Jilly shook her head.

"Richard wasn't into numbers. He liked language, phonetics interested him. Figures, particularly those used at random, he found hard work if not baffling."

They were in the sitting room sharing the settee. Davy sprawled on the carpet alongside a sleeping Benji.

Davy asked, "If Richard used words for his code, what sort would they be?"

Jilly said she thought he would have created them.

"How?"

She didn't know.

Thoughtfully Alex said, "As he was such a family man, is it likely he would have based the code on the family names?"

"That would have been too obvious," Jilly replied. "He would have been more likely to create something unique," She thought for a moment and then added without much conviction, "I suppose he could have used the letters of our names as a base. They would be easily remembered. What do you think, Alex?"

"It's a long shot," Alex told her, warming to the idea, "but it's a beginning."

The whole atmosphere of the room suddenly lifted, as Jilly said, "Let's give it a whirl, shall we? There are five names to deal with. Heaven only knows how many permutations that gives us!"

Alex said to Davy, "D'you want to tackle it? It could be a lost cause and we might not be able to crack it. Whichever way it goes it may well take us days. No time to loaf, no time to swim," he warned.

"Great!" Davy cried enthusiastically. He then looked at Jilly with unblinking eyes "Why do we need to know what's in the laptop?" he asked.

Jilly looked at Alex. Now was the time to be open and honest. They were counting on Davy to help them to find a solution. It was only fair that he should know for what they searched.

"Tell him, Alex. We can't keep him in the dark."

And so, after being warned not to repeat anything he heard, Davy was told of the situation and the fears that went with it.

"This is why Becca has been sent away, Davy. And if I'm to be absolutely honest I'm now wondering if it might be a good idea for you to stay with your mother until school starts."

"No way!" Davy shouted with unequivocal force. "I'm not going! You need me for the laptop! Oh, come on, Dad! I'm old enough to understand and I'm young enough to be ignored. I can watch and listen where you can't."

Jilly's heart raced with unspoken fear. Davy was still a boy. Had she been too hasty in involving him in the situation? She had to warn him.

"Davy, things could get dangerous. We don't really know with what we are dealing."

"I don't care!" he told her stubbornly. "And what about the laptop?" he asked again.

Helplessly Alex spread his hands. He couldn't argue with that point. They needed Davy.

Having won the argument, Davy said boyishly, "We'll be like The Three Musketeers!"

Alex laughed, "Are you suggesting Jilly looks like a bloke?"

Davy reddened and said gallantly, "Blokes are never that pretty!"

Jilly blushed.

Producing a clean sheet of A4 and using a broad, red, felt-tipped pen Jilly wrote out the family names. They were the starting point of what could be a mammoth task. To keep it simple they agreed she and Alex would create words which Davy would tap out on the keyboard.

At first it was fun as they created crazy words and even crazier sentences. But after a while of finding useless permutations the fun died.

Jilly threw down her pen.

"It's hopeless!" she said wearily. "Most of the words are unpronounceable anyway." She chewed on her knuckles for a moment and then said, "Look, Richard had a very tidy mind. He worked to patterns. At night, when emptying his pocket of change, he would stack it in order of denomination. If he was missing a particular coin then he would leave a space."

"So what are you saying, Jilly?" Alex asked with a frown.

Taking another clean sheet of paper she again wrote out the names.

BECCA. JILLY. RICHARD. OLIVER. KENWORTH.

Underlining them she said, "That's all we have to go on. If we are on the right track that's all Richard would have used. Plain English or phonetics. All of one. Some of both. But whichever way he chose he would follow it through. It's going to be a long process of elimination with no guarantee of success."

And so they began.

Time slipped by without progress. Necks ached. Minds wandered. Needing a break, Davy took Benji into the garden. Jilly thought of food while Alex, in a mixture of frustration and impatience, pressed keys and clicked the mouse at random.

'Access Denied,' hit the screen with monotonous regularity.

His frustration mounted. Then, quite by accident, the block of thumbnail photographs appeared. Scrutinising them Alex wondered how to enlarge them.

"Use the mouse," Jilly suggested, not knowing if it was a good or bad idea.

He did.

The screen went blank.

"Damn!" he exclaimed. "Just when I thought I'd got it right!"

Davy, coming in from the garden, said, "Dad that's a tricky bit of equipment." He spoke patiently if disapprovingly. "Don't mess about! If you tell it what you want it to do it will do it."

"I thought I had," Alex said grumpily. "All I wanted to do was enlarge the pictures."

"No problem!" Davy said, shifting and clicking the mouse. The screen was promptly filled.

Impressed, carefully following Davy's instructions Alex enlarged and scanned what he now called 'The Rogues Gallery'. He scanned it for several minutes and found himself latching on to one particular image. Numbered four, he scrutinised it. There was something about it that nudged his memory. Forcing his eyes away from the screen he stared into the middle distance recalling faces from the past. He recognised and named everyone except the man on the screen. Yet he was still convinced he knew him.

Jilly peered over his shoulder.

"Lunch is ready, Alex. Who's that?"

"I've no idea but I'm sure it's someone I know."

"What would a picture of someone you know be doing in Richard's laptop?" she asked sceptically.

Sighing and shrugging he knew he must be mistaken. Everyone had a double. That could explain the situation. Except it didn't. Double or original he knew the face but couldn't name it.

After lunch they returned to the laptop and tried to gain access.

Twice the 'phone rang. Both Jilly and Alex answered. Each time the line went dead Jilly trembled. Alex thought the calls were made by someone checking to find out if the house was empty. "Which means," he said, "we might not be under surveillance which in turn means – this might be a good time to tap a nail into the dining room windowframe as an extra precaution!"

"I thought you said it was jammed," Jilly reminded him nervously.

"So it is, but sometimes I'm a belt and braces man!" he told her with a wink. He then made his way to Tom's shed in search of hammer and nails.

Davy went back to the laptop commenting on how Becca had altered. "Her legs aren't so chubby and she hasn't got so many freckles, has she?"

"She thinks she has!" Jilly said. "Every now and again she pats lemon juice on to them hoping it will make them fade."

"Does it work?"

"Becca thinks so!"

As they were talking Davy brought the pictures of the men on to the screen and looked at them closely. They were all old. At least fifty. Davy wondered if Becca's father was old, too. Davy thought his own father was getting past it. He was unsure about his actual age, but he guessed it could be thirty-something. It might even be forty! Poor Dad!

Jilly suddenly cut into his thoughts asking him to go back to the man in the white shirt. He flicked the pictures.

"Him!" Jilly cried. "Is he number four?"

"Yes, why?"

"I don't know," she said, turning away from the screen. "I think I know him, but I'm not sure. Maybe if he didn't have a moustache…?"

"Who didn't?" asked Alex, reappearing with hammer and nails.

"Him!" Jilly said, pointing at the screen. "Imagine him clean-shaven and then look at his left eye…"

Alex stared intently, saying slowly, "He's number four! I see what you mean! You've found what I looked for and couldn't recognise." Narrowing his eyes he brought the picture into clearer focus.

"He could be a younger version of Arthur Armstrong!" Jilly half-whispered.

Shocked, they stared at each other.

"Arthur Armstrong!" Alex repeated. "I should have recognised him."

"Part of Richard's life! One of his staff?" Jilly said, shaking her head in disbelief.

"We don't know that for certain," Alex told her cautiously. "All we know is he's on file. We still have to find out why."

"I suppose it IS him," Jilly said, her doubts gathering. "We haven't made a mistake, have we?"

"The scar near his eye says it all. The likeness could be coincidental. The scar couldn't. I've met the man only briefly but the scar registered. When I first saw this picture I couldn't place him – the moustache threw me – now it doesn't. I'm sure it's him, Jilly."

With thudding heart Jilly agreed.

Davy, sensing the importance of the discovery, asked what he should do next. "Shall I keep working on the code?"

Alex didn't reply but went off at a tangent asking if a copy of the photograph could be made.

"Not without a printer," Davy told him.

"Can we get one?" Jilly asked.

"Maybe in Penzance tomorrow, " Davy said, unsurely.

"We can't wait until tomorrow! "Alex said.

"Have we an option?" asked Jilly.

"Yes! We have to get the Armstrongs here tonight, then on some pretext we show them the picture and judge their reaction."

"Can't we be direct and just ask them to explain it?" Jilly queried naïvely.

"Only if we know they are friends. Are they?" Alex asked, raising his eyebrows.

She shook her head. She didn't know.

Finding an appropriate reason to invite the Armstrongs was not easy until Jilly hit upon the idea of asking Marilyn to help her to shorten a dress. That was girlie enough not to arouse suspicion.

Alex didn't see the point.

"What good is that?" he asked. "We need Arthur, not the woman."

"Out of courtesy I will also invite Arthur – for a drink – compensation for depriving him of his glamorous wife!"

Alex gave a quirky smile, and said, "There are times, Jilly, when you are as wily as a fox – but – what happens if Arthur refuses?"

"Oh, ye of little faith!" she laughed. "Trust me! I can be very persuasive."

He believed her.

"When are you going to tackle the situation?" he asked.

"Right now," she told him as she moved away with her chin firmly set. She then went out of the kitchen and quietly closed the door, leaving Alex staring at her empty space.

His intention to nail down the window was postponed. Instead he used the time to open a bottle of red wine and let it breathe. He had no doubt that Jilly would return with the Armstrongs if not in tow, then due. She would not accept a refusal. Rummaging in the back of the cupboard he found half a bottle of Grouse. That might be useful. It could smooth what could be a bumpy path.

Davy was busy in the kitchen collecting all the scattered papers and pens. Tapping them into a neat pile he laid them face down on the table. He didn't know what the evening might bring but the serious look on his father's face told him not to ask questions. He felt a tremor of excitement. It was a bit like playing 'cops and robbers' except that this time it was real.

* * *

As Jilly walked away from the Armstrongs' cottage she was tingling with excitement.

At first, hinting about shortening a dress didn't appear to work, boldness did. In fact Marilyn was more than willing. Arthur didn't need persuading to accept her invitation either. He seemed pleased to get out of the house, making her feel certain they had no idea that she had an ulterior motive. Although she was nervous of what might lie ahead, she was also excited by the idea of tackling the situation.

* * *

Arthur, watching her retreating figure from the window, clenched a raised fist and yelled, "Yes! Sarah, yes!" His triumph echoed round the walls.

"Don't call me Sarah!" she yelled back. "I'm Marilyn, remember?"

"Not for much longer," he told her, striding into the kitchen and kissing her cheek. "With any luck, tonight we will begin to learn the truth."

"Pop! I'm helping Jilly to shorten a dress. We are not about to attend an inquisition!"

"It'll be what I make of it," he said sternly. "The number of times I've tried to get into that cottage and now we get invited! I can't believe our luck!"

"What good's the invitation? You can hardly go poking about in search of heaven knows what?"

"I won't need to! I wouldn't stake my life on it but I have a gut feeling that Jilly Kenworth is as much a victim as Richard was."

"Then what are we doing here?" she asked, her voice high-pitched in exasperation. "If she wasn't involved in Richard's death, then we are wasting our time."

"Not so! She may not be guilty, but someone is. She might unwittingly know who. Remember Richard was a good bloke. But he was a one-off who did things his way, which could antagonise."

"A bit like someone I know!" she told him with a half smile.

He smiled back, saying, "All righty! I know you don't approve of the way I've handled things. And I know I haven't had the results I'm looking for – but it's not for the want of trying."

"You can say that again," she sighed with resignation.

"But," Arthur went on to muse in an undertone, "we have one very big advantage."

"Oh?"

He gave a broad wink and said, "We know who she is, but she hasn't a clue about us!"

★ ★ ★

Returning home, Jilly announced with satisfaction, "They'll be here around half-seven. I think they must be bored to tears with each other. They were both quite keen to visit."

Alex was pleased. If the evening was going to be convivial Jilly's strategy may not be too painful. And whatever she had in mind he would support. Now with time to spare they could do a little forward planning and know exactly where they were going. So could they discuss her strategy?

"What do you mean, strategy, Alex? I haven't got one," she told him with dismay. "I hadn't looked that far ahead."

They were all in the kitchen, the table cleared of clutter except for the pile of papers and the laptop which was switched off. Davy sat, chin in hand, listening to the conversation.

It sounded serious.

Alex pushed his fingers through his hair and sighed, "Oh, well! With or without strategy the Armstrongs have to be confronted."

"But only after we've gone through the niceties; the welcome, the drink, making them feel comfortable. We have to put them at ease. By the way I've asked them to use the front door."

"The point being?" Alex asked.

"I don't want them to see the laptop."

"Why not?"

"I don't know," she stumbled, adding, "he might recognise it and be put on his guard."

Alex dropped his head then lifted it to look her full in the face.

"Jilly," he said, "Are you sure you know what you are doing?"

"Of course I don't, Alex," she said sharply. "All I do know is that the man is a fraud, and I'm going to expose him as such."

"How?"

"I'll think of something!"

The atmosphere was suddenly chilly.

Davy, feeling unsettled, asked tentatively if there was anything he could do.

"Shall I stay in the kitchen?"

"Would you mind?" Jilly asked. "I might need an excuse to leave the room."

"Will it be all right for me to use the laptop?"

"Yes, of course. In fact it would be a good idea."

At that Davy's eyes questioned. She didn't try to explain. She couldn't. Her thoughts were too sketchy. But a busy boy was better than a bored boy.

Alex half smiled and asked, "Strategy?"

She shrugged. She still didn't know.

Alex glanced at his watch. There was still time to spare, time to discuss and explore possibilities.

"Jilly," he said. "I'm wondering if we should look for the code in another direction."

"How?"

"Let's stop using family names and base it on the type of person Richard was."

"You couldn't slot him into a niche, Alex. He could be a pragmatist one moment, and a romantic the next."

Her skin warmed at the memory.

She took a paper from Davy's neat pile and scanned the family names. So many nonsense words and meaningless phrases had been created from them that Edward Lear would have been proud. Thinking objectively she drew the conclusion that the code would not be outlandish. It would be a reminder that meant something to Richard. It needn't be a phrase – it would more than likely be a single word! Just one word. An economy to save time so essential in Richard's world. He had lightning thoughts and worked at speed. Just one word! Many tumbled through her head. She could feel herself swimming in a sea of memories as they floated past her. She heard again Richard's voice and the language used when they were alone but now it told her nothing.

When the Armstrongs arrived Jilly's mind was crammed with words but empty of ideas. How was she going to deal with these people? If only she had given the situation more thought. It was foolhardy of her to think she could successfully pit her wits against someone who could be a hardened criminal. His wits could be honed to a fine edge against which she would not stand a chance. All she could use as a defence was the little knowledge she had and her honesty.

Knowing she could be about to play a sinister game with unknown rules she was inwardly determined, and inwardly shaking, too. She thought of Richard. The ploys he used to tackle situations, particularly those which arose from emotions. Now she remembered his words! Emotions had opposites. When sad think happy. When cold think warm.

When fearful think fearless. And laughter? What was the antonym for laughter?

Tears? No, not for Richard. He had his own word for laughter.

It was 'dyak'!

Yes, 'dyak'!

How could she have forgotten the time when she nearly wept with embarrassment?

Richard had almost fallen over with laughter.

Yes, 'dyak'! All those letters were within the spelling of the family names!

She trembled with excitement, but there was no time to explain. Before she realised it she was shaking hands with Arthur Armstrong.

His look was intense as his eyes searched her face. His clasp, firm and warm was as unexpected as his hearty words.

"Nice of you to invite me, too, Mrs. Kenworth. Not that I'm much good with a needle!"

He smiled. And as he did so the scar disappeared into the lines at his eye corner. Was this genial man the one she thought had worked for Richard? Was he connected to his death?

Smiling through her disturbing thoughts she made an appropriate reply to his banter, and asked Alex to show them into the sitting room.

"I need to have a quick word with Davy," she explained. "I won't be a moment."

Alex gaped. What was she doing? He stood indecisively and frowning.

"I'll be two minutes," she promised, giving him a gentle push, and all three disappeared.

Entering the kitchen she closed the door and laid her finger across her lips.

"Sh, Davy!"

Davy, looking wide-eyed, asked in a whisper what was wrong?

"Absolutely nothing!" she told him and quickly scribbled on a sheet of paper. "Key this word into the laptop. If it works, come and get me, yes?"

Taking the paper from her he glanced at it and asked, "What's a 'dyak'? Is it a boat?"

Jilly giggled and whispered, "I'll tell you later."

As she returned to the sitting room so Alex handed her a glass of wine and asked if everything was all right.

"I think so," she smiled. "We'll know in a minute or two. Davy is just sorting out his computer. It's gone wrong again! They are so sensitive, aren't they?"

"I never could get the hang of them," Arthur volunteered.

"You can't even use a typewriter," Marilyn joshed.

"Never had the urge. I've only just mastered the remote for the TV," he laughed. "Technology doesn't sit easy with us old 'uns."

The door opened and Davy, his face flushed, asked if he could have a glass of squash.

Alex frowned. What was wrong with the boy? Why couldn't he get his own squash?

Anticipating a reprimand, Jilly forestalled it by pushing Davy from the room.

"Dyak did it," he whispered as they hurried into the kitchen. "There are more pictures, and lots of things I can't read."

Jilly's heart tumbled so painfully it trapped her breath.

"The pictures," she gasped. "Is there another of No. 4?"

Vigorously Davy nodded, "There are lots of numbers, too."

"Numbers?"

"At the bottom of the photographs, look!"

Clicking the mouse, picture four filled the screen. It had to be Armstrong! The scar was obvious, his features well-defined. The pose, although slightly different to the previous one, changed nothing. Only the moustache got in the way.

Scanning the row of unpunctuated numbers she saw a problem. Were the numbers in units? Scanning them again she saw that 14 and 5 were repeated at what could be the beginning of two words or – two names! She tensed. Did those numbers represent A and R as in Arthur Armstrong?

Worried by her tense expression, Davy asked if he should fetch Alex.

She shook her head. Alex leaving the room could give out warning signals. No she would deal with the situation alone.

“Don’t worry, Davy,” she reassured softly.” No one will get hurt, but I do need your help. Are you game?”

Nervously he nodded.

Squeezing his shoulder she said, “Turn off the laptop. I’m going to get the others. When we return put this picture on the screen. Can you do that?”

Again he nodded, his face alight with excitement, he then switched off the power and sat on his hands.

Taking a deep breath, and clenching her fists Jilly returned to the sitting room.

The Armstrongs, sharing the settee, appeared to be comfortable and relaxed. Alex stood facing the door with his back to the window. A slant of evening sunshine showed him in silhouette, his features in shadow. Jilly wanted to see his face. His reaction to what she was about to say was important to her. As it was she felt alone.

The dress to be shortened was lying across a chair.

Brightly Marilyn confessed that although she wasn’t good at sewing her eye for line was reliable.

"Mind you," she added, "I can get it wrong, but I'll do my best not to."

Guilt-ridden by what she was about to do Jilly had to ignore the friendliness offered.

With her heart racing she turned her attention to Arthur.

Smiling flirtatiously she said, "Before Marilyn and I begin our sewing session, I would like to pay you a compliment."

From the corner of her eye she saw Alex stiffen.

Arthur sat taller and looked expectant. He hadn't had a compliment from a pretty woman in years!

Jilly gave him the sweetest of smiles and said ingenuously, "You look so much younger without your moustache!"

There was a shocked silence.

Marilyn looked at her feet.

Arthur didn't move. Eyes unblinking, face set, he stared.

When he finally spoke his voice was level.

"I think you are mixing me up with someone else, Mrs. Kenworth." His tone suggested it would be unwise for her to argue.

For a split second she believed him.

The moment passed. She knew she was right. Arthur Armstrong was the man in the photograph!

Undeterred and still sweetly smiling she said "If you would all like to come with me I have something to show you!"

Alex moved to her side.

Jilly said in a low voice, "We've got into the laptop. More pictures. More codes."

The Armstrongs' reluctance to move could be felt, and it was Jilly's sudden cold, hard look that dragged them to their feet.

Davy, anticipating their arrival, had already put the picture on the screen.

Crowding round, they looked at it in silence.

Confronted by it, knowing there was no point in denying it, Arthur held up his hands, then shrugged helplessly.

Alex said, "I think you owe Mrs. Kenworth an explanation."

With his eyes fixed on his own image he asked, "How did you know?"

Briefly he was told.

Fingering the scar he said, "I've had it since I was a lad. Took a tumble playing football. I'm so used to it I don't see it any more."

Marilyn, looking distressed, shouted," Now will you stop playing the detective! I told you you'd got it wrong!"

"Got what wrong," Jilly asked.

"Let him tell you!" she cried. "Come on, Dad. You've got to sort this out. Tell Jilly what really happened to Richard."

Jilly, looking stunned, stared and then shakily asked Arthur to explain.

Arthur, looked at Jilly's pale face. He needed her to trust him.

"It's not a pretty story," he told her kindly.

"I still want to hear it."

Alex slipped his arm about her shoulders. She was trembling.

Glancing at Davy's white face he suggested it was time he was in bed. He wanted him out of the way. If Armstrong was going to hand out unpleasant details Alex didn't want Davy hearing them.

Feeling cheated Davy reluctantly said good night and went upstairs.

Alex cut the power from the laptop and suggested they return to the sitting room.

Whatever unsavoury details Arthur was going to speak of, at least they could hear them in comfort.

As they settled themselves, the flare of hostility died.

Taking advantage of the situation, Arthur spoke at great length both quietly and without drama. Describing the day of Richard's death made him aware of how Jilly was feeling. Seeing her so pale and tense, he wondered if his guilt was as obvious as her sorrow. He had to admit to feeling responsible. Had he been on duty then this situation may not have arisen. And while nothing could be proved, the circumstances were deeply suspicious. Jack, even though his recollections were hazy, knew something was wrong. It was their joint decision to say nothing about the incident that Arthur now stubbornly pursued.

Jilly, silent and fearful, listened carefully. There were so many questions she needed to ask, where did she begin?

When Arthur finally drew to a halt, there was a long, reflective silence.

Alex suggested they all take a break.

He wanted to check on Davy.

Leaving Jilly to replenish the glasses, he went upstairs. Davy sitting on the window-seat with his head on the sill was in his pyjamas and sound asleep.

Gently rousing him he shepherded him under the duvet promising to tell all in the morning.

"Is that OK, son?"

Davy was asleep before he could make a reply.

Alex looked at him. He was a good kid. He hoped to God he was safe!

Going down to the kitchen, he shoo-d Benji into the garden. Opening a can of dog food he wondered if Benji was also part of the scenario. Threats made concerning Becca? What better way to frighten a child than to hurt a pet? And what better way to force an issue than to frighten the mother?

Angrily he clamped his jaw.

Lured by the rattle of his dish Benji, still on three legs, hopped back into the kitchen and gulped his meal.

Guiltily Alex watched. The poor dog was ravenous!

When he returned to the sitting room, the conversation had moved on. Arthur was talking about the so-called policeman and The Mariner's Head.

"The only reason we chose to drink there was to avoid contact with the locals. We didn't want to get friendly – if you get my drift. The policeman?" Arthur sucked in his cheeks. "He wasn't staying there so he was lying. The fact that Becca saw him in Truro…" Again he sucked in his cheeks, "Not good! And what about the 'phone calls? Any connection?"

"At first I was unsure," Jilly told him. "Now I'm not."

Discussion continued without reaching any kind of conclusion, there were too many loose ends. In view of those the Armstrongs decided to stick to their roles of husband and wife. Marilyn was happy with the idea except for wearing the black wig. She hated it. Removing it briefly, Jilly was fascinated by the change it made. Gone was the hard-faced, common woman, with a high-pitched Cockney accent. In her place was a pretty, fair-haired girl with a nicely modulated voice and clear diction.

Pulling the wig back on, Marilyn said, "It's been quite a challenge. Living a character is much harder than just playing the part for a couple of hours each night! Since we've been down here I feel as if I've never been off-stage."

"You are very convincing," Jilly told her with admiration. Turning to Arthur she added, "You must be very proud of her."

"She'll do," he said gruffly, but pride shone in his eyes.

The telephone rang.

Jilly looked apprehensive.

The atmosphere tightened.

"I'll take it!" Alex said, and left.

When he returned his face was set into grim lines.

"It was our friend asking if we were having a pleasant time with our neighbours."

Jilly drew in her breath.

"What did you say?"

"I invited him in – if he had the guts," Alex told her in a voice edged with cold fury.

At that the window shattered and a rock hit the settee.

Everyone ducked.

Alex charged from the room.

Wrenched the door open.

Saw nothing.

Heard nothing.

Arthur dragged off Marilyn's jacket. Glass shards fell. A sparkle of danger.

Jilly shook her hair. Splinters glinted and scattered.

Everyone was shocked but somehow calm.

Alex reached for the Scotch and poured out stiff drinks. They drank in stunned silence. A few minutes later the two men blocked up the window with plywood found in Tom's shed, and drew the curtains.

Alex said, "I suppose it's possible that the rock-thrower, and the man on the 'phone are one and the same?"

"Could be," said Arthur. "Whoever it was had serious intent, a mobile 'phone and an accurate aim. Anyone you know?"

"Maybe! Nothing positive," Alex said, rumpling his hair. "Unless we learn something from the laptop."

Arthur shook his head, "For my money it's someone – shall I say – 'local'. I doubt Richard would have anyone on file who lives in this part of the country." He shook his head again. "Unless the incidents are unconnected and we've got it all wrong!"

Marilyn, pale-faced and dark-eyed, said, "I don't think there's much point in trying to solve the mystery tonight. All we seem to be doing is chasing our tails. We are all too tired to be objective. Come on. Pop – er – husband,". she corrected with a laugh, "it's time we went home. And Jilly, I'm glad we are on the same side!"

"So am I," Jilly admitted. "We'll all meet in the morning, shall we?"

And so it was agreed.

The moment Alex closed and bolted the door Jilly shivered.

"I hope the Armstrongs prove to be as trustworthy as they seem," she said, wandering back into the sitting room. Seeing the broken window, she wondered what Tom would have to say about it.

"I expect he'll blame Hal Polglise!" Jilly said half jokingly.

Alex silently agreed, and then returned to the subject of the Armstrongs.

"Arthur seems solid enough. I think you are doubting them because you are tired," Alex assured her. "Tomorrow you will think differently, I promise."

And with those comforting words embracing her she went to her room.

That night she dreamed of Richard. The same dream. The same haunting. She awakened with her usual sense of foreboding.

Would it never go away?

Chapter Nine

Alex's decision to call on Dick Rogers was made on the spur of the moment. Regardless of it being early in the day it was something he needed to do immediately. He wanted to know about Hal Polglise and, according to Jilly, Dick was the man to ask. Although there was no proof that Hal was involved in anything, Alex needed to follow his own instinct, sharpened, he thought, when the window was smashed. Now having slept on the matter he wanted to know who was up to what and why.

Wanting to leave the sleeping occupants undisturbed he slipped noiselessly from the house. He would explain his absence later.

Dick Rogers greeting was surly. He hadn't had breakfast and a man was no good for the day without sustenance. Alex apologised and said he would return later when the time was more convenient. Dick waved his hand dismissively saying, "If it was important enough to get you out of the bed at this hour, then it might be worth listening to. Come in."

Under the glare of Dick's interrogative eyes Alec saw no advantage in being diplomatic and so he went straight to the point.

"I need information. I might have a problem with Hal Polglise," he said, adding as a get out clause, "to do with Benji."

Dick's attitude changed immediately. Sawing thick slices of bread from a large loaf he pushed them under the grill and, after telling Alex to sit down, he said he was welcome to ask as many questions as he liked.

"I'll answer what I can. You'll have a mug of tea and a bit o' drippin' toast," he suggested. "There's nothing like a bit o' beef drippin' to put hairs on your chest," he added, with the glimmer of a smile.

Dick Rogers was not given to smiling, but what he lacked in humour he made up for in his knowledge of people, particularly the Polglise family.

Eating well-peppered hot toast and drinking a mug of sweet tea, Alex listened intently as Dick outlined the family history. Some information mattered. Some didn't. Sorting wheat from chaff could be done later. Hal was the black sheep and the despair of his late mother.

"She was a good woman," Dick said. "We was at school together. Her was the mainstay of the Chapel, too. How she came to have such a bad lot as Hal, I'll never know. But you watch 'im, Mr. Hunter. He's sly, and handy with his fists. He don't like Tom Pascoe and it's likely t'was Hal who belted him round the 'ead, so you take care and keep your eye on Benji. It don't do for little dogs to stray when the roads is busy." He paused then added as an innuendo, "If you get my meaning." He swallowed a mouthful of tea and then asked, "I don't suppose you'd like to tell me what this is all about?"

Alex shook his head.

"Sorry, Dick I can't. I'd like to be more open but…"

Dick wiped his mouth on the back of his hand and said, "Don't you worry about it, my 'ansome. The best way to keep a secret is not to tell it."

On that sound advice they shook hands and Alex left knowing that in Dick he had an ally.

Walking home, Alex was pleased to have learned that Tom and Dick were very old friends and had been since their school days. Because of that he thought they could know more about Jilly's problems than they would admit. If it was Hal who had hit Tom what was his reason? Spite?

Opportunity? Or was Hal up to no good and somehow it all went wrong? It was all food for thought.

By the time he arrived at the garden gate Tom was already putting new glass into the window frame. He didn't speak, but he did shake his head as if to say 'Hooligans!'.

Jilly and Davy were in the kitchen using the laptop with great success. Jilly was elated at having made such headway. Now that Alex had returned with even more information things were beginning to take shape.

"Alex!" she cried, "We are actually getting somewhere! We might have cracked the code, too! Show him ,Davy."

Davy brought Arthur's image, complete with its row of numbers, on to the screen. Jilly said to Alex, "I remember you saying we should get away from family names and try a new direction. Knowing Richard preferred words to digits is what could have led me to Dyak. That gave us access, and that in turn made me really think. That is how I worked out the code. It's easy to follow and easy to read."

"If it's that simple, is it safe?"

"I think it is! Anyone who didn't know Richard in private life would judge him to be complicated, and the word 'simplicity' would be outside his vocabulary. Richard often projected a misleading personality just to fool people. Hence a simple code."

"And knowing how his mind worked gave you the answer? But what about all the numbers."

"They are the basis of the code," she had to admit. "That is inevitable, but translated into letters it all becomes easy."

And so it was. Easy but tedious. An hour later they had a potted history of Arthur Armstrong. All they had to do was wait for him to arrive and confirm its accuracy.

He was astounded.

"I remember having the photograph taken, and filling in the questionnaire, but where the hell did Richard get the rest of the information? Talk about naming your grandma's cat! It's all there, isn't it?"

Marilyn giggled and said, "I didn't know you had a strawberry mark on your…"

"That'll do, Miss!" Arthur said sharply." All this stuff is private and confidential."

"The thing is, Arthur," Alex cut in, "if all the photographs are of past employees, and if they all have a recorded history, then we might be able to use the information."

"It's a lot of 'ifs' and if it's all in code it'll take hours to wade through."

"Not if we check the dates first," Jilly pointed out. "Anything older than say – five years – can go to the bottom of the pile. The remainder we can look at in detail. Time-consuming? Yes! But it's got to be worthwhile!"

Davy, busily tapping the keys, suddenly stopped.

"Dad!" he shouted.

Irritated by the interruption Alex told him to wait.

"Dad! It's important," Davy insisted.

"Davy! Jilly's talking!"

Jilly was suggesting that as Delza was due and it was her day to clean the kitchen, it would be best if everyone moved into the sitting room.

"No!" Davy's voice was like a whip crack.

All eyes swivelled in ominous silence.

"Davy! What do you mean?" Alex demanded sternly.

"Dad I'm trying to tell you something."

"Rudeness accomplishes nothing! Now you apologise to Jilly!"

Touching Alex's arm she said swiftly," Hear him out, Alex!" Looking at Davy she asked, "What is it, Davy?"

"This," he told her, nodding at the screen. "I was looking through the pictures when I noticed it."

Intrigued they all crowded round to look at the displayed photograph of a stranger. Sitting upright, his arms folded, unsmiling he stared into the camera. Beneath the picture was the usual row of numbers. There was nothing remarkable or memorable about the man. In his fifties. Heavy-featured. A good head of hair and that was all.

Perplexed Jilly asked what was so special.

Enlarging the picture, Davy said, "His watch. It's unusual and I've seen it before."

Turning he looked at Arthur and then at Alex and said, "That man is Becca's policeman!"

The following silence was awesome.

"Are you sure?" Jilly finally asked.

Vigorously Davy nodded, saying "I don't remember his face too well, but I recognise his watch."

"This could be a different man," Alex told him.

"It isn't," Davy said with certainty.

Alex thrust his hands into his pockets and said, "I remember you asking about the watch, and the one he's wearing resembles the one you spoke of, so I guess you're right. Sorry I yelled at you!"

Jilly said, "We now have something to work on! May I suggest we move from the kitchen, and try to figure out who this guy is?"

After taking a few minutes to re-settle into the sitting room, the code was deciphered. And the name revealed.

Mervyn Slade.

Arthur shook his head. He didn't know him.

That was a setback but with four brains working and pooled results, they were rewarded with invaluable information.

Slade's history was interesting. For a number of years he was a Heavy Goods Driver making frequent visits to France, Holland and Germany handling various types of merchandise.

Jilly wondered if he had ever been to Pontivy.

Married and divorced. No children. Employed by Richard for three years which was until the time of Richard's death. He lived in and owned a small terraced house in Wood Green. There was no mortgage on the property that was well maintained. As a DIY fanatic he took pride in spending time and money on keeping his home in good order. He had a younger brother who bred bull terriers and lived on the outskirts of Bristol towards Gloucester. As brothers they were not close but met several times a year in various parts of the country.

Alex asked Arthur how Slade was able to take frequent leave.

Arthur explained the hours were flexible.

"And we were paid a good retainer. Escorts were not always needed. I don't think I ever worked more than two consecutive days in any one week. It would have been the same for Slade. I was always advised when I would be needed, otherwise I was on standby."

"Time-wise, didn't you find that messy?" Alex asked.

"Yes, until I got used to it. After that it wasn't a problem."

"Except for Mum," Marilyn chimed in. "Catering was a nightmare."

"I know," Jilly agreed, remembering the number of ruined meals she had thrown away.

Arthur pulled the conversation back to where he wanted it and said he thought Slade might well have been Operator 2. "Unless, when we've sorted through the remainder we find a more likely candidate. For my money Slade fits the bill. He's in the area, and he knows something we don't."

"What about the key?" Jilly asked. "Do you think he knows about that?"

Marilyn said, "If he was the guy who went through Richard's pockets the key could be what he was looking for."

Alex agreed and asked if there was a chance that Jack could identify him. "If we gave him a blown-up copy of the photograph? What d'you think, Marilyn?"

She shook her head.

"It was dark. Jack was hurt, and it's a long time ago."

Hope died under a cloud of gloom.

Tom rapped on the back door and as Jilly opened it he said, "Missus, window's all done, and I forgot to say I gotta take Delza to the dentist. Her's 'ad face-ache all night. Too many sweets I reckon. If 'er's all right I'll be back d'recly. If not, it'll be when 'er's better."

"Poor Delza," Jilly said sympathetically, looking at her blotchy cheek. "You do what is best, Tom. I hope she'll soon be all right."

"No doubt 'er'll 'ave a few tears, but tears is normal for 'er." He was about to leave when he hesitated and looked slightly awkward.

"What is it, Tom?" Jilly asked unsurely.

"I was wondering, Missus," he began, shuffling his feet, "being as 'ow Becca's away I was wondering if my Delza could 'ave a little lend of the white bear? 'Er do love it that much it'll be a comfort. I wouldn't ask, but..."

"Do you mean Pogo?" Jilly asked, knowing she would have to refuse. Pogo was a treasured toy, and if Delza lost it, then Becca would be heart-broken. Yet looking at Tom's pleading expression, Jilly had to relent. Becca would not begrudge Delza the loan of him. Collecting the bear from the bedroom Jilly handed it to Tom saying, "You will explain to Delza that Pogo must be returned when Becca comes home?"

"You leave it to me, Missus," Tom said in a voice filled with gratitude. "And it's real kind of you. Delza'll be that pleased 'er'll forget to cry."

Minutes later Jilly watched as, holding Delza's hand, Tom walked her along the garden path saying, "Missus says you can have the dolly as long as you don't cry, understand?"

Jilly saw Delza was limping.

"Tom!" she called. "Put on Delza's shoes, will you?"

She watched as Tom searched for the missing footwear to eventually find it in the hood of her anorak. What he said to her Jilly didn't hear, but she thought it would be something unrepeatable.

Returning to the sitting room she saw Alex had searched out Becca's toy blackboard on which he had written out the code. It made for easy reference and added speed to the search. Four photographs had already been discounted and their relevant history discarded.

Working as a team, following a pattern, they checked simple facts. Date of birth. Sex. Date of employment. Date of termination and reason for same. These were the guidelines. These were the essential points.

Davy asked if they needed to check the woman.

"We're looking for a man, Davy," Arthur reminded him.

Jilly, peering over Davy's shoulder, said, "If she was Richard's secretary it might be a good idea to scan her if only for the purpose of elimination."

Appreciating the point Arthur agreed.

Davy pressed the keys and her image filled the screen.

Quickly Jilly deciphered the numbers.

"Beatrice Turner. Spinster. Age 45. Richard's secretary for two years. Still in his employ at the time of his death. Previously employed by Hall and Retgood Worldwide Pharmaceuticals. Moved to Denn and Crevan Solicitors after studying Law at night-school. Speaks three languages,

German, French and Latin. Lives in a flat in Maida Vale. Hobbies include painting with water-colours, music, plays the piano for a local amateur group. Walks neighbour's dog. Has no relatives. Her only sister died ten years ago."

"It all sounds very civilised and ordinary," Jilly sighed. "Shall we discount her?"

"Not yet," Alex said then asked Jilly if she had ever owned a dog.

"Not even as a child," she told him. "Richard loved them which was why he bought Benji for Becca, but why d'you want to know?"

"No reason," he shrugged.

Arthur thought it time they had a break.

Marilyn and Jilly disappeared into the kitchen to make coffee and Davy took Benji into the garden. Although his wounds had healed well he was not his usual busy self. Jilly put that down to him missing Becca.

In the sitting room the two men decided to fine-comb the information they had gathered and try to link it all together. The only things that matched were the dates when Slade, Turner and Arthur worked for Richard.

Arthur said with studied thought, "We need much more information. Don't get me wrong, Alex, what we have is valuable but skeletal. We need something meaty. Something that will show a motive."

"We might yet get it! Davy is still finding stuff on the laptop. It's a pity we don't have the office computer. That might tell us more."

"Where is it?"

"Jilly said it was sold."

"Does she know who bought it?"

"No, but I'm sure she can find out from her solicitor. If so, maybe we could buy it back!"

Arthur held up his thumb and said, "Good thinking!"

Alex went on, "Judging by the laptop any information held in the computer will be coded, and inaccessible to anyone not in the know."

Heartened by the idea they relayed it to Jilly.

But her contact with the solicitor's office was frustrating.

Mr. Marsdon who handled her affairs was on holiday. She was told, rather pompously, by a junior partner that the information she sought was not readily to hand, but when available she would be informed. A second 'phone call to Mr. Marsdon's private secretary did not hasten results, but it did get her an apology.

Davy asked if they still needed to buy a printer. Jilly thought so and suggested she, Davy and Marilyn should take the car to Penzance and buy what was needed.

The men agreed. With everyone out of the way they could discuss the situation in depth and openly. Neither of them wanted to be overheard, particularly by Jilly.

On her way out she looked round the door and said lightly, "Alex, don't touch the laptop! You'll only press the wrong keys!"

He laughed at her, hoping she wasn't predicting a catastrophe.

With the house to themselves the two men concentrated on listing events. Alex began with Benji's disappearance. Relevant or not it was a good marker. Arthur had itemised views of which he had not spoken. When Alex read them he was filled with indignation.

"For God's sake, Arthur!" he cried in disbelief. "How could you suspect Jilly of being involved in Richard's death? Spying on her with intent to search her home!"

"I got it wrong!" Arthur admitted. "I used her as a starting point. The fact that she disappeared so quickly after the funeral and finally headed for France – where Richard had business contacts…!"

"How do you know that?" Alex asked sharply.

"I know because I went with him on several trips," Arthur said.

"The merchandise, or proposed merchandise, being...?"

"Ask me another," he shrugged. "Richard kept things to himself. He might or might not have been carrying valuables. I don't know. Anyway, the point is that I followed her, then when she returned to the UK I lost track of her." He looked at Alex with steely eyes. "The fact that she seemed to have disappeared made me doubly suspicious of her."

"So how did you eventually track her down?"

"There are ways and means," Arthur said evasively, making it clear that Alex was not privy to all information.

Undeterred Alex said, "And would Slade know of these ways and means?"

"He could," Arthur admitted. "I taught Richard certain skills and fed him – privileged – information which he could have passed on to Slade. Richard was very knowledgeable about many things connected with security. What I had to offer was a bit quirky but infallible when put into practice."

"Like what?" Alex asked.

"Sorry, Alex I can't say."

Alex looked at him through narrowed eyes filled with curiosity.

"Arthur, what did you really do before you worked for Richard? And don't give me the bunkum about you being a postman. You were no more a postman than I was a deep-sea diver!"

Arthur gave a thin smile that spread into a broad grin and then developed into a chuckle.

"That was a typographical error which appealed to Richard's sense of humour. It was left uncorrected because it was unimportant. Richard found it funny only because it was far removed from the truth."

"Which was?"

"I was a policeman who aimed for Special Branch and ended up behind a desk after taking a bad fall – in the line of duty. Although the job was interesting inasmuch that I was involved with Forensics, it was not what I wanted to do. After a lot of thought I jacked it in."

"And worked for Richard?"

"No, that came later. I set myself up as a Private Detective tracking misbehaving spouses. Not a lot of fun. Sometimes spicy, most times boring. Eventually I heard about Richard and, having kept contact with friends in the Force, I applied for the situation clutching their testimonies to my honesty. I think when he saw me he judged me to be an asset. That was it."

Slowly digesting Arthur's words Alex eventually said, "So you were able to track down Jilly because in addition to your skills you knew the right people to approach for information about her?"

"It helped," Arthur admitted.

"So how did Slade get his information?"

"By looking at the other end of the spectrum! Villains don't necessarily have problems. In fact the criminal fraternity are almost as knowledgeable in some respects as the police."

That Alex doubted.

"Tell me," he went on. "If, as you say, Richard was very secretive, how did Slade – if it was Slade – know about Finchley?"

"Ah, that's the mystery," Arthur replied, his voice flat.

The 'phone rang.

Alex took the call, and returned looking amazed.

"That was Jilly's solicitor's office. Very cagey! Almost reluctant to speak. However, it seems the office computer although bought by Beatrice Turner, was – and listen to this

– delivered by courier to an address in Lockerton. Where the hell is Lockerton?"

The bookshelf provided a dog-eared AA book that revealed, with a small dot, that Lockerton was midway between Bristol and Gloucester.

Alex cocked his head and said, "I find that interesting, don't you? Slade's brother, the dog breeder, he lives in that direction, doesn't he? Could he be one and the same? He's got to be!"

"I don't see why not! You could be right."

"I'd bet my life on it," Alex said without hesitation.

"Shall we check the laptop? It might give us more information!"

"Hell, no! If we press the wrong keys we could lose the lot. No. leave it for now, Arthur. Having made some kind of connection let's not foul it up."

Arthur stared at the map then traced his finger over a route leading back to Helston.

"Lockerton's not all that far away," he said. "I think we should go there and snoop about."

Alex shook his head doubtfully. That kind of move shouldn't be made without thinking the situation through.

Alex said, "So – we snoop, we learn he's the guy we're looking for, what then? We can hardly tap on his door and ask if he has a computer he wants to sell."

"True," Arthur said, with a wicked glint in his eye, "But we could ask to buy a dog!"

"And...?" Alex replied failing to see Arthur's aim.

"An enquiry could get us into his office – or his house – depending on where he conducts his business."

"Ah!" Alex exclaimed. "Now I see what you're driving at! We can lead the conversation round to keeping records of pedigrees, say, on a computer – and take it from there. It's a long shot and what would be the next step?"

Arthur looked slightly worried."I don't know, and that's the sticking point. Unless he's not into computers! Not everyone is. If he has a problem we could offer advice – even help."

"Particularly as we know little or nothing about them," Alex said wryly.

"He doesn't know that! Look, Alex, we've got to bluff it out!"

"So we buy a dog."

"No! We choose a dog, and then promise to return with the wife for her to make the final decision. We'll need to pay a deposit, how much cash can we scrape up? Cash speaks louder than cheques."

"Cash isn't a problem, but the idea of leaving the girls and Davy alone while we slope off is not a happy move."

"If they all stay together," Arthur suggested. "Safety in numbers and all that."

Alex remained reluctant.

"Look, Arthur," he suddenly said. "I've got to tell you this in confidence. OK?"

"You have my word," Arthur told him gravely.

"I was talking to Dick Rogers earlier. He told me Hal Polglise had been in prison for sexual assault. It was some time ago and he had time off for good behaviour, but with that kind of history, do you see my point about leaving the girls?"

"Absolutely!" Arthur said. "So," he went on his voice lowered, "Polglise has a prison record, has he? That might prove to be useful one day."

"Meanwhile?"

"I'll tackle Lockerton – you stay here." Arthur looked at his watch. "If I leave now I should be back by midnight."

"What do I tell the girls, that you've gone to see a man about a dog?"

"Spot on," Arthur laughed. "Never lie if you can get away with the truth!"

A few minutes later Arthur left with a clean shirt, just in case, and enough money to cover his needs.

"That is so typical," Marilyn said of her father when she learned he'd left.

Footsore and tired after tramping the hills of Penzance she sank onto the settee and kicked off her shoes. High heels were killers on anything except the flat. Rubbing her sore toes the pain was lost in anger at her father. What was he thinking about? Why did he have to go alone? He was no longer a young man! And one invalid in the family was enough to deal with.

Calmly Alex assured her the situation wasn't dangerous and that he was sure Arthur was skilled enough to handle whatever problems he may meet.

Jilly comforted Marilyn while drinking in the details of the new development. Progress through the tangled web was being made and faith in it had to be maintained.

Davy, excited by the news of Arthur's departure, listened intently as he set up the newly-bought equipment. Gratefully and silently he thanked his teacher for making him concentrate on the technology he was now having to apply. Proudly he felt he was an important part of the team.

Alex was saying, "Having found the possible connection between Slade's brother and the computer, we still don't know how Beatrice and Slade got together. I think that at some point Richard broke his own rule of secrecy – maybe through circumstances – and confided in her. That led to her meeting Slade and things went on from there."

Jilly thought it a strong possibility.

"Judging from the photograph, as a plain-looking middle-aged spinster, maybe she responded to being chatted up. Maybe she was easy prey. If she was looking for excitement she could have found it in Slade. He certainly captivated Becca so there must be something about him which appeals."

Davy, having set up the printer and itching to use it, asked Jilly what he should print.

"Anything, Davy. Coded or uncoded. Run it all through, we can sort it out later."

With nothing to add to the conversation, Marilyn asked if anyone was hungry. As no one had eaten since breakfast appetites were keen.

Jilly led her into the kitchen and opened the fridge door.

"Salad or a wicked fry-up?"

"What do you think?" Marilyn asked, reaching for the frying pan. "Shall I cook?"

Jilly produced a new pack of bacon. It wouldn't do her waistline any favours, but at that moment she didn't care.

The telephone rang.

Alex and Jilly met in the hall.

"I'll answer it!" Jilly told him.

He hovered uncertainly, then disappeared when Jilly spoke Tom's name.

He'd rung to say Delza wasn't well. She'd had a tooth out, and that Pogo was stained where she had kissed him with her bloodied mouth.

"If it's all right with you, Missus, I'll get Mrs. Atkins to take the dolly to the dry cleaners." He sounded upset and out of his depth.

Feeling sorry for him Jilly said not to worry about Pogo.

"When Delza's better, then you can bring him back and I'll deal with him."

"Her's so damned fond of that dolly," Tom mumbled.

Jilly re-assured him kindly but firmly that it wasn't a problem, and rang off.

Returning to Alex she said, "A mishap with Pogo! It surprises me that Delza likes a furry toy when she's so afraid of Benji. Not that Pogo looks like Benji – it's the furry bit that puzzles me."

"Why is she so scared of Benji?" Alex asked. "Or is she afraid of all dogs?"

"It's all dogs," Davy cut in and looking up from the printer.

"How d'you know?"

"Tom told me and Becca. It's something to do with when Delza was little."

Suddenly the smell of cooked bacon drew his attention and he lost interest in the conversation. Switching everything off he went into the kitchen, his mouth watering.

Jilly, knowing Davy would not always want to be using the laptop, had a contingency plan. When in Penzance she had bought a book *'How To Make a Slave of Your Computer'*. It sounded promising from her point of view, but she wondered if it was no more than an expensive hype. She had already picked up a lot of knowledge from Davy but she still had to know why certain procedures needed to be followed. Touching the keys was akin to sitting high up on a narrow ledge. If she didn't know what she was doing she could fall into oblivion. For now she would lean on Davy. Later when she had read and digested the book she would be able to contribute something positive.

The book on wood carving , bought by Becca for Alex, was on the side table. Idly she riffled through the pages. There were one or two interesting photographs of antique furniture, and the sketch of a dressing box not unlike the one Richard had bought for her. She was about to mention it to Alex when from the kitchen Marilyn called, "Grub's up!"

The box was forgotten.

After lunch, although Davy spent a lot of time with the printer, the translations, annoyingly tedious for Jilly, were not enlightening. Yet nothing could be discarded or ignored. The paperwork grew into a mountain where every word could be seen as precious, and so every word was saved. Jilly insisted upon doing all the decoding. Alex tried to argue, but she was adamant.

Marilyn, keen to know what was happening to Arthur, constantly tried to contact him on his mobile, only to find it switched off.

Alex restlessly prowling felt he should be doing something constructive, but there was nothing to do. Finally he decided it was time Davy had a proper break. Maybe they should go to the cove. A competitive swim to the raft would be fun for them both. The sticking point was leaving the girls alone.

Jilly's concentration was being constantly broken by Alex's pacing. Finally she had to bring it to a halt.

"Alex! For goodness sake! Go and find something to do. Take Davy into the garden and kick a ball or, better still, go for a walk."

"Can we have a swim, Dad, please?" Davy begged.

Silently Alex debated the situation. Asking Jilly to lock all the doors might worry her. Dare he suggest it? He decided to say nothing. By leaving the girls together they would look out for each other.

Jilly barely noticed their leaving and thought nothing of it when Marilyn said she was going home for a while so that she could take off the hated wig. And if someone came to her door she would ignore them. Perhaps she would ring Jack. Perhaps not. If she did she would have to tell him about Lockerton and, as there wasn't much to tell, she would only worry him. So she'd just settle for not talking to Jack and not wearing the wig!

Left alone, Jilly felt her neck creaking, and thought a change from decoding would be one way of easing it. More knowledge about the computer wouldn't go amiss. Picking up the book she settled down with a will to learn then found she could not concentrate. Her mind kept jumping about asking questions she could not answer. Finally she gave up.

The house seemed unnaturally still and quiet. Was it just the contrast after all the hubbub of having people around? Wandering into the kitchen she saw that Marilyn had washed and stacked away the dishes leaving all the surfaces bright and shiny. Benji was in his basket asleep and everything appeared as it should be.

Unexpectedly Tom arrived with Pogo wrapped in a plastic bag.

"This 'ere dolly be in a right mess, Missus. I 'ad to take it off Delza. 'Er would keep on kissin' 'im. 'Er do love 'im that much."

"Why is that, Tom?" she asked putting the bag, unopened, on to the drainer. "Has she no dollies of her own?"

"'Er's got plenty, but they'm all plastic. 'Er's got nothin' like Pogo. 'Tis the fur, Missus. 'Er likes the ticklin'. 'Er do want for me to get 'er a kitten but 'er 'ands is too 'eavy for a little animal. 'Er'd squash it! Not intentional o' course." He fell silent and looked at the floor.

Wanting to get to the bottom of the problem Jilly bluntly asked if Tom had ever considered getting a dog. "I know Delza is nervous of Benji, but if she had her own dog say – from a puppy?"

"No, Missus! 'Er's afraid of them," Tom barked.

"Why, Tom? Why is she so afraid? Has she been bitten?"

"No! 'Er's never been bit!"

"Then what is it?"

He looked away.

Jilly waited.

Tom shuffled.

She sensed his need to talk.

"What is it, Tom?" she coaxed "What's troubling you. Tell me. I might be able to help."

"No one can help," he told her, his head bowed his voice low. "My Delza's gone beyond... 'Er's been made dumb for life."

What did he mean? Made dumb?

"Tom, I don't understand." As she spoke she felt her blood draining away. "Delza has been MADE dumb? Do you mean born so? She has never spoken?"

Tom wiped his eyes with a grubby handkerchief and said, "'Er was fine til 'er was five then 'er was made to watch something no child should ever watch. The sight took 'er voice. If only Dick Rogers had been a bit quicker and got there in time!"

"Dick Rogers?" Jilly echoed, out of her depth. "If he had got where, Tom?" Jilly asked, her voice rising in perplexity.

"If 'e'd got to the caves on the North coast," he told her, his voice harsh. "Up along Perrondith. Dick heard there was to be a meeting there and he wanted to get proof of it."

Tom's voice had also risen, and his fists were clasping and unclasping in fury.

"Proof of what, Tom?" Jilly asked urgently, "Whose meeting?"

"Hal Polglise," Tom spat, his face dark with hatred. "Delza's dad. He took her to the cave and made her watch as two dogs shredded each other."

A physical sickness blocked Jilly's throat. She stared in horror at Tom's tortured expression.

"A dog fight!" she said in a low voice. "How barbaric! Poor Delza. Can nothing be done for her?"

Tom shook his head as his shoulders sagged. He was a man almost at the end of his tether.

At a loss Jilly did not know what to say.

How did one deal with such a tragedy. Tom must be constantly haunted by his memories. Yet somewhere she found the right words and offered what little comfort she could.

He stood back from her. Puzzled by her concern. That wasn't the way of strangers. They treated him as a half-wit, but not Missus even though she was not Cornish. Somehow she understood him *and* Delza. She'd always been good to them She could be trusted.

Gradually, as his voice filled with bitter regret, the story of his daughter unfolded.

"My Audra found out too late about Hal Polglise. I tried to warn her, but she wouldn't listen. His womanising didn't bother her, but she hated him for being mixed up in dog-fighting. She tried her hardest to stop him. No chance! For him it was easy money. So she told Dick Rogers it was Hal who was running it all. He had loads of contacts and, down this way, he had loads of supporters. Just because it was illegal that didn't mean he had to stop. Anyway, Dick had been trying for months to get one step in front of Hal…

"Is Dick in the police, Tom?" she asked for clarification.

"No, Missus, 'es just a bloke who knows right from wrong. Anyway, on the night in question, Sod's Law ruled. On his way to Perrondith in his car he got a puncture. By the time he'd fixed it and arrived at the cave everyone had scarpered. A tip-off! We never found out who. All Dick found was a dead dog and my Delza stiff with terror and as dumb as that dolly."

He looked at her with eyes dulled by the pain of the past then he went on,"Can you remember my Delza breaking a vase a couple of days ago?"

"Yes, I do remember, Tom, but it didn't matter. It was nothing special and I did try to explain to her."

He gave her a sad smile. "We know it wasn't important, but to my Delza it was. In her mind she'd done something wrong and that meant she 'ad to be punished. That's when she goes to the cliff-top and looks down into the cave. God only knows what she thinks she do see, but it do frighten her something awful."

Again Jilly was shocked. It was not difficult to imagine how Delza's poor frightened mind worked, and the agony her reactions must cause. Looking at Tom's gnarled face with its heavy-hearted expression, she felt a deep compassion and respect for him. As a man of fortitude and great courage she admired him enormously. What little good fortune there was in Delza's life was in being loved and cared for by Tom.

Silently Jilly decided that when Becca returned she would ask her to share Pogo with Delza. Eventually she might even give him to her. Meanwhile a gentle wash would restore him to his former white polar bear beauty.

As Tom turned to leave, and for no apparent reason, Jilly suddenly thought of Arthur.

Although in pursuit of a computer, wasn't the possible owner something to do with dogs?

Had she stumbled across a connecting thread? And could the other end be tied to Hal Polglise? Swiftly her mind switched to the day Tom was attacked.

"Tom," she said, "The day you were hit, could that have been Polglise?"

He avoided her gaze while admitting it could have been.

"I reckon he were out to nick something and leave me to carry the can. Then something went wrong, didn't it, Missus?"

She was tempted to tell him that at some point Arthur had arrived and scared him off. Instead she patted his shoulder and said nothing. The less Tom knew the better.

Chapter Ten

Lockerton, Arthur knew, was definitely on the map. He'd seen it as a blob in the middle of nowhere and it was proving difficult to find. There was no one to ask the way. There never was and it seemed that every signpost was either broken or pointing in the wrong direction. He finally found the hamlet tucked away in a valley surrounded by enormous oak trees.

After parking in a lay-by, he searched and found the Post Office-cum-General Store. There he bought a bar of chocolate and amiably sought information. This was eagerly given by the owner, a Mrs. Tucker, who revelled in gossip without the slightest trace of guilt.

"If you're looking to buy one of Slade's animals," she said in a heavy Bristolian accent, "you won't go far wrong. You'll pay dear, but you'll get value." She gave Arthur a sour look and added peevishly, "It'll be too much to hope that if you pay him then he'll pay me! I swear if all the dog food he owes for hadn't been for the dogs, I'd have stopped his credit long ago! And he owes the vet! Not to mention Marcia Faddon. She runs a Poodle Parlour," she sniggered. "At least that's what she calls it. The local lads call it something different – if you get my meaning."

Arthur gave a knowing and encouraging nod. Mrs. Tucker might disapprove of the seamier side of life but enjoyed talking about it.

Arthur leaned across the counter and listened eagerly.

Mrs. Tucker, relishing her audience's interest in her local knowledge, went on to list Frank Slade's misdemeanours. That he was well-known and equally unpopular came as no surprise. None of the information she gave was relevant to Arthur's cause, but reports of any kind he never ignored. Thanking Mrs. Tucker for her invaluable help and following her directions he set off down a narrow lane to find the kennels. He had no difficulty for in the distance could be heard the whining and barking of dogs.

By the time he reached Frank Slade's five-bar gate the noise had subsided. Feeding time? Plodding through mud to a scratched wooden door marked 'Office', Arthur had a feeling that Slade was likely to be shifty and short on grey matter, although not necessarily easy to handle. Lack of brainpower was often replaced with a certain slyness, but that didn't worry Arthur. He was used to human frailties.

Pushing open the door, Arthur found Frank sitting behind a rickety desk in a dingy office, that reeked of damp fur – dog fur. The dog in question was warning him off. Held by its spiked collar it reared and snarled strings of saliva from its yellow-toothed and powerful jaws.

Arthur stopped in his tracks. He knew when not to argue.

Frank spoke to the dog sharply and with unbelievable docility it went to its folded blanket in the corner, trampled a full circle and curled down. Whether to sleep or not Arthur was unsure. He'd keep a wary eye on it.

Turning his attention to Frank he saw putty-coloured skin, pale empty eyes, and long sparse brown hair that barely hid his thin neck. With his narrow head set on narrow shoulders he bore no resemblance to his brother's photograph. Had Arthur not seen the dog first he would have thought Frank better suited to selling rabbits rather than bull terriers.

That assumption would have been a mistake. For Frank knew about dogs. Any other subject baffled him, and he had no inclination to widen his world with knowledge for which he had no use. What little brain he had was crammed with information on all aspects of the canine world. He kept meticulous files on his own dogs. Anything unrelated to that subject was ignored. The only correspondence he welcomed was from people who showed a particular interest in his love for bull terriers. Otherwise he avoided human contact. He was suspicious of them unless they were into canines. Those he welcomed, others he warned off with Brutus. Brutus was a one-man dog and he was all the protection and friendship Frank needed.

Now he looked at Arthur wondering if he was going to buy a dog or demand money.

If it was money he'd be out of luck. He'd sold one pup in three weeks, and owed God-only-knew how much for dog food. He hadn't had a square meal in four days, and unless this punter was after a pup, even the prospect of fish-and-chips was remote.

Dry-mouthed and keeping a wary eye on the dog, Arthur sat on a cane chair and, after introducing himself as Jimmy Smith, asked tentative questions about bull terriers. Would a bull terrier be the best choice to guard his wife and property? How difficult were they to train, and what was their life expectancy?

Frank had all the answers coupled with enormous enthusiasm for the breed. He covered every aspect of every question, his thin face almost glowing with a kind of fanaticism. He knew everything there was to know: breeding, training, ailments. His knowledge was profound and eagerly shared.

Arthur listened while letting his eyes wander about the dismal office. There was nothing to suggest Frank had a thriving business. Paintings, photographs, and out-of-date calendars festooned the walls. Sagging shelves held fairground ornaments of dogs. There were no pin-ups of girls, cars, trains or even ships. There was nothing to suggest masculinity. The man was either gay or obsessed. Arthur thought the latter.

Frank's conversation had become more reminiscent than informative, and as he leaned back in his chair to gaze at the ceiling, Arthur's eyes tried to see into a dark corner. The shelf held something square and bulky that was covered by a ragged cloth. Arthur had a distinct feeling it could be the computer and, somehow, he had to find out.

Gently bringing Frank's memories from the past to the present, Arthur began to manipulate the conversation by standing in awe of the bull terrier brain. When he finally arrived at the point where he wanted to be, he took his wallet from the inside pocket of his jacket, and laid it on the desk.

Frank's eyes darted, and his tongue flicked across his lips.

Arthur's heart gave a satisfactory lurch. He now had Frank's complete attention.

"The only bull terrier I ever knew belonged to a friend," he told Frank in a far-away voice. "Intelligent? It was unbelievable! He even knew colours. He had six different rubber balls. Chuck 'em in the air, tell him to, say, get the blue one and he did! I tell you, Frank – it's OK to call you Frank, isn't it?" Without waiting for an answer he hurried on, "I reckon that dog's brain was more than a brain. It was something unreal! It was – I don't know – some kind of computer!"

Frank's reaction was frenetic.

"You've got to be joking," he shrieked. Striding across the room he dragged the cloth from the hidden shape. "If my Brutus had a brain like this damned thing," he shouted, "I'd bloody shoot him! See this," he went on. "It's useless! A dead dog's got more savvy than this bloody thing! My brother sold it to me for fifty quid! Said it was the best way to store all my records. Pedigrees and stuff like that. Said if there was a fire I'd lose all my paperwork.

"He can stuff his computer. I'll stick to doing things my way. Everything I need to know is kept in this office!"

"Maybe he's got a point, Frank. What would you do if there was a fire?"

"Hope the bloody computer would go up in smoke!" he said with a twisted smile. Slumping into his chair, he went on, "As for all my records, I've got photocopies. The girl who owns the Poodle Parlour told me to get them done, so I did. The computer's no good anyway," he added morosely. "It don't work."

"He's some brother!" Arthur said sympathetically. "If I was you I'd get it repaired and send him the bill! That 'ud get right up his nose!"

Frank, with wishful thinking in his eyes and a thin smile on his lips, said, "Can't do that. He'd give me too much grief! Always has, since we was kids. No, it's not worth the hassle." He sighed heavily and said, "And even if I did get it mended, I'd never use it! It's too complicated for me. No! It just sits there being a pain in the arse. In any case I can't afford to have it sorted – it's already cost me fifty quid!"

"He never really charged you, did he?" Arthur exclaimed indignantly. "What a nerve! A lot to fork out for something useless!"

Frank, feeling that in Arthur he had found someone who recognised a raw deal and financial difficulties, offered a mug of tea, a stale biscuit and to fetch a couple of puppies for inspection. If Arthur saw one he liked, providing he took it immediately, they could do a deal.

Arthur gulped. Had he lost his grip on the situation? The last thing he wanted was a puppy! But if in buying one he could get hold of the computer then that was what he had to do.

An hour and a half later, Arthur left Slade's office three hundred pounds poorer. He'd paid seventy quid for the computer which, he told Slade, he was gambling on his grandson fixing. The remainder of the money was for the little bundle of fur sleeping in a cardboard box on the back seat of his car.

What the hell was he going to do with a ten-week-old puppy?

Just after crossing the Devon/Cornwall border, a few miles along the main road, he saw a sign: 'Second Home' Boarding Kennels for Cats and Dogs. Vacancies.

Twenty minutes later and with his bank balance sorely reduced. he was back on the road. He now had two weeks to decide what to do with the puppy – cute little beggar. He might even decide to keep it.

Looking back over the last few hours Arthur felt a certain satisfaction in his achievement. Offering Frank fifty quid for his computer didn't work. Offering seventy did. The only real failure he had was in trying to get Frank to talk about his brother. On that subject Frank would not be drawn. Arthur sensed it was through fear rather than loyalty. Poor Frank! Being short on brains he understood only two things in life: that he was passionate about dogs, and terrified of his brother.

* * *

Alex, refreshed by his swim and the time spent in horseplay with Davy, suggested they should return home and clean up. "Our place, Davy," he said, "Just to save wear and tear on Jilly's bathroom. I'll go first, if that's OK with you."

Davy grinned. Who did Dad think he was fooling? He wanted to go first so that he could have time alone with Jilly. Davy could take the hint. It would take ages for him to gel his hair, anyway!

Ever since the two families had been drawn together, Davy could sense the way things were going. Something existed between Alex and Jilly that had been lacking between his parents. At one time he had hoped they would eventually be together again, but now with his mother about to re-marry he knew that was not possible. Home-life at Jilly's was different to home-life with his mother. Jilly's home was warmly lined with laughter, whereas his mother's home was somehow brittle. People came and went in an ever-changing picture. There were always lots of parties where he was constantly patted on the head and called 'chap.' And if he as much as handed round a dish of crisps everyone said, "Well done!" He hated that, too.

As if reading his mind Alex, halfway up the stairs to the bathroom said, "Davy, you do like Jilly and Becca, don't you?"

"Jilly's nice but sometimes Becca can be a brat," he said, trying to keep the edge of curiosity out of his voice. "But Jilly's a good cook!"

"And that matters?"

"Remember Mum's efforts?" he grimaced.

Alex laughed and took the remaining stairs two at a time.

* * *

Later, as he opened Jilly's kitchen door he sensed a buzz of excitement. Something had happened! Jilly's flushed and smiling face greeted him. She was keyed up. Was she sparkling and excited by something she had learned?

Yes, from Tom! Although guilt-ridden at betraying his confidence she had to share it with Alex. It was important. Finally she said, "I think there could be a canine connection between Slade and Polglise."

Alex agreed but added a word of caution.

"If there is a connection it doesn't necessarily tie up with Richard's death. We could be dealing with two unrelated issues."

"But," Jilly added, "They could both involve the same men. We know Hal is a rogue, Slade could be the same."

"If only we had something positive to go on. Uncovering the reason for Richard's death would be a concrete foundation on which to work."

Marilyn burst through the door and gasped. "I've just spoken to Pop – er – Arthur on his mobile. Guess what? He's got the computer! But it's broken."

Jilly's face fell as she said to Alex, "What if it's beyond repair? We'll have lost so much time. Will Davy be able to fix it?"

Alex was unsure,"He's pretty knowledgeable, but actual repair work? I don't know."

When Davy arrived with spiked hair and smelling of body splash, no one commented. He was content to be ignored. Perhaps in his innocence he thought no one had noticed. Becca would have. She would have said, "Pooh!" and held her nose. He missed her and wished she were home.

When told about the computer and being asked if he could repair it, he didn't know.

"If it's seriously broken," he shrugged and shook his head gloomily.

Hanging on to hope, Jilly said, "Let's wait and see, shall we? It might be no more than a glitch."

Marilyn, sounding depressed, said, "Pop'll be absolutely furious if it's a complete write-off. If it cost a lot of money and he's been diddled – be prepared," she warned.

"His pocket's safe," Alex told her. "The finance is my problem."

"Alex!" Jilly cried, shrill with surprise.

Playfully he told her to shut up.

Waiting for Arthur's return was filled with anxiety. The hours were an eternity. Playing the game of 'what if' didn't help matters. Jilly became more and more apprehensive as Marilyn, suddenly obsessed by the idea of Arthur having had an accident, could only expound her theories. The fact that his mobile was switched off exacerbated her fears.

"Something's wrong! I know it is," she said her voice sharp with panic.

"Nonsense," Alex told her briskly. "Because he's driving he'll have switched his 'phone off. He's not on a good road and he'll need all his concentration!"

The words were still echoing round the room when Arthur arrived looking pleased and smelling of beer.

"One pint!" he protested, as Marilyn harangued him for being thoughtless and selfish.

"You knew we'd be worried! You knew we'd be waiting!" Her voice held a harsh, metallic timbre.

"Oh, shut up, Sarah!" Arthur finally shouted. "You sound just like your mother! I've had a long day, and I needed a beer, all right?"

Scowling she turned away.

Jilly broke the tension by asking if he'd eaten.

"Not since breakfast, except for a bar of chocolate and a stale biscuit," he admitted. "Anything on offer?"

Marilyn thawed, smiled and said she would go home and prepare whatever he wanted.

Jilly said there as no need. It was time everyone ate something. "So what's it to be?""

"Bacon sandwiches," everyone chorused.

"With sauce?"

No one refused.

Arthur went out to his car, returned with the computer and placed it next to the laptop.

Alex found a spare double adaptor and plugged everything in.

Davy switched on. The screen shimmered and blobbed.

Arthur groaned, "Don't tell me it's really knocked out, Davy!"

When Davy made no reply Arthur went on, "Bloody 'ell! What a waste of time and money."

"It might not be that bad," Davy told him, fingering keys. "The power's getting through. I might be able to track the fault, but it'll take time."

Alex glanced at his watch. It was already late.

"Leave it until tomorrow, Davy," he suggested. "It's time you were in bed."

"What about my sandwich?"

"I'll bring it up to you! Go on, son."

Davy left with resentment written on his back. Sometimes Dad treated him like a two-year-old!.

Arthur and Alex exchanged smiles.

Arthur said, "Kids! What would we do without them?"

Thinking in terms of computers Alex said wryly, "Not a lot."

They had just finished eating when the 'phone rang.

"I'll take the call, Jilly," Alex said, "Can you go to your room?"

This was a pre-arranged strategy. Alex would listen and Jilly would look hoping the caller was near-by and using a mobile.

Running upstairs Jilly crossed to the window and peered into the moonlit garden.

It was deserted

Alex picked up the receiver and spoke.

The line went dead.

Shaking slightly Jilly returned to the sitting room. For her the moment had been unnerving, for Alex frustrating, for Arthur it held no more than nuisance value.

Jilly felt burdened.

"If Becca wasn't away I would ignore the 'phone altogether," she confessed, "but I'm never sure who is calling."

"There's always 1471?" Arthur said.

"That doesn't always have the answer, does it?"

"'Fraid not," Arthur admitted," And so it all becomes part of the game," he added knowingly. "A mild form of torture – psychological – in this case. Whoever is playing with you knows the situation, and my advice is go along with it."

"You mean if you can't beat 'em – join 'em?" Alex asked.

"Sort of," came the reply. "It sometimes pays to act dumb!" With that he patted the arms of his chair and said, "Well, I'm ready for my bed. I know we've got a lot to talk about and a lot to think about but tomorrow's still untouched." He glanced at Marilyn and said, "Come on. You look as if a good night's sleep wouldn't go amiss. And you're not walking home by yourself."

Turning to Jilly he thanked her for her hospitality and added, "Try not to worry. We are on your side." He then turned to Alex. "Tomorrow we must get down to it!"

With that he pulled Marilyn to her feet and they both left.

Alex picked up and bit into Davy's uneaten sandwich.

"I knew he'd be asleep," he munched. "Kid's never seem to know when they are tired."

Preoccupied with fingering the grimy casing of the computer, Jilly made no reply. Instead she wondered if, even though the screen shimmered, the machine really was beyond repair. If it was, and it held the answers they needed, would Richard's death ever be solved?

Asking Alex to pour out more wine, she went into the kitchen and dampened a duster. She then returned and started to wipe the computer's soiled casing. The marks were stubborn and although she rubbed vigorously they remained immovable. Alex took the duster from her, but even his heavy-handedness made no difference. The marks were indelible. Infuriated by her inability to solve such a small problem she pressed keys at random, not caring what happened. Immediately the screen momentarily cleared, then filled with a glorious sunset as a jingle tinkled.

Astonished, they both stared in amazement.

"That picture!" Jilly gasped. "I recognise it. It was taken on our honeymoon."

"Are you sure?"

"Positive! The smudge in the corner? Richard said it was my finger over the lens!"

"And was it?"

She shrugged. She neither knew nor cared. Her only thought was that the computer appeared to have righted itself. To have it in working order was all that mattered.

Now she was both eager and reluctant to touch the keys.

"If it went wrong through my ignorance…" she said, leaving the sentence unfinished

"Let's call it a day," Alex said stifling a yawn." As you say, doing the wrong thing may well cause a real disaster. We can't move on without Davy so let's play safe, shall we?"

He smiled at her and kissed her forehead.

"I'll see to Benji, lock up and then tomorrow – who knows?" He then kissed her again.

For a fleeting moment she wished he would hold her close and kiss her the way she wanted to be kissed. Then she sighed. Perhaps one day? Perhaps never. Fate could be very unkind.

"Goodnight, Alex," she said, only to find he had already gone.

Absently she plumped up a cushion. Beneath it she found Marilyn's black wig. Jilly hadn't noticed she wasn't wearing it. Marilyn had forgotten to put it on before she left. Leaving the wig on the arm of the chair Jilly picked up the book she had bought and went up to her room.

Fighting sleep she made herself read. The reward was in the retained knowledge which seeped into her brain. Things were beginning to make sense. The strange language that Davy used was being explained. Would it lead her to the answers? Would she learn about Richard?

Finally she laid the book down, snapped out the light and turned away from the window.

Bordering on sleep she suddenly roused with a sense of excitement.

Alex had spoken of seeing a woman and a camper van parked on Polglise land.

As Slade was not staying at The Mariner's Head, could he be living in it with the woman? And could the woman be Beatrice Turner? If so, could she be the woman in the shop in Pontivy? Energised by the idea Jilly sat up and rested her elbows on her knees. Concentrating her thoughts she recalled Mitzi's words when she had described the woman in the shop as being fair-haired. But Alex had described the woman he had seen as being dark.

So? It took only a wig!

Excited by the possibility of having stumbled across a lead Jilly stretched full-length and stared at the ceiling. Gradually, and for the first time in a long while, she fell into a dreamless sleep.

* * *

With the morning light peeping through his curtains, Davy didn't want to get out of bed. He was tired. He was also feeling piqued at being robbed of his bacon sandwich his Dad had promised. It hadn't arrived. Later he learned he had fallen asleep, but for now he was not in a good mood.

That vanished when Jilly, arriving with a glass of orange juice, told him the computer was working.

"At least we think it is, Davy. I sort of attacked it and it suddenly switched on."

"It could go off the same way," he warned mischievously.

"Yes, I know," she said, perching on the end of the bed, "That's why we need you to take over. It's no good me messing about with it. There could be too much at stake. So – as a bribe, how about a full English for breakfast?"

He looked at her from under his lashes.

"How about my bacon sandwich?"

She gently poked him in the chest and laughed, "You were asleep! So your dad ate it."

Sheepishly Davy grinned. He didn't really think Dad had forgotten him.

When he arrived in the kitchen his breakfast was ready and the atmosphere was buoyant.

Alex was still trying to clarify some of the coding on the laptop. Even though he wasn't having much success, he didn't feel he was failing.

Davy finally pushed his plate away and licked marmalade from his fingers. Wandering over to the computer he switched on the power. The screen again showed the sunset. The jingle tinkled. Davy moved the mouse, tapped a key, the sunset died and 'Access Denied' hit the screen.

"Oh, not again," Marilyn cried.

She and Arthur had arrived early knowing there was a lot to deal with. Marilyn was wearing a baseball cap, her fair hair tucked well out of sight beneath it. She must have been really tired to have left her wig behind. Not that it mattered. No one outside the house had seen her. Now she pushed it into the pocket of her linen skirt. For the moment there was no need to wear the wig.

Applying common sense Davy tapped in Dyak confident it was the right word to use.

It wasn't.

'Access Denied' came up.

He stared in disbelief.

Jilly too stared. The password had failed! She had felt so sure that finally they were making in-roads that would lead to a conclusion.

She was wrong.

Davy tried again. Without success.

Alex stood up and put his arm round Jilly's shoulder.

"Problems!" he said.

Dumbly she nodded.

Arthur asked heavily if, as they seemed to be back at the beginning, they would have to start looking for yet another new word by playing with anagrams.

"It's such a damned rigmarole," he grumbled." Isn't there an easier way?"

"I don't know," Jilly said. "Just give me a moment."

Metaphorically slipping into Richard's shoes she tried to think as he would have done.

Would he have used the same password twice? No. He was too cautious. If the information on the laptop had been duplicated on the computer then he would not guard it with the same password. That would not give him maximum security. So how would his mind work? What sort of word would he use, and where would he find it?

She thought deeply, drawing on all her knowledge of him. She remembered how close they were. How their thoughts and words were often spoken simultaneously. How ideas flowed between them to reach mutual agreement. She remembered how warm were their entwined fingers, and how laughter, muffled by kisses, lingered in the air. But she was romanticising. What of Richard's practical side? How did he look at every day problems?

What was he always telling her? When sad think happy. Own dross think gold. Cry tears think laughter. Her thoughts skidded to a halt.

Excited, trembling she thought Dyak and then, snatching a piece of paper she scribbled another word.

"Try that," she told Davy.

Alex peering said, "That's not how you spell it!"

"I know!" she said. "It's a 'phonetic. It might work! Try it,Davy!"

Davy tapped in 'KYAK'.

The screen filled with figures. Column after column.

Davy yelled with excitement.

Jilly closed her eyes and silently thanked Richard.

Alex said, beaming and almost bursting with relief, "I've a feeling that somewhere there is a story to tell."

She looked up at him and laughed. Yes there was and one day she would tell it.

Chapter Eleven

To escape the tension in the house Jilly and Marilyn moved into the garden to sit in the warmth of the mid-morning sun. The amount of information found on the computer was both overwhelming and disappointing. Most of it, found by Davy and de-coded by Alex, was understood only by Arthur but their mutual apprehension was almost tangible. The possibility of the computer breaking down again served to concentrate their male minds.

Jilly was glad of the break. It was an opportunity to put thoughts into words to another woman. Alex was a wonderful listener and a loyal supporter, but he didn't always understand the female mind.

Unexpectedly Marilyn asked, with a blade of grass jutting from her mouth, "How did you line up someone in Pontivy with someone in Cornwall? It seems a bit surreal, doesn't it?"

"Yes, it does," Jilly agreed, "but it all boils down to part intuition and part – what shall I say – deduction?"

"Clever you!" Marilyn smiled. "So what's the connection?"

"Polglise and the woman camping on his land! Alex thought she was odd – unfriendly. She said the right words without feeling, and disappeared at speed."

"That doesn't mean anything," Marilyn said lazily." Lots of folk are distant with strangers. And," she added, "A man on his own? Looking for a lost dog? I think I'd have disappeared at speed, too!"

Undeterred Jilly went on, "I think it would be a good idea to check the woman out. She could be Beatrice Turner and she could be connected to Slade."

Marilyn snatched the blade from her mouth.

"Slade!" she echoed. "How do you work that out?"

Clasping her hands behind her head and looking at the sky, Jilly didn't explain but she did say, "I also think she could be the woman in Pontivy."

"Oh, come on!" Marilyn laughed. "That's way out – screwball thinking!"

"Could be! Except that I might be able to prove it." She let her hands fall and gave Marilyn an open and direct look. "Well – I might not be able to prove it – but you might!"

"Me?" Marilyn cried. "Where do I fit in?" she asked with wide-eyed astonishment.

"Look," Jilly said, "we have a picture of Beatrice, so she can be recognised. All you need to do is get close enough to identify her. I can't do it. It's possible she knows me by sight. You? You're a different matter."

"She could know me by sight," Marilyn argued.

"Not as a blonde, she wouldn't. If you leave off your wig, and dress down, I'm sure you can get away with it! Please, Marilyn. If I've got it wrong we've nothing to lose, have we?"

Marilyn didn't reply. She needed to think. What was at stake? Nothing. And what could be gained? Reprisal for Jack! That was a worthy cause dear to her heart.

Suddenly she laughed, "Tell you what, Jilly, I have the most horrendous ginger wig in the cottage. I brought it down just in case – if you know what I mean. I can do fake facial piercing, wear a truly awful make-up and…" she paused. "Ah! Clothes might be a problem."

"Torn jeans and a grotty T-shirt do?"

"Brilliant! Yours? You're slimmer than me!"

"Since when have ragbags cared about skimpy clothes?"

"Since never!" Marilyn laughed. "Are we going to tell the blokes?"

"Better not. They might think we're being silly, even rash."

"They might be right!" she replied, her voice holding a warning. She then added, as she creased her brow, "There is just one small problem. Although I've seen the photo of Beatrice, I can't remember what she looks like."

"No problem. I ran off a copy on the printer. In fact I made copies of everyone."

"You did?" Marilyn said with admiration. "The book you bought seems to have paid off."

"That and watching Davy!" Jilly confessed.

"Everything appears to be working in our favour, doesn't it? The next question is when do you plan on all this happening?"

"How about today?"

"Why not?"

Why not indeed, Jilly thought as she went to her room! Delving into the back of her wardrobe she found an old pair of jeans and a sleeveless blouse that had green paint splodged on it. Pushing the two garments, along with a worn-out jacket meant for the jumble sale, into a raffia shopping bag, she collected the photographs and returned to the garden.

* * *

In Jilly's absence Marilyn decided the character she was about to create should have a Scottish accent. Nothing too regional. She didn't want to be caught out. Her portrayal had to be totally convincing. Worthy of a Bafta if not an Oscar!

Returning to Marilyn's side Jilly's thoughts were sober. Now that the decision had been made she wondered if it was the right one. Should she tell Alex of her plan? If he disagreed with it she would not change her mind, but she would feel safer.

Lost in thought she was startled when Marilyn nudged her and said in an unrecognisable voice, "Thart wee lardie hars hus aye orn yeou."

For several seconds Jilly's face was blank then, when she understood, she blushed.

Marilyn laughed.

"It's true!" she said, "That guy is crazy about you. Anyone could tell that from a mile off!" Scrambling to her feet she said, "Now, come on! Let's go to my place, find the ginger wig, and try on this clobber."

* * *

Indoors the men worked in silence speaking only when there was something of importance to say. The correspondence found on the computer was, in some cases, years old. Even so Alex insisted everything should be read thoroughly. Skimming was pointless.

Messages, both open and coded, arrived in a constant stream and work on them was made more tedious by the continuous ringing of the 'phone.

There was never anyone there. Only intimidating silence. That would have affected Jilly, but not Alex. All it did was make him wonder if the caller was becoming desperate.

"Just silence! No mention of the key," he told Arthur. "So what's he got in mind?"

"Nuisance value," Arthur assured. "It's a method of keeping things edgy. Ignore it."

Sound advice. Difficult to follow.

Arthur asked Davy if the now idle laptop had given up all its secrets. If so, it might be a good idea to put it away.

"What do you think, Alex?"

"Fine by me! Less clutter for Jilly! By the way, where are the girls?"

"In the garden, I think," Arthur said.

Davy said, staring at the computer screen, "I've found something in the recycle bin!"

They crowded round and read the un-coded message:

"S. LEFT WITH KEYS. SENT 2 COLLECT. N E 10-20. NORWICH."

"That's a bit of a riddle!" Arthur said baffled.

"What on earth can it mean?"

"At a guess I'd say Beatrice Turner, alias Smith, went off with the office keys. She was on her way to Norwich and Agent 2 was sent to collect them."

"From?"

"Who knows," Arthur shrugged. "Somewhere North East? 10-20 could be a map reference."

Davy said, "Dad, when I come home from school and I stay with Mum, I always have to go by coach."

"So?"

Sheepishly Davy suggested NE could stand for National Express.

Arthur said, shrewdly, "That's a distinct possibility, Davy! Thanks!. Alex, let's say Smith went off with the office keys? Slade was sent to collect them from – well – we don't know where – but we can track that with a 'phone call or two. That would be how they met! And in allowing them to meet, Richard broke his own cardinal rule – that of not letting his right hand know what his left hand was doing."

"Which might prove to be a good thing. Davy, have we a date to say when this took place?" Alex asked.

"August the 24th two years ago."

Gleefully Arthur said, "Leading up to the Bank Holiday. There's the connection we were looking for – Bank Holiday! The office would have been closed."

"It's a bit flimsy!" Alex said, cautiously. "It proves only that they could have met. They don't necessarily know each other – in the full sense of the word!"

"OK, Alex, I see your point. Lets consider the facts. There was an incident in Pontivy; unexplained. Likewise on the beach with the kids, followed by a happening in Truro. These are connected, yes?"

Alex nodded.

Arthur went on, "And that makes me think that the game being played is two-handed if not three."

"We are dealing with Slade, Smith and Polglise?"

"That's my guess."

"Which is fair enough, but we still don't know the motive."

"We'll find it eventually," Arthur said resolutely. "Meanwhile we've got to stick at it. And we've got to be careful. If there is a league table for villains I'd say this team is near the top!"

"That bad?"

"That bad," Arthur repeated heavily.

Alex frowned and said, "I know it's only a detail, but why would Richard keep a record of Slade collecting keys?"

"I'd say he was merely tracking Slade. If he was on duty before the holiday and diverted from his normal course, Richard would automatically put the incident on file. Missing keys had to be accounted for, holidays or not, and so the incident went on file."

Alex digested the information. It seemed to fit Richard's pedantic attitude; his way of thinking. His next question to Arthur came as a surprise to both.

"I don't suppose the key being demanded was part of the bunch Smith had, was it?"

Arthur gaped.

"Now there's a question!"

Davy, who had been diligently working on the computer, said, “There’s another message, but it’s coded.”

Alex groaned. They had followed so many paths leading to dead-ends he wondered if they would ever find one which would show them something worthwhile. Reaching for a clean sheet of A4 he settled down to work.

The first stroke of luck was the date. So far, everything that could have been important was too old to be considered. This date was new. Only a week before Richard’s death.

> “WHITE ICE INC.
> INFORMATION RECEIVED OF PLANNED RAID DURING TRANSPORTATION. DATE MOVED FORWARD. 24 HOURS. EARLY FLIGHT. ALL UK BOARDINGS MONITORED.
> DEBRON. W.I.I.”

Alex read the message twice and said to Arthur, “White Ice? Transported by a courier? Could it be diamonds?”

“It could! It also suggests a large consignment! Worth waiting for and worth nicking.”

“And if the thieves thought Richard was carrying the gems…”

“Which he wasn’t because the date had been changed…”

“The key in demand could be to a safe-deposit box.” Alex paused. “Wait a minute,” he said cautiously. “How did all this come to light? How did they know about the diamonds in the first place?”

“That could have been a simple communication which Smith could have known about. Richard had a kind of jargon he used and bits of information could be gleaned by what *wasn’t* said. He could have replied to the original communication within Smith's earshot and she could have acted accordingly. It’s likely she didn’t know about the rearrangement.”

Although Alex could see the possibilities in Arthur's reasoning, it was still based on supposition, and he said so.

Arthur shrugged, "That's how it works, Alex. You have to grab anything that could have potential."

With that Alex had to be satisfied.

"What about the safe deposit box? Where's that, Arthur?"

Arthur shook his head.

"I've absolutely no idea, sod it! I don't even know if it actually exists! It's all conjecture! Talk about one step forward and six steps back!"

Alex laughed and slapped Arthur's slumped shoulders, "Look on the bright side! Using your format we could eventually know who and what we are chasing, and that's got to be a step forward."

"I suppose," Arthur growled.

Davy cried excitedly, "Dad, there's another message and it isn't coded."

The men turned back to the screen.

Dated the day before Richard was killed it read:

> "REQUEST FOR LAND DEEDS TO BE
> TRANSPORTED TO PARIS A.S.A.P.
> IF COMMISSION ACCEPTABLE COLLECT FROM
> TOLBEN MEWS FINCHLEY TOMORROW AT
> 21.00.
> SIGNED
> PRIME LAND SURVEY CO."

This was followed by a note accompanied by Richard's initials:

> "All details checked on P.L.S. Viable Co handling only worldwide land sales. Assets 14 million. Paris Office. Accepted."

"This is vital information," Arthur said through clenched teeth. "We now know what Richard was doing in Finchley."

"The rest is guess work," Alex pointed out, "but can we assume that both commissions, as far as collection was concerned, were to take place on the same date? Can we assume Richard was carrying the diamonds when he went to Finchley?"

"Except that he wasn't," Arthur cut in. "He wasn't carrying anything. Unknown to the bad guys the schedule for moving the diamonds had been changed. Because deeds have no particular monetary value, it's likely Smith would have known about them, told Slade, and they seized what they thought was an opportunity to relieve Richard of the stones."

"I wonder if Prime Land Survey really exists?" Alex asked idly. "Or was it created as part of the set-up?"

"It could have been. We can check. Jack and Richard met up after Richard had presumably collected the deeds from Tolben Mews. I say 'presumably' because Richard would not have disclosed his movements. Jack didn't need to know what they were and so he would not have been told."

"Why was he there in the first place?"

"It was the norm for Richard to have a guard. My guess is Richard was going to collect the diamonds *after* he'd been to Finchley."

"How could he?" Richard queried. "If he didn't have the key with him?"

"Problem!" Arthur said morosely.

"If all this conjecture has even a modicum of truth to it, then it's no wonder Jilly is being given hell."

"Yes. They are assuming Jilly has the key and they won't go away until she gives it up."

"She hasn't got the damned thing!" Alex said harshly.

"They think she has and they are playing a waiting game until she collects."

"So they don't really want the key! They want Jilly to use it! For God's sake! How much would the diamonds be worth?"

Arthur sucked in his cheeks and said, "Well over ten million if not more."

"How do you know? Or is it a guess?"

"It's a fair assessment. Private security is not cheap. Richard was a top man, handling big business. He didn't skimp anything. Everything was checked out. Every commodity used – such as taxi firms, private hire, hotels – they were all scrutinised, assessed and the time he used to make those assessments had to be paid for."

"Yet he still slipped up," Alex quietly pointed out.

"He was human!" Arthur replied just as quietly.

"This is all very well, Arthur," Alex said briskly, "but we don't really know how this information came to light. Could Smith have hacked into the computer and, unable to understand the coded stuff, just homed into everything else."

"Egged on by Slade?"

"Why not?"

"Meaning you think he had some kind of hold on her, and it was strong enough for Slade to manipulate her. Poor cow!" Arthur sighed. "She'll have a helluva price to pay eventually!"

"If she's guilty! We don't know anything. We can't prove anything."

Arthur gave a wry smile.

"Frustrating, isn't it? It's a policeman's lot. There are villains walking free because there's no proof! There are hundreds of them all thumbing their noses at the Law!"

Alex swallowed his rising anger at the scum blighting innocent lives.

At that moment the door opened and all Alex saw was a white face scattered with metal rings and red straggling hair.

"What the hell?" he shouted.

Marilyn pulled off the wig and said, "Don't panic. It's me."

Jilly, following behind gave a thin smile and said, "It seemed a good idea at the time."

"What did?" he demanded.

The confession was made at the end of which Arthur said, "Of all the hare-brained schemes."

"Say what you like," Jilly said defensively, "It worked by a process of elimination. The woman in the camper van is not Beatrice Turner – Miss Smith – whatever you like to call her."

Arthur swore under his breath.

Alex, angered by the risk the girls had taken, made no attempt to hide his feeling while refusing to give a reason. All he would say was he thought the whole thing was totally irresponsible and he had credited them both with more sense.

Marilyn collapsed into a chair and sliced through his reprimand saying sharply, "Alex! Just shut up, will you?"

"Sarah! Manners!" Arthur barked.

"And you shut up, too" she shouted.

"Let's all calm down," suggested Jilly.

There was an uneasy silence laden with anger and resentment.

Alex sent Davy into the garden suggesting he take Benji with him.

"He needs exercise to keep him mobile."

Disappointed at being prevented from hearing what could have been an exciting adventure, he called to Benji and reluctantly took him outside.

Jilly made a pot of tea with hands that were not quite under control. She had not expected Alex to be so brutal in passing his opinion. All right, maybe the actions taken by Marilyn and herself had been unwise, but he hadn't allowed them to give the result in its entirety. All he had heard about was their failure. Their unspoken success was still to be told. And why did he have to be so ratty? Were his feathers ruffled because of the initiative shown? She didn't know and at that moment she didn't care.

Marilyn, looking at Jilly, said, "Are you going to tell them or am I?"

"You are. You'll tell it as it was, I might get it wrong."

"OK." She looked at her father and said, "Slade was in the camper van."

Arthur stared in disbelief.

Alex sucked in his breath.

Pleased at having shocked them, she went on, "When he came to the door I recognised him by his watch. The woman with him was not Beatrice Turner. She was much younger than the woman in the photograph."

"Not that we hung about hoping for confirmation," Jilly added. "It was a bit nerve-wracking not knowing what we could be getting into."

"It was a bloody stupid thing to do," Arthur raved. "What if you'd been recognised?"

"In this get up?" Marilyn grimaced, "No chance!"

Alex, his voice clipped, asked where Jilly had been whilst Marilyn was begging for a slice of danger.

Ignoring his sarcasm she said curtly, "I waited by a farm gate. I thought it the wisest thing to do."

"I'm glad you showed some sense!"

She ignored him.

Marilyn unhappy about their reception, tried to shrug off the incident.

"Oh, well. What's done is done. If nothing else we now know where Slade is, and if no one minds my adding my two-pennyworth I reckon Polglise is also somewhere in the picture."

Neither Arthur nor Alex was drawn into discussing that possibility – even though they agreed with it. Jilly, sensitive to the atmosphere, ignored it. She was looking for answers and was not about to be put off asking questions to find them.

"Does anyone think it possible that Beatrice could be the woman in the Pontivy shop?"

The reaction was one of tense silence when, infuriatingly, no one offered an answer. Frustrated, she let the subject go. But that was not the end of the matter.

Davy wandered in and, having settled Benji into his bed, returned to the computer. Glancing round at the gloomy, set faces he knew he'd missed something interesting.

Jilly sighed and said tenaciously, "I'm inclined to send Beatrice's photograph to Mitzi. She might recognise her." Turning to Davy she went on," Davy, I wonder, can the photograph be altered. Can you make Beatrice blonde?"

"I can make her bald if you like," he told her mischievously.

"Blonde will do fine," she laughed. "And if you can do it straight away I can post it today."

Davy suggested to save time they could send it by e-mail.

"Does Mitzi have a computer?" he asked.

"Mitzi has everything, Davy! And somewhere I have her e-mail address."

"Right," Davy said, putting Beatrice's picture on to the screen. "Tell me what to do, and when to stop."

With that he set to work.

Jilly was amazed at the transformation.

Marilyn, sounding blasé, said, "Changing hair colour offers a quick and easy disguise – or am I stating the obvious?"

"You could be! Let's hope Mitzi is able to prove your point."

★★★

Because Slade was back on the scene, nothing was said about the information, newly-found, on the computer. Alex thought it a wise move. If Mitzi confirmed the identity of the woman in Pontivy as Beatrice it would add strength to their growing suspicions. With the risk of being wrong-footed lessened, only then could the girls be told of the new development.

Jilly, thinking to warn Mitzi that an e-mail was on its way, decided to 'phone her.

There was no success with her landline but contact was made via her mobile.

After listening to Jilly, Mitzi said, clearly concerned, "Oh, heck, Jilly! My computer's crashed. I'm waiting for someone to fix it. I've tried to put it right, but I'm not much good with that sort of thing."

Disappointed, Jilly said she would post the photograph, and if Mitzi could identify the woman would she ring immediately?

"What if I don't recognise her?" Mitzi asked, "What if she isn't the woman I saw?"

"We can deal with it, Mitzi. Just do your best – please?"

"Of course I will!" She paused slightly then asked, "Jilly are you in some kind of trouble? Is it financial? If so then let me help."

Touched by the offer Jilly had to refuse it. "No, honestly, Mitzi. We are fine! In fact Becca is having a wonderful time with my parents. They've taken her on a cruise!"

Again Mitzi paused and then breathed, "Oh my God, Jilly! You're not on your own, are you?"

"Of course not! I'm surrounded by friends. Stop worrying! Just let me know about the picture as soon as you can. It's important."

"Please tell me why," Mitzi coaxed. "You know I hate mysteries."

"Don't we all!" Jilly replied lightly. "Truly, Mitzi, there's nothing to worry about, and eventually all will be revealed."
"Promise? Cut your throat and hope to die?"

"Absolutely!" And before Mitzi could question further Jilly rang off.

Mitzi's crashed computer was a disappointment for Jilly. Having thought things were beginning to move forward, she now had to accept the setback.

"I suppose getting it repaired will take a couple of days," Alex said. "Unless she gets hold of a really good technician then it might be only a couple of hours. Whichever way it goes I'm sure Mitzi will ring you."

"Perhaps," she shrugged disconsolately.

Marilyn appeared about to make a comforting comment when Alex shook his head.

Marilyn, seeing that as a signal for her to depart, said it was time she went back to the cottage and changed into more comfortable clothing. Arthur too wanted to get back. He needed to write up his notes.

Davy, aware that people were leaving on purpose, followed suit by taking Benji on yet another walk. At the rattle of his lead Benji scrambled from his basket, nosed the door, and pawed Davy. They left at an unexpected trot. And despite Benji's three-legged gait, he was a lot fitter than everyone realised. Watching them walk away, Alex made a mental note to remind Davy to eventually take Benji to see the vet.

As they finally disappeared, Jilly sighed, "At least Benji is getting better so something is going right for us."

He put his hands on her shoulders, drew her close and kissed her forehead.

"You girls were very foolish," he gently chided. "That camper van is in an isolated spot. How did you find it?"

"I rang Tom and asked him how to get to it. He told me to take a turning off The Narrows, which we did. You found it the hard way!" She made no attempt to keep the laughter from her voice.

"It's all very well to treat the situation lightly, Jilly," he told her sternly, "but had anything untoward happened…"

"Well, it didn't!" she cut in." We took a risk and found Slade."

With that he had to agree, but he still made her promise to leave any future questionable situations alone.

After returning to the kitchen he silently debated about his next move. It was unfair to keep her in the dark about the information found on the computer. At the same time he did not want her to be more worried than she already was. In the end he decided he had no right to make decisions for her and so he explained about the missing keys and the bus station. She listened intently forming opinions only after Alex told her of the connection between Slade and Beatrice. "I think they are both in this scam," he said. "She was able to provide information, and he acted upon it."

"And if Mitzi can confirm the identity of the woman in the photograph..."

"Things will start to fall into place," Alex smiled.

"Thanks to Mitzi," she smiled back.

"You're fond of her, aren't you?"

"Very! She's been a good friend."

"From your school days?"

"Oh, no! She's the widow of Pierre Penober. He died some time ago. He and Richard did a number of business deals and while I knew of him, I never met him. Mitzi took over the business and, eventually, Richard introduced Mitzi and I at a dinner party. We kept in touch and finally met again some months later. She was with the new man in her life, but it didn't last. Since then she's gone solo apart from Guy."

"Who's Guy?"

"Her brother on whom she dotes. He's rather nice. Intense, but also a bit flirty."

"With you?"

"Yes," she laughed. "Having caught him out a couple of times, Mitzi took him to task, and he quietened down – apart from footsie under the table whenever he got the chance."

"Did you tell Richard or Mitzi?"

"Of course not! I didn't want to spoil a business connection or a blossoming friendship. Guy I could handle if I had to. And so Mitzi and I became very close. She was wonderful to Becca and I when Richard died. I suppose being a widow herself she knew what we were going through."

"At such times that kind of friendship is invaluable, isn't it?"

"Very much so."

"It could prove to be even more valuable. If Mitzi can solve the mystery of the photograph, then maybe we can solve the other mystery."

"What other?" she asked with a slight qualm, his tone of voice suggesting she was about to learn something only he knew.

He cocked his head, and looking at her with deeply penetrating eyes, said, "The mystery of why I love you, Jilly Kenworth!"

Stunned she turned away. She didn't want to look at him. She was too afraid. Now was not the time for tender thoughts. The beat of her heart was suddenly captivated with an emotion she thought long dead. She was afraid of it. Deep down she wanted it to fly freely. She wanted to be rid of haunting fears and foreboding. To do that she had to be strong and focused. She had to emotionally close down and shut Alex out. Desperately searching for something to divert her thoughts she snatched up the plastic bag from the drainer. Fumbling she opened it. Inside was Pogo. Bloodied by Delza he needed cleaning. Turning on the tap she was about to sluice him when Arthur, followed by Marilyn, Davy and the dog arrived. Turning the water off and putting Pogo back on to the drainer she forced herself to offer a cheerful greeting. Davy and Benji disappeared, but Marilyn looked worried, and Arthur was agitated. Purposefully he crossed to her side, took her hand, led her to the table and sat her down. Taking the chair opposite he said, "Jilly, I'm sorry to ask this of you but it is important."

Her eyes flickered with uncertainty.

Arthur went on, "It's usual, after a fatality, for everything belonging to the victim to be returned to the next of kin. Have you kept anything of Richard's?"

Looking at him, her eyes holding pain, she said, "His clothing I dumped. The remainder is still in a sealed bag in the bottom of my wardrobe."

"Can I see it?" he asked gently.

"Why?" she asked in return.

"I wondered about the key. Could it be in the bag?"

"I don't know," she said tightly. "I've never looked. But the bag's clear plastic. I would have noticed."

"Would you have remembered?" he probed.

"Perhaps not," she admitted.

She looked at Alex with eyes so clouded and hurt he knew that touching Richard's things would open her wound even wider than it already was.

He switched his attention to Arthur.

"Do you have to follow this path?" he asked. "It's not easy for Jilly."

"Of course it isn't!" Arthur told him brusquely, then softening his tone he said to Jilly, "You don't need to do anything. Tell me where to look and I'll do the rest."

Challenged by the inference that she was some kind of a weakling, she squared her shoulders and said, "No! I'll get it."

With that she went upstairs to return seconds later with the bag.

Arthur fingered it for a moment then said, "When you are looking for something as elusive as evidence look at everything twice. If you see a coin, for instance, and it has a dent in it. Look twice. That dent might mean something."

Davy had returned and had slid onto the chair next to Jilly. He was round-eyed with curiosity and excited by what he was hearing.

Arthur carefully squared the bag. Pulled open the self-seal strip and shook the contents on to the table. There wasn't much to see. Twenty seven pence in change. A Parker pen. House keys, identified by Jilly. An office key, Jilly held a duplicate, and a wallet. Calf leather with gold corner pieces it housed four business cards which were later identified by Arthur, and twenty pounds in five pound notes."

"No euros," Alex observed. "Odd as he was on his way to the continent."

"They could be in the safe deposit box along with his passport."

"Ah!" Alex said, "I missed that!"

Arthur gave a smug smile.

"But no key," Jilly said with sinking heart. She looked at Alex with tear filled eyes and said in a small voice, "I want this to be over, Alex. I need to move on."

"You will," he told her, slipping his arm round her slumped shoulders, "We all will! I promise."

Davy, wanting a better view, now hovered at the edge of the table. Intrigued he watched and listened thinking Richard should have carried a gun. He should have carried two guns. Maybe they were in the safe deposit box along with knives and poison pills! Maybe he would be a detective when he grew up! He felt his father's eyes watching him and his own face reddened.

"Are you all right, Davy?" Alex asked.

Sheepishly grinning, and without taking his eyes from the scattered belongings, Davy nodded.

It was the movement of his head that changed the angle at which he saw the wallet.

One of the gold corners was slightly out of shape and a smear of some kind had travelled an inch or so along the leather. Davy cocked his head and squinted. He was looking twice!

"What is it?" Alex asked.

"I don't know," he said.

Alex reached for the wallet.

"Don't!" Arthur warned. "Don't touch it. We don't want to mess it up with prints. What is it, Davy?"

Davy, without knowing what he was looking at, explained what he could see.

Arthur asked Jilly for two forks, and then gradually manipulated the wallet so that the bent corner and the smudge were brought into his sight line.

"The smudge might be blood," he said cautiously. "A finger caught on the metal corner could have been nicked sufficiently to make it bleed without being noticeable or hurting."

"A blood stain proves nothing," Alex said. "The blood could be Richard's."

"So it could," Arthur agreed. "DNA will prove it one way or another."

"DNA!" Jilly cried her voice shrill." Where do we get that kind of information?"

Carefully prodding the wallet back into the bag and sealing it, Arthur said, "Leave it to me. I have friends in high places!"

Davy stared at him in total awe. Wow!

Jilly was unsure how she felt about this new development. Would it mean looking into Richard's death? Would she have to go through all the formalities, the trauma again?

Would the result prove he was murdered? Or would it confirm he was the victim of a hit-and-run attack after all? The need to search for the missing key seemed to be opening a huge can of worms. And when the key was found, where did she go from there?

Frustrated by her inability to find answers, feeling she was being tossed on a sea of mystery, she needed to be otherwise occupied. Leaving her chair, she crossed to the drainer and picked up the little toy bear. Poor pathetic thing! What a mess. Delza had all but covered him with blood. Putting him into the washing machine as he was was not a good idea. He would have to be unstuffed.

Using the kitchen scissors she snipped open the seam on Pogo's back thinking the finishing wasn't very good. She then remembered it was her own work. Ages ago Delza had shown her where the stuffing was poking out. Jilly had pushed in some cotton wool, and hastily re-sewn the gap.. Now she was removing the cotton wool and the soft filling that made Pogo so cuddly. With only the head to do, and an enormous pile of filling to eventually replace, Jilly's fingers probed and bit by bit pulled out the packing.

Her fingers then touched something hard. Pogo's plastic eyes! Gripping with her fingertips she slowly withdrew her hand from Pogo's empty body to find, whisped by threads of white stuffing, glinting and silvery, a key.

Uttering a small cry she dropped it. It clattered into the stainless steel sink to wink at her like a malevolent eye.

Chapter Twelve

Tom rocked himself rhythmically in his oak chair. It was old and it squeaked with a comforting familiarity that belonged to his childhood. He let his mind drift back. He remembered the times when his mother held him. Her ample and soft bosom was a pillow of safety as she sang lullabies that gently kept time with the squeaks. Dora, his long-dead wife, had rocked Audra, their daughter, with the same love and tenderness. In turn he had rocked Delza, his rough clumsy hands comforting her as best he could.

Now he listened to her.

She was on her bed crying. The noise she made was pitiful. No more than the mewing of a day-old kitten. How he wished she could cry like Audra. Audra bawled. When she opened her mouth the village listened in amazement. How could such a dainty little girl make such an awful noise? He didn't know. Now Tom would give everything he owned to hear the same noise coming from Delza. But that would never be.

At that moment she was crying over two things: a sore mouth and being deprived of Pogo. Both problems were more of an inconvenience than being irresolvable. Her mouth would heal and Pogo she would eventually hold again and so he was unworried by her tears. His real concern was her future. Delza was growing up and with her maturity would come women's problems. Tom knew he was not qualified to deal with them. When he mentioned the subject to the doctor he was very understanding. He suggested that when the time came the Community Nurse would be able to help. All Tom had to do was contact her at the surgery.

Now Tom recalled his feeling of mortification. The very idea! An old man talking to a young woman about something so private! How could he? Did he have an alternative? Might he confide in Mrs. Kenworth? No! That would be even more embarrassing than talking to the nurse. Mrs. Kenworth he saw every day. The nurse? Rarely. With the problem unresolved he closed his eyes and gently rocked as he listened to Delza's mewing.

Delza was spread on her bed looking at the ceiling. Seen through her tears the Mickey Mouse lampshade wobbled. Her eyes were swollen, her face blotchy and her left cheek scarlet. It felt as if it was on fire and it hurt. Her mouth was bleeding and she could make it bleed more if she poked her tongue into her gum. Papa had given her one of his big handkerchiefs to wipe her tears, and now it was wet like Pogo. Papa told her that Pogo had to have a bath. Papa also said her face hurt because she ate too many sweeties. But she liked sweeties! And if she liked them then they should like her. She didn't like turnips, but they didn't make her face hurt – well – they should, shouldn't they? Papa said that as soon as she was better they would go to Mrs. Kenworth's and she would see Pogo. She would not see Becca. Becca had gone away. Had she gone to the Angels like her mother? If she had, Delza thought, then maybe she could have Pogo for ever.

Delza would like that.

* * *

As Jilly laid the key on the table, astonishment was written on every face.

Several seconds passed before anyone spoke. Arthur then said, "Alex, I think you were right. It could belong to a safe deposit box. It has that look about it."

Momentarily fingering, he went on, "Don't ask me where the box is, I don't know. If its location isn't on file, then we've no chance."

Only half listening Jilly was unable to grasp the situation. Now that the key had been found, why didn't she feel a sense of relief? Because of her own stupidity! She blamed herself for not recognising the signs. They were all written on Pogo. Why hadn't she found them sooner? They were so obvious! How could she have missed them?

Arthur, having listened to her angry self-recriminations, ignored them. Now they had the key, its hiding place was irrelevant. He was far more concerned with Richard's wallet. That stain needed to be investigated. Although Arthur was sure it was blood, it had to be an established fact before they could move forward. Gravy stains were for sloppy eaters! And Richard was no sloppy eater.

Without discussing what he intended to do he made several 'phone calls to London leaving his mobile number with requests to ring him back if they managed to track down Don Tragg.

Don was a backroom boy in the Force who owed him a favour, and he now needed to call it in. After failing to make direct contact, Arthur prowled. He didn't explain or apologise. The only gesture he made was to hold up his crossed fingers when the 'phone finally rang.

Everyone listened anxiously. The one-sided conversation revealed only that Arthur knew what he was doing. He ended the call with a grunt of satisfaction. Scooping up the plastic bag with its contents he said, "We're on a roll. I need to catch the London train in twenty-five minutes! Any offers?"

"I'll get the car," Marilyn said and left at speed.

Davy, caught up in the excitement, begged to go to the station just for the ride. Seeing no harm in it Alex agreed and within minutes they were on their way.

Although ignorant of Arthur's intentions Jilly felt both optimistic and nervous. Where would this twisting path lead, and at what cost? Although the key had been hidden in the most unlikely of places she still blamed herself for not finding it.

Holding it in the palm of her hand she said, "Alex, how could I have been so slow on the up-take? All the signs were there and I failed to see them."

"It was a thin trail, Jilly. Manicure scissors in Becca's room. Delza crying because Pogo was losing his stuffing, due to Richard's lack of sewing skill. Why didn't I pull it all together?"

He shook his head. Answers, once known, were so obvious. Obscurity caused the problems.

Having possession of the key did not tell them where it belonged. There had been no mention of it on either computer. Not even the smallest clue had emerged. Did that mean there was nothing left to learn? Was it down to deduction? It seemed to be the only answer.

Alex took the key from Jilly and turned it over several times studying it closely. There was nothing unusual about it. Smaller than a Yale and slightly jagged it suggested lack of use. Perhaps newly cut and/or newly acquired? What little he knew of Richard he thought he would not have handled extremely valuable commodities every day of his life. Therefore a safe deposit box was not necessarily an every day need. Scrutinising the metal he saw, below a row of four digits, the outline of a ship. Was it the Mayflower? He couldn't decide but felt he'd seen the logo before. Where? A vague memory stirred.

Suddenly he looked up sharply and said, "I'm making a connection! I'm not sure to what, but there's something in the back of my mind."

She looked at him expectantly.

The 'phone rang.

Startled, and swiftly moving into the hall, she lifted the receiver.

The line was dead.

It immediately rang again.

"Jilly, let it go," Alex called.

"It might be Becca!"

It was Tom. He'd had an awful time with Delza and had only just coaxed her into taking a nap.

"'Er do keep lookin' for Pogo. I do keep tellin' 'er 'e's 'avin' a bath, but 'er's too upset to listen."

"I'm so sorry, Tom," Jilly said sympathetically, "I can't help at the moment. Pogo is very soggy and it'll take time for him to dry out."

"That's all right, Missus. Us'll be back to you in a couple of days. As long as she do 'ventually see 'im, 'er'll be 'appy. Is everything all right with you, Missus?" he asked sounding doubtful.

"Yes, thank you, Tom. Why, is there a problem?"

There was a slight pause before he said. "No. I just wondered being as 'ow you did ask me about the Polglise place." Again he paused." You take care. Goin' on to 'is land ain't safe."

His voice alone held a note of warning.

Heeding it she thanked him for his concern and assured him she would do nothing foolish. With that she rang off.

Returning to Alex she found him deep in thought and drumming his fingers on the table. The key lay in front of him.

"Who rang?" he asked absently.

"Tom. Warning against going on to Polglise land."

Alex appeared not to hear.

Pogo's limp and empty body was still lying on the drainer. Wrapping him in a tea towel, Jilly took him up to the airing cupboard hoping he would dry out quickly. If Delza saw him as he was she would not understand.

Returning to the kitchen she wondered if Arthur had been in time to catch the train. If so, would his skills at detection be of use to him?

"Alex," she said, "In view of what Arthur hinted at and if his trip to London could be connected with a DNA test on the wallet, what if the stain is blood but *isn't* Richards, what do we do?"

"We've got to leave it to Arthur. If there's no match to be found then we plod on."

"And if there is a match?"

"Then I presume it's evidence that the person involved could have been at the scene of the crime."

"Could?" she cried. "Only could?"

Alex shrugged, "I don't know, Jilly! I suppose it's possible the stain could have been there for weeks if not months."

Seeing her look of hopelessness he wished he could have given her a more positive answer that would close the whole business, but he couldn't.

As a diversion he suggested she continued to search through the computer, "You never know, you might discover an earth-shattering secret."

"Like the real name of the man in the moon?" she half smiled.

"I dare you to find out! And it wouldn't surprise me if you did. You've become very adept at using this newly-acquired bit of technology."

Sliding into Davy's chair, she said, "I've learned a lot from the book I bought. It's very informative. Not that I'm an expert..." Her voice tailed away as Alex sped from the kitchen, thundered upstairs, clumped to his room then hurtled back down to Jilly.

"Alex!"

"Sorry," he gasped. "There's something I need to check."

She gave a questioning glance at the book he was now holding. It was the hardback on wood carving, bought by Becca in Truro.

Sitting at the table he riffled the pages anxiously chasing back and forth through the leaves.

"I'm sure it's here somewhere," he muttered. "I've seen it recently."

"Seen what, Alex?"

He pushed the key towards her.

"That emblem – logo. I thought it was the Mayflower, but it isn't. It's the Golden Hind and I've seen it or something like it within the last few days."

Jilly squinted at the key and said, "There's a small carving of a sailing ship on the lid of my dressing box, could that be it?"

Snapping his fingers he said, "Of course! That's where I saw it! When I was looking for your mobile!"

"The day Becca and I went to Truro," Jilly said remembering.

Alex returned to his book and searched out a line drawing of a magnificent writing desk.

"There!" he said slapping the page.

"What?" she asked peering. "Oh, a very imposing piece of furniture! Has it a logo?"

"I don't know. It isn't detailed enough, but I'm pretty sure I did a restoration job on something similar. It was a while ago, so my recall is a bit hazy."

"So you can't be certain about it?"

"Not without a bit of research. I think the firm who do the actual wood carving are pretty exclusive as a company and they work to a very high standard. They specialise in family crests. Coats of Arms, that kind of thing. So it's possible whoever owns the desk I worked on uses this logo and might know about this key! If it's a family crest I'm inclined to think whatever business they are in will be exclusive. Not in the public domain as such. Does this sound like the type of company Richard would have used?"

"Every bit," she told him. "So what do we do now?"

"If I'm going to track it down, I'll have to go to Norfolk."

"Norfolk!" she echoed. "Why Norfolk?"

"Because that's where the company is that I need to talk to."

The idea of Alex being away filled her with dread. She didn't want to be alone, and so she made a mild protest.

"I don't see why you have to go to Norfolk! If you know the name of the company who carved the original logo, can't you telephone them for information?"

"I can. But they wouldn't tell me. They may not tell me even when we meet face-to-face. This is a huge find, Jilly," he said, holding the book open with the flat of his hand. "And if I'm right and I did have indirect contact with the company who owned the desk, then the information might be among my papers."

"And where are they?"

He didn't try to hide his grin as he said, "In my loft! Where else?"

Alex had only just left when Marilyn and Davy returned. Davy, flushed with excitement, listened open-mouthed as Jilly explained the new situation. After being warned not to talk about it to anyone Davy promised, quite seriously, that he would not tell a soul. He then asked if he could walk Benji. Reminding him not to let the dog jump about she said, "We still have to be a bit careful with him."

"I'll keep him on the lead, walk him and then I'll go and see Dad," Davy told her. "Benji can stay in our kitchen. If Dad wants help I'll be there for him."

Seeing nothing to object to, Jilly agreed, and Davy left.

"So what's this about a logo?" Marilyn asked, sitting at the table and peering at the key. After a moment she said, "That's the Golden Hind, isn't it?"

"How do you know that?" Jilly demanded, amused by the unexpected.

"I played Elizabeth the First in a school play and to make it authentic we had to mug up that period of history for costume making and the like."

"Did you have to wear a ginger wig?" Jilly giggled.

Marilyn laughed and gave her a playful push.

Returning to the book, Jilly scanned the picture and then said doubtfully, "Are you sure this is the Golden Hind? It's quite a small image."

"It's still the Golden Hind. Trust me!"

Not that it mattered, the real importance lay in identifying what it represented. Jilly wondered if logos were exclusive – protected by copyright? If not they could be heading for another nightmare where every bit of cheap tat bore the same stamp.

For the first time in days her feeling of foreboding returned and she shivered.

Marilyn looked at her narrowly.

"Are you all right, Jilly?"

"I'm fine," she smiled. "Now tell me about Arthur."

"I expect you've already worked out he's aiming to get a DNA test done on the wallet."

"Will he succeed?"

"Oh, yes! Pop's a stubborn old devil. He'll get a result."

"Let's hope it's the right one! Alex wants to follow up on the logo, that means he has to go to Norfolk. Tomorrow."

"Norfolk?" she repeated, lifting her eyebrows. "That's off the beaten track! And you don't sound too happy about it."

"I'm not. I don't like the idea of being on my own. Not that I will be. I'll have Davy."

"If you want me stay with you I can."

"Will you?" Jilly asked with gratitude.

"Why not! We can send Davy to bed early and have a girlie night. You do the grub. I'll do the plonk!"

"You make it sound like an adventure," Jilly laughed.

"So it is! You and me without the blokes, there's no telling what we might get up to!"

Jilly giggled. Sometimes Marilyn had a wicked sense of humour!

Alex returned in triumph. He'd found the papers he was looking for, and they confirmed what he thought. There was a detailed letter of the damage done to the side panel of a writing desk. It had been caused by the pawing of a large dog. If the panel could not be made good, then it would have to be replaced, and the crest carved to match those already in place.

"So I've got the name of the company I need to see."

"Alex," Jilly began with a frown, "I'm not following you. You know the company who handled the commission, but not the owner of the desk, yet you did the repair. I can't work that out."

"Only because the repair was made on the premises of the company who retained me to do the carving! To do the work in situ would have involved moving staff and tools. It was easier to move the desk. I spent a week or so in Norfolk copying the logo. Once that was completed I went back to my own workshop. I was duly paid and that was the end of the matter. For me it was just a job and it held no significance other than helping my reputation," he added with a modest smile.

With the situation clarified, Jilly asked when he intended to leave.

"Early in the morning. I thought to drive up and, if I can get hold of Arthur, we can come back together – if he isn't already on his way."

"No he won't be," Marilyn said. "He'll still be digging around. I had hoped that by now he would have rung with some kind of news. Seems there's nothing to report."

With that her mobile rang.

It was Arthur. Things were taking longer than he thought so it was likely he'd be away for a day or two.

"Pop, have a word with Alex, will you?" Marilyn said. "He's got a lead which might help you!"

Handing over her 'phone she said to Jilly," I hope they get together, there's safety in numbers! And Pop'll be going in to see my Jack and if it can be arranged I expect he'll take Alex and they'll stay with him overnight."

Alex hung up and said, "It's all arranged. I'm going to Norfolk, then I'm meeting up with Arthur and with any luck we will have cracked the mystery. He's asked me to take the key. Is that all right with you, Jilly?"

"Absolutely!"

Marilyn stretched and yawned saying, "I think I'll take myself off. Have a bath and an early night."

"You'll do no such thing!" Jilly said firmly. "You're not staying on your own. Stay here. That's what we had intended – we're just doing it a day earlier!"

"Good idea," Alex said. "I can sleep at home." He paused then asked if Davy could stay, too." Just to save moving him about. He'll want to come with me tomorrow and I can't take him, so staying here with you two will solve the problem. Is that all right, Jilly?"

"Of course it is, Alex," Glancing about she asked where Davy was.

"He's in my loft poking through all the junk stored up there. And Benji is on his bed!"

"Davy is all right, isn't he?" Jilly asked with concern. "He's not feeling neglected or anything? This last few days we haven't paid much attention to his needs, and he's been so helpful."

"He's fine," Alex assured. "And once everything is sorted out, he'll get his reward."

"Which will be?"

"A waterproof watch that does everything except cook!"

"There's always a snag, isn't there?" Marilyn said straight-faced, then added, "Still, a snazzy watch is better than a cook who can't tell the time. Now I'm going to nip back to the cottage, pick up one or two things, plus a bottle of plonk, and I'll be back 'd'reckly' as the Cornish would say!"

"Not too 'd'reckly'," Alex suggested.

Smiling knowingly, she left.

Alex, taking Jilly by the hand led her to the sitting room and gently pushed her on to the settee. Sitting next to her, separated only by a narrow space, he said, "I'm not happy about leaving you, Jilly. I know Marilyn will be with you, and Davy but..." he paused and gave a half smile. "I want everyone to be safe and I don't want Davy to be a liability."

"He won't be!" she protested. "He's a super boy, both sensitive and sensible."

"He's also a boy with a mind of his own. He can be stubborn to the point of pig-headedness if anyone stands in his way."

"That's not likely to happen, Alex. Please don't worry about any of us. We'll take good care of each other, I promise."

His eyes, full of indecision, rested on her face. He knew her promise had not been made lightly. She would take care of Davy, but the question was 'would she also take care of herself?' Not if Davy was in trouble. Under that circumstance she would think only of him. The other possibility that disturbed him was the idea that between them she and Marilyn might dream up another hare-brained scheme from which they may not escape. So far all the threats had been low-key, full of menace but without action. That situation could change leaving all three vulnerable. If he was absent for more than a day, which seemed likely, what could he do to safeguard them? Letting life appear as normal was not possible. With both Marilyn and Davy staying with Jilly that was a cover blown. He then thought in terms of the telephone.

"Jilly, how many people have your mobile number?"

"I'm not sure. There are quite a few. Family, friends, the village shops, the vet, the school, Becca's friends, shall I go on?"

"No," he smiled. "I think I've got the picture."

"Why did you ask?"

"I just think it might be a good idea if you keep in touch with the family – and they with you – on your mobile. Can you ring your parents and suggest it?"

"Giving what reason?"

"Er – say – a fuzzy line – bad reception. Anything to discourage them from using the house 'phone."

"What about Tom? Shall I give him my mobile number?"

"No! We can't cut out the house 'phone entirely, but your mobile will give you some peace of mind. You'll know that those calls are from people you can trust which includes me and Arthur."

"And what do I do about the house 'phone?"

"Answer it as usual. Try to keep everything sounding normal. Knowing what to expect is easier to deal with than the unexpected."

"I'm still unsure about Tom, particularly as Delza is not well. If he rang late at night I would not answer – and he might need help."

"It's a risk to be taken, Jilly."

"But how do I explain, what do I tell him?

"As little as possible and nothing about your mobile."

The whole conversation had chilled Jilly. She knew Alex was trying to protect her, so why did she feel trapped? It was almost as if he was hemming her in. In some obscure way she felt restricted and it was nothing to do with the loss of the house 'phone. Was it the curbing of freedom?

"Alex I understand what you are trying to do, but what happens if I need to go to the village for shopping?"

"Send Davy! He and Becca are always out and about. I expect everyone knows Becca is away, and so Davy on his own will not raise eyebrows."

At that Jilly felt even more trapped. Was she being unreasonable? She was certainly being ungrateful.

Moving from his side she crossed to the window. The sun had travelled round and now slanted across the sea. Vapour trails patterned the sky and she wished they were still part of her life. She wondered if Becca was as enthralled by travel as she had been. She thought of Dyak. She thought of Kyak. She smiled mistily. It was all a long time ago.

She was suddenly aware of Alex's hands on her shoulders. They were warm, firm and yet somehow gentle. Leaning against him she no longer felt chilled and trapped, she felt at ease. He rested his chin on the top of her head and said quietly, "It'll be all right, Jilly."

"I know," she softly replied and believed it to be true.

Davy, with Benji still on his lead, crashed through the door looking pale and apprehensive.

"What's wrong, son?" Alex asked in alarm

"It's Benji."

The dog was shivering and holding up his damaged leg.

Jilly crouched and saw the wound had partly opened and was bleeding.

"What happened?" she asked.

"He tried to jump over the wall," Davy said sounding distressed. "But because he was on the lead he fell backwards and..."

"It's all right, Davy," Jilly told him calmly. "I'll bathe it and if it's no better tomorrow we can take him back to the vet."

"I'm really sorry Jilly," the boy said his eyes downcast. "Sorry, Dad," he added.

Alex scooped the dog into his arms and carried him through to the kitchen.

"You were asked to be careful with him," Alex said crisply.

Davy's face crumpled with remorse.

"I'm sorry, Dad. He just decided to jump. I think he was after one of his bones."

"You should have taken more care!" Alex told him relentlessly.

"Alex!" Jilly cried sharply. "Let it go! Davy has apologised. Let that be the end of the matter."

Carefully swabbing Benji's leg with warm water she said, "I think he's popped a couple of stitches. I'll bandage it and see how he goes."

Again Davy started to apologise.

"Davy, it really is all right. These things happen." As she carried the dog to his basket she told Davy that sleep was the best thing, "So we'll let him snooze."

Turning to Alex she removed the heat from the situation by saying, "I'd better think about getting a meal ready. Would you get the wine from the cupboard, please? And, Davy would you like to raid the garden for lettuce?"

Left alone Jilly looked at Benji's twitching paws. He seemed comfortable with whatever dream was racing around in his head. If only life was always that simple for everyone.

★ ★ ★

It was mid-evening when Alex unexpectedly decided to leave for Norfolk. The roads would be clear, and if everything slotted into place he and Arthur could be home by tomorrow night. Had Jilly been on her own with Davy, who was already in bed, he would have waited until the morning. But with Marilyn under the roof, leaving the girls together he considered to be a fairly safe move.

As he left, Jilly again realised she didn't want him to go. Somewhere deep inside she was afraid she would never see him again. She pushed the thought away. She was thinking like a simpleton!

"He'll be back," Marilyn said quietly.

Of course he would.

The void he left was only temporary.

Twice the 'phone rang.

Jilly, mentally prepared, dealt with the inevitable silences calmly.

Fear had to be held at bay and she was gradually learning how to do it.

After the second call, Marilyn said, "If it rings again let me answer it. I'll give them something to think about!"

Recalling their earlier escapade, Jilly said, "You might have already done that with your ginger wig!"

"That was a hoot, wasn't it? Not at the time! It's only with hindsight that I feel brave. In actual fact I was quite scared."

"You didn't look it!" Jilly told her, sounding surprised.

"For that you must thank RADA. It's down to them that I can act."

"They did a good job."

As Jilly topped up the wine Marilyn asked about the dressing box.

"I'm not quite sure what it is. Is it a glorified sewing box?"

"Not at all," Jilly told her and promptly retrieved it from the bedroom.

Setting the box on the coffee table she said, "Ignore the dull patch on the lid. That's where Becca spilt the remains of my Chanel N°. 5, and that's the result."

Opening the box, and on seeing the contents, Marilyn gasped,"Jilly! How beautiful," and feasted her eyes on the silver-topped bottles and jars slotted within the tailor-made compartments. Lined with plum-coloured velvet it was a perfect background for the contents. The ivory-handled button-hook and the silver thimble. The delicately embroidered étui, all faintly imprinted with the Golden Hind, all in lovely condition.

"How long have you had it?" Marilyn asked.

"About four years. Richard saw it, liked it and bought it."

"A man of excellent taste! Has Alex seen it?"

"Not properly. But it was seeing the logo on the lid that triggered off his memory."

"So, I suppose this box could have once belonged to the family Alex is trying to find?"

"It may have done. And if it did, I wonder if that will be of any significance?"

"It will certainly illustrate how small the world is!"

The house 'phone rang.

Angrily Marilyn shouted, "Can't the telephone people stop the calls?"

Jilly had already left the room.

As she returned she shrugged and said. "Silence! Nothing! As for having the calls stopped, Alex and I did talk about it but thought such an action might provoke more trouble in the shape of someone coming to the house!"

"That you can do without!" Marilyn said. She searched Jilly's face for a moment then added, "The calls don't seem to worry you as much as they did."

Jilly explained why. "As long as I'm able to keep in touch with Becca and my parents, that's all I care about. Calls on the house 'phone are a nuisance not a problem. I can anticipate, and deal with them accordingly."

"Thank goodness for mobiles and technology, eh?"

Benji scratched at the door. He'd been quiet all evening and refused his food. Not a good sign. Now he needed to go out.

"I'll take him!" Marilyn volunteered. "If you take him and the 'phone rings I'll be very tempted to have my say! Incidentally, have you tried 1471?"

"Number withheld!"

"Sod technology!"

Jilly laughed.

Marilyn was still in the garden when Alex rang.

"I'm just checking all is well. Any problems?"

"Not really. Benji's a bit off colour. Marilyn's walking him in the garden. Davy went to bed early. I think he was a bit miffed when you left. I looked in on him earlier and he was sound asleep in a slightly rumpled bed."

"On the whole it sounds peaceful. Good! I wish I was sharing the quiet with you."

"So do I!"

"'Phone calls?"

"A couple. The usual."

"No word from Mitzi?"

"Not yet. Once she has something to say she won't waste time."

"As soon as you hear, you'll let me know, won't you?"

"Of course! Take care, Alex." And with that she switched off. It had been good to talk to him.

Marilyn returned from the garden white-faced and clutching a piece of paper.

Handing it to Jilly she said in a low voice, "It was stuck on the side door with Blu-Tack."

Heart pounding Jilly took the sheet of cheap writing paper from Marilyn's trembling hand. The message was stark. The letters cut from a recognisable tabloid.

TIME IS RUNIN OUT.

Illiteracy! Immediately she thought of Hal Polglise and paled.

Had he approached the cottage? Did he know the menfolk were away? If so, what did the message mean?

Chapter Thirteen

Arthur drew on his cigarette. He was on his second packet of twenty for that day and his tongue felt like it was wearing a squirrel's tail. He and Don Tragg, talking in low tones, were sitting in the Pig's Ear pub not far from Trafalgar Square. It was long after closing time but the landlord, being a mate and a staunch supporter of the Force, readily made his back room available when needed.

The men had been there for several hours, part of the time sipping best bitter and munching pork pies.

"Let me get this straight," Don was saying between bites. "You think this wallet ties up with someone trying to steal diamonds, and a suspected hit-and-run in Finchley?"

"It's no more than a gut feeling, Don. I've no proof unless the wallet turns up something concrete."

"Even if it does, it's not necessarily conclusive evidence. There are always alibis – fake or otherwise – to prove or disprove. And quite frankly, Arthur, after all this time, who's going to remember what?"

"So you keep saying," Arthur replied tetchily. "But can we wait for the DNA result before we admit to getting it all wrong?"

Don's eyes drooped. He was tired. He and Arthur had been discussing all the possibilities connected to this case and they'd ended up chasing their own tails. That was very wearying.

There had been no report of diamonds having gone missing during the last year, so Arthur could be on the wrong tack. A young couple passing by had found Richard Kenworth's dead body and Jack Mason injured. They had been investigated and cleared of any involvement in what was believed to be a hit-and-run incident. Despite the best efforts of the police the vehicle involved had never been traced, nor had the driver.

Now, Arthur turning up with Kenworth's wallet meant the case could be taken from the sidelines and brought into play. With no other possible evidence in sight Don saw no point in refusing a DNA test. He owed Arthur a favour and, if the result was what they wanted, he could end up owing him another. Cracking this case could spell promotion! Maureen, his wife, would be pleased. She was an 'I always wear my hat to a tea-party' lady. His promotion would buy her a new hat not to mention the joys of his increased pension. She would be very happy.

Dawn was streaking the sky by the time the men parted. Arthur had intended to stay with Jack. The early hour changed his mind. Instead he checked into a private hotel in the Sussex Gardens area. He was known and welcomed despite disturbing the bleary-eyed owner.

Within minutes Arthur had crashed out and was later roused by his mobile vibrating under his pillow.

It was Alex calling from Norfolk.

Norfolk already? Blimey!

The time was nine a.m.

Alex asked could he and Arthur meet up later?

"If we say round about four this afternoon. By then I should have all the information I need."

At this prospect Arthur's sleep-clouded head cleared. Things were beginning to move!

If Alex was successful, and Don came up with the right answers, the whole issue could be sorted within hours! Having arranged a rendezvous with Alex, Arthur showered, dressed, ate a full English and arrived at Don's office in just over the hour.

Don wasn't there.

He'd been called out. It was something to do with a body found in the Thames. Arthur shuddered and sighed. Not easy. Not nice.

He'd have to sit it out. A young, pretty WPC provided him with a mug of dark brown, sweet tea. Thanking her he held it up and said, "Cheers!" Her white teeth flashed in a smile. As she walked away, he thought her trim. Very trim! He grinned into his mug. WPCs might get prettier, but the canteen's stewed tea never changed.

* * *

Alex, parked on a wide grassy verge, ran his battery shaver over his chin. The result was not as good as he would have liked but it would have to do. He'd had a good trip up from Cornwall and had even managed to sleep for a couple of hours. Cutting across country he was now within five miles of Potter Heigham and even fewer from where he wanted to be. A quick 'phone call to Arthur had put him in the picture, and a further call to the company in question had paved his way to a meeting with Henry Garlby the owner. Alex was flattered at having been remembered and looked forward to meeting the old man again. He knew asking for the information he needed could put him on delicate ground and he anticipated and expected difficulties. What he did not expect was Garlby's absolute refusal to disclose anything about the family beyond that which was common knowledge. Henry Garlby was of the old school and any confidences held by him were strictly kept.

"I would like to help you, Mr. Hunter, but all I can tell you is that the Golden Hind is used as a logo by the Drake family. It is no secret that they are in banking, and have a small and exclusive retail outlet but beyond that I can say no more. I am bound by my own code of conduct to disclose nothing about anyone who has given me their trust. Anything I may know about Mr. Drake's business I cannot divulge. The only thing I can suggest is that you contact Mr. Drake and that you address your questions to him in person."

For a moment he paused to contemplate his position, his eyes in the middle distance, and then having come to a conclusion he said, "Drake can be quite difficult and he doesn't suffer fools gladly. However, it is in your favour that he was delighted with the restoration work you did on his desk."

Surprised, Alex asked, "Do you think he will remember my name? The repair was made quite a while ago, and I didn't actually meet him."

"He will remember. Indeed he will! He's interested in anything and anyone connected with wood. He dabbles in carving. Nothing ornate and," he added with a twinkle, "not very well executed." Smiling he went on, "But, there! If he were a craftsman he would not have needed our services, would he? Would it help if I rang him and told him you are on your way? No guarantee he will see you, but he might."

Grateful for the help Alex thanked him.

Driving away from Garlby's rustic premises Alec had been impressed by what he could only describe as 'Old World Charm'. He had forgotten that Henry Garlby belonged to a bygone age, that his attitude and outlook was that of a true gentleman. He had also forgotten that the seemingly mild and gentle manner hid an iron will. Yes, any secrets Henry held would be absolutely safe. He was not a man to give way under any circumstances. Would Drake be of the same ilk?

Alex was soon to find out.

* * *

Don Tragg reeked of Thames mud. It was nowhere near lunchtime and, despite the stench, he was hungry. Kicking off and changing out of his caked shoes he grumbled to

Arthur, "Why the hell do people choose to die by drowning? The water's bloody cold even at this time of year. Still, there you go! D'you want a snack, Arthur, or shall we see if the DNA results are through first?"

"That'd suit me best. I've arranged to meet Alex Hunter later on, so if need be I can eat on the hoof."

"Right! I'll grab a sarney from the canteen. No breakfast! No time. My stomach thinks my throat's cut! D'you want anything? Packet of biscuits, crisps?"

"No thanks, Don. I'd rather get on if it's all the same to you."

After leaving the canteen they trudged endless corridors in search of the vital results. Wriggling through red tape, the enquiries discretely made finally led them to a dingy office set in the bowels of the building. They sat in silence listening to the rattle of the central heating pipes. Vaguely, Arthur wondered if the boiler was about to blow. It certainly sounded like it. He shuffled in his chair contemplating what might be his ignominious end.

The waiting time was interminable. Eventually Don was handed a buff envelope by a plain-clothed man who didn't hang about. Wordlessly Don undid the metal clip, peered inside, then resealed the envelope saying, "We'll sort it in my car, Arthur. I hope you appreciate that what we are doing is strictly against the rules and if caught…"

He didn't say any more. He didn't have to. Arthur understood.

In the car Don withdrew a sheet of paper from the envelope. Hand-written the lines were closely packed and dense with black ink. Don scanned them and said, "It's from Nevil."

"Nevil Hammond? What's he saying?"

"You don't want to know, Arthur. All you need to know is the result. Beyond that – nothing, OK?"

"OK," Arthur agreed unhappily. Of course the result was important but the nitty-gritty would have been interesting to learn.

Don read in silence muttering the odd expletive. Finally he said, "There's a load of jargon. Nevil ain't nothing if not thorough! So I'll skip the technicalities and just name names, yes?"

"Fire away!"

"Before I do, let me warn you – you get only one bite of this cherry. What's written here has to be wiped out – burnt – no evidence left to show it ever existed. So listen and remember. And the next time you see Nevil think in terms of double Scotch and your zipped lips. Get me?"

"Every bit."

"Right," Don said, spreading the paper on his knee and smoothing it flat. "The name that Nevil's come up with…" he paused and squinted." His writing is bloody awful! I think the name is Porglost."

"Could it be Polglise?" Arthur asked, pulse fluttering.

"Could be. First name Harold?" Again he squinted, "Lives in Thewden?"

"Treveden! Hal Polglise!" Arthur corrected quickly. "That's him! Did time?"

"Yup! Inside he got the name of being something of a bully-boy. Up for sexual assault. A sixteen year old girl! Sounds a nice bloke!"

"That's him!" Arthur repeated triumphantly.

Folding the paper and slipping it back into its envelope Don said, "So, having found the villain, can you prove he was at the scene of the suspected crime?"

"Not yet, I can't," Arthur admitted." But if he's got an alibi I might be able to crack it. Polglise sometimes crews for Dick Rogers. I'll have to talk to him."

"Crews what, and who's Dick Rogers?"

"Our local butcher. He runs boat trips in the holiday season."

"What? Any more for the Skylark jobs?" Don asked laughing.

"You can take the Mick!" Arthur grinned, "but with Dick's help your Maureen might well get a new hat!"

Laughing louder Don said, "You never miss a trick, do you? Let me know how you get on. And if you want help – you've got my number."

Wiping the windscreen clear of mist he said, "I'll have to move, Arthur. Paperwork to do for the body in the river. And I've got to clean my shoes. Maureen won't let me into the house unless I do."

* * *

Alex, determined to gather as much information as possible was prepared to battle verbally for it. Having been forewarned that Drake was tough he'd steeled his nerves and felt able to ward off anything thrown at him. Now, taking a deep breath, he turned into the wooded driveway leading to the home of the Drake family. A large, elegant house built of mellow stone glowed in the sunshine. As he drew up at the massive double doors bearing the carved family crest, he knew he'd taken the first step in the right direction. Two Great Danes bounded round the side of the house and, barking ferociously, held him prisoner in his car.

Eventually the house doors opened and a balding, middle-aged man approached. Calling the dogs to heel and scowling at Alex he tapped on the window and asked for identification. Having inspected the offered driving licence and without introducing himself he then invited Alex into the house.

It was opulent. The hallway with its sweeping staircase was richly carved and carpeted. The ancestral portraits, hanging on the walls, were beautifully painted. By contrast the small ante-room into which he was shown and left alone was gloomy. The only point of interest for Alex was the writing desk. He recognised it as the one on which he had worked all those years ago. Again gouges scarred the side panel. It seemed that Great Danes had long claws! Another restoration? Could be! Out of interest he crouched to finger the scars and the crest. Yes, it was the Golden Hind. It couldn't be anything else – Drake being the family name!

The door opened and an older version of the original man walked in. This was Wallington Drake and he looked formidable.

He was.

He glowered.

He barked.

Crouched, and feeling at a disadvantage, Alex straightened up and met the man eye-to-eye. The coldness in them told Alex the next few minutes were not going to be easy..

Nor were they, as he told Arthur later when he surreptitiously rang him.

"He's a tough nut to crack. He gives nothing away and he's very skilful in re-phrasing the same questions. Luckily I recognised what he was doing, stuck to the truth, and always gave the same answers. What he seems unable to grasp is the fact that I need nothing more than access to Richard's safe deposit box."

"And?"

"He's refused. He wants Richard's written permission or, failing that, his password."

"Jeez! Another password! How did you get out of that?"

"I didn't. I had no option but to explain the situation. Richard's death shocked him. Although he hadn't seen him in a long while, that was not unusual. Beyond giving him the details of Richard's death everything else was only in outline."

"Why the caution?"

"At that point I didn't trust him any more than he trusted me. So I gave him personal details he could check but I made no mention of you or the DNA test."

"Did that ease the situation?"

"No. He accused me of playing some kind of game." Alex's voice hardened. "I'll tell you this, Arthur. It took a lot of self-control to remain calm. When I thought of Jilly's fear and what she'd had to deal with I wanted to hit him – hard. Instead I told him I didn't have time for games. Lives could be in danger. Not mine. Not his, but the lives of Richard's widow and his small daughter."

"Did that do the trick?"

"No!"

Arthur swore under his breath.

Alex said, "That was when I ran out of patience. I was getting nowhere, and it seemed I'd nothing to lose, so I decided to speak my mind. However he suddenly opened up."

"How d'you mean?"

"He started to feed me information. He said that anyone wanting to bank with Drakes had to prove they held assets to the value of a million pounds – minimum."

"He wasn't talking peanuts, was he?" Arthur breathed.

"With that sliver of information I understood him better. His attitude is rock solid. This isn't an ordinary bank. They aren't interested in your mortgage repayments, or your water bill. They deal only with money. Real money. Consequently penetrating their security at any level is almost impossible."

"So whatever Richard kept in his box had to be valuable enough to justify the cost of keeping it there," Arthur said reflectively.

"That's my guess, too! Drake then went on to tell me that he was used to people spinning tales of hardship and danger. That the bank was regularly targeted by villains which made him extremely careful at all times. However, he was prepared to give me a chance, but he would need to check me out first. He had to be sure I was who I said I was. I told him as long as he did it quickly. Too much time had been wasted and too much hung in the balance."

"What did he say to that?"

"It's unrepeatable," Alex told him, laughing quietly.

"Where are you now?" Arthur asked.

"Didn't I say? I'm still in Drake's study waiting for him to come back and give me the all clear."

"You cheeky sod!" Arthur bellowed. "What if he walks in on you?"

"I'll deal with it!" Alex laughed and pushing the 'off' button on his mobile he slipped it into his pocket.

An hour later Alex left Drake, having achieved his aim.

Drake had spent most of the time on the telephone talking to various people including Springton, Alex's bank manager. Finally he appeared satisfied that Alex was who he said he was. He still had doubts about the scenario but he was prepared to take the risk. Drake then telephoned his own bank and left instructions that Alex only was to be allowed access to the safe deposit box, for which he had a key. Alex was then given Richard's password that he had to commit to memory and sent on his way.

Once beyond the house he jubilantly rang Arthur again and arranged to meet him in Soho. Arthur pressed for further details that Alex refused to disclose. They could discuss them later.

He rang Jilly. Was all well in her part of the world?

"Absolutely," she said, sounding slightly breathless. "What about you?"

"Things are moving slowly on," he told her. He was guarded for her own safety. Again it was the maxim 'what you don't know you can't talk about'. He told her just enough to keep her spirits high adding he hoped to meet up with Arthur and be home within hours.

"But don't wait up, Jilly. If we are very late Arthur can go back to his place and I'll go back to mine."

"But how will we know you are home?"

"I'll bring you a cup of tea in the morning! Is Davy all right?"

"He's great and being really helpful. We still haven't heard from Mitzi so she must have a real problem with her computer."

"Have you rung her?"

"No. I'm trying not to use the 'phone at all – just to keep the line clear. Although I did ring the vet about Benji, his leg looks a bit sore so if it's no better we'll need to take him to the surgery."

They talked on for a few more minutes each enjoying the contact and warmth it brought. If there was fear in Jilly's voice, Alex didn't hear it.

When Jilly rang off she was trembling. Sinking on to the settee she felt utterly drained.

She had desperately wanted to tell Alex about the threatening note Marilyn found, but couldn't bring herself to do so.

Marilyn looked at her in absolute amazement and said, "What a performance, Jilly! You were brilliant. Your voice didn't waver, the pitch was at its most convincing." She poured a glass of wine and said, "Drink that. You look as if you need it! I gather there has been some success in Norfolk."

"It sounds promising. I think maybe Alex knows more than he's telling."

"That makes two of you and it might be a good thing. You know how things go! Telling you all his news might have encouraged you to tell him yours – that would not have helped, would it?"

"No. *We* have to deal with this note problem. And I still think the best way is to ignore it. We mustn't appear worried or perturbed."

"Shrug it off? What about Davy?"

"We won't tell him. He doesn't need to know we've been threatened. And if we all remain together we should be safe until the men get home. After that they can take over."

"You make it all sound very simple," Marilyn sighed.

"I wish," Jilly said forlornly and shivered as the fingers of foreboding scraped her spine.

The house 'phone rang.

The atmosphere tensed as nervous glances were exchanged.

Marilyn said, "I'll get it," and before Jilly could argue she disappeared.

Returning moments later she said, "That was weird. The message was that the key would be collected within the next twenty four hours. Put it in a brown envelope and leave it under the bush by the gate."

Someone was approaching the house! Did they know the men were away?

"I don't know," Marilyn said shaking her head. "But what struck me as weird was the sound of the message. I think it was recorded. There was a noise in the background that I couldn't quite place. And another thing. Your voice must be familiar to them but I was addressed by your name and the whole thing sounded sort of tinny."

"They *must* know the men are away," Jilly concluded tightly.

"What shall we do?"

"We don't have an option. We have to obey."

"We don't have the damned key!"

"They don't know that! So any old key will do. We must play for time. Whoever is collecting it might not check immediately."

"And the messenger may not be recognisable!"

"You mean they'll be disguised? Or use a courier?"

"A courier makes sense! Complete with leathers and helmet, and probably on a motor scooter. I've seen a couple of them tearing through Helston."

So had Jilly. Whoever was making the plans was being careful and clever.

Hurrying to the kitchen they searched the drawers and Jilly found a discarded Yale key.

To what it had once belonged to she neither knew nor cared as long as it served a purpose now.

Suddenly, angrily she slammed the key on to the table covering it with her palm

"What?" asked Marilyn sharply.

"What are we thinking about!" Jilly said harshly "Doing as we're told! Obeying orders!"

"Why? I think we should contact the police."

"No!" Marilyn cried, in a voice laced with experience. "There's no point. By the time the information reaches the upper echelons of those who make decisions, it'll be too late."

"OK, but we can't just let it happen. What about asking Dick Rogers to help? He knows from Alex that something is wrong".

"Dare we involve an outsider, Jilly? Wouldn't we do better to ring Pop?"

"Why? All he can give is advice. Both he and Alex are too far away to be of any real help. No. We've got to deal with the situation."

"How?"

Jilly shrugged and shook her head. "There's got to be a way. What if we barricade ourselves in the house or attack the courier?" She half smiled and said, "Which is a pretty stupid idea born of desperation."

"I'm not so sure," Marilyn said thoughtfully. "I think the answer could be to hand over the key and *then* barricade the house."

Jilly laughed thinly saying, "Thoughts of stable doors and horses spring to mind."

"It might prove to be the best way."

The 'phone rang.

Jilly's nervousness heightened as she took the call.

The usual male voice said, "Becca can't sail for ever. Let's hope she finally comes home."

The line went dead.

Ashen faced and shaking Jilly returned to the kitchen and relayed the message adding in a trembling voice, "I'm really frightened, Marilyn. If they harm Becca…" Her voice trailed away.

Swiftly Marilyn put her arm around Jilly's bowed shoulders and said softly, "She'll be all right, Jilly."

Anxious and needing to know if Becca was safe she rang her mother. Fighting hard to have a calm and chatty conversation she was also desperately trying to find an opening for the vital question when her mother bridged the gap.

"We are having the most lovely time! I do wish you were here," her mother said wistfully. "Becca is in a constant state of excitement. Although at one point she did have a little tantrum."

"Oh?" Jilly said with dread.

"It was nothing serious. Just disappointing," her mother said lightly. "I'd told her so much about the shops and market in Algeciras then when we arrived, everywhere was closed. I never do remember Siesta time," she said with a shamed laugh, then added," But everything was back to normal within minutes. Becca can be so mercurial!"

"Tell me about it," Jilly said in what she hoped was a level voice. "How is she otherwise?"

"Absolutely fine!"

"No falls or cut fingers. You know how accident prone she can be."

"She's absolutely fine," her mother repeated. "You sound edgy," she added. Then assuming the cause was due to Becca's absence her mother said with conviction," Becca really is having a super time, and we never let her out of our sight. I'm watching her now. Talking to a little boy called Toby. Shall I call her over?"

Although Jilly desperately wanted the contact she refused saying skittishly," Mummy! How can you interfere in what could be Becca's first big romance!"

Laughing her mother said, "With Toby? Hardly! He's not yet five."

"Ah! A toy boy!"

To Jilly the conversation verged on the hollow and flippant but at least she knew Becca was safe. For the time being. Her parents would take good care of her. If they literally never let her out of their sight, then that was how things would be.

Reassured, but still deeply worried, she rang off knowing Becca was being used as a very potent threat.

Later, when discussing this new twist, the big question was how did *they* know? The only conclusion Jilly could draw was that after having been followed to Plymouth, Becca and her grandparents were now being stalked.

"It seems to be the only answer."

At heart Jilly thought the idea flimsy, but it was the only one she had and so she hung on to it.

* * *

Alex picked up Arthur in Greek Street. Not the most salubrious area but convenient for where they needed to be. The premises they wanted were found tucked away in the corner of one of the many squares. Drab and without any form of identity except for the brass number eleven on the door, it did not ask for a second glance.

Parking in the private bay the two men sat and exchanged information. Being able to put Polglise in the picture was an enormous step forward. Arthur said, "Now that we know about Hal, I was going to tackle Dick Rogers about him, but it might be best if you approach him."

"On what score?"

"Hal's alibi. He'll swear he was out on the Blue Gull! Now we have proof that his blood is on the wallet we have to prove he wasn't at sea. He was in Finchley on the evening in question. So how do we prove it?"

Alex thought about the problem for several minutes and then said, "Let's start by asking Dick about tide tables. He might have kept a log of sailings and crew-members' names. If we need written proof. I dare say there are official records kept somewhere and they can't be refuted. What about the DNA, can that be dated?"

"I don't know, but if we need to I can get hold of Don."

They grinned at each other. Things were on the up!

Just before Alex got out of the car to go into the bank, Arthur asked about the diamonds.

"What will you do about them? I know you can't remove them – even if you could it'd be too dangerous to carry them about."

"I'll have to leave them where they are." For a moment he banged the heel of his hand on the steering wheel and then said, "One thing that really puzzles me, Arthur, is although we know where the diamonds are, why has the loss of such a quantity remained unreported?"

"They probably have been but not to the Yard. The French don't always work in tandem with us."

"Really?" Alex said "Then the French could be chasing *their* tails!"

"It's a happy thought," Arthur guffawed.

Walking into the bank was a strange experience for Alex. Its atmosphere was heavy and hushed, even muffled. He had thought to find armed guards discreetly placed. Instead there were several dapper little men moving briskly and officiously about. The only imposing figure was that of Elland Drake the man he had first seen, only that morning, with the two Great Danes. Why was he there? To check out the situation? To ensure Alex was bona fide?

He greeted Alex with rather more warmth than he had done earlier, but did not explain his position. It was only when one of the staff appeared and asked for his signature that Alex realised Elland Drake worked for his living.

As they descended a flight of stone steps leading to a well-lit corridor conversation was polite and banal; the weather, the latest cricket score and the crashing of one of the big fashion houses. Probably one of Drake's clients!

When they were halfway along the corridor Alex had a mild panic. He had forgotten the password!

Drake, with his endless chatter, had driven it from his head.

As they turned a corner they were forced to a halt by a grille of floor to ceiling iron bars, behind which stood a uniformed guard.

Drake said, "This is where I leave you, Mr. Hunter. Mosten will open the barrier and then close it behind you. You will then pass through the vault door. That too will be closed behind you. When you are ready to leave, press the button on the far side, a light will flash and Mosten will open the door so that you may leave."

"And the password?"

"You may or may not be asked for it. Not knowing keeps people on their toes. After leaving the vault you will be collected and escorted to my office." He smiled and added, "It all sounds rather dramatic, but it isn't, not really. It's all part of our safety precautions. We have tremendous responsibilities not only for valuables but also for people – you – for instance. So all this 'drama' is just our normal procedure."

With that he smiled again, nodded and left.

Mosten pressed a button and the iron grille slid silently open. Alex was about to step through when Mosten said, "Your password, sir?"

As he spoke Mosten's barrel-shaped chest filled the gateway. Although his manner was not threatening his bulk was.

Alex's brain raced. The password! What was it? What had Drake said? "Nothing."

Delivered with a gleam of mischief for a moment Alex had not understood. Then Drake had laughed and patted him on the back saying, "Nothing's as good as anything, Mr. Hunter!"

Now Alex recalled smiling at the neat ambiguity.

With the password spoken, the grille passed through, and the vault door closed behind him, he stood and gazed around the high-vaulted chamber. Surrounded by shelf after shelf of small, numbered metal doors, each bearing the Golden Hind logo, he idly wondered what value lay behind them. If Richard's safe held several millions, what did the remainder hold? He couldn't imagine.

Taking the key from a slot in his wallet, he searched for the matching number. Oddly they were all at random. Another safety precaution? His search was frustrating and time consuming. No door contained less then four numbers and there were no clues to lead him forward.

With the time slipping by he thought Arthur would be getting restless.

There was nothing he could do about that. Every number had to be read. Relentlessly the minutes flew by. Alex's eyes darted about. The box had to be here somewhere!

And then he found it.

With pulses racing he stared at it. Behind that metal door lay the root cause of Jilly's fears. Once the contents were handed over to the police that would be the end of her nightmare. No more stalking. No more smashed windows. No more silent 'phone calls. Her life would be smooth, easy and happy. Even very happy given time.

Content with his thoughts he inserted the key and opened the door. As he did so a metal tray slid towards him and docked into place. Within the recess was the safe deposit box. This also slid forward to slot and lock into position on the extended tray. Again he had to use the key.

Excitement ran through him. His hand trembled as he fumbled for the keyhole.

The lock clicked and the lid flew open.

An inner lid held a notice reminding the user that once the lid was closed the box would reset itself and could not be reopened for one hour.

Another safety precaution?

All he had to do now was carefully insert the key one more time, check the contents, lock the box and go home to Jilly.

Tense, holding his breath he carefully turned the key.

The lid flew open.

The box was empty!

Chapter Fourteen

The offices of Prime Land Survey Co. in Tolben Mews, Finchley had been unoccupied for several months. The owner of the shop next door gave this information. He was Chinese and ran the family take-away. No, he did not know where the owners were and he didn't care. He was more concerned about his loss of trade. That he attributed to the boarded-up premises. He did not consider that his own dingy and depressing shop might be at fault.

On the other side of the closed office was a launderette called "Bubbles". The owner, a plump, dark-haired girl, was pleasant and helpful. She remembered that after the owners moved out, which was not long after they had moved in, there were one or two enquiries about them and one man in particular had stuck in her mind.

"He didn't seem very happy at finding the place closed. I told him as much as I knew – which wasn't a lot – but he seemed a bit – I don't know how to put it – sort of suspicious. I don't know why! I wasn't telling porkies!"

Alex and Arthur exchanged glances.

"Can you remember when this was?" asked Alex.

"It was sometime last summer and it was around closing time. We shut at nine every night. I've had enough by then. Talking to him made me late getting home. That's how I remember. I missed me telly programme."

"Any idea what he looked like?"

She screwed up her face and shook her head.

"Not really, but he talked posh. I remember that. Posh don't come to this sort of place!"

She spoke easily, and remained unperturbed by the questions. For that Alex was grateful. He had just one more to ask. Giving her his most winning smile he thanked her, told her she'd been of enormous help and then went on, "Can you cast your mind back again? Do you remember hearing anything about a car accident that happened just along the road?"

Her eyes and mouth rounded with intrigue.

"O-oh yes! It wasn't him what was killed, was it? Poor bloke! I read about it in the paper. Old Wang next door asked me about it. He wanted to know if I'd seen anything. I told him no, which was the truth. I think he was disappointed. You can't tell with the Chinese, can you?"

Inscrutable, Alex thought.

* * *

The decision to go to Finchley was made to counteract the shock of finding the safe deposit box empty. They sat in Alex's car bowed down under a heavy silence and it was several minutes before Arthur said, "We have to go back to the beginning, Alex. We have to trace Richard's movements."

"What's the bet his secrecy will get in the way? The man was obsessed."

Arthur couldn't argue. Richard had always been the same. He revealed nothing about his business and very little about his private life. His philosophy was that silence was a safety net. Through which he finally fell, Arthur reflected sadly. He liked Richard. He was a good man to work for, and he didn't deserve to die as he did. There would be a lot of satisfaction in catching his killer.

Alex drove away from the area in silence. Although he was angry at having undertaken what he saw as a wasted trip, it had led his mind to explore a different channel. He drove some way in silence and then said with conviction, "The more I think about the situation the more I'm convinced Richard was set up. I also think he knew it. He knew he was walking into a trap. Although finding deserted premises must have been more than he anticipated."

"How do you come to that conclusion?"

"With difficulty and lots of unanswered questions," he replied wryly. "But I'm sure I'm on the right track."

Arthur dropped his chin onto his chest. Alex could be right. If Richard hadn't done his own security check on Prime Land Survey Co., if Smith or Slade had somehow manipulated the situation, then Richard would have fallen into the trap.

"Tell you what," Arthur said, "Let's go back to the Pig's Ear – I could sink a pint – get Don Tragg to meet us there, then we can talk the whole thing through."

Alex wasn't keen. Within himself he felt restless and said so.

"I'd rather not, Arthur. I'm worried about Davy and the girls being alone."

"They'll be all right," Arthur assured him. "I can't see the situation changing in the next few hours. Why should it?"

Although Alex had no answer his doubts remained.

Slowing to a halt at the traffic lights he waited impatiently to move on. Was everything determined to hold him back?

As they finally pulled away, Arthur said, "If you take a left at the next corner, we can short cut to the pub. I know you'd rather get home, but meet me on this. Don might be able to help. If he can he will, but only face-to-face, not on the 'phone. Once we've picked his brains for a couple of hours we can leave, OK?"

Reluctantly Alex agreed. Driving through the night could be quicker than journeying with daytime holiday traffic.

Perhaps it would be a good move to make.

He made a left turn and within minutes Arthur was downing his pint. Alex settled for tonic water while Don, still panting, having made a hurried exit from his office, held up a Scotch and said "Cheers!"

An hour later Don said, "So, Alex, let's have this theory of yours again. You know it's flawed, don't you?"

"So you say," Alex replied, adding stubbornly, "It might be incomplete – I don't pretend to know all the answers – but theoretically it's feasible."

Don sighed and contemplated the bottom of his empty glass. When it came to serious crime, why did every man think he was Sherlock Holmes? Half-brained ideas offered with complete conviction were the norm. While there was no satisfaction in proving theoreticians to be wrong, they tried his patience.

Alex swirled the remains of his tonic water.

"I think," he said, "that the Finchley arrangement was a well planned hoax."

"Set up by?" Don asked.

"Smith and Slade."

"Can you prove it?"

"No. Not yet."

Don raised a cynical eyebrow and asked him to explain further.

"They knew Richard was due to fly with the diamonds that night. Creating an extra mission would tighten his schedule. That meant he would be carrying the stones or the key to the safe deposit box. Either way they couldn't lose – so they thought."

"But," Don cut in, "he carried neither. You found the key – deliberately hidden. The diamonds are still missing. There has been no report about the theft of stones, so where are they?"

"I think they are with the rightful owners in France!"

From the corner of his eye he saw Arthur's jaw drop.

Don looked sceptical.

"And just how did they get there?"

"Let me go back on the story," Alex said. "According to Elland Drake, Richard called at the bank three days before we know he was killed. He went to the vault, and I think that was when he collected the stones. Then the day before he went to Finchley he travelled to France and back. Easily done these days."

"Jilly said he was missing from early morning until late at night. When he returned he looked exhausted. The following day he hid the key in the toy bear – another safety precaution – no doubt intending to retrieve it when he'd sorted out the problem. What he did for the remainder of the day no one seems to know."

"He rang me," Arthur volunteered, "And I suggested Jack should accompany him to Finchley. They were to meet outside the pub. Jack thought it a bit odd – so did I for that matter – but Richard had his own way of doing things."

"Did Richard collect the Land Deeds? A fairly bulky package!"

"Not according to Jack. He came from the alley empty-handed.."

"Did he say why?"

"No. But his expression was grim."

"Then what happened?"

"They started to cross the road and that was it."

Alex, listening closely, cut in, "I think either Slade or Smith was driving and that Hal Polglise did the searching only to find nothing. No diamonds. No Key. They then reasoned Jilly had the key."

There was a short silence then Don said, "I can go along with you so far, but what about the time lapse? A year? I can't see villains waiting that long."

Alex said, "My guess is that because Jilly moved about so much they lost track of her. That didn't matter at first. They had Richard's computer and they thought all the data they needed would be on that. They were wrong."

"I thought you said he had a laptop?"

"Kept at home and packed away, probably on the day he died. Another safety precaution!"

Don pulled on his bottom lip and said, "He was something of a fanatic, wasn't he? So – having had their plans fall apart, believing Mrs. Kenworth had the key, they had to find her."

"That's how I see it," Alex told him with conviction. "They think she's biding her time before she collects the diamonds, and they are determined to stop her."

"Does she have the diamonds?" Don asked sharply.

"Don't be a bloody fool!" Alex replied harshly.

Don shrugged.

"This is all supposition," he pointed out. "Don't get me wrong. I can see where you are coming from, but you've nothing to back you up. No hard evidence."

"I disagree!" Alex told him doggedly. "We can put Hal Polglise in the picture! And that's got to be worth something. We can also contact the company who I say have the diamonds. If they have then they can be removed from the equation. If they haven't…?" he shrugged, "I don't know."

"OK, Alex, I'll do what I can. Let me have the details of the diamond company and I'll contact them. The British Bobbie carries more clout than the British citizen!" He gave a half grin adding, "It'll cost you another Scotch!"

Alex grinned back. It was a small price to pay.

Chapter Fifteen

It was late afternoon when Davy appeared complaining of hunger. Jilly wasn't surprised. She hadn't seen him since lunchtime. Not that a meal was anywhere near ready. Food had become a very low priority for Marilyn and herself. However, Davy was a different matter.

"Will you settle for an apple, just to stem the pangs until tea-time?"

He eyed the fruit bowl on the dresser, selected an apple and then picked up a banana.

"Can I?" he asked. "Please."

"Of course!" she smiled and went on to ask what he'd been doing all afternoon.

"Not much," he shrugged. "There's no fun in being alone on the beach."

"You've been out?" she asked, her voice sharp with surprise. Had she been so preoccupied with her own thoughts she hadn't missed him? How careless and neglectful.

"You must tell me when you leave the house, Davy!" She spoke with unintentional severity.

"Sorry," he said and hung his head.

Guilt-ridden by her attitude, she tried to make amends.

"Dad rang," she told him brightly. "He and Arthur have met up and hope to be home soon. I think they aim to travel through the night, so you'll see him at breakfast."

He looked at her nervously with eyes which questioned. She knew what he was thinking. He was worried. He needed to know the situation.

She looked away. There was nothing she could tell him other than her own theories. To pass those on to him would achieve nothing. Ignorance could be unsettling, but suspicions could be frightening. But which was the lesser of the two evils? Davy was sensible and bright. And left to his own thoughts might he draw the wrong conclusion?

Uncertainty ruled.

And uncertainty to Davy was unacceptable. He needed to know. He needed reassurance.

Earlier, he had been on the landing when the 'phone rang. And when Jilly didn't speak he knew there was trouble brewing. After Jilly had returned to the kitchen he crept down the stairs and listened at the door. Having heard part of a conversation about Becca and a courier he was apprehensive and worried. Becca might be hurt? But she was with her grandparents! On a ship! Surely she was safe? And what about Dad? He was supposed to be on his way home. Was that the truth? Or was Jilly telling lies?

He had to find out.

"Jilly, is Dad all right? He's not hurt or anything?" He watched her closely. When his mother lied she always fiddled with her hair. Jilly did nothing except smile and say, "Hurt? Gracious, no!"

Something told him she spoke the truth, but he still had to press her.

"Where is he? Has he found out about the logo?" he added, pursuing his thoughts.

"Davy, you know where he is," she said patiently. "He's on his way home. As to the logo I think he's sorted it out," she added unsurely." He didn't want to say too much on the 'phone, but he did want to know if you were all right. I told him you were taking good care of us."

Reddening, he looked away. He was doing his best, even so his doubts returned and he wondered if Jilly could read his thoughts. He hoped not. He wanted to believe her.

Marilyn, sensing a diversion was needed, changed the subject by asking what was to be done about Benji.

"His leg still looks sore."

Jilly crossed to his basket and as she touched his muzzle she received a feeble lick on the palm of her hand.

"His nose is hot and dry! But as he's no longer shaking, perhaps we can wait until tomorrow and then see the vet."

Marilyn looked doubtful.

Davy, reaching for the lead, asked if he could take him into the garden. "Maybe fresh air will help. I'll be very careful with him."

At the word 'garden' Benji looked up and then struggled from his basket.

Jilly felt a refusal would be unkind, and so smiling she said, "Off you go, and don't do anything silly."

Attaching the lead Davy encouraged Benji out of the house promising to find him a bone.

Jilly watched them leave wondering if Davy was at ease with everything.

"He looks very unsure," she told Marilyn, adding for her own comfort, "I expect he's worrying about Alex."

"He's also hungry! So what are we going to eat?"

"Salad's no good. Davy needs bulking up."

"What about Spag Bol? I do a mean dish of that – or so my Jack says."

"You miss him, don't you?" Jilly asked with her head to one side.

"Like crazy," Marilyn coyly admitted. "I know I don't talk about him, but he's always in my thoughts."

"I know the feeling," Jilly admitted mistily. "Although my thoughts are less intense these days. There is not so much welling of pain."

"Due to…?"

Jilly smiled and said, "I refuse to answer that question on the grounds of self-incrimination."

Quick to see through her defence Marilyn said, "If I wasn't a happily married lady you might find yourself facing stiff competition for your grounds of self-incrimination! Not that I'd stand much chance!"

Jilly laughed and turned away. Were her feelings for Alex beginning to show? If so, did it matter? Not one iota!

Smiling to herself she opened a cupboard door and took out a new pack of spaghetti.

"We'd better cook the lot. Spag Bol is Davy's favourite so it won't be wasted."

"What about the men?"

"I expect they'll eat on the way."

The house 'phone rang.

"I'll take it!" Jilly said grimly.

It was Mitzi.

Jilly sighed with relief. She'd forgotten to tell Mitzi about using her mobile number. Not that it mattered. She had called to say the photographs had finally arrived.

"They came after I'd left this morning. I've been out all day, which is why I'm ringing now." She paused and went on in a low voice, "Sorry. I don't recognise the woman in the picture. Is it important?"

Jilly hesitated and hid her disappointment before replying. "Not really. Not now."

"I do wish you would tell me what's going on," Mitzi said, "Shall I come over? I can be with you by tomorrow. Guy will run me to the airport, and there's a flight more or less every hour."

"No, truly, Mitzi. I'm fine. Give me a few more days and when Becca comes home then you come and stay with us, yes?"

"Shall I bring Guy?" Mitzi asked." He still hankers after you. And now that you're free…?"

Jilly laughed and said, "Mitzi your brother is a delightful man, but I don't really think we are made for each other."

"Neither do I!" Mitzi laughed back. "I'm teasing! In any case he's got himself engaged to the Mayor's daughter."

"Really? When's the wedding?"

"Ah! Guy won't be pinned down to a date so don't hold your breath. But what about the photograph? Are you sure you don't want to tell me about it? Are you sure I can't help?"

"Positive. And I do value your offer, Mitzi. We'll meet soon, I promise."

"Take care, Jilly. See you. Bye." And with that she rang off.

Jilly immediately rang back. She had forgotten to ask if the computer had been repaired. As a quick method of communication it might be useful for arranging a visit. There was no reply. How like Mitzi! Ever the butterfly, she would already be off doing other things.

* * *

Alex and Arthur having eaten a good meal were replete. After taking two hours to get on to the motorway they had left it to find a restaurant. Arthur had adamantly refused to eat at a service station. Over-priced inedibility was his claim. In view of the meal they had just consumed Alex had to agree they had made a wise choice. The other advantage was mobile reception. It was crystal clear and took only one call to contact Dick Rogers. So far things were going well. If only he could be sure about the situation at home. Needles of doubt kept stabbing. Not a good sign.

Arthur, having helped himself to the cheeseboard, was spreading Bleu de Bresse on to a cracker. He liked the idea of cheese being foil wrapped. Not too many fingers touching it. He bit into the cracker spreading crumbs beyond his plate. All part of the enjoyment. Crumbs at home led to nagging. Here, no one would dare.

Alex's mobile, in silent mode, alerted him. It was Dick returning his call. Alex listened, said little, then slipped the 'phone into his pocket.

Sounding cheerful he said, "One of the good things about living in a village is that eventually everyone is in the know about everyone else. It doesn't happen overnight, but it happens eventually. Dick has just come up with more information than we could have hoped for."

"Tell me!" Arthur said, scattering more crumbs.

"Remember when Tom was attacked in Jilly's hall? Tom said all along that it was Hal Polglise who hit him. He was right.

"Hal hadn't heard about Benji going missing, but having seen everyone out and about, he assumed the house was empty. He went in hoping to find rich pickings in the shape of Benji – but had to deal with Tom. Having hit him he then couldn't find the dog and so left empty-handed."

"How the hell did Dick get hold of that story?" Arthur growled.

"From the lad who works for him. Seems he was in the pub a couple of nights ago where Hal, in his cups, was spilling out the story as a triumph."

"Why? He hadn't achieved anything."

"But he had! He'd clobbered Tom. And that was a victory for any feuding family. Benji could be dealt with at another time."

Arthur pushed his plate away and wiped crumbs from his mouth with his paper napkin. Screwing it into a ball he tossed it on to the table. People and their feuds were a pain in the butt!

"What about the real problem?" he asked. "Was Hal in the village on the day in question, the day Richard was killed?"

"Not according to Dick's log for the Blue Gull. Dick said Hal wasn't around for three days. He wasn't available. He wasn't even in the vicinity. The tides were right, the weather was good, but there was a shortage of crew. The demand for sailings was more than they could cope with so some trips had to be cancelled. When Hal finally surfaced, he told Dick he'd been home with a bilious attack."

"Had he?"

"No. Dick went round to Hal's place two days running and he wasn't there. The house was locked and his car was missing."

"Bloody 'ell! Was that the car which hit Richard?"

"I doubt it. Hal's car was two-tone brown and cream. Anyway according to Dick it's since been scrapped. Burnt out."

"Insurance scam!" Arthur said sourly.

No doubt, Alex thought and called for the bill.

"We'd better move on, Arthur. If I put my foot down we could be home by midnight."

"D'you want anything to eat on the way? Crisps? Chocolate? I wouldn't mind a bar of something."

"Arthur! You've just had an enormous steak!"

"And an enormous bar of chocolate would round things off very nicely!" he grinned.

Alex laughed, shook his head and moved off towards the car park. Arthur could eat himself into a stupor if he wanted to. Alex just wanted to get home.

As Arthur slipped into the passenger seat his mobile rang.

It was Tragg sounding pleased.

"Arthur? You can tell Alex he was spot on! After pulling a few strings I spoke to one of the Big Boys at White Ice. His English was not good and my French was even worse but between us we communicated the facts. They have the diamonds! Delivered by Richard the day before he was killed. White Ice had been tipped off by someone at the airport about a possible heist and so Richard was warned. He made his own arrangements, and as far as White Ice is concerned there isn't a problem. Richard's death was a shock to them, though. Any progress at your end?"

"Confirmation that Polglise was not in Cornwall at the time in question."

"It can be proved?" asked Tragg

"A written log. Word of mouth, and DNA."

"That'll do!" Tragg said firmly. "Keep in touch." And he rang off.

* * *

If Hal Polglise had one attribute it was that of patience. If by spending time waiting there was a reward to be gained then he would wait. Tracking Mrs. Lang and her Pekinese had taken months, but he now had the timetable of her movements logged to the last second.

Every Sunday, weather permitting, she walked the dog to the cove known as 'The Cauldron' which was something of a misnomer. Two hundred years ago it *had* been a cauldron. A cauldron of seething treacherous water into which desperate people flung themselves. Now it was different. Over the years coastal erosion and shifting sand had left most of it, literally, high and dry.

The locals ignored it, and visitors never explored it. Being no more than a narrow semi-circular beach it was thought to be boring. Guarded by dark cliffs, the tide, even at its highest, never reached the foot of the stark, grey granite and so most of the beach was always dry and sheltered. Because of the topography no matter how hard the wind blew never a breath stirred a grain of sand or a hair of Mrs. Lang's head. She always sat on a smooth rock, honed by the elements into the shape of a chair, and read. Hal never knew what – maybe a love story – maybe the Bible – she was a staunch Methodist. But whatever it was it completely absorbed her. Wheeling, swooping and screaming gulls could not break her concentration and they certainly did not worry her dog. She ambled daintily avoiding shallow rock pools and ignoring the debris-fringed shoreline.

On most Sundays Hal sat in an elevated cleft and watched as the dog waddled about. He was not over keen on the breed. Too much fur. Too much looking after for his liking. Still – Peke's were some folk's fancy – and in short supply. Once nabbed it would mean driving up to Scotland with it – after he'd nicked a car – but what the hell! The further away the better. Less chance of being found with either commodity. He could bide his time. There was no rush. His customer was happy to wait. That suited Hal. He had it all planned. Before he took the Pekinese, he wanted to get hold of Benji. He would bring in real money. He'd had an amazing offer. The tricky bit was meeting the deadline. The dog being unfit didn't matter. If it ran off it wouldn't move all that quick. The snag was the lack of routine. Now that the kids were no longer together, their routine had fallen apart. With the girl away the boy's movements were unreliable. But – and that but could be a bonus – because of the family's preoccupation with the missing key, the boy was coming and going as he pleased.

Now Hal was just a few yards away from the Kenworth cottage and about to play the opportunist. Biding his time. Waiting for his cue. Concealed, he watched with patience. There was something to be said about lax councils who didn't cut back hedges. Cow parsley, all of five feet tall, made an ideal cover, but didn't blot out the view. Hidden as he was Hal felt safe. The only thing that made him recoil from his hide was the snails. They were repulsive and made him shiver. How anyone could eat them he couldn't imagine. But he could see himself heading an international hate campaign against the French for their disgusting habit. He wasn't keen on Chinese fried rice either That place in Finchley? He could still smell it. And German sausage made him throw up. Give him local food any time.

He shifted uncomfortably. His legs were beginning to cramp. An hour was a long time to crouch. Not that it was time wasted, it wasn't. He'd used it to polish his plans and make sure he'd got them right. He knew exactly what he was going to do. And this time next week he'd be stashing a considerable amount of cash under the hearth of his cottage. All he had to do was shift a flagstone. The Kenworth's place had a similar secret hide. In fact all the cottages were the same. Smugglers were not fools, his ancestry told him that. His own village of Treveden might be a mile away from the rocky shore, but that didn't make his cottage any different to the rest. Years ago, carrying a stolen keg of brandy a mile inland was a rich reward for the effort made. And if the soldiers got too close there was a network of underground passages to follow which offered safety if not escape.

Hiding a dog? There were many places. Once that was done, finding the key would fill his coffers to overflowing. Meshing the dog and the key together? Brilliant!

The slamming of the Kenworth's garden gate shattered his thoughts. The boy, with the dog on its lead, was in the lane. The dog was hopping on three legs but other than that seemed to be alert. They turned away from where Hal crouched and walked towards a spot where the dividing stonewall dipped. Hal knew the dog would be unable to jump it – even at its lowest point, so what was the boy thinking to do? He was too far away to hear what the boy said except for the salient points. "Sit," which the dog seemed unable to do, and "Stay". The command obeyed, the lead was laid across the dog's back, the boy hopped over the wall to be hidden from view. The dog remained motionless.

Hal moved.

Quietly, quickly, running low he scooped up the dog.

Teeth sank into his upper arm.

He smacked its snout.

Crouching, he ran back into the cow parsley and, struggling with the dog, he waited.

Bared teeth and silent snarling took over. Clumsily he looped the lead round the dog's muzzle and jerked it tight. The animal kicked and gouged the fleshy part of his arm. He jerked the lead even tighter. The dog quietened.

Moments later Davy clambered back over the wall carrying a blackened bone, one of Benji's treasures. There were several scattered about but this was the nearest. Jilly would laugh when she saw it, and Benji…

Benji was not there.

"Benji!" he called repeatedly.

Shrilly. Panic-stricken he didn't know what to do. Where was Benji? He never moved once the lead was on his back! Now he had! Davy raced along the lane, past the clumped cow parsley, calling for him. Where was he? He couldn't be far away – he was lame. How lame? Had he picked up the scent of a lady dog? Dad said that boy dogs, once they had the scent of a girl dog, went their own way. Had he gone back to The Narrows?

* * *

Some twenty minutes later Jilly dropped a generous amount of spaghetti into a pan of boiling water and said, "Davy's taking his time. I hope he hasn't walked Benji too far. I don't want his leg popping open any more than it already has. Would you give them a call, Marilyn ? He'll be over the wall looking for bones."

"He wasn't being serious, was he?" Marilyn said dubiously.

"Every bit! Benji's bones aren't hard to find. When it comes to burying, Benji is not the best in the book. Becca has been known to follow him around and bury them deeper."

"Get away!" Marilyn laughed.

"True!"

The door burst open and Davy appeared.

Flushed, his eyes dark with despair he gasped, "I've lost Benji!" Tears of guilt swamped his face. "I went to The Narrows – he isn't there. I'm sorry, Jilly.I don't know what else to do." Ashamed he wiped his face with the heel of his palm.

After the initial shock Jilly put a comforting arm about his shoulders and said, "He won't be far away, Davy. He's too lame."

"I wish I hadn't left him!" Davy said in a small voice.

Jilly and Marilyn exchanged glances.

"Left him, where?" Jilly asked.

And the whole story came out.

"He was alone only for a few minutes," Davy explained. "Just while I found him a bone. With the lead across his back I didn't think he would run away. He's never done it before."

"That means his lead will be trailing!" Jilly said with a worried frown." If it snags…!"

She said no more. The possibilities didn't bear thinking about.

Davy slumped at the table and putting his chin into his hands asked if he should go back to The Narrows and search again.

"Not a good idea," Jilly said cautiously. "It's Polglise land and we've been warned to keep away."

"But what about Benji?" Davy asked in desperation.

She didn't know, but Davy needed to calm down. Smoothly she suggested they should eat.

"After that we'll work out what to do. In any case, by the time we've come up with ideas, Benji may well be home?"

"He wasn't the last time he went missing," Davy said drearily.

"That was then. This is now!"

Marilyn put a piled plate of steaming food in front of him and said, "Eat up, Davy. Troubles get smaller as your tummy gets bigger!"

He didn't believe her, but he hoped it was true.

Aware of their vulnerability Jilly made up her mind that no one was to leave the house on their own, then reluctantly relented when Davy said he wanted to keep watch for Benji by the gate. This she agreed to, adding the rider 'no leaving the garden on any account'.

"But what if I see Benji, and he needs help?" Davy argued

"Call me!"

Frustrated, he accepted.

Once he was out of earshot Jilly said, over the clatter of stacking dishes, "We can do without this episode! Too much is happening. It's as if we are being attacked from all directions. Could this be tied up with the threat to Becca's safety? I found that very frightening."

"Of course you did. But bear in mind that Becca is in safe hands. Even if someone was actually watching her I doubt they'd get near enough to touch her. In any case," Marilyn went on calmly, "I don't see the connection between Becca and Benji. He's merely gone a-courting. He wants to finish what he started!"

Jilly had to smile at the idea of Benji going a-courting. It conjured up silly symphonies in her mind. Perhaps Marilyn was right. Yet some sixth sense said she was wrong. Benji's disappearance could be a lure to get them out of the house. Why? Or was she being melodramatic? She couldn't decide. The only thing of which she was sure was safety being tantamount to life. No one must be put at risk. Benji was missing either by design or accident. Whatever the cause she would do nothing. Once the men were home she would feel safer, more protected and probably better advised.

Meanwhile foreboding returned to haunt her.

Chapter Sixteen

Due to a motorway pile-up the men were late getting home. Some fool had hit a patch of dense mist in which three vehicles had already come to grief. The result was carnage, chaos, and a three-hour delay until they reached a slip road. Trying to make up for lost time, Alex drove through the sleeping village of Indian Queens faster than he intended. A wandering cow made him slow down.

Arthur was asleep with his head jammed against the side window, his breathing rasping above the purr of the engine. He finally roused as they pulled up at Jilly's gate. The house was in darkness. That surprised Alex. He had somehow thought Jilly would wait up. Using the front door key they slipped quietly indoors to find Jilly asleep on the settee, and Marilyn cosied into a duvet in one of the armchairs. A table lamp in the corner furthest from the window glowed softly, leaving the window area in shadow.

Suddenly Jilly was awake roused only by instinct. On seeing Alex, flooding with relief, she stood up and stretched out welcoming arms.

"Alex!" she cried. "It's good to see you."

"Hi, Jilly!" Alex said, holding her in a bear-hug and kissing her forehead. Marilyn emerged from her cocoon and said sleepily, "Hullo, Pop. Everything all right?"

And so began the exchange of information they all needed to hear. There was triumph in the achievement, and worry about the circumstances to which they could find no solution. Their lack of constructive thinking was due to tiredness. What they all needed was less coffee and more sleep. After that they would conquer the world. Although said light-heartedly each wished it was possible.

When, the next morning, Davy was roused by Alex, his first stumbling words were, "Dad, about Benji..."

Alex ruffled his hair.

"Don't worry, Davy. No one is blaming you. We'll find him, or he'll just turn up. Right now we have other things to sort out."

"I heard Jilly say something about a courier and Becca in... in...," he floundered, unable to remember.

"It doesn't matter, Davy."

"But is Becca safe?" he asked with alarm.

"I'm sure she is," Alex soothed. "And the business about the courier? It was only a guess made by the girls. I don't think that's going to happen."

"But what will?" he persisted.

"I don't know," Alex admitted. "We'll have to wait and see."

"But, Dad!" Davy protested.

"Leave it to the grown-ups, son! Now up you get! Breakfast is ready and we need life to appear as normal as possible."

"Does that mean I can go out without asking? Because yesterday Jilly said..."

"Whatever was said it was for your own good," Alex cut in brusquely. "And if you want to go out, you still have to ask. Get it?"

"Yes, Dad."

It was just after breakfast when everyone had disappeared that Tom and Delza arrived. She looked pale and dark-eyed. She still wore her anorak and constantly zipped and unzipped it. Jilly wondered if it was some kind of compulsive behaviour. She was also wearing new shoes, clumsily shuffling them to show off the silver buttons.

Tom told her to be still and then went on to explain he had bought her the shoes because she had been so upset. She hadn't slept much since having her tooth out.

"Neither have I," he grumbled. "'er do make such a fuss! 'er do pull off my bedclothes and rattle my bed something awful. So I don't get much sleep."

Helpfully Jilly suggested he had another day at home.

"That's good on you, Missus, but I'm better off being busy. And Delza's got to learn her can't have 'er own way all the time. She do try it on. 'Er's not always as simple as she do try and make out!"

Jilly lapsed into thought for a moment and then said, "Tom, Benji's gone missing again. Would you and Delza like to look for him?"

Tom frowned, "You'll not want us to go to The Narrows, will you? Me and Polglise…"

"No, no," she hurriedly assured. "Searching along the lane will be a help."

"In that case it'll be all right. Delza'll like that. Her do like to pick the flowers on the lane. Tis only dandelions, but 'er do like the colour. First, though, I'd best put a bit of slug bait round they young lettuce – unless they've already been got at. Slugs is little blighters."

Turning from Jilly he was about to speak to Delza when he realised she was no longer there. Looking perplexed he said, "Where's 'er to? 'Er was here a minute ago."

Of Delza there was no sign.

Tom shook his head then said with some relief, "I expect her's in the shed. Her do like to twirl your bicycle pedals. Keeps 'er 'appy," he explained and wandered off muttering. Jilly followed wondering if her bicycle was still in working order. Delza could be quite heavy-handed.

Delza was not in the shed.

* * *

Delza was looking for Pogo.

Papa said Mrs. Kenworth had given Pogo a bath because Delza had kissed him so much she'd made him dirty. Now that the dog had run away again, and Papa and Mrs. Kenworth were talking about slugs, Delza would find Pogo, and hold him against her face so that he tickled her. Delza liked that. When Papa kissed her goodnight his face was prickly. It didn't bother her. She just wished it had Pogo's softness. Delza clumped across the kitchen nervously eyeing the empty dog basket. Mistrusting what she saw she looked under the big table. What if he was hiding there, ready to pounce and bite her? But he wasn't. He didn't seem to be anywhere. Maybe he had gone to find Becca. Delza missed Becca. Becca understood her. Becca sometimes played with her. Davy didn't. He was silly. He couldn't hold a string under his nose. Delza could. Becca had shown her how.

Her mind switched back to Pogo. If he'd had a bath he would be wet. When Delza had a bath Papa always gave her the big stripy towel to use. Sometimes she put it into the bath. It was nice to sit on. But then Papa would get cross with her and make her dry herself with little towels. They were not as nice as the big towel. They didn't have stripes. Mrs. Kenworth's towels had flowers on them. They were pretty. And Becca had a towel with a picture of Rupert Bear on it. Pogo would like that. She would get it from the airing cupboard, go into the bathroom, and wrap Pogo in the towel so that he was nice and warm and dry. Looking back over her shoulder she saw that Papa and Mrs. Kenworth were near the shed. They didn't know she was going to talk to Pogo, and make him warm and dry in the Rupert towel. He would be very pleased to see her.

Fumbling with the catch on the airing cupboard door, her fingers were clumsy and trembling with anticipation. Moments later there was a rewarding click and the door swung wide.

Smiling, her eyes lit upon Pogo, then blind terror hit her.

His head lolling. His body flat.

No fat arms.

No fat legs.

Horrified she backed away.

Pogo was dead.

Delza had killed Pogo!

Papa had lied. Pogo did not have a bath. He was dead.

Stumbling away she groped towards the front door and fled.

Running with an awkward gait, crying, her mind confused she looked towards the clifftop. She was wicked. She had killed Pogo. Now she must be punished. She must look into the cave.

Breathless and frightened she sprawled on the ground her face pressed against the hard rock and peered into the darkness below.

She was five years old again.

She could hear the dogs snarling.

She could see flesh and fur being shaken by ugly mouths.

Men roared. Men laughed. Men jeered.

She tried to cry out, but no sound came.

Scrambling to her feet, losing a shoe, her face wet with fear, she stumbled home. But the sights and sounds that lived in her head followed her. She would make them go away. She would lie on her bed and hold her red spoon until Papa gave her a bun in milk. Then everything would be better.

* * *

Finding the shed empty Jilly asked Tom where Delza might be.

"'Er'll 'ave gone 'ome. Sometimes she do please herself. Then there's no reasoning with 'er, so I just lets 'er go." He spoke philosophically as if it was the only way he could ease his burden.

Jilly looked at him uncertainly," Tom, if *you* want to go home – just to check that she's safe…"

"No need, Missus. Her'll be 'appy with a picture book. She'll 'ave 'er red spoon and if she's a mind to she'll put some milk on 'er bun. Save me a job," he half smiled.

Although Jilly still felt unsure about the situation she had to accept that once Delza was away from the house, she was not Jilly's responsibility.

Alex and Arthur, sitting in the garden, were trying to piece together the jagged edges of the puzzle.

"Arthur, I know nothing about police work, but something tells me this whole business has been set up by a gang of amateurs? I don't understand why they haven't yet worked out that if Jilly had the key she would have handed it over by now. *No* mother would leave her child's safety in jeopardy."

"Criminals don't always see things in black and white, Alex. To me there's a kind of cruelty in the situation. A deliberate torment. Almost a hate campaign."

"But why? Wouldn't the diamonds be enough?"

"It depends."

"On what?"

"Who wants them."

"Surely the answer to that is Slade." Alex said. "He's gleaned all the information from the unseen Miss Smith, and then he set up Richard in what he thought to be a simple situation. When it back-fired that left Slade to deal with circumstances which were beyond his grasp. Now he's making all these clumsy moves in the hope of acquiring something that no longer exists – at least – not where he can get his hands on it."

At that point Alex fell silent and searched for more ideas.

Arthur nudged him out of his thoughts and, looking up, he saw Jilly crossing the lawn.

"I've just spoken to Becca!" she said brightly. "She sounds as if she's got a cold!"

"That's good," Alex said unexpectedly.

Jill looked startled.

Alex went on. "It could keep her in her cabin instead of going ashore."

"Ah! I see what you mean! Out of harm's way. And knowing what a doting granny my mother is."

"There you go, then. She'll be as safe as the Crown Jewels!"

For a moment Jilly looked completely carefree and then her brow puckered as she asked Alex if he'd been to the airing cupboard.

"Only I found the door open."

"Not guilty, Maam! Is it a problem?"

"No. I just wondered." Dismissing the matter she then asked, "Where's Davy?"

"At home. I think he still feels guilty about losing Benji so he's keeping out of the way."

"Still no news about the dog?" Arthur asked.

"Not yet," Jilly sighed." I thought I'd walk to The Narrows – just in case."

"Not alone, you won't," Alex told her bluntly. "How can you even contemplate such a thing?"

"I wasn't planning on going alone," she replied in a flare of heat. "I was going to ask Marilyn."

"Unwise!" Arthur cut in. "You stay away from that area. To be seen there is not a good idea."

"I didn't intend to go barging through," she said further enraged by their opposition. "Credit me with some sense! I do know the score!"

"Jilly, take it easy!" Alex said mildly. "We know Polglise is connected to Richard's death and, although we can't yet prove it, so is Slade. The Narrows is connected to both men."

"Alex! Stop preaching! I do understand! All I want to do is look for Benji. I can do it quietly and discretely. I don't have to rush in with all guns blazing!"

"No, of course not," Alex said, trying not to smile. The idea of Jilly even swatting a fly was, for her, violence beyond belief. Guns blazing? No way!

Steering away from further argument Alex suggested that he, Jilly and Davy should stroll to The Narrows together.

"As a family. Just a casual outing. Nothing specific."

Jilly gave him a long, searching look. "And?" she frowned.

"Nothing," he shrugged," We'd just be – ambling."

"And?" she repeated, probing.

"All right," he said holding up his hands. "Going on to Polglise land is tricky. We know Slade hangs about the camper van even if he doesn't live in it. For three of us to openly wander about that particular patch might be a bit foolhardy but it could look innocent. If we are seen by the woman who I spoke to…" He shrugged. "That could be a stroke of bad luck. We'll just have to be careful."

"Alex, all I'm trying to do is find Benji! Admittedly I want to see the place again, I'm curious about it."

"OK," he said sighing with resignation. "But I don't think you should show your face."

"Are you asking me to hide away from the people who were involved in my husband's death?"

"Yes, Jilly. I don't think you should show yourself. You'll be able to see as much as you need from the cover of the wood."

"And what about Davy?"

"He'll stay hidden with you. I'll go forward. If I'm spotted and asked what I'm doing I'll say I'm looking for Benji – again! That is the whole point of this trip, isn't it?"

Jilly made no reply. Suddenly she felt troubled and uneasy. She had that feeling of someone standing close behind. What if there was someone there who couldn't be seen?

Someone they didn't know about.

Such as who?

Slade's brother! He was family. He could be involved.

This possibility deepened her fears for Becca's safety. She had assumed she was out of harm's way.

If Slade's brother was watching Becca, who was watching him?

She was now guilt-ridden by her own complacency. The clumsy warning about holding the key, and about time running out told her she did not have the upper hand.

Shivering she knew she was trapped. Giving up a fake key may bring a few hours of respite, beyond that it solved nothing. The dark clouds of foreboding gathered around her as the hopelessness of the situation became clear.

These tumbling thoughts fell into her head in less time than it took her to blink.

Alex was saying, "I'd rather take Davy with us than leave him here. I know Tom will be around, but look what happened last time." Seeing Jilly's dark expression he swiftly added, "Not that I think there'll be a repeat performance. We've all moved on. We're all aware."

Jilly turned to Arthur. "What do you think we should do?"

"Follow Alex's lead," he told her bluntly. "I will keep watch from up the lane. If anything moves – I'll be on hand."

Jilly still hesitated. She was nervous and unsure.

Alex put his arm round her.

"Think positive," he said. "We're going to look for Benji, and that's all. No cloak-and-dagger stuff."

"Hiding in the woods is cloak-and-dagger!" she said.

"No, it isn't! It's ferns and trees!" He smiled. "Now I'm going to get Davy. Back in a mo'." And he left.

Hesitantly Jilly said, "Arthur, do you think Slade's brother could be involved?"

Arthur appeared surprised by the suggestion.

"I've got my doubts about that! I can't see him leaving his dogs for any length of time. And I don't think he's got sufficient grey matter to deal with this sort of situation. What's made you ask?"

"I'm unsure, but do you think someone else could be involved?"

Arthur sucked in his cheeks.

"That's some question, isn't it? As to the answer, Jilly, I've no idea."

Jilly looked disappointed. Somehow she thought Arthur would know – or at least have a fresh theory to offer. It seemed he was as much in the dark as everyone else.

When Alex and Davy returned they were both wearing jeans. Alex suggested Jilly did the same.

"Should we decide to go into the woods we need to be covered. The whole place is pretty dense with ferns and brambles."

"As an alternative we can go via the lane – the one Tom told me about."

"Not if we're trying to find Benji. We know the route he took last time, so perhaps we'd better follow it this time."

"Can we go along The Loop?" Davy asked. "Sometimes Benji goes that way."

"What's The Loop?" Jilly asked.

"It's what Becca calls the narrow path that goes along the top of the cliff. It's not a short cut. It's just more fun than going along the lane. Sometimes when there are rabbits about Benji chases them."

Not today he won't, Jilly thought pessimistically.

The path was narrow. Very narrow. It was also overhung with vegetation, including the odd blackberry bush. This must be where Becca had picked the fruit last Autumn, Jilly thought.

The path wound along, rising gently until they reached a vantage point and could look down into the cove. Alex and Jilly paused to look seaward at the vast expanse of blue water. Davy, full of energy, ran on leaping and bounding at will.

Jilly watched him. "Oh, to be young again," she laughed. Looking back along the path they had just walked, she said, "I've never been along here before, have you?"

"Never! It makes a nice change, doesn't it? Mind you it would lose some of its charm in wet weather. Not that the grass would be so tall but the bushes would. And in winter you'd get a pretty cold shower!"

Davy came racing back gleefully shouting, "Look what I've found. And it's new."

In his hand he held a shoe on which glinted a silver button.

Taking it from him Jilly said, "It's Delza's! Where'd you find it, Davy?"

"Along the path."

"Show me."

Running ahead Davy halted by a narrow fissure in the rock and pointed to a patch of flattened grass.

"It was here. This is where Delza comes to look into the cave."

"Why?" asked Alex.

"It's something she does when she's upset," Jilly said trying not to sound disloyal to Tom." It's all to do with her childhood. And punishment. Tom did explain, but it's very complicated."

Alex looked bewildered, "What do you mean?"

Jilly made no reply. She was remembering the open airing cupboard door. Had Delza seen Pogo and been frightened? In her poor simple mind did she blame herself for how he looked. Had she come to this spot because of it?

Alex stood, hands in pockets, looking down at the narrow fissure. He then crouched to lay full-length, cupping his face against the light.

"I can't see anything much," he said, his voice muffled. "Maybe a vague outline of rocks, but nothing else."

"There's nothing *to* see," Jilly said, "It's all in Delza's mind! She must be so frightened."

Getting to his feet Alex gave her a questioning look. She ignored it. Brushing the sand from his jeans he asked Davy if this was the cave in which he and Becca played.

"What's the fascination?" he asked. "Caves, to me, are usually cold and smelly."

Davy grinned and confessed he thought so too.

"When I hold my nose Becca calls me a wimp."

Dismissing the subject, Jilly said tersely, "This is all very interesting, but what about Benji? We're supposed to be looking for him!" On that note she moved away, carrying Delza's shoe and the worry that went with it.

By the time they'd walked The Narrows and, after some debate, entered the woods, Jilly was glad of her jeans. Within minutes they were wet and snagged by thorns. As Alex had already pointed out the undergrowth was dense. So dense she could not imagine Benji pushing his way through it. Davy had already taken a different direction in the belief that he would find Benji by the fallen post with its tangle of barbed wire.

Such optimism, Jilly thought enviously.

Pausing to rest by a split and gnarled tree, filled with disquiet, she asked Alex what was the real purpose of being where they were.

He looked slightly guilty and said, "Apart from searching for Benji? I hoped seeing the enemy camp again might reveal something I'd missed."

"Such as?"

"I can't even guess. In any case they might have already decamped. Mission unaccomplished!"

"I don't think they'll give up that easily," she said shrewdly. "Too much is at stake." She paused and added, "Life seems to be in a constant state of unease. Living happily in rural Cornwall has become a shattered dream."

"Don't say that, Jilly. Eventually everything will return to normal. In fact life will become so normal it might even be boring."

"I don't do boring," she replied with a quick and challenging smile.

"That's my girl! Come on!"

They were within ten metres of the clearing when Davy caught up with them. He was out of breath and his arms were scratched.

"I tracked you!" he declared proudly. "But I didn't find any paw marks by the barbed wire. Maybe Benji didn't come this way."

"We had to make sure," Alex said. "Ideally we need to cover all his haunts."

"This isn't one of them," Davy said. "Not in the woods. *We* never brought him down here. He likes the clifftop, his bone yard, our cove and the bay next to it. He sometimes went the other way, and down a really steep path near the holiday cottage. So he might be there."

"I think Tom's going to search in that direction – or he was until Delza disappeared," Jilly said thoughtfully. "But if

Benji is trapped in some way I doubt Tom would be able to do much about it."

"I could!" Davy said swiftly. "I've been down that particular path loads of times – and Becca has. If Benji is down there I'm sure I can coax him back up."

Jilly looked unsure. It might be dangerous – but what Davy did was not for her to say.

"Alex?" she said.

Nodding he said, "Worth a try as long as you take care, Davy. No heroics! Just good common sense!"

Davy, bright-eyed, asked with anticipation, "Shall I go now? It won't take me long. I'll race you home!"

"You'll do no such thing! You'll take care! Hear me?"

"Yes, Dad," he replied, only slightly chastened.

"There is just one thing, Davy," Jilly said, "Should you meet Tom, be tactful. He might be offended if he thought we had asked you both to look in the same area."

Looking perplexed Davy asked what he should say.

Alex suggested, "Ask him if he knows where I am."

"But I know where you are!" Davy said, missing the point.

Alex cocked his head.

Davy grinned. "Oh, I get it!" And, turning from them, he headed back through the wood.

When they were alone Jilly experienced a surge of misgiving about Davy.

"Should we have let him go alone? Will he be all right, Alex?"

"I hope so. He's usually sensible, but holding him back might have aroused too much curiosity."

"How do you mean?"

"Being where we are he might have asked too many questions. He doesn't know the full situation, and I don't want him to. My son has that rare trait known as gallantry, and I don't want it to lead him into danger. So while he's looking for Benji – doing a boy thing – he's not playing Sir Galahad."

Having clarified the situation he went on. "What do you want to do, Jilly? Shall we go forward, or turn back?"

She hesitated, undecided. She then found another aspect to consider. While Slade might recognise her, he did not know that she would recognise him – even if it *was* only from a photograph. To walk up to him, address him by name and see his shocked expression would give her enormous satisfaction. She knew it wasn't possible. It was too dangerous. But having the advantage bolstered her confidence.

"Let's go forward," she said. "I'd like to see Slade in the flesh."

"He might not be there," Alex warned." The place could be deserted."

"We'll see," she half smiled and silently they moved nearer to the clearing.

Pausing, they squatted behind the ferns, to watch and wait. There was a dank smell and an unreal silence. No birds sang and no breeze rustled the leafy tree tops.

The camper van appeared deserted although a gas cylinder was still connected to an inlet pipe.

Silently they watched and waited. Nothing stirred. A cloud of gnats swarmed around their faces. Impatiently Jilly wafted them away. They dispersed into a wild dancing cloud only to return and bite.

Jilly began to think they were on a fool's errand until the door of the camper van opened and a woman stepped into the sunlight. Shabbily dressed and unkempt, she shielded her eyes against the glare, scanned the site and returned indoors.

Then at the window Jilly saw someone else.

For one electrifying moment her world shook as her shocked cry was muffled with her hand.

Alex saw disbelief sweep her face as she sank against him.

Baffled he held her. What was wrong?

She made no reply.

Foreboding had become a reality, and words could not describe the shock.

Chapter Seventeen

Passing within yards of Arthur's cottage, Davy ran at full speed to the top of the cliff and, panting, peered over the edge. What he saw frightened him. Halfway down the crumbling path Tom was clinging to a tuft of grass as the path trickled from under his searching toes. Davy hovered uncertainly. Doom was written all over Tom's face. Davy knew that if Tom fell he would certainly die. He had to get help.

Tom was breathless and running out of strength. He'd been a fool to tackle the path. He knew it was unstable and dangerous. As a lad he had watched his friend slither and tumble to the bottom. He got away with a broken arm. Tom knew he wouldn't be so lucky. One false move and he could be dead. How much longer could he hang on? Letting go would be easy. But what would happen to Delza? He gripped the tuft of grass more tightly, and buried his face in the shifting soil. Despairing, and desperate for help, he then forced himself to look upwards.

Above him, dark against the blue sky he saw the crouching figure of Davy. Using what little breath he had Tom called out.

"Davy!" he gasped. "I'm stuck. I'm all out of breath. I can't move."

Davy remained crouched. Rigid with fear he knew he had to get help. He couldn't save Tom alone. Would Arthur know what to do? Would he have a rope?

Wordlessly he ran to find out.

Tom closed his eyes. His whole body had shut down. He no longer had the strength to hang on. Even his power of thought was slipping away. But he had to hold on for

Delza's sake. Pressing his feeble body against crumbling soil, forcing his tired brain to stay focused he struggled with the death wish. It would be so easy to just let go. The fight weakened him. He lost all sense of time. Numbness set in. He sighed. His head sagged. And darkness welcomed him.

The next thing he knew was Davy straddling his prone body and struggling to fasten a rope round his chest. The rope suddenly tightened and as Davy scrambled away Tom felt himself hauled inch by inch up the cliff face. The distance was short, but to Tom it was the longest journey ever travelled. As the rope crushed his chest, he feebly helped himself over the edge to sprawl gratefully at Arthur's feet.

Twenty minutes passed before Tom was able to get his trembling body under control. Sipping sweet tea under the watchful eye of Arthur, he was glad to be alive. Arthur could hardly believe Tom had gone to such lengths to search for Benji.

"What on earth made you tackle the cliff path, Tom?"

"I was worried in case the dog was down there and couldn't get back up."

"And a fat lot of good you would have been," Arthur said, not unkindly. "But it's understandable," he went on. "It's all to do with adrenalin. Once that gets going we think we are Superman and can take on any situation. Too late do we realise that we are mere mortals!"

"I'm old enough to know better," Tom said by way of self-recrimination. "Silly old fool! If anything had happened to me, what would have happened to Delza?"

Before Arthur could reply Davy said, "We found her shoe."

Tom looked at him sharply.

"Delza's shoe? Are you sure?"

"Jilly said it was Delza's. I found it on The Loop."

Tom's face fell into worry lines as he struggled unsteadily to his feet.

"I've got to get home," he said.

"Why? What's wrong?" Arthur asked.

"Delza's upset. She'll be in a state." His sketchy reply explained nothing.

"In a state about what?" Arthur pressed.

"Something'll have frightened her. It's best I get on. I'm grateful for all your help. But for you I might have been…" He floundered to find appropriate words and failed. Turning to Davy he said, "Tell your mum I'll see her in the morning."

Nodding to Arthur, moving unsteadily, he left without a backwards glance.

It was only then that Davy realised he and Arthur were alone. It was they who had rescued Tom – just the two of them. Where was Marilyn?

As if in answer to his question she walked in through the door.

"Where the hell have you been?" Arthur barked.

"To the shops. I told you! What's wrong with everyone? I've just seen Tom. Who's rattled his cage? "Heaving her heavy shopping bag on to the table she went on, "He totally ignored me!"

Briefly Arthur offered the reason.

Open-mouthed, Marilyn listened

"What next?" she asked."Benji's disappeared. Delza's having a panic and Tom almost kills himself." Turning to Davy she said she hoped he wouldn't do anything silly, and then asked where he'd looked for the dog.

"I went to The Narrows with Dad and Jilly."

"But he wasn't there, was he?"

Davy sighed and shook his head.

"Where are Alex and Jilly now?"

"I'm not sure," Davy shrugged. "But what if they spied out the camper van and it looked empty?"

"The birds could have flown," Arthur said morosely.

"Why should they?" Marilyn asked. "They haven't achieved anything yet."

"As far as we know."

"What d'you mean."

"We've lost track. Our net is so wide it's difficult to know how to haul it in. We know a lot, yet at the same time we know nothing."

"Such despondency!" Marilyn accused. "I know we keep getting sidetracked, but is the missing Benji a related issue? I doubt it. So why are we wasting precious time trying to find him? Other things are far more important."

Davy's face crumpled. Benji was a waste of time? He wasn't important?

Quickly Marilyn tried to cover her tactless remark.

"Davy, I'm sorry! Of course Benji is important! But there are other considerations. Think about it. How did all the problems begin? Is Benji part of the mystery, or is he just an adventurous dog?"

Davy, burdened by the questions, shook his head. He had no answer and didn't understand half of what was happening.

Arthur snapped, "Sarah! Let it go! He's a child!"

She shrugged and turned away. To be called Sarah meant she was on dangerous ground with Pop. He was tense and his point of explosion was very near the surface.

Arthur, frustrated by lack of progress and physically strained with helping Tom, swore under his breath. He could do without side issues. As for a lost dog and the diamonds, where was the connection? He couldn't see it.

Davy, cutting into his thoughts, said he wanted to go home.

Arthur said no.

"Stay with us until your Dad gets back, Davy."

"I've just bought some ice-cream," Marilyn said temptingly.

Davy stubbornly refused. He wanted to go home. That was what he told them, but his intention was to look further afield for Benji.

Finally, trusting his word, Arthur gave way.

Davy left feeling triumphant.

* * *

Tom found Delza on her bed rocking herself. A bad sign. Hurrying down to the kitchen he took the bun from the bread bin, put it in her favourite dish, and poured milk over it. She would enjoy that. Her red spoon she already had. It was on her blood-stained pillow. She'd been poking her gum again.

For a moment Tom perched on his rocking chair. He was weary. The incident on the cliff seemed to have robbed him of all resilience. Davy had been a really good lad. A life saver. Literally. If Tom had slipped – poor Delza. Her father wouldn't have cared. He was a rogue, and he was up to something. Mrs. Lang said she'd seen Hal hanging about The Cauldron on more than one occasion. She felt she was being watched. Why? She couldn't imagine. Tom could. Hal wasn't watching her. He was watching her dog. It wasn't a run-of-the-mill breed any more than Benji was. That was Hal's interest! Eventually he would have a lot to answer for.

Carrying the dish up to Delza's room he set it on her bedside table, then wiped her face with his handkerchief. She smiled at him. Her fears forgotten. She ate her milky bun being careful not to hurt her mouth with the spoon and listened as Papa told her he had found her shoe. Missus had it and tomorrow he would take Delza to see Missus and get her shoe back. That pleased Delza. It was a pretty shoe. It had a shiny button on it. Delza liked shiny buttons.

Papa was talking to her telling her what a good girl she was for eating up her milky bun. Later, if she was still a good girl, he would buy her some chips for supper.

Delza beamed. Delza liked chips.

★ ★ ★

Davy raced towards the cove. Instead of following the lane he kept to the clifftop bending low as he passed Jilly's cottage. If Dad saw him he might stop him. Davy had made up his mind to search meticulously. First the cove, then the cave and finally the bay. Benji could have been in all three or none of them. If there were tracks in the sand he could follow them. If? He should be so lucky! But there were tracks! Footprints belonging to small children, and shoe prints belonging to grown-ups. A family? They led down to the edge of the tide where the rising water had partly demolished a sand castle. The tracks moved towards the bay. Davy, realising he could be cut off by the tide if he followed, retraced his steps and turned towards the mouth of the cave.

There he found more prints belonging to the family. Pointing both in and out, they could have explored it.

He ventured as far as the craggy mouth feeling jittery. In the past whenever he'd been in the cave he had always been with Becca. Now, being alone, he found it creepy. The familiar smell of dankness, overlaid with an unfamiliar pungency he had smelled only once before. That was when some of the local lads held a beach party. Becca said it was stale beer. Davy wasn't so sure. Cautiously he stepped into the gloom. He knew there was nothing to be afraid of, so why was he scared?

Was there something living in the cave? Something awful which only Delza could see?

He paused. Why go in? There was nothing there except rocks! So why did he feel so uneasy? Hovering. Undecided. He suddenly squared his shoulders and plunged into the darkness.

Cautiously climbing, finding familiar footholds, his disquiet faded

Suddenly he slipped.

In his head he heard Becca's laughter.

A jagged rock gouged his knee but, protected by his jeans, it was no more than a graze. Resting for a moment he looked up into the cavernous height to see a faint line of light. That must be from where Delza looked down.

What did she see? Did she have special powers? Dad said the Cornish were a mystical race. Was mystical the same as magical? And did that mean that Delza really could see what others couldn't. Of course not! That was a stupid idea! That was the sort of thing Becca would dream up. No. When Delza looked into the cave she would see nothing. It was too dark. Looking back towards the mouth of the cave and the sunshine on the sand, it was where he wanted to be. There was nothing in the cave. There was nothing to see. And he hated the smell.

Again, in his head, he heard Becca's voice calling him a wimp.

Goaded, he reached and recoiled.

He slipped.

Clung.

Searched for purchase.

Panting.

Afraid.

He reached again.

Groping, he touched.

Shocked, he recoiled.

He touched again, felt soft fur and a warm tongue licked his hand. A nose butted him. He'd found Benji!

Tied by his lead to the mooring ring embedded in the rock he was on a narrow ledge without food or water, and he was shivering.

Excited and frightened, Davy fumbled to free him. Benji squirmed making small noises in his throat. Trying to keep him calm Davy talked gently as he struggled with the knotted leather lead. It was damp, swollen and each time Benji moved it tightened. Gradually and with shaking fingers Davy pulled it free of the ring and together they made a slow and precarious descent.

Emerging into the sunshine Davy blinked and came face-to-face with the menacing figure of Hal Polglise.

Terrified. Giving no thought to consequences, Davy, dragging Benji, ran to the water's edge and plunged into the surf. Towing the dog, not knowing if they would survive, he struck out and swam for the raft.

⋆⋆⋆

In the woods, Jilly pushed and backed away from Alex then blundered through the dense undergrowth, careless of the noise she made.

She said nothing.

She heard nothing.

She was white faced and dumb.

Moving swiftly and sinuously she dodged the trees.

Following her path Alex paused only long enough to call Arthur.

Jilly was in trouble. No time to explain. But Marilyn was needed.

On reaching The Narrows, Jilly's pace quickened.

Alex ran at her side.

She ignored him.

Talking was useless.

She paid no heed. All she did was run.

They reached the cottage.

The side door was ajar.

Jilly went straight to her room and slammed the door.

Marilyn burst in and cried, "Oh, My God!"

It was only then that Alex saw the chaos.

The kitchen was wrecked. Ransacked. Shelves cleared. Drawers emptied. Contents strewn. Pottery smashed. Papers scattered.

Stunned they stared at each other. What? who? Unknowing they started to salvage what they could.

Was Jilly's state of mind such that she hadn't even noticed?

Scooping up broken china Marilyn told Alex about the incident with Tom.

"Davy was really brave," she said.

Feeling both proud and angry Alex asked where Davy was.

"Is he with Arthur?"

Registering surprise, Marilyn replied, "No! We thought he would be with you."

Well, he wasn't!

Then where was he?

"He might have gone home," Alex said. "Sometimes when he's worried he goes to his room. I'll check him out in a minute."

"What about Jilly?" Marilyn asked. "Why is she in such a state?"

"I don't know. I can't get her to talk. She's seen and recognised something or someone but she won't say what. She seems shocked." He pushed his hands through his hair and said with agitation, "Look, I'm worried about Jilly, but I'm also concerned about Davy. I'm sure he's all right, but I do need to know. I don't want him wandering off. Will you stay here with Jilly?"

"Yes, of course. If Davy isn't home, do you want me to do anything?"

"Just take care of Jilly. If Davy has gone walkabout I'll check the cove and maybe the bay." He paused as if overwhelmed by indecision. "Maybe I should call the doctor first. It could be Jilly needs some kind of professional help."

"Leave her a while, Alex. I'll take care of her."

He stood, thumbs in waistband, gazing at the littered floor. All that smashed pottery! It would break Jilly's heart. Small ornaments, little vases, tiny containers all smashed beyond repair. The thought that any one of them could have held the key hit him in the pit of his stomach. The fact that no key would have been found hit him again. The intruders' frustration could lead to revenge. Smashing up a house was one thing – but people?

Would that be their next move?

* * *

Polglise, the non-swimmer, swore. The boy, the dog, both on the bobbing raft were beyond his reach. Furiously he hurled pebbles at them. His luck had run out. He hadn't found the key despite smashing everything he could lay his hands on. No key. No cash.

That key was valuable. A lot of people wanted it. If he could get it. They would pay.

Now this kid had just cost him even more money. Even though the Lang dog was in the pipeline and a Dandie Dinmont was on the cards, this dog was the real prize. And he'd lost it thanks to the kid. Now the kid was in big trouble! Staring at the raft with blazing eyes he flung a final pebble. It was nowhere near its mark! That served to fuel his already raging temper. Well, the kid couldn't stay there for ever. Eventually they'd have to come ashore. So he'd wait and get the kid and the dog later. Kicking off his trainers he decided to go back to The Narrows via the bay. It would save time and he wanted a word with Slade. Slade owed him money. The deal was that each time Hal carried out an order, Slade would pay him. Cash in hand. On the dot. That hadn't happened and Hal didn't like cheats. Rolling up his jeans as far as they would go, barefooted, he sloshed through the tide trying to avoid the breakers.

Shivering, Davy held on to Benji and watched Hal disappear.

Benji's leg was bleeding. Could he swim? Somehow they had to get back to the shore and while he knew he could manage the distance, could Benji? Dare he leave him on the raft and go for help? What if Polglise came back? Kneeling he held the shaking dog and talked to him while smoothing his wet coat.

A sudden shout from the shore made him look up.

His heart leapt with relief.

"Dad!" he yelled. "Dad!"

Pausing only to pull off his shoes, fully clothed, Alex plunged.

Strong strokes and foaming speed took him to the raft. Grasping the edge he shook water from his eyes, and looked into his son's face. Pale. Brave With only the slightest tremble of his bottom lip, Davy said,"Hi, Dad."

"Hi, son! You OK? Can you make it back to the beach?"

"What about Benji?" he asked through chattering teeth.

"He'll be fine! You go. We'll follow."

Davy dived and made for the shore.

Minutes later, looking seaward he saw his father, using a slow breaststroke, had Benji draped across his shoulders. The dog, held in place by its lead, started to struggle. Alex sank. Davy bordered on panic. Alex appeared spouting water, and moments later gasping and spluttering he reached firm sand, and crawled onto a patch of pebbles. Prone he looked up at Davy and grinned as Benji, dragging his lead, scampered off.

"I reckon he could have made it on his own," Alex said. "You all right, Davy?"

Silently Davy nodded not knowing what to say to the best Dad in the world.

They had both showered and changed into dry clothes before Davy told Alex why he had swum out to the raft with Benji.

"I didn't know how else to get away from Hal. He kept swearing and threatening and trying to get hold of Benji."

"You did the right thing, son. However, I think it can be our little secret for a while. Benji's home, and that's all that matters."

Davy looked doubtful and said, "He's wet."

"So? You found him on the beach, didn't you?"

Davy grinned.

Alex ruffled his hair and said, "I think you've had enough adventures for one day – yes – I know about Tom, too!"

Again Davy grinned. Life was quite exciting!

When Arthur arrived at Jilly's Marilyn had already swept and tidied the kitchen and Alex was examining a broken drawer.

"Can you mend it?" Arthur asked

Looking at it from all sides Alex said it wasn't a problem, but Jilly was. She had locked herself in her room. Marilyn had taken up a cup of tea leaving it on the landing where it remained.

Alex still felt the doctor should be called. He was deeply concerned at Jilly's lack of communication. No one knew who or what had triggered her reaction. How did one deal with the unknown?

"The doctor might be able to help – maybe get her to talk – to offload."

Marilyn suggested they wait until morning.

"Give her time, Alex. She obviously needs to be on her own. Once she's thought things through she will cope."

Alex finally agreed. Yes, Jilly would cope. If only she realised she didn't have to cope alone.

Davy was in the sitting room watching TV. Banished there by Alex he wasn't really interested in what was on the screen. He wanted to know about Jilly. What had happened to her? Dad said that once he knew then Davy would be told. Meanwhile he had to stay in the house. He'd had enough excitement for one day. Yes he had. Hal had really scared him.

Being near to his father made him feel safe. He turned back to the TV. News! Not again!

Benji, having been bathed, fed and watered was in his basket asleep. The open wound which had worried everyone appeared to be clean and healthy. Even so Alex didn't entirely discount a visit to the vet.

"Leave it for a day or two," Arthur suggested.

"Why are we all being so indecisive?" Alex growled. "We're doing nothing. We are in crisis and treating the situation almost flippantly."

Arthur shook his head understanding how Alex felt. He was at the same level. It was par for the course.

"We can do nothing until Jilly tells us what's bothering her. It's got to be something serious. It will need to be dealt with and she will have to decide how it is to be done. She has to make up her mind."

"I can't," she said in a small voice. Head bowed, standing in the doorway she looked lost and vulnerable. There was a childlike helplessness about her asking, not for sympathy, but for strength. She felt burnt out. Is that how shock affected people? Not that it mattered. She now knew that Becca was no longer in danger; Jilly was the victim and always had been She should have seen that from the beginning. Had fear robbed her of reasoning power? Was it part of the sinister game? Was she being manipulated?

Looking up with troubled eyes and a smile that was touchingly sad, she said, "I'm sorry I behaved so badly. I know it was the wrong thing to do. You were all there for me, and I pushed you away." A gentle colour washed her cheeks as she went on, "I'm now back to normal – at least I think I am."

Alex, visibly relieved, put his arm about her shoulders and led her to the table. As she sat down, she ran her hands over the well-scrubbed surface. Because it was solid and familiar it was a comfort.

Marilyn had found an unbroken bottle of wine on its side, and salvaged four glasses.

At least some things were untouched.

Jilly shook her head and shrugged. What was done could not be undone. Broken pottery was better than broken bones. She was saddened by the loss of one or two little treasures, other than that she appeared unworried.

Arthur stood hands in pockets gently rocking on his feet.

With his back to the window he looked at Jilly. Somewhere inside that pretty head lay the answer to the mystery that was plaguing them all. Because he knew there was always a pattern to a crime he was certain more action was to follow. Even though their wide spread net could be eventually tightened, whether or not it contained holes remained to be seen. They needed to get Jilly talking. Whatever it was she saw needed to be explained. It could be a red herring, or it could be a sprat!

Alex was now quietly talking to her, leading her gently back to the woods, and then taking her right back to the beginning. Finchley, Gloucestershire, Norfolk and Soho. Skilfully weaving all the strands, creating a warp which needed only the weft to hold it together. It was now down to Jilly. What she knew might not complete the picture, but an outline could guide them and maybe lead them to answers.

Toying with the stem of her glass, she swirled the remains of the wine and said wearily, "Nothing fits. If I've found the answer I still don't understand it." Looking at Alex she went on, "You saw the woman at the door of the camper van, didn't you?"

"Yes, I did, Jilly but I didn't recognise her."

"Neither did I," she said looking away.

Alex was stunned. He was sure it was the sight of the woman that caused Jilly to panic! Now confused he stumbled, "But I thought..."

Jilly gave a mirthless smile and looking at him said, "So did I! But it was the face at the window that I recognised."

"What face? I didn't see anyone."

"I did! It was Stenning!"

"Who the hell's Stenning?" Arthur barked.

"Guy Stenning. Mitzi's brother!" she said and buried her face in her hands.

Chapter Eighteen

It was midnight when Tom's 'phone rang. Delza, having sobbed herself to sleep, wakened mewing. Stumbling into Tom's bedroom she dragged the covers from his sleeping body. Pulling the bedding back he mumbled, "'Tis all right, my bird. 'Tis only the 'phone. Go back to bed like a good girl, and I'll bring you a drink in a minute."

Delza smiled. Papa would bring her some milk in her Mickey Mouse mug. Delza liked Mickey Mouse, and Rupert Bear and Pogo. Pogo tickled her face. She did not remember how he last looked only how he used to be, and so she smiled and wandered back to her bed.

Tom padded downstairs. After hitching his braces over his shoulders he then fastened the top button on his trousers. Whoever was ringing at this hour would be looking for help. Best be prepared.

Lifting the receiver he heard Dick Rogers say, "That you, Tom? I've been trying to get hold of Alex Hunter, but I can't find his number. Do you know it?"

"I've got Mrs. Kenworth's."

"No. That won't do." He paused and then went on, "I need to pass on a bit of news."

"What sort of news?"

"About Hal Polglise. You know he's been causing a bit of bother?"

"So tell me something I don't know!" Tom said tetchily.

"I will if you'll give me a minute," Dick said brusquely. "I've just been talking to my lad Bernard. He was on his way home from the pub when someone said the ambulance was at the harbour. Down he went and got there just as they was loading."

"What? A body?"

"In a black bag! That's what they do these days, isn't it?"

"Who was it, then?"

"Hal Polglise!"

"Never!"

"Barefooted too!"

"Get away! He never went near the tide unless he was on a boat."

"Could've fallen overboard. Been doing a bit of fishing."

"Who'd take him fishing? No one you or me could name."

"That's as maybe, but he's a goner. I know Mr. Hunter was having bother with him, so I thought to warn him."

"What for?"

"Well – what if he was the last one to see Hal alive?" he said with meaning. "And another thing, if it is Hal, will you tell Delza?"

"No point. 'er wouldn't understand. And you keep your mouth shut. What we knows about Hal and Delza is not for the ears of everyone, all right?"

"Course it is. Now, will you tell Mr. Hunter about Hal?"

"As long as Bernard's got it right."

"I don't think there's much wrong. No one's seen Hal since this morning and he hasn't been in the pub, so I reckon my lad knew what he was talking about. Hal's a goner all right."

And good riddance Tom thought as he hung up. He knew he should have been feeling sorry for the bloke. But how could he mourn someone who'd never done a good turn in his life? Even his death would inconvenience folk. Typical! His thoughts turned to Mrs. Kenworth. No point in waking her with that kind of news. Best leave it 'til the morning and then tell Mr. Hunter.

With his thoughts put to order he went into the cluttered kitchen yawning and scratching his head. After rinsing Delza's Mickey Mouse mug he half filled it with cold milk and went back upstairs, still yawning. It was likely she would be asleep. Best thing for her.

★ ★ ★

Earlier that evening Jilly's sitting room was airless. Everyone was sprawling and grey-faced with tiredness.

So much had been discussed. Every incident leading up to Richard's death and those beyond it had been analysed and slotted into Jilly's memory. Going back to the time before Richard's death had been difficult. Some memories were recalled with great clarity – some were shrouded. Then there were others. They fell into another category. They were taboo. Never visited or aired. They were just there. Indelible. A darkness of which Richard always made light. She never understood why. Maybe it was a man thing. A kind of perverse flattery. Glory-basking in the knowledge that other men, Guy Stenning in particular, were ardent admirers of Jilly. Richard could afford to watch. He knew she was his and always would be. He had nothing to worry about. Sometimes, when across the room, she silently begged him to rescue her, he would just smile and watch. He was confident she knew how to handle any man who overstepped the mark. What he didn't know was that Guy Stenning was a different animal. Charming, attentive, silver-tongued and forceful in a subtle way, Jilly became his obsession. She knew things were not right. Guy had an attitude that bordered on intimacy. His penetrating looks made her feel and look uncomfortable. Mitzi appeared not to notice, but gradually Jilly learned that Mitzi's devotion to Guy was unwavering. Whatever Guy wanted he could have.

Because of Richard's business commitments they all met frequently and Guy and Richard shared several lucrative deals. If only Guy's relationship had remained at that level, but it didn't. Each time he met Jilly, irrespective of where or when, he blatantly sought her company. He once tried to give her a single uncut diamond. She refused it. He merely smiled a smile that said her refusal was unacceptable. He would try again.

Not wishing to spoil her burgeoning friendship with Mitzi she said nothing about Guy's behaviour and dealt with it as firmly and tactfully as she could.

Now, with the memories crowding in, she looked at Alex with troubled eyes and went on, "Then a few weeks before Richard died we threw a dinner party inviting mainly business associates, with just a few chosen friends to lighten the atmosphere. Although Mitzi was welcome, Guy wasn't, but I felt he still had to be invited." Here Jilly paused as her face shadowed with pain. Her audience sat in apprehensive silence wondering what was to follow. When she finally spoke her voice was low and flat.

"It was an incident I have been unable to forget. Guy was drunk. I was careless and unguarded."

Sensing her discomfort Alex cut in, "Jilly, you don't have to go on."

"I do," she said quietly. "I need to. This ghost has to be laid." She paused again and then went on in a stronger voice, "One of our lady guests, while standing on the terrace, had dropped her glass of wine. She bent to pick up the pieces and cut her finger. I was on the terrace with Guy, who was being his usual manipulative self. Mitzi had just returned indoors.

"Obviously, although the injury was minor, I had to take care of my guest. After bathing her hand in the downstairs cloakroom, I went upstairs to find a plaster. Guy followed me into the bathroom then slammed and bolted the door. I don't want to talk about what happened next. Sufficient to say that he and Mitzi left in a hurry.

"I thought that would mark the end of the friendship between Mitzi and myself – but no. She rang the following day to apologise for Guy's behaviour and promised that in future he would behave himself. She then told me she had decided to live in France permanently, instead of constantly crossing the channel as she did before her husband died. Guy was going to help her to move into a new property, and then he intended to remain abroad and freelance as a courier. I was left with mixed feelings. Sorry to lose Mitzi. Relieved to lose Guy. But for a while we lost touch altogether, then after Richard died our friendship was resumed – but – without Guy! He was building a reputation for himself, and travelling worldwide, which left little time for socialising."

Marilyn asked how, if he was so busy, he'd managed to get himself engaged to the daughter of a French village mayor?

Jilly gave a bleak smile, "He's a man of great charm, and his home base was with Mitzi. Presumably he spent just enough time doing social rounds to make his mark. It wouldn't have been difficult. Handsome, well-connected and on the face of it a good catch, any girl would have her head turned."

"So why is he over here getting involved in something pretty nasty?" Alex asked.

"And another thing," Marilyn cut in, "If he's lost interest in you, why is he trying to harm you?"

Alex shafted in, "And what about Mitzi? Does she know what's going on?"

"No!" Jilly said vehemently. "We are really close friends! She's even offered to come and stay with me. You know she has, Alex! I spoke to her only the other day."

"And where was she?" Alex asked.

"At home. In France!"

"Are you sure?"

"Of course I'm sure!" Jilly said angrily.

"What are you getting at, Alex?" Arthur asked, his head to one side.

"I don't know. I'm just exploring intersecting avenues."

"Leading where, and to whom?"

Before he could reply Jilly said harshly, "Don't include Mitzi! Guy, yes! Mitzi, no."

The atmosphere was tense

Arthur and Alex exchanged glances.

They were asking themselves the same probing questions.

Was Mitzi somehow involved? If so, how and why?

Jilly's face had taken on colour. She was angry.

Mitzi was her friend. How dare Alex try to condemn her.

She would listen no more. She would not allow a friendship to be destroyed no matter what.

Standing up, looking at each face with hostility, she said, "I hope you can all live with yourselves." Turning, she said over her shoulder, "Mitzi is a true friend!"

Alex, unprepared for such intensity, said, "Jilly, wait."

"It's late," she told him coldly. "I'm tired and I'm going to bed."

With that she walked out of the room.

Helplessly Alex spread his arms letting her go. There was nothing else he could do.

* * *

To Jilly the hours of darkness were lonely, but her sense of isolation forced her to make decisions. The shock of seeing Guy had left her world rocking. Getting back on to an even keel was difficult, but in the quiet of her room she was beginning to think with a level head.

Guy: charming, obsessed and manipulative. Was he also vengeful? Was this his revenge because she had rejected his advances? Surely not! Didn't all men suffer rejection at some time? Wasn't it part of life's pattern? But did rejection turn them into fiends – murderers? No! They moved on to other targets! Mitzi couldn't know what was happening.

Although she seemed to control Guy it wasn't for reason of exacting power, it was because he was deeply loved. What he delighted in – so did she. If he was hurt – she felt his pain. Jilly's speeding thoughts skidded to a halt. The incident in the bathroom? But that had been long ago. It had no bearing. Guy was now engaged. Would he still carry a grudge? Would he plot and scheme? Jilly shivered. Yes, he would! Would Mitzi? No! Mitzi was not from the same mould. But Guy was her adored brother! Could there be a dividing line over which Mitzi would cross? It was possible. Again Jilly shivered. Was she being a blind fool? There was only one way to find out. She had to tackle the situation head on and expose the truth. But how? Thinking deeply while tossing and turning there seemed to be no answer. Then finally a simple idea fell into place. Buoyed by optimism and with a sense of achievement she drifted into sleep leaving behind her sense of foreboding.

The sun-streaked dawn found her energised, and eager to put her ideas into practice. Should she discuss them first? It might be naïve not to do so.

Alex had a probing mind, Arthur's had years of experience. They would offer advice. Marilyn, on the basis of all girls together, would be supportive. If she'd got it all wrong she'd just have to re-think the issue. The only thing that worried her was Davy. She wanted him out of the way. Sometimes he could be a little hot-headed and that could have consequences. Where could one send a boy to keep him out of harm's way? Why not out to sea? On the Blue Gull? Weather permitting? A day's fishing? What if Hal was crewing? Not a good idea. What about Tom? Sometimes he took Delza to one of the beaches for the day. If she gave him time off, would he take Davy, too?

Would Alex let him go? Of course he would. Tom may be old but he was reliable. She would ask him. He could refuse, but somehow she didn't think he would.

The next thing was how to pull everything together to make it all happen in sequence.

⋆ ⋆ ⋆

They were at breakfast when Tom, holding Delza's hand, arrived earlier than usual and looking solemn. Delza cowered as Benji hopped out of his basket to scuttle past her into the garden.

Tom said, "Delza, my bird, you go to the shed and twirl the pedals on the bike. I'll be with you d'reckly. Go on, now. Don't worry about the dog. He's gone up to the front gate."

Fearfully Delza ambled away.

Tom looked at Jilly and said, "I got a bit o' news, Missus. Bad news what's good news."

Jilly looked puzzled.

Tom went on. "'Tis Hal Poglise. Been found drowned."

Davy dropped his spoon.

"Say nothing!" Alex hissed.

Jilly looked stunned. Hal dead? He couldn't be. He was connected to Richard's death.

They had proof. If Hal was dead would he be left to carry the entire blame? Would the others get away, literally, with murder?

She stared at Tom not knowing what to say.

He stared back at her, his rheumy eyes full of understanding.

"'Tis a bit of a shock, but no great loss." He shuffled uncomfortably and said, "I'll get on, Missus. Got a bit o' catchin' up to do. Weeds don't stop growin' just 'cos my Delza 'ad face-ache."

He walked away, looking more bent than usual.

Jilly slumped into her chair and murmured, "Hal dead? I can't believe it!"

There was an electrifying silence, and before Alex could stop him Davy had blurted out the whole incident of the previous day.

Jilly looked stunned as Davy, red-faced, dropped his head and said, "Sorry, Dad."

Jilly finally said, "Alex?"

Abruptly he cut in saying sharply, "That's an incident we must forget. There's bound to be an investigation and I don't want Davy involved. If, in due course, everything leads back to us then we will have to deal with it. Until that time we know nothing. OK?"

Jilly agreed. It was the wisest course. She then added, "We'll have to tell Arthur and Marilyn. After all the incident might be relevant. Maybe Hal's death will take the pressure off us."

"I wouldn't count on it," Alex said grimly

Benji limped in from the garden with soil on his nose and the hairy seed heads of herb-bennet clinging to his coat. Davy, carefully picking them off, asked if he should take the dog to the vet adding, "His leg doesn't look much better. Maybe that's my fault for making him swim to the raft."

Alex said sharply, "Davy! What did I tell you? That incident never happened."

Shame-faced Davy mumbled, "Sorry, Dad. I forgot."

To soften what she saw as an edgy situation Jilly said a visit to the vet might be a wise move.

"Benji is a bit subdued so, if it's all right with you, Alex, Davy taking Benji will save me a trip, yes?"

"Put like that, how can I refuse?" Alex said mellowing. "All right, Davy, just be careful this time, we don't want to lose him again."

"Shall I tell the vet he went into the sea?" Davy asked unsurely.

"Yes, if he asks. But don't tell him why."

Within minutes of Davy leaving, Arthur and Marilyn arrived to be shocked by the news of Hal's death. The possibility that Davy could have been the last person to see him alive gave Arthur food for thought.

"Ah, complications could arise," he said, wise from past experience. "We don't want Hal's death to lead the police in this direction."

"I don't see why it should – not if his death was accidental," Jilly said.

"The police always have to probe," Arthur told her darkly, "particularly if the victim has a record. Sexual offences can breed and lead to revenge. Hal could have been got at. Who's to know?"

Jilly said impatiently, "Look, before we get bogged down in a hypothesis concerning Hal, I really need to run ideas past you."

"Apropos, what?" Alex asked.

"Guy Stenning!"

As she spoke his name, she was filled with self-doubt. Was she being impractical? Had the security of her darkened room led her, blindly, to contemplate an idea that was impossible?

Now was the time to find out.

Taking a deep breath she said, "I want to ask Mitzi to come and stay with me."

The atmosphere tightened.

"And then what?" Arthur asked.

"Tell her about Guy."

Hurriedly Alex said, "Hold your horses! You know what's at stake, don't you, Jilly?"

"Yes, I do," she told him levelly. "And I'm prepared. If Guy is proved to be mentally unstable, I know he could be extremely dangerous."

"And out of control."

"This is why I must ask Mitzi for help. She knows how to handle him."

"But will she help? If you tell her he is involved in serious crime, will she believe you? And if she does, will she want to go against him? Will she be strong enough to do that?"

"I don't know," Jilly admitted. "I'm just hoping that when she sees that he is a very sick man, then she will do what is best for him."

"Which might be to defend him! But whichever way it goes you will lose her friendship," Alex predicted sombrely.

"I know," Jilly said on a sigh of regret," But I have no option. She has to know what is happening, and it's better I tell her. To let her just find out would be too cruel."

"It's a big gamble," Arthur said. "She may choose to disbelieve you."

"Her argument being?"

Arthur shrugged, "Pure defence in the guise of blind family loyalty."

"That suggests Mitzi, too, could be unstable?" Marilyn offered.

"Don't be so ridiculous!" Jilly said hotly. "Mitzi is the most down-to-earth person I know. And even intense loyalty would not preclude her from acting in Guy's best interests. And that covers her having to accept the truth about him!"

Calmly Alex suggested they just take one step at a time, adding. "And if we slip we'll be prepared and have time to recover. When were you thinking of contacting Mitzi?"

Picking up her mobile she switched it on and said, "Right now."

Mitzi answered almost at once.

Jilly asked her if she would come to Cornwall.

Of course! If Jilly needed help then she would give it.

Mitzi went on, "The last time we spoke I knew there was something wrong. You sounded so worried. It's all to do with a key? Which you've found and someone else wants? It all sounds very mysterious. We'll sort it. I can be with you tomorrow. I'll ask a neighbour to run me to the airport."

"Can't Guy do it?" Jilly asked, her heart hammering.

Mitzi's voice crackled along the line.

"Guy's in the States closing a big deal. He's been negotiating for months."

Jilly felt her blood run cold, but she kept calm.

"That's a pity," she said. "Having a man around would make us safe."

Comfortingly Mitzi said, "I'll ring him later! If he's closed the deal I'm sure he'll fly to the UK to be with us. It might take a day or two, but I know he'll do what he can to help – if Collette will let him!"

"His fiancée? Possessive?"

"Very! But nothing he can't handle! Now leave me to find out about flights, and I'll ring you as soon as I'm organised. Try not to worry."

"Thanks, Mitzi."

"No thanks needed, Jilly. We are friends and friends help each other."

Comforted but pale-faced, Jilly laid down the 'phone and said, "Mitzi's under the impression that Guy is in the States negotiating a business deal."

"And she believes him?" Alex asked.

"She has no reason not to," Jilly told him. "He's a courier. He does deals. He travels. Why question?"

Alex shrugged. For a family who were believed to be close, there was now a doubt hanging over them. If Guy could lie and deceive his sister, what would he do to Jilly?

Davy arrived with Benji to say his leg was on the mend and the vet was pleased with his progress. Putting the lead on the hook behind the door, Davy went on "The waiting room was packed. Dogs, cats, birds, there was even a tortoise. Everyone was talking about Hal! He paused and looked at his father. "I didn't say anything, Dad. I just listened. Someone said a rowing boat was missing and that Hal could have taken it to go fishing. Maybe I wasn't the last person to see him alive."

That we may never know, Alex thought.

Jilly said, hopefully, "I think with Hal out of the equation the pressure will ease off."

"I doubt that will happen," said Arthur matter-of-factly "Hal's demise does not devalue the worth of the diamonds. If anything it increases them. Fewer people to take larger cuts."

Alex said, "What really worries me is what will happen when they learn the truth? When they discover the stones are not in the bank?"

"We have to make sure they don't. Not until it suits us," Arthur said.

"This is where we really need Mitzi!" Jilly pointed out. "This is where I have to persuade her that the picture I paint is in true colours."

"Easier said than done," Arthur said mournfully.

"I'm sure Mitzi will be on our side," Jilly said with conviction. "And I'm equally sure she will know how to handle Guy."

"What about the others? Slade, his brother and is it Smith the secretary? It's not a one-man show," Marilyn said thoughtfully. "They'll all have some kind of input. And all be holding out their sticky palms for rewards."

"And if it leads to fighting among thieves – couldn't be better," Arthur said with glee. His expression of mischief made everyone smile and the tension eased.

Alex said to Jilly, "As Mitzi could be on her way fairly soon, your idea about asking Tom to have Davy for a few hours might be a good one. The fewer faces around the better. In fact just you and Mitzi, might be the best way."

The house 'phone rang to startle everyone.

Nervously Jilly answered. There was the usual silence. Involuntarily she shivered. As it wasn't Hal on the line, was it Guy? Was he taking some kind of sadistic pleasure from the situation? She thought it very possible.

Feeling enclosed by danger she immediately thought of Davy. After a brief word with Alex she went into the garden to find Tom. Davy had to be in a safe place for a little while. Intuitively she knew Tom understood the urgency. His rheumy eyes told her so. His suggestion was better than she could have hoped for – his sister had a chicken farm Padstow way. They could all stay there for a day or two. If it suited everyone they could leave later that day.

"My sister, Morva, won't mind if we just arrive. Her'll be glad of the company. I dare say Davy will make himself useful collecting eggs. Delza do love doing that. All free-range. None of your cooped-up-in-cages rubbish, so it's a case of hunting in the hedges. Hens is not fussy about where they do lay.

"Yes, Missus. The lad'll be fine with us. Just pack him some jeans and a couple of T-shirts and maybe some wellies. It do get a bit muddy after a splash of rain."

And so it was arranged.

The ease with which everything was settled amazed everyone. Alex was visibly relieved. Davy's safety, after the raft incident, was an acute source of worry. For the problem to have been solved so quickly was a blessing.

Davy did not see it that way and sulkily said he didn't want to go. He wanted to stay and share the action. And Delza wasn't much fun to be with, he added scowling.

"Maybe she thinks the same about you," Alex told him lightly. "In any case it's only for a day or two."

"Can I take Benji?"

Alex scornfully raised one eyebrow.

"Delza, free-range hens, and a dog? Not a good idea."

Davy gave a sheepish grin. It was a rotten idea but it was worth a try.

Once Davy had left, a full discussion of Jilly's plan could be completely open. Spread out in the sitting room they all looked at ease, although the atmosphere belied the calm. Moving into the unknown was never easy for anyone but the apprehension was shared.

Jilly said in a low voice, "The hardest part will be telling Mitzi that her beloved brother has lied to her. That he is nowhere near America, but he is here. She will be deeply hurt."

"Less hurtful than your taking her to the woods and letting her see for herself," Alex said. "That would be a total shock. At least telling her face-to-face can be done gently. It's still going to hurt, though."

"If she believes you," Arthur said with doubt." She might not and then lash out verbally if not physically. Which ever way it goes Guy is in serious trouble."

"This is why she must know the full story, "Jilly said.

"Beginning to end?" Alex asked.

"Yes! I need her to understand – even get her sympathy. Perhaps then…" her voice tailed away and she stared at the floor in silence.She was hoping for a miracle while building on shifting doubts.

"Meanwhile," Alex said, "We have to get through the day. It might pay to sit tight until we know Mitzi's plans, and then we can move on. Any comment, Arthur? Any words of wisdom?"

"No," he said, clasping his hands behind his head and stretching out his legs. "Let's just stick together."

The house 'phone rang.

Silence.

It no longer had a deeply telling effect. It was so much part of life that little notice was taken. Even so Jilly's palms were damp. She was dreading Mitz's call and her eventual arrival. She hated the thought of confrontation. She could not imagine what the revelation would do to Mitzi, or how to deal with her inevitable reaction.

Her mobile rang.

Sudden happiness surged as she heard Becca's voice. The cold she thought she had was no more than a sniffle.

"The doctor was nice, Mom. He gave me a lollipop. Can I talk to Davy?"

His absence led to questions and Jilly had the feeling that Becca thought she was missing out on an adventure.

"It's a chicken farm. Becca," Jilly laughed. "He's not going to be branding bulls or riding wild mustangs."

"What are mustangs?"

Sidestepping Jilly said, "Let me speak to granny."

When granny came on the line she unwittingly solved a problem.

"Jilly, I meant to tell you we are due to dock tomorrow evening."

Before Jilly's heart had time to sink, her mother went on, "Can we take Becca home with us? It's the church fête on Sunday and Becca really wants to go to it. She wants to be in the Fancy Dress Parade."

"What as? What will she wear?"

"I've still got your fairy costume. The one you wore when you were about Becca's age."

"Becca as a fairy?" Jilly laughed. "I can't quite see it but – if that's what she wants to do."

"Oh, she does! She's so excited. And you don't mind her staying with us for a few more days?"

"As long as everyone is happy," Jilly told her.

"Then we'll ring you and tell you if she wins a prize. You did. So history might repeat itself." She then paused and went on to ask in a lowered tone, "Are you all right, Jilly? You sound – er – stressed?"

"I'm tip-top! Benji's been a bit off-colour but he's better now. Life is really good."

"If you're sure," her mother said uncertainly.

"Mummy, don't fuss! Everything is fine."

After ringing off, Jilly reflected that if her mother could sense things were not quite right, would Mitzi do the same?

It was agreed that until Mitzi's time of arrival was known they would remain at Jilly's.

After that Alex would move back into his own cottage, giving Jilly and Mitzi the privacy Jilly wanted. Arthur and Marilyn would return to their cottage, from where Arthur would keep watch.

Meanwhile, Arthur settled down to snooze.

Jilly and Marilyn occupied themselves with chores. Linen changing and dusting being a necessity.

Alex was restless and unable to settle down.

Time dragged.

Twice the 'phone rang, followed by the usual silence.

The only certainty that came out of that situation was that Hal was not the perpetrator.

Jilly now wondered if he ever was.

Needing something to do, Alex asked if he could look at the damage on Jilly's dressing box. Going to her room, she collected it and, returning to Alex, set it down in front of him.

Viewing it with expert eyes he said, "It shouldn't be too difficult to put right. Spilled perfume usually does no more than superficial damage to wood. The biggest problem is the logo. Where the perfume has filled and laid in the hollows, the polish has been stripped."

Arthur roused to ask how that logo ended up on what looked to be an antique box.

Alex said he didn't know, but he did know Drake did wood carving as a hobby. "And frankly," he went on, "this does look a little amateurish. Maybe he did it as a favour to Richard. But that's a guess."

Marilyn asked about clean linen for Becca's room.

"I'm presuming that's where Mitzi will be sleeping. So what do I want? Duvet cover? Linen and towels?"

"All in the airing cupboard, which reminds me – Pogo! I must get his innards. It's time he was put back together."

With that they both went upstairs.

Jilly was in the bathroom folding clean towels when Marilyn called out to ask if she could look at the photograph album on Becca's bedside table.

"Help yourself," Jilly called back. "Most of the pictures were taken by Becca, mainly of Benji and Pogo so don't look for artistic merit. Everything is labelled, so read about what you don't recognise."

A long-ago memory slipped into Jilly's mind. Richard had bought the camera for Becca when she was seven. It was expensive and not really a toy. Richard didn't care. Nothing was too good for Becca. He always wanted her to have the best of everything. And she did. She was also taught values. Consequently she took care of things. Maybe the pictures weren't all that good. Heads and paws were often missing, but the camera was faultless in its detail. The only crisis was when Richard insisted that Becca should buy her own films and pay for developing and printing. That caused foot-stamping and tears for several minutes, after which Becca went happily to the local chemist clutching her used film.

Misty-eyed, Jilly remembered. It was all such a long time ago.

"Jilly!"

Startled by Marilyn's voice Jilly turned towards the door.

Marilyn stood rigidly clutching Becca's album in both hands, her face strained.

"Marilyn? What's wrong?"

Dumbly she shook her head.

Jilly, draping the towel she was holding over the edge of the bath, took the album from Marilyn's nerveless fingers and said, "What?"

Marilyn, her eyes wide in disbelief, said in a barely audible whisper. "The woman I saw at the camper van. The day I wore the ginger wig. Her picture's in Becca's album!"

Chapter Nineteen

Morva Pascoe shielded her eyes against the glare of the late afternoon sun. In the distance, moving along the farm lane, a cloud of dust was enveloping a car. That was Tom for sure. How many times had she told him about speeding along the track? It scared the hens, they refused to lay and she lost an income that could never be made up.

Still, it would be nice to have a bit of company for a day or two. Vaguely she wondered who the young boy was. Tom hadn't said. Not that it mattered. A drop of young blood to collect the eggs would take the strain from her back. And it was a strain. She was getting too old to be crawling under bushes in search of the big, brown eggs for which she was well known. Let a lad do it.

Delza would be a joy. Poor love. She was the child Morva had always wanted. It might have been – once. That was years ago. When she found out the man she worshipped had been doing to other girls as he did to her, Morva whipped him with her tongue and sent him packing. After that no man had his way with her. Delza was her substitute child. Morva had the knack of keeping her happy. She found the time to play with her and read stories from the books which once belonged to her dead mother. Strange how Delza remembered them. She never remembered much else. Not that she could say, but she could give a look that was full of words.

Later, after the fuss and excitement of settling the children in. After answering all the question young Davy asked. After they finally went to bed, Morva produced a bottle of whiskey, and poured out two generous tots. The house was quiet. The lime-washed walls, streaked pink by the last rays of the sun, glowed comfortingly. Quietly Tom told Morva about Hal.

The news was met with an indifferent shrug.

"He was a bad lot! Got what he deserved! Though in my book the sea was too good a place for him to die in. Let the Devil have him and good riddance! What's going to happen to his cottage?"

"It's Delza's by rights. She's his next of kin."

"Got it sorted, have you?"

"Years ago."

"What will she do with it?" Morva asked scathingly." She can't look after herself never mind a cottage. Even if it is only a two-up, two-down with an outside lavvy."

"You do always jump to the wrong conclusions, our Morva!" Tom sighed. "I've worked it all out. When it's legally hers I'll sell it and put the money in the building society. When I'm gone she's still got to be cared for and with a bit o' money behind her she should be all right."

"As long as another Hal don't come along!" Morva warned.

"Oh, no! It'll all be done legal" Tom told her cannily. "No one will get their hands on it except Delza and even that will be only bit by bit."

Morva gave him a quizzical stare.

"How do you know about all this legal stuff? How d'you work it all out?"

Tom laughed, winked and sipped from his glass.

"Jilly Kenworth do tell me a lot and I do listen to her. She do understand about Delza."

"As long as you know what you're doing, our Tom! In any case, should the Good Lord take you before he do take me then our Delza'll live with me."

"I'd thought about that," Tom said slyly, "So I made provisions for that, too!"

Morva laughed, showing cream and brick-red dentures.

"You're taking me for granted, you cheeky old sod!"

"Takes one to know one," Tom laughed back.

* * *

Jilly's eyes, glistening with unshed tears, gazed at the snapshot. It was a coloured, clear, close-up of Mitzi. Shocked and angry, she said nothing. The hurt was too deep for words. The picture was familiar. She even remembered when it had been taken. It was the day of the toy telephone. The last picture on the film. Posted back to the UK on the same day. Jilly wanted to wait. Becca didn't. And so it was sent home from France.

Now Arthur said, "It looks to me as if this vendetta started some long time before Richard's death."

"For what reason?" Jilly asked in despair.

"An act of revenge?" Alex offered. "Except it was an act that went too far."

"You mean it isn't against me?" Jilly queried.

"Well, I suppose it is now – but only because you are in the way."

"How d'you work that out?" Marilyn asked

When Alex replied he did so in measured tones.

"This is how I see it. Richard was a top man in his field. He and Jilly had an excellent lifestyle. They mixed with the right people and were seen in the right places. What an achievement to knock him down! To rob him of his status, his business, by having him branded as a thief. Who would believe him when he pleaded to the loss or theft of millions of pounds worth of diamonds? He was well-known for his meticulous planning and safety measures but – even if he was believed – his image would have been tarnished. Who would have trusted him? No one."

"But why would Mitzi be party to such a vicious act? Robbery is one thing but murder?" Marilyn said.

"I think it could be because of the bathroom incident – in part," Jilly offered, hesitantly.

"In part?" Alex said.

"Yes, there has to be more to it than that."

"D'you think you will ever know the true reason?" Marilyn asked with doubt.

"Oh, yes!" Jilly said steely-voiced. "Eventually I'll find out."

"How?" Alex asked.

Jilly said in a flinty voice, "With lies, duplicity, and deceit."

"To give as good as you get?"

"Absolutely. I'll expose Mitzi for what she is: a thieving liar!"

There was a heavily-laden silence and uncomfortable shifting. This was an unfamiliar Jilly. There was a harshness about her. She seemed to be harbouring some kind of plan that no one could even guess at.

Finally she said, her voice brittle, "I intend to give her the key…"

There were audible gasps.

"…for safe keeping. I will give it to her on trust. I will tell her nothing of importance. I won't mention Pontivy, Slade or Hal. All she will learn is that threats have been made over the 'phone and there have been intruders in the house. I will tell her that you have all been supportive but you know nothing of the true situation."

"And the lack of police intervention?" Alex asked.

"They were not called because, apart from a broken window, I could prove nothing."

Arthur, sounding foxed, could understand that point but couldn't see the point in parting with the key.

"I'm playing a long shot," Jilly told him. "Because of the business connection I'm pretty sure Guy uses the same bank. That means he too could have a key to a safe deposit box"

"And access to the vault," Alex added.

"Ah! Now I see what you're getting at," Arthur smiled. "Mitzi will give the key to Guy and he…" Arthur came to an abrupt halt. "Hang on a minute, what happens next? What if she doesn't give the key to Guy?"

"That's the tricky bit," Jilly confessed. "But I think it will work out."

Although it was agreed the plan was incomplete and what existed was sketchy, it was also agreed it could be workable. After reaching that point they each remained with their own thoughts.

Later, when Jilly and Alex were alone, the subject was brought up again, and they tried to anticipate what could go wrong.

Alex said, "You seem fairly sure about Mitzi giving Guy the key?"

"I've got my fingers crossed," she told him with a hesitant smile. "If my theory is right, and Mitzi runs true to form she will pass the key on. But it is a gamble."

"So," Alex continued," Guy has the key and he goes to the bank alone. Once there he opens Richard's box. What does that prove?"

"That he illegally accessed the property of a dead man."

"And if Mitzi is with him?"

Jilly blinked. She hadn't thought of that.

Alex said, "As you gave her the key in the first place, that could be interpreted as permission to use it, then there would be no case to answer."

"Maybe not, but what about shock value?" Jilly asked with sudden inspiration. "They are expecting to find diamonds. Imagine the fury – the shattered dreams – when they find the box empty."

"I suppose the idea will work providing Guy also uses that bank. The situation is hanging by a thread and…" He reached for and held Jilly's hands, "…an empty box proves nothing. With nothing to steal, no one can be accused of theft."

Withdrawing her hands to anxiously wring them Jilly said, "I know, but looking ahead, if Guy does go alone and I'm sure he will, when he tells the others the box was empty, will he be believed? They know he lies and schemes, why should they trust him?"

"When you say 'the others' you mean Slade and the other woman who could be the secretary who we know as Smith?"

Jilly nodded.

Alex went on, "And you're hoping that when Guy turns up empty-handed the thieves will fall out!"

"Oh, yes!" she said fervently, "I'm also hoping to discover the unknown element. There has to be one. All this mayhem can't be resting merely on the bathroom incident, can it?"

"Maybe an unstable mind has a distorted view on what is right and wrong. Perhaps Guy saw you as a possession he had lost."

"But that's insane!" she protested.

"Isn't Guy?"

Jilly's skin turned cold at the thought.

During the course of this conversation Alex had been exploring Jilly's dressing box, examining more carefully the damage done by the spilled perfume. One by one he had removed the silver-topped jars, then lifted the fitted tray, beneath which lay several documents.

"They are the usual things," Jilly explained. "Birth and marriage certificates – and death," she added, her face bleak.

"And what's in the pocket in the lid?"

"My school photographs. And, no! You cannot look at them. I was buck-toothed, straggly-haired and skinny!"

"No change there, then!"

Playfully she slapped him.

"And what about the secret drawer? Does that also hold telling evidence of your girlhood?"

Jilly's face was blank.

"Secret drawer? What secret drawer?"

Alex's eyebrows lifted with surprise, and then lowered into a frown.

"D'you mean to tell me you don't know about it?"

Jilly shook her head.

"Richard never mentioned it. Perhaps he didn't know about it either. Show me."

Alex pulled a silver filigree knob on the lip of the box and removed a long, slender spindle. As he did so a shallow, velvet-lined tray slid into view."

Jilly gasped and smiled.

"Wow! I had no idea. That is amazing!"

Lifting that tray Alex revealed yet another compartment in which lay an envelope marked 'Jilly'.

Astounded, Jilly stared at it. Instantly her throat tightened with anguish. Her name, boldly written in black, felt-tip, was in Richard's hand and dated the day before he died.

The house 'phone rang.

Jilly sat, unable to move.

The ringing shafted, knife-like, into her head.

She winced.

"Jilly," Alex said gently. "You must answer it."

As if in a dream she went into the hall.

"Jilly? It's Mitzi. It's all arranged. I'm booked on an early flight tomorrow. I can get a connection to Newquay, and then take a taxi to you. I'll be with you in time for lunch. Is that all right?"

"Perfect," Jilly said, her voice flat.

"What's wrong? You sound odd."

Making a supreme effort Jilly forced lightness into her reply.

"I'm amazed that you were able to organise everything so quickly. What about Guy?"

"He'll be here as soon as possible. He sends his love and says you are not to worry about anything. We'll look after you."

And how! Jilly thought as she rang off.

Having listened to Mitzi's lies Jilly's reaction was not what she thought it would be. She had expected to be consumed by rage, hostility or even hatred. She felt nothing except a deep calm. Now she knew who her enemies were. She didn't care about their reasons. She wasn't even curious. Returning to Alex, with a hand that was steady she picked up the envelope bearing her name and carefully tore it open.

* * *

The camper van was stifling, the atmosphere tense. Mitzi, her blouse undone to expose her ample cleavage, laid her 'phone down, picked up yesterday's newspaper and gently wafted herself.

Smiling with satisfaction she said, "No problems! All we have to do now is kill time until tomorrow. Guy, you can then run me to the nearest cab stand where I can pick up a taxi and arrive suitably travel-weary at Jilly's door."

Guy scowled and said nothing.

"Pity about Hal," Slade said, having heard the news on the local radio station, "We've lost our fall guy."

"We don't need him," Mitzi said. "No one knows anything. That part's over and done with."

Slade gave a half smile and nodded. Yes, it was in the past as was Richard's death. He regretted that, even though

Richard was an oddball. He was fanatical about safety, and always tight-lipped. But he slipped up. That was how Slade met Mitzi. He was escorting Richard to a meeting with Mitzi's husband. She was there, and Slade held open the door for her. It was as casual as that. But something between them clicked.

Now here he was, almost two years and two dead men later, still hooked.

He was sweating profusely. Heat didn't agree with him. Except the steaming moments he shared with Mitzi. And her voluptuous body created plenty of those. But that was a different kind of heat. That he could deal with when he had to which, sadly, was rarely.

Memories stirred his loins.

Restlessly diverting his thoughts he glanced towards the corner where Beatrice Turner sat. She was Richard's secretary and known as Miss Smith. Name-changing was another Richard rule. All in the cause of security.

Now Slade wondered what was going through her mind. Not that he cared. She had served her purpose. She was the one who had provided most of the information about Kenworth's movements. She learned about the diamonds through a contact at the airport who worked in security. Who he was Slade didn't want to know. There would be no future deals. This was a one-off heist. Its success would suit him, it would keep Mitzi happy and they would share a good life.

Guy he was unsure about. He was unstable. Clever but unpredictable. He had this thing about Jilly Kenworth which only Mitzi was able to control. Lust was a powerful emotion with which to deal.

Beatrice was lustful in a diluted way. She didn't know much about the workings of the human body. Over the months Slade had kept her happy with little or no effort. Saving his energy for Mitzi had given him many hours of anticipated pleasure, not always fulfilled, but still enjoyed. His next dream was to be somewhere with Mitzi breathing in cool, clear air and attaining heights of passion never before reached.

Licking his dry lips he wiped the sweat from his beaded brow.

Beatrice sat in the corner of the camper van with a window on either side of her thin shoulders. Her brown, shoe-button eyes, darted from face to face as each one spoke. If her eyes rested at all they were on Mervyn. She never tired of looking at him. Maybe he was heavy-jawed, but he had full, passionate lips which drove her wild when they touched hers. That pleasure had been curtailed since moving into the camper van. The presence of Mitzi and Guy had negated the promises made by Mervyn. He had spoken of a love nest.

It was a love nest but not for her. Female intuition told her that Mitzi had replaced her. Not that Beatrice had seen any indications, she hadn't. She just knew. Oh, yes. One could sense there was more to the situation than pure business. It was only upon reflection that she saw she was a mere pawn in the game. The game which would never have been played had she not set it up. At first she saw it as an exciting intellectual challenge. She had far more computer skills than Richard knew of and she used them to probe into his secret world. Some things were encoded. That was frustrating. But she still learned as much as she needed. For Richard to lose a few diamonds would not hurt him financially. The insurance would cover him. Her big mistake was in confiding in Gerald Williams. It was Gerald, working in security at the airport, who got her the job with Richard. Knowing how Gerald felt about her she was sure of his support in anything she did. It didn't work out that way. He found out about her and Mervyn and that finished the friendship. She dismissed it without heartbreak. Gerald was all spotted ties and Adam's apple. Mervyn was different.

Although she couldn't prove it, she was certain it was Gerald who warned Richard about the planned robbery. She also lived with the fear that one day Gerald might open his mouth about the part she played.

Richard's death was a complete shock. The fact that Mervyn had been driving left her numb for days. Even so, she promised to be an alibi should Mervyn need her. If he chose to use Mitzi he would end up in jail. Mitzi was untrustworthy. The only thing she cared about was her deranged brother. Although she loved him fiercely, she remained a spiteful and malicious woman. She was full of cunning ploys. Ploys used to create mystery and fear. She was a terrorist, and Beatrice hated her.

Guy watched Beatrice from beneath half-closed eyelids. Leaning back against the partition, his naked chest, covered in coarse, dark hairs, hardly moved. It was too hot to breathe deeply and fresh air was in short supply. Cooped up in this dump everything was in short supply except his simmering anger at Mitzi. Why tell Jilly he was in the States? Where was the point? And to anchor him to a French fiancée was ridiculous! Mitzi knew his sole aim in life was to be with Jilly and to make her deliriously happy. Once he had his share of the diamonds the richness of their lives would be beyond anything she had ever known with Richard. To invent a mythical fiancée could make Jilly seethe with jealousy, that would be flattering but not what he wanted. He wanted her to smile at him as she had smiled at Richard. He wanted to be touched, as she had touched Richard. To make her do that would not be easy. He could not push her. He had to lead her. He had to show how misguided her love for Richard had been. Then he had to prove how much more he loved her – worshipped her. Eventually she would be convinced. Fighting for her was exciting, challenging, and a game he desperately wanted to play. His victory would bring its own magnificent reward – Jilly.

Now, looking at Beatrice, he was sure she would be an easy conquest. She had that look about her. That look of a sex-starved spinster, a dried-up virgin who would be grateful for anyone. It might be fun to egg her on. Get her going then turn his back on her. Was there a greater insult to a woman's femininity? He thought not. Unwittingly he smiled in her direction.

She smiled back.

He froze. Bloody hell! Not now! There was important business in hand.

Mitzi was saying, "Why hurry things? Taking everything slowly is safer. Jilly will need careful handling. She will need to be assured that I'm there to help her. I can't do that by pushing her along. I'll have to coax her into letting me have the key."

"And how will you do that, dearest sister?"

"I haven't yet made up my mind," Mitzi admitted.

"Why not offer to safeguard it?" Guy asked lazily. "That's what a true friend would do. Take on the burden."

"No, Guy. Jilly has to make that move. To do as you suggest would make me vulnerable should things go wrong. Whatever I can lead her into doing she must do willingly. She's no fool. She won't be hurried and so slow is best."

"And where am I when all this slowness is taking place?"

"Here! Then once I have the key, you take it to Drake's. You go to your own safe deposit box and then you move on to Richard's and remove the contents."

"And if I'm challenged?"

"Why should you be? You're a legitimate customer, brother-in-law to my late husband who was a good and well-respected customer for many years."

Guy chewed on his bottom lip. His frown was ugly.

Mitzi said, "Don't look so worried, darling. Jilly and I will cover all eventualities by exchanging notes. Mine to say I have the key. Hers to say she has given it to me. All right?"

Guy's face cleared and he said, "You think of everything! It's as good as in the bag!"

Slade said, "As long as you don't do a bunk!"

"As if," Guy said, his voice intimidating. "My motivation is down here. I'm not likely to shoot off in another direction – not even for several million."

"Is she worth it?"

"Every penny."

Beatrice interrupted, her thin voice sharp, "I hope you've remembered this is a four-way deal. I've earned my share and I expect to get it."

"You will, my love!" Slade told her. "Without you none of this would have been possible."

Mitzi held down her laughter. His love? No chance!

Inwardly Beatrice glowed. He showed he cared. And in front of the others. His dalliance with Mitzi was a façade to keep her happy. Once everything was concluded they could all tread their chosen paths. Mitzi would be rich but floundering in a sea of loneliness. Mad Guy? Rejected? Suicidal? More than likely. And Mervyn? A sharp thrill rode the length of her spine to explode inside her brain. She closed her eyes in anticipated ecstasy. Suddenly the blind hatred she had felt for Mitzi evaporated. Now she felt sorry for her. Poor, Mitzi! She wouldn't have much to live for. Her best bet would be to stay with Guy. She smiled to herself. Guy? Suicidal? Mitzi sharing his fate? Two birds killed by the same stone? Such a comforting thought.

Mitzi had stopped fanning herself with the newspaper and was now pretending to read it. She'd picked up the vibes radiating from Beatrice. She had the hots for Mervyn! She was welcome. As an amusing diversion he was acceptable for a limited time. Preferably with long breaks between their encounters. His company was now beginning to pall. A month with him in any situation was far too long. But the present one had to be endured.

Guy was getting truculent. Secret glimpses of Jilly only served to disturb him. He was so obsessed, and even more so since being in such close proximity to her. He'd taken to watching her when she was in the garden. It was easy enough to do. High hedges made ideal screens. At first, when the children had been around, watching had not been easy. Becca in particular was given to unexpected activity. One minute she would be sitting quietly, the next she'd be charging about. Her unpredictability annoyed Guy. It robbed him of many hours of secret observation. Observation that filled him with an overwhelming desire to grab Jilly and carry her off. Such was his dream. Mitzi warned him that this must not happen.

"You'll scare her off. Stick to the plan, Guy. Do as we agreed – arrive from America in two days' time. Meanwhile I'll persuade Jilly to let you stay with us in the house – as a safety measure. She is so nervous she won't refuse. By then I should have the key! You will then receive an urgent business call. Something is in crisis, and you need to go to London – only for the day. You will be back by nightfall If we stick to the plan there will be no ruffled tempers or doubts. Offloading the stones is not a problem. A buyer is ready, willing and waiting, and..." she added her eyes suddenly sparkling with malice, "he was one of Richard's clients! How's that for payback?"

Guy didn't reply. He had his own idea about payback. His would be much more satisfying. He intended to take over where Richard had left off. Stepping into a dead man's shoes was a challenge Guy was eager to accept. He would become the focal point in Jilly's life. He would not allow other men to seek her out as Richard had done. Jilly would be his prized trophy and he would never share her with anyone. Not even her child. She would go to boarding school. If, when the summer holidays were due, he was in the right frame of mind, then he might allow her home. At all other times Jilly would be far too busy with her new and extraordinary lifestyle to have it interrupted by Richard's child.

Jilly already believed that her life with Richard was the epitome of excellence.

Jilly had yet to live.

As for Mitzi, as far as Richard was concerned, she had stood no chance. No amount of manipulative moves or seductive glances had any effect upon him. Though what Mitzi could see in Richard, Guy never understood. Jilly, being pure and innocent, would have been dazzled by him – but not Mitzi.

These thoughts along with his conversation with Mitzi had taken place earlier in the day. It followed an argument caused by Guy wanting to watch Jilly secretly. Mitzi said no, it was unwise. The whole plan was almost complete. If he was observed everything could be ruined. And that was a risk they couldn't take. Guy, as usual, sulked. Why was it her caution always overruled his chance of excitement?

Now his mind switched back to Beatrice. Might it be fun to lead her on? Looking at her thin, shapeless body and pallid skin, he decided she wasn't worth the effort. Frustration was fuelling his temper. A few days ago Hal had promised to introduce him to a couple of willing local girls. That had blotted Jilly from his mind for a few hours. But now that Hal was dead he'd lost interest. Jilly would be his fulfilment. Damn Mitzi for delaying it.

Inside the van, as the heat built up so the atmosphere deteriorated.

⋆ ⋆ ⋆

Jilly's cottage was calm, yet there was also an undercurrent of excitement. Now that the scenes were set she was no longer afraid. The 'not knowing' part of her life no longer existed. Even though the climax was still in the realm of the unknown it held no fear for her. Whatever transpired she knew it would be the final piece in the jigsaw. And the picture it would reveal, no matter how awful, would bring an end to all that which had darkened her life.

Alex, sitting next to her on the settee, said gently, "Don't let things appear so simple, Jilly. We are not dealing with ordinary, honest people, This bunch are complex and as such they are likely to do the unexpected."

"Such as what?"

"If I knew that it wouldn't be unexpected, would it? All I'm saying is we must be careful. You will be very vulnerable. Don't be lulled into a false sense of security. If Mitzi tells you it's raining – go outside and check!"

Jilly laughed.

Alex looked at her gravely and said, "I'm being serious. Trust nothing she says." He sighed heavily and went on, "I just wish I could be here when she arrives. I know we have agreed it will be better if you are alone. I just wish…"

Jilly looked at him in silence. His face, now dearly familiar, was creased with anxiety

Yet there was a re-assuring calm about him. She felt safe. Although within a few hours she could be in danger she knew Alex would be guarding her.

Richard's letter lay folded in her lap. Fingering it with reluctance she finally un-folded it and read it for the third time:

My Darling Jilly,
God willing you will never read this letter. Should you do so you will need to understand what has been happening over the last few weeks. Someone, somewhere is trying to ruin us not only financially but also by reputation. Who it is, and what their reasons are I have been unable to discover. If the worst should happen and I am unable to care for you and Becca, inside Pogo you will find the key to my safe deposit box which is empty. Should you be asked for this key by anyone then just hand it over and call the police. They will then need to make contact with a company called "White Ice", who will confirm that the contents of my safe deposit box are in their possession. I delivered the contents earlier than arranged, but the company understood why.
I have one small commission outstanding that takes me to Finchley. Once that has been completed I hope to track down whoever is causing trouble. None of the staff are aware of the problems but of the three the most trustworthy is my Number One. He can be contacted by 'phone and he's listed in my private 'phone book under 'Arthur.'
I can hear your laughter at what you think is yet another cloak-and-dagger situation.
Yes. I am cautious. I have to be. With so much to care for that is precious I will take no chances.
I love you
R.

The shock of finding the letter had subsided. The pain she felt had ebbed away. She now needed to move forward. Silently she refolded the letter, blinked away threatening tears and said,"We were right to trust Arthur, weren't we? He's going to contact Tragg and pass on what we have learned. Other than that we can only wait. If only we had known of this situation sooner, Alex. Richard must have forgotten to tell me about the secret drawer. I wonder if he told Becca? It is possible. They often shared little secrets. This could have been one of them."

"Finding it was lucky – thanks to Becca spilling the perfume. Although I have a feeling that Richard expected to solve the mystery. The letter was purely precautionary and not intended to be found."

Jilly remained silent. Alex had spoken her thoughts.

Unsure of the reason for her lack of response he channelled the conversation in a new direction.

"I've been intending to ask you for quite a while, and now seems a good time. Tell me about Dyak and Kyak – the latter misspelled."

Jilly's eyes suddenly creased with laughter.

"Oh, that! Just a resounding clanger dropped when we were in rather grand if not pompous company. Richard said something about Dyaks – which of course is a tribe, but at that moment I thought Dyaks were boats."

"You mean Kayaks?"

Laughter bubbled from Jilly's throat.

"Yes Kayaks! Richard never let me forget my faux pas. But eventually it served its purpose, didn't it?"

The laughter fled. Tears gathered.

Alex said" I can imagine your blush of embarrassment. Edam cheese?"

Her laughter returned.

"Every bit!" she admitted.

Alex became serious again.

"Looking at Richard's letter and seeing his problem he really was at a loss, wasn't he? And for my money I still think this vendetta against him was based on revenge. I would also include jealousy and even lust. It all seems to be there. Although in which order it falls is anyone's guess."

"It seems unreal. Perhaps one day we will learn the truth. As we seem to be theorising, what are your thoughts on the dressing box carving?"

For a moment Alex sat in deep thought and then said, "I think it might have been done as a gesture of friendship or maybe a favour. Perhaps Richard wanted the box to be unique and Drake's talent could make it so. The carving isn't perfect, but it's acceptable. Although I didn't get the feeling that Drake was particularly friendly with Richard there could have been some kind of mutual respect and the carving could have been the seal on their relationship."

"That is possible. I know Richard would have had his reasons for wanting the carving, but he wouldn't necessarily share them."

"A bit of a dark horse?"

"Somewhat – though in the nicest possible way."

Alex knew Jilly was defending Richard. And why not? Secrecy was not a crime.

Yet for all Richard's secrecy and caution he was still conned and killed.

Would Jilly be next?

Chapter Twenty

Don Tragg was in his back garden sprawling in a deck chair. Holding up a brimming glass to the last rays of the sun he could think of nothing better to do than drink cold beer on a warm evening. Having cut the lawn and dead-headed the roses he was at one with the world. He'd waved his wife off to one of her meetings. One that demanded she wear a hat. A meeting that was genteel, important and charity-conscious. She would be happy. He would put her out of his mind for an hour or two.

Now he turned his thoughts to Arthur. Things seemed to be moving in Cornwall – shakily – but nevertheless, shifting. He wasn't sure Arthur had given him all the facts. Not that it mattered. He'd learn them eventually. What Arthur had to keep in mind was that criminals never expected to be caught. Each was sublimely confident that his plan was perfect. This led to a lack of caution, omission of details, and unguarded words uttered in pubs. This kind of neglect could trigger an explosion of police investigation. Arthur had to take care and not get in the way of that.

Tragg's brain scrambled about. Pity he didn't know all the details, but Arthur was right to be guarded. Telephones were not all that safe to use as Mrs. Kenworth discovered. When calling a mobile number the recipient could be anywhere. She thought her so-called friend was in France. And where was she? Less than two miles away. A clever and deceptive move. That potentially dangerous situation was why Tragg had sought personal contact with Drake. Face to face was safe even if Tragg found him difficult to deal with. Drake didn't like trivia. He grasped situations without needing to know the ins and outs. He was very focused. If his bank was about to be robbed he would do all within his power to prevent it. Motives didn't interest him, but he did make a suggestion. Instead of leaving the safe deposit box empty, why not substitute fake diamonds? Not difficult to come by. A little theatrical shop just off Charing Cross Road sold them by the handful. A contact in Hatton Garden would supply an authentic pouch, and Drake would be happy to make all the arrangements. What did Tragg think? He thought it a splendid move.

While discussing this idea Drake's eyes had taken on a hard, glittery look, but once the plan was accepted his expression softened and he spoke kindly and with regret about the Kenworth family. He made mention of a carved box. One Kenworth had bought for his wife. It was Drake who suggested embellishing it with a carved decoration and offered to do the work himself. It was his hobby and to put it to good use would be very rewarding. The gesture was also made out of regard for Richard. Since when Drake had often wondered if it had been appreciated. Kenworth had never said. Tragg could offer no explanation, but silently thought it might be because Richard was tight-lipped. Had he not been so then perhaps this situation would not have arisen.

Outlining the expected robbery to Drake, Tragg offered a timescale of a couple of days. Nothing was certain, in fact most of it was speculation, but a theft would be attempted. Every angle was covered as far as possible. All Drake had to do was be alert and say nothing to his staff. That was something Drake could handle. He was not a man to share explosive information.

Now Tragg squinted into the sunshine and drained his tumbler. He had to play a waiting game. Not something he enjoyed. He debated whether to tell Arthur about the ploy with fake diamonds. Then decided he should. He'd ring him. Contemplating his empty glass he wondered if he had time for a refill. Why not! It gave him something to do. The sun disappeared behind a purple cloud and chilled the air. It was time to go indoors. Heaving himself upright he wandered into the house. There was a psychological thriller on the telly. Maybe he'd watch it from the comfort of his bed. It was the best place to fall asleep, if sleep was on the agenda. That he doubted. He had a lot to think about. Picking up the 'phone he dialled Arthur.

* * *

Earlier Jilly had listened intently to Marilyn's advice. They had been heads-together in the sitting room for over an hour. Alex and Arthur, not wanting to appear over-anxious about their safety, had strolled down to the Harbour pub in search of cold beer. It had been a worrying day. It had also been a scorcher and thirsts were in need of quenching. The girls declined the invitation to join them. They had some important things to do and very little time in which to do them.

Marilyn was sitting straight-backed, her hands palm uppermost in her lap.

"It's a technique, Jilly. Palms down you tend to press and tighten up. Palms up – you relax. Empty your mind. Make it into a blank screen. Remember how you once felt about Mitzi. How you valued her friendship. Relive the emotion and adopt it. You have to become what you were and not what you are."

"It's hard," Jilly said. "The anger, the sense of betrayal, keep getting in the way."

"I know," Marilyn said sympathetically, "I also know you can do it. You have to. You must not show anything but warmth and friendship towards Mitzi, and toward Guy when he arrives."

Jilly shuddered, "Guy? He's a snake!"

"No, he isn't. He's a good friend and an admirer! You are thankful for his company and you bask in his devotion to you."

Staring in horror Jilly protested, "I can't do this!" Her desperation was ignored.

"You can and you must!" Marilyn told her forcefully." For God's sake, Jilly! Look! The night Richard was killed was also the night my Jack was injured. I was playing Juliet in Rep when the police came to the stage door and told me he was in hospital. What did I do? Did I have a choice? No. I finished the play by blotting out the news and remaining as Juliet who loved Romeo. Sarah did not exist until the curtain fell. And that's what you have to do, Jilly. Wait until the curtain falls."

"I can't! I'm not made of such stern stuff," Jilly told her.

"Yes, you are! We all are when motivated. Think Becca. If you make a mess of this what will happen to her? How will you deal with her in relation to the consequences? And what about Alex – and Davy for that matter? How will you explain your colossal failure to them? Come on, Jilly! You must convince yourself that Mitzi and Guy are your biggest supporters in this dangerous game."

"And it is dangerous, isn't it?"

"Very! Now, come on. Palms uppermost and remember how fond you are of Mitzi."

"And Guy?"

"And Guy!"

"Masochist!"

The time was well spent as Jilly gradually learned to react as Marilyn suggested. The men returned, peeped round the door and silently withdrew. Finally, sighing with relief, the girls called a halt and took pride in their accomplishment.

Jilly did not sleep until dawn. It didn't matter. Outwardly she was in charge of herself, thanks to Marilyn.

Inwardly she remained in turmoil. Outwardly she had learned how to projected a rather naïve and helpless woman who needed friends to lean upon. She now knew how to appear incapable of dealing with a situation she did not fully understand. Not a halfwit; just someone who was at a loss. She knew how to convince Mitzi and Guy that they were her salvation, and her gratitude towards them would know no bounds. She was controlled. She would not effuse. She knew how to underplay and how not to overplay. She learned how to look her enemies in the eye without flinching. She showed no expressions of mistrust and her newly-acquired aura told everyone they were loved.

Even Guy?

Yes, even Guy!

She shuddered.

Just before she finally slept her thoughts turned to Alex. Where would she be without his strength? She knew that whenever she'd turned to him he was always there. He was so steadfast and that made her feel – what? She was unsure. She knew how he felt, but her own feelings were no more than friendship towards him. Or was she refusing to read the message her heart was beating out? Or was it too soon to listen to such an exciting rhythm? If only she could decide.

* * *

The curtains in the camper van were drawn, but the windows were open. Within, Mitzi and Mervyn were talking in hushed tones. Guy was out, no doubt spying on Jilly hoping to catch a glimpse of her.

The man was quite mad.

So thought Beatrice. She was outside listening at the window. No one had missed her. They were used to her nightly disappearances. Before retiring she liked to walk. Just along the path she had beaten over the last few weeks.

It was a ritual that helped her to sleep. Sharing a minute sleeping space with Mitzi was not only claustrophobic it was also noisy. Mitzi mumbled, grunted and snored her way through the hours. Beatrice needed her nightly stroll to help her deal with the disturbances.

Now she turned towards the open window and listened to what she was not supposed to hear – the conversation between Mitzi and Mervyn.

Mitzi, her voice quivering in agitation said, "Guy's decided he doesn't want to follow our agreed plan."

"Jeez!"

"Yes, I know. You'll have to keep him here, Mervyn. By force if necessary!"

"Oh, come on, Mitzi! When has anyone been able to make Guy do anything against his will? Yes, all right! I can use force – not a problem – but not a wise move."

"Then you'll have to reason with him. Convince him that arriving at Jilly's before he's expected will not fit in. He's supposed to be flying in from the States. In view of that he cannot possibly arrive tomorrow. Not only that, but I need time to work on Jilly. I need to coax her into handing over the key. And that might be difficult and time-consuming."

Mervyn hunched his shoulders. Everything was getting too complicated for his liking. He hadn't anticipated things getting so involved. When Mitzi first approached him, apart from the inevitable planning and homework, the remainder was easy. Get the key. Go to the bank. Scarper. But now there was Guy to deal with. And his fixation for the Kenworth woman. Jeez! She was a nice looker, though.

He glanced at Mitzi. She was a real turn on, which was why he was here – well – that and the diamonds.

Sighing, he said, "I'll do my best with Guy, but you know what he's like." He paused to stare at the smoke-stained ceiling and then said, almost to himself, "I wonder if Beatrice could tempt him?"

Mitzi chortled, "What? That silly cow? No chance!"

"Oh, come on, Mitzi! If it wasn't for good old Bee we might not be here."

"I suppose," came the churlish reply

Seeing her mood was about to slip into that of a bad temper, Slade suggested they again recap the moves for the following day

"It might be a good idea," he said, unsure as to whether it was or not.

Sighing at his constant demands for repetition she said in a monotone, "Tomorrow Guy runs me to a taxi rank. The time fits in with the Paris flight on which I'm supposed to arrive. Right? That means I get to Jilly's around midday. Guy should be back here by then. That's when you step in. You have to hold him back for another twenty-four hours. Only then can he show his face at Jilly's."

"And what about Beatrice? We can't just ignore her."

"Don't worry about her. As long as she gets her slice of the cake she won't be any trouble." Mitzi then laughed softly and said, "I'm sure you can find a way to keep her happy if you have to."

There was an atmospheric silence broken only when Mervyn said, "D'you mean in the same way I keep you happy?"

"Mmm, if you must!"

Beatrice turned away from the window and silently threw up.

* * *

Guy stared up at Jilly's darkened bedroom window. Wanting to see her he had willed her to appear and failed. Sometimes he felt empowered and he would stand and silently command her to do as he said. Only once had she obeyed him. Then she had stood breathing in the night air. But not tonight. Tonight there was no movement. The curtains remained open and still. In his mind's eye he saw her wearing something diaphanous as she drifted about her room. With his blood pounding in his head he again willed her to appear at the window.

It was not to be.

Verging on fury at his failure he moved silently away. It would not always be like this. Eventually she would be his for all time.

Making his way back to the camper van he wondered if Beatrice would still be on her nightly stroll. She was no substitute for Jilly but better than nothing. And nothing was the result. Despite following Beatrice's worn path Guy did not find her. Had she been on the beach she would have left footprints, then he would have found her. That would have been a stroke of luck. As it was, Beatrice remained in the way. She irked him with her cow-eyed looks, her simpering and fawning. And so he decided she was disposable as was Hal. He was an ill-mannered lout and should not have talked about Jilly as he did. He was disrespectful and lascivious. He drooled with lust for her. He described her in foul language, and boasted that he once had her in the alleyway at the back of the Seaman's Mission. He was a liar! And could not be trusted.

Jilly would never have consorted with such a man. She was too gentle, ethereal. Long ago, when he had trapped her in the bathroom, her hands, beating his chest, were like an injured bird fluttering. Had she really wanted to push him away she would have been tigerish. That's how she would have been with Hal had he tried to hold her against her will. That was the thing about Jilly, as far as he, Guy, was concerned she just went through the motions without realising that in her heart she belonged to him.

As for Hal he deserved what he got!

More than once Guy had seen Hal hidden in the darkness and loitering in the bushes in Jilly's garden. He would stare up at her window. Waiting. Watching. He had no right and Guy had told him so. Hal had sneered. But no more.

Now Guy smiled remembering the look of shock on Hal's face when he found himself on his back in the sea. A look that turned to terror as Guy straddled him and held him beneath the incoming tide. It didn't take long and no one saw Hal die. Only the rocks in the far bay, and they wouldn't tell. Later, when he arrived at the camper van in wet, stinking clothes no one questioned him. They wouldn't dare. He was his own man and he would do as he pleased.

Now the fact that he had been unable to find Beatrice taking her nightly walk didn't bother him. She was old. She was dull. She was not Jilly. Pushing his hands into his pockets he strolled towards the camper van to wonder if Mitzi would be sharing Slade's bed again. If so, how the hell did he put up with her snoring?

* * *

Alex watched from the silence of his side door. He knew Arthur and Marilyn had gone home and that Jilly had retired. This was his final check before he too went to bed. Scanning the darkness his eyes suddenly jerked. What was that? Did something move or was it just the shadowy bushes stirring? How? There was no breeze? He waited and watched eyes fixed on Jilly's garden. Was everything as it should be? He was unsure. He hovered uncertainly while remaining alert. After several minutes he concluded his imagination was playing tricks and, finally, he went indoors. Everything seemed peaceful. Even so there would be no sleep for him that night.

★ ★ ★

In the holiday cottage Arthur was half-way through his second packet of cigarettes and Marilyn had all but run out of air freshener. The session with Jilly had left her feeling proud and triumphant but drained and her mood was not of the best.

"You are going to kill yourself, Pop!" she warned, as she emptied the piled ashtray, "And me," she added for good measure, "Secondary smoke is just as lethal as the original!"

"I know," Arthur told her testily while grinding out his newly-lit cigarette into his saucer. "And once this little malarkey is over I'll give it up. Promise!"

Marilyn shook her head in despair. She'd heard it all before.

He half smiled at her and said, "I'm glad you were able to help Jilly. She's pivotal to our plans and if she fails we all fail."

"She won't. She's much more gutsy than we give her credit for. I'm not saying she isn't scared – she is. But fear won't stand in her way. Now I'm off to bed. No more fags, OK? 'Night!"

"'Night," he said and reached for another cigarette.

In his head the next couple of days were mapped out except that people were not puppets. His plans were based on what he wanted to happen. But life was never that accommodating. His biggest comfort was that he and Don Tragg were of the same mind about how events would fall. They could both be wrong – it was a gamble. Ideally the direct route was for Guy to have the key. They were banking on that. If Guy and Mitzi were convinced it was their ball game they would play it their way. If, for some reason, Smith or Slade had the key then the outcome would be different. But whoever had the key they would end up clutching a bag of worthless stones – thanks to Tragg. They would also be in the frame for murder. Proving it might be difficult with Hal dead, but sometimes the dead spoke from the grave.

Arthur sighed. All his ideas, while based only on conjecture, left him feeling he was not far off the mark. Tragg shared his views and that gave him a sense of satisfaction.

Stubbing out his cigarette on the now empty packet he tossed it into the fireplace.

Perhaps he would cut down on the fags. Cutting them out was a bit drastic.

Chapter Twenty-One

The following morning Jilly saw no one. It had been agreed that was the wisest plan. She could be under surveillance. The less she saw of friends and neighbours the less she would have to worry about. She felt strangely alone. So much was missing from her life. Becca's chatter. Alex's laughter. Davy dashing in and out. Even silent Delza was missed. Only Benji remained. Now fully recovered, he hung about to paw her legs from time to time as if telling her not to worry. He was there and would take care of her. As she fondled his ear he licked her wrist. It was comforting but no doubt he was merely asking to be taken for a walk. They would go later. Meanwhile he would have to be content with the garden.

Just after noon, tense with apprehension, she sat on a hard chair. Straight-backed and with her palms uppermost in her lap she closed her eyes. Within moments she became calm. All the hatred and animosity she felt towards Mitzi and Guy just drifted away. Marilyn had promised it would as long as Jilly followed the rules. Well, she had and now she was reaping the reward.

It wasn't long before she heard the slam of a car door. That would be the taxi! Her heart raced. From now on she would be playing a dangerous game. She needed to be careful – very careful.

Mitzi arrived in a cloud of silk and perfume, carrying a small suitcase and a large handbag. In the doorway she effusively air-kissed Jill's cheek with the usual "Mwah. Mwah." And then, oozing affection, said how good it was to see her again after so long.

"I'm just so sorry you have had such a trying time. You must be scared witless. I know I would be. Guy was horrified when I told him you could be in danger,"

She prattled on while Jilly made appropriate noises without actually saying anything.

They were at lunch when Mitzi, rolling crumbs of bread between her finger and thumb, said, "You know, Jilly whoever is making these demands could be dangerous. As for the key, couldn't you just hand it over?"

"Why should I? The safe deposit box must hold something valuable. They know what it is and I don't. But valuable or not it is rightfully mine. Why should I give it up?" As if to give emphasis Jilly banged her hands on the table. Not too hard, just enough to suggest that while she was brave she was also timorous.

"Can't *you* go to the bank?" Mitzi asked.

For a moment Jilly looked troubled and then said in a small, plaintive voice, "I'm too scared. I'm almost too scared to leave the house."

"Oh, darling!" Mitzi cried, covering Jilly's hands with her own." I hadn't realised just how serious things really are."

Almost visibly shuddering Jilly steeled herself not to withdraw, saying, "I'm also terrified that someone will break into the house. There has already been one intruder – although nothing was taken."

"Do you think they were looking for the key?" Mitzi asked, glancing about as if to suggest they were being watched at that very moment. "If so then the quicker you are rid of it the better." Drumming the tips of her scarlet nails for several seconds she then said, "Would you give it to me? I can hide it or even post it home to France."

That was a new angle! Looking grateful Jilly said hurriedly, "Mitzi! I couldn't do that to you! I couldn't put you into such a dangerous situation."

"Who would know?"

"I don't think anyone would actually know, but those connected to me become vulnerable. Becca and her friend Davy have both been got at. Even Tom my gardener was attacked."

"Noo!" Mitzi breathed with incredulity. "Is he all right? Where is he now?"

Jilly sensed the enquiry was not out of concern but purely to check on Tom's whereabouts. Without blinking she innocently supplied the information.

"Away?" Mitzi said with eyebrows raised. "A precautionary measure?"

"No, just a family visit. He's also taken Davy – just as a treat."

With that information stored Mitzi sighed," Poor you. You're completely on your own!"

Deliberately Jilly let her features droop.

"A couple of neighbours have been kind, but you can't confide in neighbours as you can in close friends."

"Which is why I'm here," Mitzi smiled.

Inwardly Jilly seethed at the duplicity. Mitzi sounded so concerned, so sincere. Her eyes were gentle, her expression sympathetic. How could she be so false, so evil?

Mitzi said, "Yet despite all the worry and turmoil you look amazing and you are so calm."

"That's because you are here," Jilly said sweetly and looked down at her now upturned palms. Yes, she was calm, but it was no thanks to Mitzi.

After lunch, while Mitzi was unpacking, Jilly went to Tom's shed and rang Alex. Words tumbled from her in a torrent of dismay and anger.

"Alex! How can she be so two-faced! She pretends to be genuinely concerned. She even looks concerned. How I kept my temper I don't know."

"But you did!" he told her, "and you were not fooled. We both know Mitzi thinks in terms of diamonds rather than friendship."

"That's so true," Jilly agreed with a soft laugh, "And I'm pretty sure I'm fooling her just a little bit more than she thinks she's fooling me."

"That's my girl!" Alex praised. "Keep it that way, but be careful."

In Becca's room Mitzi swiftly unpacked the few clothes she had earlier thrown into her case. They were crumpled, but it didn't matter. She didn't intend to stay long enough to wear them. Cautiously peering from the window she rang Guy. His 'phone was switched off. Was he in a mood? Swiftly she called Slade to find out.

"Where's Guy?" she demanded. "He's not answering his 'phone."

"It's out of juice and the electric point Hal fixed up isn't working."

"That's all we need!" she replied acidly. "Loss of communication will really mess things up."

"Don't worry," Slade soothed. "Electricity is not a problem. I can sort it."

Changing tack he asked if she had the key.

"Not yet. My dear friend might take a bit more persuading than I expected. She thinks giving it to me will put me in danger. She is so naïve!"

"Not really! You are just cleverer than she is. I'm sure you are playing everything exactly right. You'll win! I've never backed a loser yet!"

Flattered, Mitzi primped at her reflection in the window.

Guy came on the line.

"Hi, Sis! Everything going to plan?"

"So far," she told him, relieved to find him calm. "Just don't do anything rash. Jilly is really looking forward to seeing you again."

She spoke with a smile knowing Guy would preen. Bolstering his ego was one way of getting the best out of him. And for the next few hours he had to be kept happy.

"Jilly pleased to see me?" he asked, elated. "I must have gone up in her estimation."

"She's always been fond of you, Guy, but as a married lady she had to be careful. Now you must take things slowly. She is cautious, and you must be the same, but I do know for certain that you will not be pushed away."

The fact that Jilly had hardly mentioned Guy was neither here nor there. He would never know. "Be patient, Guy," she went on. "Don't play the caveman," she mildly reproved. "Tomorrow will soon be here, so don't spoil things. Stick to the plan, yes?"

"Of course, sister dear. I don't want to ruin the chance of spending my life with Jilly. I won't rush things. I'll be the perfect gentleman."

"You promise?"

"Cross my heart!"

Satisfied that everything was under her control she switched off her 'phone.

Hearing voices coming from below she went down to the kitchen.

Jilly smiled, "Ah! There you are Mitzi! Come and say hello to Alex my neighbour. He's going to the village. Do you need anything?"

Mitzi offered a limp hand liking what she saw. Blond, chunky, strong features. Nice firm touch. This was the man Jilly had spoken of but hadn't confided in. Mitzi didn't judge him to be a threat. He looked too ordinary, too solid, too much of a good citizen.

She gave him a girlish smile and confessed to having forgotten toothpaste. Would he mind? Any brand would do.

It was no trouble, he smiled back.

Jilly watched without expression. She knew Alex had his finger on the situation's pulse. His body language told her so. He conveyed that things were in hand. She wondered if he had set up something with Arthur.

Alex was telling Mitzi that, later, he intended to walk Benji.

"Since Davy, my son, has been away I haven't been getting enough exercise. I thought to go to The Cauldron, Jilly. What do you think? Good for me and not too far for Benji?"

Again Jilly knew he was telling her his intended direction rather than his destination.

"It's fairly rough terrain," she said unsurely and then smiled, "but Benji will love it. So yes. It's a good idea."

To her surprise Mitzi suggested they go shopping.

"With no dog to worry about – what do you think? It will do you good, Jilly. I know you are nervous of leaving the house – but – it will be a break for you. And there's safety in numbers!"

Mischievously Alex asked if he should still get the toothpaste.

For a moment Mitzi's eyes flickered uncertainly. What was he doing? Leaving the way open for another meeting? Before she could decide Alex gave her a lingering look and left.

After staring at the closed door for a moment Mitzi said, "He's rather nice."

"Not my type," Jilly laughed. "Given a choice I prefer tall, dark and handsome."

"Like Guy?"

"Like Guy," she repeated, amazed at her ability to lie with such conviction. "Alex seemed quite smitten with you, and he is nice. A bit stolid and not very imaginative."

"And you don't go for him?"

"Like I said he isn't my type."

Mitzi fell silent while again drumming her fingers. Finally she said, "Have you ever considered giving the key to Alex and asking him to go to the bank on your behalf?"

Jilly looked wide-eyed with shock and gasped, "I couldn't do that! I hardly know the man. What if there are valuables in the bank? Could I trust him to bring them back?"

"Could you trust me?"

"Of course! You're my friend! My misgiving is nothing to do with trust. It's fear for your safety. I don't want to put you in danger."

"Darling," Mitzi sighed. "Aren't you being a little over-cautious. Who would know? How could they? I'm just a visiting friend. A slightly dizzy female who forgets her toothpaste."

Jilly smiled. Again sitting with her palms uppermost she exuded an aura of doubt and concern while remaining firmly in command of the situation.

Mitzi started to pressurise.

"Think about it, Jilly. If I go to the bank, what does it involve? Taking a train to Town, a cab to the bank, then the procedure in reverse. What can go wrong? Look, darling, if you don't want me to go alone, why don't we both go?"

Jilly shrank, protesting she couldn't.

"It would leave us vulnerable and open to attack."

"By whom?"

"I don't know!"

"You must have some idea!"

"I haven't!"

"Then you are over-reacting!"

"I'm not!" Jilly told her, wringing her hands. "You don't understand! For weeks whoever it is always seems to know what is happening in my life."

Mitzi gave an exaggerated shudder, and then squared her shoulders.

"This situation is out of hand, Jilly. I think you should call the police." Inwardly Mitzi laughed. She was playing Jilly like a fish on the end of a line.

Jilly marvelled at the coolness of the bluff and replied helplessly," How can I? Anonymous 'phone calls are not evidence of a crime, are they?"

"Your gardener was attacked."

"That was put down to being a family feud. And in any case the attacker is now dead."

"Poor man," Mitzi said without sympathy

Who said it was a man, Jilly thought?

Again, glancing at her hands, she felt a surge of pride, and silently thanked Marilyn. Now having fed information to Mitzi, Jilly needed time on her own and so she suggested Mitzi should stroll to the cove.

"It's quite pretty, I'm sure you'll enjoy it. And the other thing is that before we go out I must write a letter to explain Becca's absence from a friend's party. If I don't she'll never get another invitation! You know what children are!"

"Letter writing! How tedious! A necessary evil! I'll leave you to it. Shall I take Benji?"

"Better not. Let Alex have the pleasure."

Mitzi twiddled her hair and smirked, "I would pleasure Alex any time!"

Jilly forced a laugh while resisting the urge to slap her.

After borrowing a pair of Jilly's flip-flops Mitzi left the house. It was amazing how everything kept falling into place. There she was silently worrying about finding an excuse to be on her own when Jilly suggested walking to the cove. What could be better? She had reached the overhang when, on realising she was hidden from view, she rang Guy on Mervyn's number. Mervyn was not pleased. Mitzi didn't care. Talking to Guy she said, "Just to keep you in the picture. The house will be completely deserted this afternoon so there's no point in you hanging about. Jilly and

I are going shopping. Her neighbour Alex is walking the dog to somewhere called The Cauldron, so the house will be locked up, and not overlooked."

"This so called neighbour," Guy said with an edge to his voice." What is he to Jilly? A friend? A lover?"

"Guy! Stop being paranoid! He's a neighbour and that's all."

"You're sure? Good-looking?"

"Not in Jilly's eyes," she told him evasively.

"How d'you mean?"

"She likes her men tall, dark and handsome."

"And?"

"He's nothing like."

"And he's just a neighbour," Guy persisted." You're sure? He's not touchy-feely with her?"

"Guy!" she cried in exasperation. "Stop it! He's not even a close friend! You have no reason to be jealous!"

Guy grunted and rang off, leaving Mitzi unsure whether he believed her or not.

On reaching the tiny beach, Mitzi found nothing of interest and so she stood by the tide mark thinking of Guy. Of late he'd become more and more moody. She understood why. He was frustrated. With his goal in sight he was impatient. He wanted and needed Jilly to himself. And he wanted her now! He loved her to distraction and wanted to give her a fabulous lifestyle in any part of the world she chose. She was on the highest pedestal from which he would never let her fall. Success would be his, it always was.

She was the one who failed. She had failed with Richard. She was the one who bore his rejection and suffered the pain. Given the chance she could have loved him deeply, but he denied her. Her face crumpled and then twisted at the memory. He didn't want her love, so she gave him hate. It was true what they said about a woman scorned, and she had been scorned. Ruining him would have exacted a very sweet revenge, but even that failed. His death was not on the agenda, and it left her feeling cheated and lacking sorrow. She wanted him alive and grovelling. But it wasn't to be. Now she had to concentrate on Guy and persuade Jilly, among other things, that he was right for her.

Returning to the house she found Jilly stacking dishes, and a stamped envelope lay on the table.

The 'phone rang.

Jilly deliberately dropped a plate. It crashed to the floor and shattered.

Mitzi, ignoring the shards of china, calmly asked if she should take the call.

"Please," Jilly quavered. "It'll be the usual silence! Just hang up!" She spoke rapidly, nervously. Marilyn would have been proud of her.

Mitzi disappeared and then Jilly heard her say, "Hello, my little darling! It's Aunty Mitzi! Yes – just for a few days."

What was Becca doing calling on the house 'phone? Didn't she know to use the mobile. Not that it mattered. Not now.

Excitedly grabbing the receiver, Jilly cried, "Becca! It's Mom. Are you having a lovely time?"

For next few minutes Jilly forgot the dangers in her life. Caught up in Becca's exuberance she heard how she'd won a teddy bear by answering twenty questions on the seaside.

"I didn't get them all right," she confessed. "But I got more than anyone else."

Jilly was filled with an overwhelming surge of pride and love. Gratefully she thanked God that Becca was out of harm's way. If only she could keep her so. Jilly's mother came on the line and for the first time ever did not have to wheedle for Becca to stay a few more days.

"I know you're letting her go to the church fête but, after that we've had an invitation to a garden party for the grown-

-ups and a barbeque for the children. Daddy doesn't want to go, so I thought…"

Jilly's relief was so intense she cut into her mother's words.

"A barbeque? Becca will love that!"

"You mean she can go?" her mother asked with surprise.

"I don't see why not. School is still a couple of weeks away. Davy is on a chicken farm near Padstow -"

"And you have Mitzi for company," her mother chirruped." What could be better! Do give Mitzi my regards. Perhaps when you collect Becca you could bring Mitzi and we can all stay together for a few days. That would be fun. Daddy would like that. Let me know. Bye, darling." And with that she hung up.

With Mitzi standing so close Jilly was unsure how much she might have overheard. And so, smiling brightly, she passed on the invitation, adding that Guy too would be very welcome.

"That would be lovely," said Mitzi. "Once all this ghastly business is over! I gather your parents don't know anything about it."

"Nor must they!" Jilly said sharply.

"Your secret's safe with me,"

Alex arrived with the toothpaste, refused payment, and asked if they were ready for the off. Turning to Mitzi he told her it was ages since Jilly'd had a friend to stay. It had been on the tip of his tongue to tell her it had been ages since she went shopping. Then he realised Mitzi might just know that wasn't true. He wondered if Jilly had already made the same mistake. Jilly covered the situation by confessing that, although she had been out, it had been a worry.

"But now," she smiled, "I feel safe, confident, and I intend to treat myself."

"Good for you! And don't worry about Benji. He and I are good pals so he won't fret."

Taking the lead from the hook behind the door, he folded it and held it in his hand.

"Come on, Benji! Let's go and find Mimosa."

"Who's Mimosa?" Mitzi asked, hoping she wasn't another problem.

"A little Peke. She lives near The Cauldron."

"And her owner is young, pretty eye-candy?"

Alex threw back his head and laughed.

" Mrs. Lang? Eye-candy? She must be sixty if she's a day," he told her still laughing

"You know what they say about new tunes on old fiddles?" she bantered.

He winked at her.

"I've yet to find out."

Mitzi fluttered her eyelashes. Alex had made a definite pass! And why not? She did not consider herself to be an old fiddle, but maybe she could give Alex a few months.

Jilly stood silently by and listened. Alex was leading Mitzi on. And such was her conceit she thought he was being serious.

It was only then that Jilly understood how she would have felt had Alex been serious. He would have broken her heart.

Now having agreed to go shopping Jilly left Mitzi fixing her make-up and went to get the car. In the garage she rang Marilyn and outlined their movements adding those of Alex's. "I had a feeling he wanted to see Arthur but didn't want to say anything in front of Mitzi. He's keen for us all to keep in touch."

Armed with this knowledge Marilyn roused Arthur from a deep sleep spattered with strange, confused dreams. He was relieved to awaken to his familiar problems. Alex wanted to see him. Good. That meant things were on the move. Groping for a cigarette he found the packet empty. Blast! Life did not get into gear until he had a smoke. There was no point in asking Marilyn to go to the shop. She wouldn't and her refusal would be adamant. Rightly so. Cigs were slowly killing him; but once Jilly's problems were resolved he'd give up the weed. A bout of coughing shook his frame leaving him watery-eyed and breathless.

Bloody fags.

Although pressed for time Arthur hurried down to the village store. After pushing two packets of twenty into his pocket he left the shop and waited at the kerb to cross the road. It was then that a car, slowed by the queue of traffic, halted in front of him. Arthur's heart lurched.

The driver was Frank Slade! His dog was on the back seat its nose pressed against the window clouding it as it breathed.

What the hell? Was Frank involved in the heist, too?

Swiftly turning back into the shop he bought another pack of twenty and then fingered the rack of postcards near the window and kept watch.

Yes, it was definitely Frank. And now the traffic was moving, where was he going? To the camper van? Arthur guessed so.

Hurriedly he headed back to the cottage.

"I think I'll catch up with Alex."

"You know he's walking the dog to The Cauldron!"

"So? I've got legs haven't I?"

"You've also got fags judging by your pockets."

Arthur snorted in disgust. He couldn't get away with anything.

* * *

Driving towards Penzance, Mitzi said, "Guy is really looking forward to seeing you again. Will you be pleased to see him?"

"Immensely so!" Jilly told her, startled by the conviction in her voice. Within herself she smiled. Maybe she should become an actress. She was certainly experienced in drama!

* * *

Guy stood in the camper van, rocking on his heels and looking at Slade through narrowed eyes. He didn't like Mervyn Slade. Had he not been useful he would not have been tolerated. But, as things stood, Guy had no option but to accept the situation. And that included Slade's molestation of Mitzi. Not that she cared. It was all to the good and what did a little bit of flesh sharing matter? It was the end result that counted.

Guy curled his hands into fists. He just didn't like the man.

Beatrice had gone out. She was into all things natural and so she spent time foraging in the wood for roots and berries. The concoctions she produced were pretty revolting, but she didn't appear to mind when no one appreciated or shared her enthusiasm for them. With malicious glee Guy hoped she would one day gather and cook deadly nightshade. It would solve a problem.

Slade was playing patience with a grubby deck of cards. It was a way of killing time. With luck two more days would end his stay in the Godforsaken hole. He and Mitzi would then be off to more civilised and glamorous climes. He couldn't wait.

Guy said, peering over his shoulder, "You've put a spade on a club."

"I know!" Slade said with ill-temper. "I'm working on it!"

Loser, Guy thought with a sardonic smile.

Finally Slade tossed down the pack and pushed the remaining cards into a heap. He was frustrated with playing straight. He liked to cheat. But how could he with Guy hovering in the background?

Unexpectedly Guy said, "You're familiar with this area, aren't you? What's The Cauldron or, more to the point, where is it?"

"Local beauty spot on the other side of the village. Bottom of the cliffs overlooked by a big house."

"Who lives there?"

"Some old dink. Why?"

"No reason. Just wondered. Thought I might stroll that way.

Slade looked at him through half-closed eyes. What was he up to? Not a lot at The Cauldron. Dull and deserted he couldn't cause much harm there. So – was it the woman?

"Interested in the old dink?" he asked. "She's no oil painting – unless you're hard up," Slade sniggered.

"I'm not but *she* might be."

Slade guffawed.

Guy gulped down his rising gall. How dare Slade suggest he would even look at any woman other than Jilly. She was the only one he wanted.

Had it not been for the unexpected knocking on the door he would have launched into a vitriolic verbal attack. Instead he pulled open the door and barked, "Yes?"

"Is Mervyn in? I'm his brother Frank."

God! Not another problem!

Guy jerked his head in Slade's direction and snapped," He's in there." He then pushed Frank aside and made his way along the field to the five-bar gate. Although it would have been safer to go through the wood, bumping into Beatrice might just have made her the victim of his simmering rage.

Swinging open the gate he crashed it shut, the noise of squeaking hinges screaming through his head. The fencing, made of rotted wood, leaned drunkenly. The stakes had jostled for the upright only to fall into useless, decaying heaps. Scrambling across the rutted verge he tugged a gnarled stake from the ground. Holding it firmly he swung it as a cricketer might when batting for the Ashes, and smiled. What an injury that would inflict! He smiled again and caressed the timber ignoring the splinters that gouged his palm.

He felt invincible. He was invincible.

★★★

Mervyn was not pleased to see Frank. Frank got in the way. He was too principled. Right from wrong mattered. Dogs versus people was no contest. Dogs always won.

Now instructed by Mervyn, Frank drove towards the coast. He drove erratically along a badly potholed lane. Mervyn braced his knees against the dashboard. He didn't know which was worse, having his liver shaken from his body, or the slavering of the dog whose head was on his shoulder.

Since getting into the car Frank had been begging for understanding and trying to justify the reason for his visit. But, being incapable of driving and talking coherently at the same time, Mervyn told him to shut up.

Finally Frank, calling on what little courage he had, stopped the car and said, "I heard on the grapevine that come the weekend there'll be a meet involving bull terriers. It's not on, Merv! No dog's put on this earth to fight."

"Oh, come on, Frank! It's a bit of sport! God knows there's little else to occupy the mind in this neck of the woods."

"I don't call it sport, Merv. And if I can stop it I will."

"All right! I'll show you the venue. Just don't involve me. I've got more to think about than a few mangy dogs. And get this mutt off my shoulder, will you?"

"Brutus! Get down! Get on your blanket."

Obediently the dog shifted.

"See!" Frank said with pride. "He's as good as gold. Harmless. Docile. He's not into killing."

Angrily Mervyn swivelled in his seat and hissed, "Frank, I don't give a sod what he is, just don't involve me! OK?

"Now if you want to see this place, do it on the quiet. You're just a bloke walking your dog. Get it? Now push off. Follow the lane to the stile. Cross it. Go down to the beach. Second cave along. Go into the mouth about ten yards. On your right there's an opening. Duck, go through and you'll be in the arena – that's where it all happens. At the far end there's another passage. An escape route. Leads into a series of passages. Some are dead-ends, some are get-outs so don't get lost. And take your torch you'll need it."

Hurriedly Frank tugged Brutus from the back seat and left.

Mervyn Slade slid down in his seat and closed his eyes. He'd done as much as he wanted to do. He'd given Frank the late Hal's instructions. It was now up to Frank.

* * *

On Morva Pascoe's farm everything shimmered in the heat.

The chicken shed was stifling. Its strong, musty smell hung like an invisible veil. Dust danced at ground level as Davy stared in helpless dismay. The clutch of smooth brown eggs had been reduced to a pulp of shattered shells and yellow feathers oozing on to pale yellow straw. Why had Delza stamped on them so ferociously? Why had she run away with her shoes covered in the evidence? Auntie Morva had said not to touch those eggs. They were ready for hatching. If the chicks survived they would grow into strong healthy birds. Delza's breaking of one egg had been an accident. She had just hugged it too hard. The baby chick was already dead. Davy tried to explain and failed. He tried to comfort and failed. Delza's fear took over and after stamping on the whole clutch she fled.

Alerted by Delza pounding across the yard Tom and Morva exchanged horrified glances. They recognised her gait. It was the pattern of self-punishment. Davy, white faced, hovered. Lost and unsure he didn't know what to do. Telling him not to worry, they knew where Delza would go. She would make for the beach. She would take the short cut across the fields, find the cave and be traumatised. Leaving Davy staring at the shattered remains they ran across the yard. Morva, wild-eyed, shouted. "My car, Tom! I'll drive!"

***

Tom didn't care who drove as long as Delza was found.

Inside the cave the smell was foul. Rotting seaweed, tar and God only knew what else hit the back of Frank's throat and made him retch. He covered his nose with a grubby handkerchief only to discard it. The place was pitch black and he needed light. The torch beam shafted the gloom and lit what he saw to be the arena. It was roughly circled by fist-sized rocks and the odd coils of wet rope. Water dripped down the rocks faintly cutting the silence as it plopped into shallow pools. The atmosphere was eerily unsettling. Brutus growled and his hackles stood on end. He could sense things. He knew. There was a blood smell. His deep-throated growl rumbled round the rocks to bounce and increase in resonance. He reared. Frank shortened the leash. The growl died into a whimper and then burgeoned into a threatening and chilling howl.

***

Only feet away, cowering between the rocks, crouched Delza.

She broke the egg. She killed the baby chick.

Papa would be angry.

She was wicked and must be punished.

The full-throated howl of the dog shocked and terrified her.

Covering her ears, panic-stricken, her body shaking she opened her mouth and screamed.

Outside, running and stumbling into the mouth of the cave, Tom heard the mind-numbing cry. His body shrivelled with disbelief.

He knew that voice. It was that of his dead daughter. It was Audra!

"Audra!" he shouted. "It's Dadda! I'm coming, my bird."

But it wasn't Audra. It was Delza.

Hunched on to her knees she was beating the sand with her clenched fists, the dark, hoarse voice bursting from her throat.

Tom crumpled, his head hitting a rock as he fell.

Morva did what she always did. She coped.

Frank fled. Dogs were his life, but it seemed death was in the air.

Brutus dragged at his lead and howled.

Frank, sobbing with terror, stumbled after him, blindly heading away from the nightmarish noise.

Was it human? It couldn't be!

Chapter Twenty-Two

Benji, free of his leash, rooted among the tussocks of coarse grass that fringed the top of The Cauldron. Delighting in all the new smells he snuffled with canine fervour. Below, Mimosa, her plumed tail wafting, daintily picked her way between the low tide rock pools. Mrs. Lang read her book. Fancy being able to tell the age of the cliffs by their bands of colour. She knew about counting rings on tree trunks, but this was something else.

Standing on the lower level of the clifftop, many feet above her, Alex looked down and saw how the cove came to get its name. It must have been a place of absolute terror before erosion widened and softened the contours. Now he felt there was something romantic about its seclusion and grandeur. It was a place to which he would like to bring Jilly when all her worries and fears no longer haunted her. This was a place in which they could be close and talk of their future – God willing. But that couldn't happen yet.

First her enemies had to be routed. Then her spirits had to be restored along with trust and self-belief. They had been crushed by viciousness and greed dressed in the guise of friendship.

Thank God for Arthur and Tragg. They knew how best to handle Jilly's situation. Once Guy had the key and opened the safe deposit box authority could step in and take action. On what score Alex didn't know or care. All that really mattered was bringing the whole gang down. Yet there had to be some kind of evidence to do that. Theft? There was nothing to steal. Richard's death? Could they prove it was murder even if the main suspect was dead?

Alex didn't know but he believed that eventually truth would out.

Meanwhile Jilly was safe. Shopping with Mitzi in crowded streets was hardly a venue for harm. Slade and the Smith woman seemed to be no more than puppets. That left only Guy. Sinister and dangerous, he was the one to watch.

⋆ ⋆ ⋆

Arthur, still half a mile from The Cauldron, was already gasping for breath. Halting he leaned forward and pressed his hands on to his thighs. He was out of condition. His lungs blackened by smoke, his heart banging in his throat and his watering eyes distorting his vision, pointed him towards an unhappy and short future. That was not what he wanted, and so he'd change it. Get this little drama was out of the way. Get all the villains banged up, and then get a new lifestyle. He had a puppy to train. He'd have to walk it at least twice a day. That would do them both good. That'd put good clean air into his lungs! And the fags? He'd dump them. Straightening up, he looked ahead. In the distance he could see the house on the hilltop. It wasn't all that far away. Ten minutes at an easy pace should do it, then he and Alex could get their heads together. It shouldn't be too difficult to sort out a plan of action for this end. Tragg had the other end covered, and once Guy showed his face the ball would start to roll. All Jilly had to do was give him the key and then sit back and wait.

Now breathing more easily and motivated by his thoughts, Arthur moved forward.

⋆ ⋆ ⋆

Guy, using the wooden stake, lashed out at the hedge of cow parsley decapitating the flower heads and reducing the stems to pulp. The action filled him with deep satisfaction.

He likened the result to that of reducing Alex to the same end. He couldn't wait. He had it all planned. In his mind's eye, once Alex was in sight, all Guy needed was stealth. Alex wouldn't be expecting an attack. Dutifully he would be watching the dog. The dog wasn't a problem. Even if it saw Guy it couldn't bark a warning. So much for dumb animals – literally!

Striding along the deserted clifftop, Guy paused. Alex was not in sight. Momentarily unsure he hovered. He then reasoned there must be slight hollows along the way, even though the terrain appeared level. Cautiously he hunched himself. Skyline silhouettes could give the game away.

⋆⋆⋆

Arthur hadn't travelled far but was again breathless and forced to halt. Had he needed to run for his life he couldn't have done so. Such was his condition. He knew time was slipping by. Time he needed in which to talk to Alex. The house on the clifftop was so near he could see the colour of the curtains, and he wondered if he would ever reach it. All he needed was a few minutes and a bit more breath. He squared his shoulders and took in the landscape with a sweeping glance. It was empty. There was no sign of Alex. Had he moved on? Had he returned to the cottage?

Arthur looked down and toed the grass. What should he do? He was undecided. Should he return or continue? It was then he recalled there was a gentle slope of several feet leading down towards the cliff's edge That would be why Alex was out of sight!

And so he continued, his breath rasping.

⋆⋆⋆

Ahead, Guy was following a narrow path running between steep banks. Well-trodden, it was firm underfoot and offered excellent cover. He quickened his pace eager to do what had to be done. He felt The Cauldron couldn't be all that far away. Mounting a slight rise he could clearly see the striped curtains in the upstairs windows of the house on the cliff. Alex was near. Very near. Guy licked his dry lips. Gripping the wooden stake with a knuckle white hand, he smiled, advanced and letting his eyes slide towards the rim of the cliff he saw his prey. His brain produced a shaft of hatred as he silently screamed, "Alex Hunter, you're a dead man."

He licked his lips again and waited to taste sweet revenge.

Alex was looking down into The Cauldron watching Mimosa. Mrs. Lang appeared to be engrossed in her book and unaware that Mimosa was worrying a length of rope that was trapped between two rocks. She was tugging furiously, her long-haired body jerking energetically and spasmodically as her feet searched the rocks for purchase. Alex watched with amusement. She was such a little animal to have so much stamina. She'd been tugging for several minutes and showed no sign of tiring. Well done, little dog!

Benji stood at Alex's side. He too was watching Mimosa his tail flicking in canine envy. It was ages since he'd had a tug-o-war and even longer since he'd seen a pretty girl! Now that his leg was better maybe? But no, he was on duty and had to take care of his charge.

* * *

Guy moved cautiously. He had not anticipated a slight drop to reach the level on which Alex stood. Digging his heels into sand-filled crevices he silently made his way down. Nothing moved. The scene was that of a painting. Still life! Soon to be still death! Now he stood a few paces behind Alex the stake aloft ready to strike. His face contorted with both rage and triumph. Rage at the man who had soiled Jilly, and triumph at bringing about his end.

Just one mighty blow and his unconscious body would be pushed over the cliff to crash on to the rocks below.

No one would see. No one would know. Everyone would assume he had fallen. People did fall. They were careless and lost their footing. Guy raised the stake higher, gripped it tighter and silently moved forward.

Arthur saw.

Yelled.

Froze.

Alex spun, arm raised. The stake smashed into him. He felt the crunch of bone.

Benji leapt, hit the back of his knees, felling him.

The stake crashed again fracturing his shoulder. Unaware of pain Alex rolled away, grabbing grass. He was too near the edge.

Guy was screaming in triumph has face contorted. Stamping on Alex's hand he again raised the stake and with a maniacal laugh swung it at Alex's head.

Benji leapt. Ears flat. Teeth bared. He ripped and gouged Guy's face.

Guy screamed, fell and, rolling out of control, grabbed at Alex and together they went over the edge.

To Alex the world was suddenly black. There was no pain. No sound. No sense of time. There was nothing. Only a long, dark void into which he endlessly fell. Was this Death making a claim? If so he didn't care. Nothing mattered anymore.

★★★

Mrs. Lang called for the Air Ambulance. She was shaking from shock. She always knew that one day someone would fall. But two people was more than she could grasp. One man was dead. No one told her so, but she knew about body bags. The other was unconscious. She wanted to look at him to see his injuries, but she was held back by a paramedic. Perhaps the sight was too gory, too much of a mess. A fall like that could seriously mangle flesh.

The third man, who scrambled down from the clifftop, was so distraught he could hardly breathe. He arrived just before the helicopter took off. It had taken him that long to get to the beach! He seemed to know at least one of the victims and the little dog seemed to know him. Not that the man was of any help. All he could do was gasp. Poor soul.

Mimosa had tar all over her ears. What a nuisance! It was so difficult to remove, thought Mrs. Lang. What an awful day! She was still shaking. No doubt the police would want to question her about what she saw. Not that it was much. Just the actual fall, really.

That was bad enough. Those poor men. Holidaymakers no doubt. What a way to go. She would have liked to know the full story so that she could have told the police.

Not that it really mattered. Her picture would still be in the local paper. That would be nice. She took a good photograph.

Duty-bound, Arthur got a lift to the police station to report some of what he'd seen and to name Alex. The other man involved? He didn't know. He wasn't going to name Guy and complicate matters. Arthur knew about procedure and followed it. He knew how to make a statement. He understood the jargon and how not to waste time and words. To mention Tragg would have given credence to the story that stretched beyond two men falling over a cliff. But that he wouldn't do. A young policeman who stood in awe of the situation laboriously recorded Arthur's words with much licking of his pencil stub. Arthur watched him knowing how he felt. Poor lad. This would be his day to remember.

By the time Arthur returned to the cottage he was exhausted.

Marilyn was furious. Where had he been? It was not until she noticed his haggard face that she knew something was wrong. When he explained her anger turned into shock and concern.

Was Alex dead?

He didn't know.

Haltingly and speaking in a low, hopeless voice he said, "I saw them fall, but I couldn't reach them. I had to backtrack along the top of the cliff. By the time I'd done that and then clambered down to the beach it was all over." He dropped his head into his hands. "There was nothing I could do. And no one was talking."

Marilyn poured him a stiff brandy and made him drink it neat. "Come on, Pop. You need it!"

Arthur gulped it down. The raw liquid scraped his throat.

He asked about Jilly.

"She's home," Marilyn told him. "She rang about an hour ago." At that she paused uncertainly.

"And?" Arthur said, pressing for information.

Marilyn chewed her lip and then said, "She's given Mitzi the key!"

Arthur gave a low whistle, "And?" he added.

"Mitzi went for a walk! And we know what that means, don't we? She'll be making a move, won't she?"

Arthur nodded. He'd better warn Tragg that she could be on her way. But he'd have to check first.

Marilyn said, "Pop, before you do anything we've got to talk to Jilly. Prepare her for the worst. It's best we tell her rather than some well-meaning but clumsy policeman."

"Of course! If Alex is alive he'll be injured. God willing it will be nothing serious. That's me being optimistic," he added with a thin smile. "The fall was considerable, so I feel the outcome could be bleak." He took a cigarette packet from his pocket only to return it unopened. Hunching his shoulders he said "I rang the hospital but I didn't get anywhere. Nothing unusual there."

"So we don't really know anything, do we? And what about Davy? No matter what the outcome we have to think about him."

"And we have to think about Mitzi," Arthur told her.

"Why?" she snapped.

"The woman is deranged! If Guy is dead can you imagine her reaction? She will tear Jilly apart! So, as you suggested, Jilly must be told. I think we'd better call on her now, don't you?"

* * *

When they arrived at Jilly's cottage she was in a state of agitation. Benji was home, but Alex wasn't.

Silently Arthur cursed. Why hadn't he thought about the dog!

Jilly went on, trying to smile, "I expect Benji was bored or hungry or something! Anyway, I'll have words with Alex when he gets back. Mitzi has also disappeared. The moment I gave her the key she took off – I think for London! Now I'm worried about Guy arriving. Which is partly why I'm cross with Alex. When he's not here I feel vulnerable. But I suppose..." She suddenly halted and looking from one to the other she finally sensed all was not well.

"What is it?" she asked, her head to one side. "Something's wrong!"

Telling her was not easy for Arthur. He wanted to be brisk and official but couldn't. Watching the colour drain from her face, hearing her catch her breath and seeing her crumple on to the settee undermined him. Clumsily he tried to comfort her, but when she suddenly straightened and sat stony-faced with disbelief he knew his words had fallen on deaf ears.

Throwing a pleading glance towards Marilyn he said, "Look after her, will you? I'm going to the camper van to find out who's there. If the birds have flown I'll ring Tragg. He'll get them at his end. If they are still here, we'll have to play for time. Guy dead or alive has not been identified so the police will not be knocking on doors. My guess is that Mitzi will put Guy's disappearance down to his normal erratic and unpredictable behaviour. She might even assume he's here with Jilly. That being the case you girls stay together and don't open the door – particularly to Mitzi."

"Pop, you will be careful, won't you?" Marilyn asked her voice nervous and low.

"I'm the epitome of self-preservation," he told her, wishing it were true. If he was attacked, even by someone as weedy as Frank, he wouldn't stand a chance. Forty years of fags had made sure of that!

Arthur had barely left when Jilly said in a strong and steady voice, "I can't sit here and do nothing. One way or the other I have to know about Alex. I'm going to the hospital."

"Jilly, you're not in a fit state, and you're not a relative – you won't learn anything."

"I've got to try!" Jilly said doggedly. "Will you come with me?"

"Of course!"

★ ★ ★

The doors of Casualty wafted warm, disinfected air as they swung open allowing Marilyn and Jilly to enter the brightly lit reception area. Most of the seats were occupied, as were several trolleys. The first person Jilly saw was Davy. She froze. What was he doing here with Delza and was that Tom's sister? Davy flew into her arms gabbling about Tom and chickens and Delza, none of which made sense. Morva proved to be a rock of sensibility. First she explained, then she listened, and seemed to deal with this added burden with practised ease.

Jilly was in turmoil and tears were near the surface. She blinked them away and steeled herself. This was not her time. This time belonged to Davy. Talking quietly she gently explained. Davy's lower lip trembled and his eyes, dark with fear, bore into her own.

What was Jilly saying? That Dad might be dead? He couldn't be.

Morva listened and knowing how he felt kept a plump and comforting arm about his shoulders whilst holding Delza's hand. These poor children!

Briefly Jilly asked about Tom and learned that although he'd had only a bump on the head he might have had a small stroke. "We're just waiting to find out," Morva said, almost matter-of-factly. "I had to bring the children. I couldn't leave them alone, could I?" Her homely face searched Jilly's. "I'm sorry to hear about the boy's Dad. Let's hope it's not real bad news. But no matter what, we'll do what we can, won't we, Delza, my bird?"

Delza smiled.

Davy had moved away to stand with his head down and his body sagging. Jilly moved to him, and drew him close. "Davy, now that you know what's happened, are you brave enough to ask how your Dad is?"

Davy's eyes flickered.

"He might be dead," he whispered.

"That's why you have to be brave," Jilly told him gently. "Two men were involved in the accident and one didn't survive. As the son of one of the victims you have a right to know what happened."

"Can't you find out?" he begged.

"I don't think they'll tell me, Davy. But I will stay with you while you ask."

With his young, boyish face tear-streaked, he took Jilly's hand and together they approached the nurses' station

★ ★ ★

Arthur found the camper van empty. It looked vandalised. Drawers spilled contents. Gaping and grubby cupboard doors, revealed grubby shelves. The place stank. Propped against an empty beer-can, on the greasy drainer, was a handwritten letter scrawled in apparent haste:

Guy,
It's all arranged. I have the key and Jilly's Passport. She's rather careless. You'll have to take her in hand. Slade is driving us to Town. His weird brother has left. Three plane tickets have been booked for Vancouver. Coax Jilly into letting you drive her car so that you can take her "out to dinner". Then make straight for Heathrow. Customs won't be a problem. Richard being a perfectionist will have left the correct documentation with the stones, which will see me through.
Slade and Smith will be flying to Spain believing we will be joining them tomorrow.
Just remember to handle Jilly carefully. Sweet-talk her and the world will be yours.
Love,
Sis.

Arthur gave a satisfactory smile. So that was what they intended to do. Outside he saw fresh tyre tracks leading across the field and out through the gate. He immediately rang Tragg.

"They're on their way. At least three of them are. The fourth might be dead."

"What do you mean, might be?"

Arthur explained adding, "So that leaves you looking for one man and two women. One of the women has the key, and they are all involved in Richard Kenworth's death. Right?"

"Got it! Thanks, mate! Leave it with me. Are you OK?"

"Fine! Did I tell you I've bought a dog?"

"You? A dog?" Tragg chortled. "You must be bonkers! Walking it'll be like pounding the beat again."

Arthur laughed. Yes it would. But no heavy boots this time. Just trainers. He'd be well away!

Pushing the letter holding the vital evidence into his pocket he turned towards home.

* * *

Delza's voice was coarse and dark. Her vocabulary limited to an interrogative, "Papa?"

Morva chaffed her hand and explained, "Papa has hurt his head and he's having a little lie down 'til he feels better. Soon he'll be asleep and then you and me will go back home and feed the chickens. And get the eggs. Then tomorrow we'll come back and see Papa. All right, my bird?"

"Papa?" Delza said with an innocence which told Morva she had already forgotten about the broken eggs and the dead baby chicken.

Morva looked at her, her heart joyous. She had never believed in miracles until now. For Delza to speak, even if it was only one word, had to be a miracle. How it had happened she didn't know. It was something to do with the cave and, she thought, a dog baying or barking or just making noises that terrified Delza. And they were real noises. Morva heard them and so did Tom. That was partly why he was in hospital. Shock no doubt. The unexpected cry from Delza could have come from Audra – except that Audra was dead. But for that moment, to Tom, she was alive. To hear the voice of the dead was frightening. No wonder he collapsed. As to the noise in the cave that was a mystery, but mystery or not it had served its purpose. When Tom was better they would talk about it. But first she must wait for him to fully recover. After that they would all go back to the farm where she would teach Delza more words and maybe teach her to read. But for now they had to wait and see.

"Papa?" Delza asked anxiously.

"He's all right, my bird. Don't 'e worry none."

Delza smiled.

* * *

Sitting on a hard bench in the corridor Jilly held Davy's hand. She could feel him shaking. She wanted to comfort him but didn't know how. She could not raise his hopes, and her own cowardice filled her with shame. She could have volunteered to identify the body but she was too afraid of who she would find. If it was Alex she knew she would fall apart. And what use would that be? She had to remain strong for Davy. Better to identify the living rather than the dead.

All around them was the hum of activity. There were people bustling and machinery providing life. Hushed voices and squeaky shoes. An organised chaos which dealt with life and death. In its midst sat those who waited in a welter of both hope and despair.

At the far end of the long, white corridor with its grey shiny floor, two swing doors barred the way. Above them an illuminated sign read 'Theatre Four'. Beyond those doors the surgeons were striving to repair the body of a man. That much Jilly knew. Who the man was she didn't know.

In Turton Ward, Tom was tucked up in bed, the cut on his head neatly held together with stitches. He was tired and slightly disoriented, but he had all his faculties. Delza was at his side saying in her new found and gruff voice "Papa".

Tom's tears welled and through them he saw those of Morva's.

"You'll be fine, Tom," she told him. "They're keeping you in tonight, and I'll fetch you tomorrow. By that time they'll know how you really are."

"'Tis nothing but a bang on the head," he grumbled.

"They'm just got to check your brains didn't fall out," she told him, her eyes still bright with unshed tears.

"Never did get no sympathy from you," he scolded lovingly.

She laughed and said, "Me and Delza'll get on now. We still got to see to the hens."

"Where's Davy? I saw him just now. Is he all right?"

"He's gone to the lavvy," she lied. "Don't you worry none about him. He can stay with me and Delza."

Bending she kissed Tom's cheek. Something she hadn't done in years. There was a mingling of tears reminiscent of childhood.

"See you tomorrow, Tom," she said gruffly, hiding her concern.

"Papa?" Delza said touching his brow. "Papa hurt?"

Tom smiled at her. Another word? Was she finally escaping from the prison in which she had been locked away for so long? He held her hand in his gnarled fingers and said slowly, "Papa loves Delza."

Delza smiled and was led away. After a few paces she halted, turned and said with only the slightest stumble. "Bye, bye, Papa."

Tom smiled with pride. Delza had taken one more step towards freedom.

He watched them disappear from view and gazed at the ceiling. Years ago old Doctor Fletcher had told him Delza's condition could have been caused by terror and it was likely that terror would un-cause it. Tom didn't believe him. The old doctor was getting on and he was forgetful. And sometimes he prattled, telling tales which didn't seem to have conclusions. Now it seemed that was not one of his tales. He knew what he was talking about and what he had predicted had come true. Pity he hadn't lived to see the day.

Chapter Twenty-Three

The Indian summer had lasted well into October. Autumn was beginning to colour the trees and hedgerows with soft yellows and vibrant reds. Late evenings sometimes needed a touch of warmth to make them comfortable, but the days were balmy.

Life had settled into an easy and slow-moving pattern which embraced firm friendships, shared memories, and a comradeship that bridged the age gaps.

It was Tom's idea to have a group photograph taken.

"We'm like one big family. We all looked after each other, so 'tis only right we have us picture took. We'm family!"

They had to wait a day or two until Morva could leave the chickens. She'd had trouble with a fox but, as Tom explained," Her's a dab hand with a twelve bore. Her'll not kill'un. Her'll just scare him out of his skin."

Dick Rogers offered his photography skills. The end result was excellent, after his third attempt. He blamed Jilly's digital camera for his initial failure. He didn't go along with such complicated inventions. Give him a Box Brownie any day.

"A what?" Jilly laughed

Dick winked and laughed back.

Arthur, having bought the holiday cottage, given up smoking and taken to walking Bullah, his young dog, twice a day, was fitter than he had been in years. The rounding up of Mitzi and the rest had given him a real sense of achievement. Even though Tragg had executed the final move, Arthur enjoyed basking in the reflected glory. They still laughed at the silliness of Mitzi's downfall.

★ ★ ★

Although the evidence was still mounting up Tragg remained worried. If they slipped through the net and fled the country…! It could take years to bring the whole thing to trial. And then a simple mistake was made.

At Mitzi's insistence Slade parked in the private No Parking zone. This was the opportunity for which Tragg had been waiting. Having kept watch since Arthur's 'phone call Tragg, playing the part of a genial private citizen, pointed out the parking problem. Slade more or less told him to get lost. At that Tragg produced his ID Card and watched as Slade broke out in a sweat. With stumbling tongue Slade explained he was just collecting a friend. Beatrice, white-faced and trembling said, from the back seat, that the lady was her sister who wasn't very well. Tragg, all heart, said kindly, "In that case she won't be very long, will she?"

At that moment Mitzi appeared hugging a package. Tragg's heart flipped. If that was what he thought it was…! Courteously he opened the car door for her then stood back for her to enter. Before she could do so he arrested her on suspicion of theft. Immediately there was a crash of gears, the car mounted the pavement, swerved and sped away. Tragg hit the ground, his shoulder crashing into the kerb as the full weight of Mitzi fell on to him. Swearing, screaming writhing with rage she fought like a tigress. Two burly officers hauled her to her feet. Tragg, wincing with pain, hoped to God the back-up he had yelled for was in place. Minutes later, after bundling a fighting Mitzi into a patrol car, the message loud and clear announced that Slade and a woman had been arrested and were on their way to Headquarters. Mitzi screamed hysterically. She was not the thief. She was the victim. Jilly Kenworth was the guilty one. It was she who had planned everything. She was the real thief. To prove it, all Tragg had to do was contact Guy her brother. He would verify her story. He would prove who she was. He would prove her innocence. The other people? They were crooks in league with the Kenworth woman. They had forced Mitzi to go to the bank where her late husband had a safe deposit box. Threatening to kill her brother if she didn't do as she was told they had turned her into something she wasn't. They were trying to make her a criminal. That was so wicked. She was just a simple widow trying to make the best of her life.

Tragg listened with outward sympathy. She was almost breaking his heart!

Inwardly he had heard it all before. He had mopped more crocodile tears than he could remember and most of them had been more convincing than those that rolled down this woman's face. Handing her and her companions to the Desk Sergeant gave him quiet pleasure. Although he was not yet in a position that warranted buying his wife a new hat, once the trial began that situation would change. Wouldn't Maureen be pleased! And Arthur. That was a celebration they could look forward to.

* * *

Jack and Sarah, after spending several happy and peaceful weekends together, decided it was time to start a family. Their weeks spent apart had drawn them together and Sarah, having cast aside the character of Marilyn for ever, was content to be ordinary. Although in the back of her mind she thought that one day she might start a Stage School. That would be fun. Becca, she thought, could prove to be quite talented.

Jack discovered that his hobby of dabbling in oil paintings had developed into something very artistic. Sarah was so impressed she wondered if he might prove to be another Degas. Why not? He could paint realistic ballet shoes!

From the centre of the group Jilly smiled. There was a radiance about her that stemmed only from the man at her side. Although he was still on crutches Alex beamed with pride and happiness.

Surviving the fall with a broken shoulder, a smashed ankle and a damaged spleen made him the lucky one. Having Jilly and his son near him, made him even luckier.

For Jilly and Davy, the not-knowing was over. The hours they had to wait before learning Alex was alive were behind them. Now all they wanted to do was look forward.

Tom looked less careworn and smiled more often, particularly at Mrs. Atkins. Standing next to each other they appeared to be slightly self-conscious. If one looked closely entwined fingers could be seen. But that was an observation Jilly kept to herself.

And so the photograph held a fund of memories for everyone.

At the very front of the group Benji sat upright and alert with Becca's hand on his head. He was a very happy dog. To Becca's left stood Davy. To her right stood Delza. Each wore an anorak and each held drooping hood strings under their noses.

Three Mandarins!

"Look, Papa," Delza said, pouting whilst hugging Pogo.

Everyone, enveloped in a cloud of great happiness, looked and laughed.

Foreboding? It no longer existed.

Printed in the United Kingdom
by Lightning Source UK Ltd.
117562UKS00001B/1-12

9 781844 264001